THE
MEMO

THE
MEMO
· · · · · · · · · · ·

A Novel

RACHEL DODES AND
LAUREN MECHLING

HARPER ⬤ PERENNIAL

NEW YORK • LONDON • TORONTO • SYDNEY • NEW DELHI • AUCKLAND

HARPER PERENNIAL

THE MEMO. Copyright © 2024 by Rachel Wortman and Lauren Mechling. All rights reserved. Printed in the United States of America. No part of this book may be used or reproduced in any manner whatsoever without written permission except in the case of brief quotations embodied in critical articles and reviews. For information, address HarperCollins Publishers, 195 Broadway, New York, NY 10007.

HarperCollins books may be purchased for educational, business, or sales promotional use. For information, please email the Special Markets Department at SPsales@harpercollins.com.

FIRST EDITION

Designed by Jamie Lynn Kerner

Library of Congress Cataloging-in-Publication Data has been applied for.

ISBN 978-0-06-331935-6 (pbk.)

24 25 26 27 28 LBC 5 4 3 2 1

For Gráinne

THE
MEMO

· · · · · · · · · · · ·

PART I
· · · · · · · · · · ·
MEMO-LESS

1
..

ANOTHER MONDAY MORNING, RACING AROUND THE APARTMENT, praying I wouldn't be late for work. Hal was at our kitchen island, spooning gluten-free granola into his beautiful mouth while I lifted objects and slammed them back down in desperate pursuit of my keys.

"You sure you haven't seen them?" I sounded frantic.

Hal gave one of his shrugs. "What do they look like?"

"They look like . . . my keys, with a fob." The bright green, droplet-shaped entry device had been a fixture of our butcher-block countertop only ever since we'd moved in. "Forget it." I flung open more drawers. We really needed to get one of those wall hook contraptions.

Hal and I had been in Pittsburgh for a little less than a year, covering the maintenance of a spacious if somewhat dilapidated loft that belonged to a distant contact of Hal's. My boyfriend had a way of drawing interesting people to him, like a six-foot-two magnet. I'd never met the owner, an artist named Glen who was currently in Marfa, Texas, for reasons that were never made clear. Clarity wasn't really Glen's thing. I'd informed our landlord of the bedroom closet door that was falling off its hinges and the leak in the kitchen ceiling, but his stock response was "no problem," as if I was asking for forgiveness and not help. Hal and I came up with our workarounds. We crammed our clothing into the hallway closet, and I placed a braided-trunk ficus tree beneath the source of the water drip. A housewarming gift from Geeta, the tree had been more valuable than my best friend could have imagined.

At last, my keys! They were on the shelf in the entryway, nearly obscured by a thicket of junk mail and receipts. At the top of the pile was a letter from my alma mater. I averted my eyes but not quickly enough to miss the words emblazoned on the envelope: "Attention Jennifer Green, Coleman College Class of 2007! Two Weeks to Go!"

Down to four days, actually. I was due to head out of town on Friday for a full weekend of catching up with a group of people who, based on their social media feeds, were all living their absolute best lives. I'd only been dreading this getaway for five years, ever since the ten-year reunion, which I'd managed to skip. Hal and I had not been getting along at the time, and I'd assured myself—promised myself, really—that I'd be in a better place by the time our fifteen-year reunion came along. Lo and behold, I wasn't.

My two best friends from college, Geeta Brara and Leigh Sullivan, were furious with me for bailing the last time, and my absence had made Geeta all the more zealous that we all attend our fifteenth. I could hardly believe it myself—fifteen whole years since graduation. Leigh and I were no longer in close touch, but I doubted that she required the same type of hard sell I did. After all, Leigh had no reason to be reluctant. She could dazzle our classmates with her glamorous style, confident gait, and stunning success. But I couldn't shake the conviction that, for me at least, the whole weekend would be a recipe for nostalgia and regret, not so much on account of all the stupid things I'd done, but for all the things I'd failed to see through. On the plus side, I had my keys.

I bounded back into the kitchen, waving the green fob in the air. "Mission accomplished!"

Hal's mouth puckered in what I took for amusement.

"What?" I said.

"Nothing," Hal said. "You're just super cute when you get flustered."

This statement only made me more flustered. Hal was super cute in all emotional states. He was textbook gorgeous to a degree that bordered on the comical. He had big hazel eyes and thick honey-colored hair just long enough to pull back in a low bun, and a tall, lanky body that never managed to put on any weight. Even more attractive, though, were the intangibles. Hal gave off a zero-fucks, no-stress energy that made putty of pretty much everyone. Everyone except for my mom.

Hal cocked his head to the side. "Jenny," he cooed.

Oh lord. He wanted a quickie.

I shook my head. "I have to go to work, like, five minutes ago."

"Come on." He patted his lap.

"I gotta go," I said.

I really did have to go. Probably in more ways than one. Hal was a good-time guy, the kind of dude you were meant to hook up with for one summer, in your early twenties—not stick with until you were in your mid-thirties. We'd met in Costa Rica, the site of my brother's destination wedding. Hal was living in a funky tree-house on the edge of the luxurious but ecologically sustainable resort that my sister-in-law had chosen for their nuptials. He was working at the resort, doing some groundskeeping by day while reading philosophy books at night, thinking big thoughts and talking big talk, his specialty. It felt thrilling and preposterous to get together with this broke yet insanely intelligent guy who looked like a hot caveman.

I wrote epic emails to Geeta and Leigh about this dream man and all the treehouse sex we were having, sex that rang through the canopy for all the tourists, resort workers, and exotic animals to hear. What a week! But at the end of it, we'd ended it. I was going home. My destiny was not to cling to a guy who lived in a tree in Costa Rica like an oversized sloth. Then, a couple of years later, Hal and I ran into each other at my freshman roommate's barbecue in Brooklyn. Hal happened to be her neighbor, living with three other guys in a one-bedroom with a tiny home office where he slept when he wasn't on one of his crazy trips. We'd picked up where we'd left off, and I'd fallen so hard for him. By wintertime, we had matching travel backpacks. Hal and I stuck together through our thirtieth birthdays, an engagement, a disengagement, and a pandemic. Now the world was opening back up, and here we were, untransformed and static, petrified skeletons at Pompeii.

"What's the deal with tonight?" Hal said in a matter-of-fact tone. He was over trying to seduce me, now reading his phone.

"The deal?" I repeated.

"You have singing, right?"

"A cappella is on Tuesdays," I said, not taking the bait. My schedule in this city wasn't that hard to follow. I had exactly one standing activity that didn't involve Hal—the embarrassingly named Looney Tunes—and our group met on Tuesday every week. "I'll be home at the normal time," I said, going over to kiss him goodbye.

Hal didn't need to start getting ready for hours, possibly not at all. He worked at a gallery located in a converted mattress factory on the north side of town. He was one of their art handlers, part of the team of strapping men responsible for setting up and dismantling shows and building the occasional display case. He particularly enjoyed philosophizing with his coworkers over their many coffee breaks.

"Oh!" I said. "There are muffins in the bread drawer if you want to bring them with you to work. Hazelnut crunch."

Hal raised his eyebrows, his I-would-never look. He'd recently gone paleo, which I'd been trying not to take as a personal affront.

"Babe, you know I'm against the grain," he said.

"I didn't say you have to *eat* them," I called out as I darted to the front door. "You can share them with your team."

Back in the entryway, I gave myself a final once-over in the mirror. Dark shoulder-length hair, brown eyes that were neither excessively big nor small, a light dusting of freckles across my cheeks. And, of course, my prominent nose, a feature that I tried to think of as regal. I smoothed my hair and took a step back. I was bordering on presentable, if not more than the sum of my parts.

No wonder Hal's attention had faded. After what I'd believed to be two fully monogamous years, my boyfriend had taken an interest in a swishy-ponytailed woman who had recently moved into our apartment complex. Brie—yes, that was her name, like the cheese—had a little toffee-colored dog and a bounty of yoga outfits that showcased her waffle abs. I tried to keep my suspicions to myself. I focused on staying busy, going on movie dates with my work wife, Sophie, and reconnecting with my love of baking, which I had neglected in New York. But no matter how hard I pounded the dough, I was never quite able to knead away the sense that I was committed to a guy who would never be fully committed to me.

Twenty minutes after Hal rejected my muffins, I was waiting in line outside SteelHaus, the coworking space where I spent most of my waking hours. Members had to go through an elaborate sign-in process at the front desk, like we were ticketed guests to a performance of our own work lives. I pulled out my phone and saw that three new emails had come in since my T ride over. They were all from Alice. Typical. A good portion of my maniacal boss's ideas came to her during her morning workout, tossed word salads dictated while sweating it out on one of those Internet-connected stationary bikes that every upwardly mobile professional suddenly seemed to be into. I took a deep breath and closed my inbox. I deserved a few more minutes of peace.

As I inched forward in the line, I pulled up my most recent text thread with Geeta. The night before, she'd sent me an image of my face that an app that her company was developing had generated to reflect the answers that Geeta had selected (on my behalf) to a personality quiz centered on my "embodied self." This was what rising tech stars did while nursing their twins, apparently: toy with technology that nobody needed yet everybody desperately wanted. My embodied self had huge Bambi eyes and a jawline that could cut glass. My nose looked the same, which made me feel a tug of warmth for Geeta. My mother had, apropos of nothing, offered to fund a nose job back when I was in college. Geeta had objected, maintaining that my nose made me look dignified, like a socialite in a John Singer Sargent painting.

I pinched the screen to expand the view. It was me and not me. I tried to imagine what this Jenny's life would be like. The version of me who didn't spend her Sunday nights consumed in dread about the coming workweek and her psycho boss. The Jenny who didn't analyze hairs on her boyfriend's jacket collar to see if they matched with the coat of the pretty neighbor's dog (they did). The Jenny who didn't have a slew of problems that she hid from her mother on their increasingly infrequent phone calls. This embodied Jenny. She would love phone calls with her mother!

"Hello? Are you going in?"

I spun around to see who sounded so irritated. Sophie smirked at me. "Goodness, Jenny," she said. "You'd think you're not psyched to clock in and rock out."

Sophie was the best thing about my job, way wiser than her twenty-four years on earth. She was always good for a sympathetic side eye or a snack break. Today she was the portrait of Gen-Z perfection in her ironically adorable mom jeans and a cap-sleeve sweatshirt, every fiber undoubtedly sourced from a sustainable farm. A topknot sat on the crown of her head.

"Sorry, Soph." I stepped toward the front desk.

"I didn't think you would ever use FaceTune," Sophie said, hot on my heels. "You've always been more of an au naturel type." She gave me a playful smile and gestured to my outfit. I had thrown together a prairie skirt, a loose cotton sweater, and brown clogs that dated back to my early twenties.

"It's a vintage look," I said quickly.

"Right. Cool." Sophie bit her bottom lip.

I really needed to take Sophie up on her standing offer to be my stylist and take me shopping. But that would require accepting the fact that my body was never going to resemble the limber figure I'd once taken for granted. The only thing about me that was getting leaner was my bank account balance. This skirt had an elastic waist and was getting a lot of wear.

Sophie brandished her ID card at the SteelHaus receptionist and consulted her watch. "We can do this. Three hours, then we get to order lunch."

"Three hours of saving womankind," I told her.

"We are heroes, Jenny. You know that, right?"

I pumped my fist in the air and followed my work wife inside.

2

THE BEST WAY TO DESCRIBE WHAT I DID FOR A LIVING WOULD BE TO say I was a professional beggar. I raked in contributions for the Aurora Foundation, whose mission was to demolish structural barriers to gender equity. In more tangible terms, this meant directing small grants to girls clubs and female entrepreneurs across the nation, but mostly in western Pennsylvania. It was stable work, occasionally inspiring. Well, it used to be occasionally inspiring, when our pockets were a bit deeper. We would have had a lot more money to invest in demolishing structural barriers to gender equity were it not for our executive director's exorbitant personal expenses that somehow were always "work related."

I reported to Executive Director and Founder Alice Hustad, who happened to have graduated from Coleman College a few years ahead of me. She had already tried her hand at becoming an actress, a stockbroker, and a raw foods restaurateur before settling on philanthropy as an occupation. She'd come up with the idea for the foundation while adventure-vacationing in the Arctic and named it for the northern lights, those gorgeous disturbances in the magnetosphere that turn the night's sky into a swirl of green. An astrologer told Alice that, as a Taurus, her aura was green like the northern lights and that she had the power to bring out the best in other people through her bull-like determination. It was at that moment that Alice realized the universe was speaking to her.

As the foundation's key relationship officer, I was responsible for securing our financial support. But since we had to trim staff of late due to a precipitous fall in philanthropic donations across the board, I was wearing a lot of other hats, too: media strategist, spokesperson, and therapist. It fell on me to soothe the increasingly fragile ego of my insecure boss. I had to remind Alice repeatedly how astute her vision was, how important the foundation's work was, and how essential our objectives were, not just for women, but for society. Without people like us, the world would spin off its axis, swinging the arc of the moral universe away from justice. At first, I believed all of this. As a woman who hadn't exactly been served by the system, I was a pretty easy mark.

The rest of the world took a little more work. There were other, more pressing causes out there than helping stay-at-home moms launch their low-sugar brownie and event-planning businesses, as potential donors were quick to remind me. But Alice had her network of Pittsburgh millionaires looking for an easy tax deduction, and they usually could be relied upon to continue their dwindling contributions, provided that I continued flattering and wining and dining them at the city's finest restaurants, regaling them with inspiring stories of entrepreneurs seeking to save the world. Alice's latest pet investment was a woman-founded start-up that specialized in portable bidets for children. Putting the bill on my corporate credit card was getting a little harder, though, given that Alice had said I needed to tighten my belt. I was now expected to split the check with putative donors, which was not a great look.

My first task of the day was to reply to an email from Christy Spector, the director of marketing at Pittsburgh's Slime Museum, the site of a Father's Day Parade after-party we were hosting. I was behind schedule, as I'd spent the previous month trying—and failing—to secure a partnership with a more august local institution.

I'm soooooooooooo sorry, but a request for a big birthday party just came in, Christy wrote. We're going to need the main slime stations. Your group can use the basement room. Let me know if you're still interested—and how many slime dumps we should plan on setting up!

The Slime Museum basement seemed a poetically just place to celebrate our Feminists for Father's Day float, an idea that Alice had dreamed up during one of her spin sessions. After failing to convince her that Father's Day might not be the right holiday to market a women-oriented foundation, I'd mapped out the route of the float, approved the designs, and followed up with a few potential sponsors, securing their participation. A local jazz band led by Alice's ex-husband, Deck—who worked at the foundation as a vice president of operations, but rarely showed up for video meetings, let alone made in-person appearances—was set to perform on the float and perhaps at the after-party too. I prayed he wouldn't be too deep in his beer by then.

I replied to Christy:

That's fine! We can do it in the basement, I typed. And I think just one slime dump will be perfect. A surprise for Alice. She'll love it!

Just as I was hitting "send," a new email from Alice popped up in my inbox. She must have sensed that I was plotting the destruction of one of her silk outfits. Now she was haranguing me about some inane thing she'd seen on Instagram: an account with fifty-five followers, all of which appeared to be bots, was impersonating her. Hadn't she warned me that there were saboteurs lurking everywhere? I was about to respond in a perfectly professional message—As per my previous email, I began—when my phone went off again. It was a text from Hal's number.

Yum.

For a second I wondered if he'd reconsidered the muffins.

My mouth fell open. This was not about a muffin. Was this my first dick pic? Why yes, it was. I stared at it in disbelief. Weren't we a little too old for this type of behavior? I checked to make sure nobody in the communal work room was close enough to see the contents on my screen, then glanced back at the image. This organ was certainly Hal's. As I tried to come up with reasons he had chosen to send this to me at this moment, it dawned on me that perhaps he intended to send the picture to someone else. Hal barely even texted, believing abbreviations and emojis to be two of the Four Horsemen of the Apocalypse. (The other two were social media and reality television.)

I tried to steady my breathing and pulled up Geeta's number.

Emergency update: Hal just texted me a picture of his penis with the word "yum." I don't think it was for me. Help me process this, I wrote.

Yuck. I was trying to eat my breakfast, Leigh replied.

Crap. I suddenly realized that I had accidentally responded to the long-dormant, recently resurrected thread that included both Geeta and Leigh. Geeta and I were still best friends, but Leigh and I had had a falling out and were just recently back in touch. I didn't want Leigh to be receiving my most intimate cries for help. Dealing with someone else's vulnerability was not her forte.

Leigh Sullivan, former champion rower turned noted queer artist, and I had drifted apart years ago. We no longer even qualified as Facebook friends since she quit the network, though she would occasionally "like" my Instagram posts—typically steamed-up images of baked goods—from her checkmark-verified account. Every time Leigh engaged with something I shared on social media, I'd get an influx of new followers, a gnawing reminder of her ever-expanding sphere of influence. I wished she hadn't bothered. To me, going from practically being sisters to tapping hearts on an app was heartbreaking. It was worse than if we'd had a blowout fight. She liked my content even though she didn't appear to like me.

Meanwhile, Geeta wouldn't accept Leigh's and my ever-widening rift. Optimistic to the point of delusional, she believed that all we needed was some actual face time—not FaceTime—to rekindle our relationship.

Just minutes earlier, Geeta had sent Leigh and me a text saying how excited she was for the reunion, sharing that she'd heard that her college crush Dave Smalls was going to be there.

Maybe this will finally be our moment, Geeta wrote, followed by an upside-down smile emoji.

I'd responded by telling her there would be no judgment from me. I didn't think Geeta would ever cheat on her husband—but she did believe that the reunion was just the thing to summon all the energy of our youth, and I was willing to play along. And now I'd sullied the thread with a confession that my commitment-phobic, probably-cheating boyfriend had just sent me a dirty picture I highly suspected wasn't intended for me. A great way to show my fabulous friends that I was progressing in life.

Adulting FTW, I wrote, then added an embarrassed-face emoji.

I saw the three dots indicating that Geeta was composing a message. She sent a smile emoji followed by a gentle reminder:

Much as I love and embrace all forms of adult entertainment, no more texting me about anything until you've signed up for the reunion. We won't let you ditch us this time. Can't wait to see you. I'll even try to be nice to Hal.

She tacked on an eggplant emoji followed by another embarrassed face.

I groaned. We'll be there, I replied.

Statement of intent is not enough, Geeta shot back. Send proof of registration.

Given my decision to bail on our last big reunion, her due diligence wasn't entirely unwarranted. I'd never been much of a planner. This bothered Geeta to no end. She was the kind of person who mapped her weekend getaways in a multitabbed spreadsheet of the hotels, hiking paths, and dinner reservations she'd scored, replete with links to reviews and maps. Ever the power entrepreneur, Geeta always wanted documentation, agendas, projections, and action items for follow-ups. She and her husband, Matt, even scheduled sex via their shared calendar when their lives were getting too busy. Rather, her life. Matt was never that busy.

U got it, I fired off begrudgingly.

I searched through my email for the various reminders from our alumni class president, Alessandra D'Ourous of East Sixtieth Street, New York City, formerly known as Allie Dourous of East Lansing, Michigan. Somehow she had become a wildly successful independent film producer. At the bottom of Alessandra's note detailing the links to the registration page was a bullet-point request:

- Record a quick video on your phone re-introducing yourself to the Class of '07.

- Upload the video to this Google Drive! And please don't peek at the other videos till you've submitted your own :)

- Keep it fun!

Fun. Right. Another thing I had forgotten to do. I looked at my watch and I had some time before my next phone call. There was no way I was shooting a video in SteelHaus's bustling common area, so I made sure no one was watching me, and sneaked off to Alice's private office, the last place she'd be at nine a.m., even though the rest of us were expected to be at our desks by then. (Her hair took ages to blow-dry into barrel curls; it couldn't be helped.)

The latest issue of *Moment* magazine was on Alice's coffee table, a reminder of another impossible task she'd asked me to complete. Alice felt entitled to be profiled in the magazine's annual Changemakers List, a roundup of women making an impact on society around the world. The problem was, nobody cared about a forty-something white woman who'd inherited millions from her industrialist father and rented out space in a coworking facility in Pittsburgh. Stop the presses.

I took a seat at Alice's desk and opened my browser to the reunion's registration page. Not only had I missed the deadline for the 30 percent early-bird discount, but the Coleman College class of 2007 bulletin board was now full of impressive information, more than I could possibly absorb. I scanned the bios sent in of some of my former classmates. Certain words kept coming up: CEO. Cofounder. Head of Something. Chief of Operations of Something Else. Partner. Leader. Chairman. Producer.

Even though the woman formerly known as Allie had urged us not to look in the video folder, I couldn't help myself. I saw her thumbnail and clicked the little triangle. There she was, introducing herself as "Alessandra." She was on a movie set in what appeared to be Venice, Italy, and she was speaking in a vaguely Italian accent.

Amanda Rosenbaum, a know-it-all from my American studies class, shared that she had won a Peabody Award for an online series exposing war crimes in Myanmar. Lyndsey Bogatsky, a poetry major, was now a rocket scientist—a true rocket scientist!—at SpaceFisch, one of a handful of entities run by Levi Fischer, a billionaire fixture of the tabloids who was always getting sued by someone. Alexis Wilson, a math prodigy who'd lived directly across the hall from Geeta during sophomore year, was an archeologist with her own lab at UC Davis. "I just returned from Egypt, where I co-led a dig in collaboration with Oxford University and uncovered a cache of teenage mummies," Alexis said. "Our discovery of new clues helped deepen our understanding of human adolescence. I can't wait to see you and hear your news!"

My news. What was my news again? What the hell *was* I doing with my life? This was the question I tried to constantly keep at bay. I grabbed a handful of licorice allsorts from the antique glass jar Alice kept on her desk and nervously stuffed them into my mouth. Then I walked over to the wall where Alice hung her prized photography collection, swallowed hard, and turned on my phone's camera. I held the device a few inches at an angle above my head to suggest the existence of cheekbones, a neat trick Sophie had taught me. I tapped the red "record" button.

"Hey there," I said, "your old friend Jenny Green here. You remember me, the eco-chic econ major, raging against the machine, writing papers on Engels while dreaming of becoming America's favorite artisanal baker?" I paused and thought about what to reveal next. "You probably read about how I burned down an Italian bakery right after college. Not just any Italian bakery—an official UNESCO cultural heritage site. Impressive, am I right? More recently, I moved, perhaps against my better judgment, from New York to Pittsburgh with my boyfriend, who is annoyingly good-looking and used to organize the most fantastic exotic vacations for the two of us but now seems to be busy drooling over one of our new neighbors. So . . . that's cool. And what am I doing? I am now working as a professional groveler at a non-profit organization that none of you has ever heard of. I have two friends in the city: a coworker who isn't old enough to rent a car and a man I met in my a cappella troupe, the Looney Tunes. He is awkward as they come and currently estranged from his wife. And yes, I am still baking! But my boyfriend has sworn off gluten, so I eat everything I bake and as a result no longer fit into most of my clothes. But on the plus side, he just texted me a picture of his dick that I think was intended for that neighbor girlie. Don't be too jealous!"

I pressed play to review the recording and chuckled. Yes, I'd squandered my potential, but at least I could make fun of myself.

"That. Was. Epic."

Sophie was standing in the doorway. Had she seen it all? The humiliation made me go stiff.

"I'm in the middle of something, Soph," I said.

"Evidently."

"It was just a joke," I said. "I was just doing a warm-up. Making sure the sound levels were okay."

"Yeah, sure," Sophie said. "Are you okay, Jenny?"

"Me? Of course I'm okay," I said reflexively.

But I wasn't. I could feel my mouth begin to tremble the way it did when I was about to cry. And not only because I wasn't okay. Nobody had asked me if I was okay in such a long time.

"I don't know," I said. "Maybe not?"

Thankfully, Sophie had a plan for everything. She handed me her jumbo water bottle and proceeded to turn off all the lights except for a neon plaque—the words "Interactive Reactive" glowing in yellow—that hung on the wall. The piece was by an acclaimed artist named Ezra Lightfoot who I knew about through Hal.

I took a sip of water and wiped the corners of my eyes.

Sophie came over to where I was standing and wrested the phone from my hand. "Don't you dare move. The lighting is perfect."

She ran off and in a moment was back with her enormous makeup bag. Sophie knew more about contouring than any Sephora employee. She opened the bag and took out what looked like mascara, but explained it was brow gel.

"I came looking for you to see if you wanted to order smoothies from that new organic place. Thank god I found you," Sophie said, in a voice slightly sweeter than her usual tone, brushing my eyebrows. "You've got this, Jenny. Those college friends are going to be blown away by your refreshing realness. Just don't be so real that you self-sabotage at your reunion!"

That was another thing about Sophie. I had told her about my reunion months ago, when I first began stressing about it, and she remembered everything.

"Easy there," I said when she started yanking on my hair.

Sophie frowned, then stepped back, looking pleased with her work.

"Ready to start over?" Sophie asked. She was still too young to know just how good starting over sounded. I hoped she never would.

3
..

TOTO'S "AFRICA" WAS THE LAST SONG OF THE EVENING, AND I WAS giving it my all. I was no Adele. But my mezzo-soprano voice had the ability to dazzle at a karaoke bar. Not that I was big on the bar scene anymore. Which was why I now spent my Tuesday nights at the J. T. Carnegie Community Center in central Pittsburgh, jamming with the illustrious Looney Tunes.

I watched my friend Gabe sing along from his spot down the row from me, his brown fleece jacket with the red pockets draped over the back of his seat. Gabe was wonderful. We'd recently started hanging out after these weekly singing sessions, at first with a larger group, and we'd mostly talk about music. Lately, we'd head out to the bar, just the two of us. We'd fallen into an easy rhythm. I liked Gabe's way. Saying the right thing was never his priority, nor was trying to impress other people. The details that most people would brag about tumbled out of his mouth like accidental revelations. It turned out, for instance, that Gabe was studying Russian—which came up only when I mentioned my great-grandmother Rivka. Oh, and another thing—he used to sing and play lead guitar in a punk band, a band that had once opened for the Strokes before they were famous. Not that you would have any idea from the looks of him. He was cute, with his dimples and bright blue eyes, but he seemed a bit worn down by life. Gabe kind of reminded me of a stuffed animal a kid had out-grown but couldn't stand to toss out.

Gabe now poured his musical passion into our a cappella ses-sions. He had a lot of feelings to work through here. Gabe's wife, Thea, a bankruptcy lawyer with long hair and longer legs, had left him for a partner at her firm because, she said, she found Gabe exhausting. She told him she wanted to have a "big life." She was feeling the momentum in her career and needed someone who was excited to take on the world with her. And somehow Gabe had ended up here, in a community center with a motley crew of this city's eccentrics. See? He really didn't care what other people thought.

Something about seeing Gabe go for broke inspired me to sing what remained of the song with even more emotion. When I sang, I wasn't hung up on the past or the future. I was suspended in time, just a bundle of vibrations ricocheting off the plaster walls, crooning about doing the things we never "ha-aaaaad."

When the session was over, our ringleader, a white-haired soprano named Barb McGregor, beamed at us and clapped as if we were all in on an incredible secret. Which, I guessed, we were. To think of all the money I had wasted on therapists, the years of experimenting with antidepressants. It turned out the most dependable way to shake off my troubles and improve my mood was to lose myself in a cluster of loud, searching souls.

In New York I would never have joined a group so undeniably uncool. I had enough friends there to ensure my social calendar was always packed, sometimes more than I wanted it to be. I'd worked for a local radio station doing fundraising and between my demanding work schedule and meeting up with people at night, I didn't have much time to bake, much less take up a new hobby.

By the time we moved to Pittsburgh, Hal knew five people and I knew none, which meant he was the de facto driver of our social lives. Within months, he had more than two dozen close friends and seemed to know about every concert and party in Allegheny County. That was Hal's magic; he always had new things for you to try, up-and-coming music to listen to, and new places to check out. His unquenchable wanderlust complemented his go-with-the-flow attitude. Thanks to his sense of adventure, I'd slept under the stars in Joshua Tree, and my passport had stamps from Nicaragua and Greenland. But I was eager to have something in my life that was entirely mine once again. Enter the Looney Tunes.

I glanced down the row at Gabe. There was something familiar about him that I couldn't place. I chalked it up to the fact that we both had similar backstories, both transplants from New York, persuaded to move here by our significant others, both of us struggling to put down roots in this unfamiliar town. Gabe had outgrown the punk scene and embraced his life as a high-school math teacher. Now he spent his free time playing hockey and hanging out with his eight-year-old daughter, Ramona, named after the beloved children's book heroine Ramona Quimby. He had mentioned once that his late mother had been a school librarian, which I found incredibly endearing.

GABE WAS UNUSUALLY QUIET ON TONIGHT'S WALK TO THE TAVERN. WE took our regular table in the back and hung our stuff on the backs of our fraying wicker chairs, recapping the highs and lows of our singing session. He was acting strange. He kept running his hand through his scruffy hair and he'd barely touched his beer since the waiter had plopped it on the table five minutes earlier. And he kept checking his phone.

"Everything okay?" I asked, gesturing at Gabe's frosted mug.

He gave me a reluctant smile. "It's my anniversary," he said in a barely audible mumble. "My separation anniversary. One full year since Thea pulled the plug."

"Sheesh, I'm sorry," I said, searching for something more helpful to say. I took a sip of my wine. Then I remembered the olive focaccia loaf I'd made the night before, and grabbed it out of my bag. I watched him rip off a chunk and chew appraisingly.

"Mmmm. You used those wrinkly olives?"

"Salt-cured." I nodded and watched him eat some more.

Gabe took a sip of his beer and sighed sadly. I'd never seen him this down in the dumps.

"Look, at least you *got* married," I said at last. "A for eff—"

"Getting married is hardly any kind of achievement."

"Tell that to my mother." I forced a chuckle.

"Want to see something?" Gabe held up his hand. My heart twisted when I noticed that his ring finger was bare. Until now, he'd still worn it. Its absence made me sad.

"God, I'm so sorry," I said.

"I'll eventually get used to it, I suppose." Gabe shrugged. "Or maybe not."

"You know what they say. Relationships are complicated," I said, trying to fill the silence. I quickly realized that I was hardly one to be offering advice. "How's that for a useless pep talk?" I asked.

"Supremely not helpful." His dimples became deep crescents when he smiled. "Let's talk about something else. Anything else. Tell me about your exciting life."

"Okaaaay," I said, trying to remember something that might qualify as remotely exciting. "How about this? In addition to being on my case about casting 'rad dads' to ride this ridiculous 'Feminists for Father's Day' float that Alice wants me to organize, she emailed me to say how excited she was to learn that I am friends with Leigh Sullivan."

"The artist, right? The one who makes those sculptures of . . ." Gabe waved his hands in the air and averted my gaze.

"Celebrity vulvas," I said, finishing his sentence. I hadn't gone into too much detail about Leigh, somebody with whom I hadn't had a real conversation in years, but Gabe's memory was a steel trap. While I had to be reminded of the names of everyone in our singing troupe, Gabe knew all the Looney Tunes' first and last names right after meeting them—and a lot of their phone numbers too.

"Alice, being the stalker that she is, saw that Leigh had liked something of mine on Instagram," I told him. "She wanted to know how Leigh and I could possibly know each other, which was borderline offensive, but before I could even reply to explain that we lived together in college, she was off to the races, following up to ask if I could help get her a Leigh Sullivan sculpture without the gallery markup."

"It's not like she could afford one at full price. Her great-grandfather only owned what, half of the railroads in America?" Gabe raised his eyebrows.

"Exactly," I said.

"What did you tell her?"

"I said that I would bring it up with Leigh at our college reunion this weekend," I said. "Which, by the way, I am not going to do."

"You're not going to the reunion?"

"I'm not going to bring it up. I have to go. I can't not go."

"You don't sound too thrilled."

"It was going to be fun. But now I'm not so sure." I took another gulp of wine and proceeded to tell Gabe about how ashamed I'd felt when scrolling through all the videos of my classmates boasting about their accomplishments, how it put my lack of any discernible life achievement into sharp relief. "To add insult to injury . . ." I pulled out my phone, careful to scroll past the dick pic, and showed him the photo Geeta had texted me, the portrait of my embodied self.

"Cute," he said in an unconvincing tone.

I screwed up my mouth. "She's trying to be encouraging, but it can sometimes have the opposite effect. It's almost like my friends are getting tired of my lack of . . ." I petered out, trying to locate the right word.

"Lack of . . .?" Gabe sounded confused.

"It's like . . . they don't know what to do with me." I thought about how Thea told Gabe she found him exhausting. My friends and family members felt the same way about me.

Gabe listened as I told him about my older brother, Andrew, who, despite being a certifiable meathead, managed a hedge fund and lived in a dream home with his fitness-instructor wife. I told him about my mother, and how we used to be so close, and how the only thing we seemed to talk about anymore was her disappointment in my choices and concerns about my future. I told him about Sophie, who was more than ten years my junior and excelling at work all the while amassing an army of TikTok followers with her snack-related content.

"Hold up. I thought we liked Sophie?"

"We do! I do! She's the best! She just puts me to shame sometimes. I don't know how she does it. She left a terrible controlling boyfriend who I know she's still hung up on, but she never even mentions him. She just powers through. Seriously, she's so disciplined and confident. She kills it at work and she does Pilates four times a week. I bet she's going to run the Gates Foundation by the time she's thirty. Which would be great, as I'd be more than happy to go work for her." The alcohol was going straight to my head. I was rambling.

"I still don't see what you mean by this supposed 'lack,'"

Gabe said, leaning back in his seat. "You're smart enough to understand that our whole culture is powered by manufacturing feelings of inadequacy to sell us something to fix the fake problem. It's how the bastards grind us down."

"Ugh, I know," I told him. "But, sometimes, when I'm with my friends—who aren't bastards, for the most part—I feel worse than down. Like I'm cursed."

"Jenny, take it easy."

"Okay, maybe I'm not cursed, but I definitely feel like—"

"Like what?"

"It's hard to explain. It's like I have no chance. Like I'm doomed to fail over and over again. Like I never got the memo."

Gabe chuckled. "There's a memo?"

"You know, the 'I didn't get the memo' memo."

"From my perspective, you're doing great things." He took another bite of bread.

"Thanks." I felt my cheeks flush. "That makes one of us."

"Forget the other people! Their opinions don't matter. Do you think I care what anyone has to say about my becoming a high school math teacher?"

"That you're good at math?"

"More like: 'Look at that guy who used to pull in mid-six figures and is now teaching fractions to kids who are playing with their phones.'"

"I'm not following."

"You know, I briefly worked as a Wall Street quant, trading derivatives," he said.

"You did?" I shook my head, a little embarrassed. Sometimes I worried I was a terrible listener. "Did you tell me that already?"

"Why would it have come up?"

"Okay," I said, feeling relieved. "So you were a wolf of Wall Street *and* you were on tour with the Strokes? Anything else you want to put out there?"

"It was one show."

"Still," I said. "Wow. Tell me about your mid-six-figure days."

"I was on a team of math nerds who evaluated what was going on in the market, but not based on investment fundamentals. We ran algorithms, using mathematics to discover arbitrage opportunities. We were killers."

"You? A killer?"

"Good point." He took a gulp of his beer. "I wasn't so much of a killer."

"You say that like it's a bad thing."

"The guy who ran the firm was a total tyrant. He wore Belgian loafers and had three baseball bats in his office. When Ramona was born, I became the first person who used the company's paternity-leave policy, which we were expected not to do. Then, right before I was ready to go back to work, I started having the worst stress headaches. The thought of returning to that job was literally making me sick. Thea is the one who encouraged me to quit."

"That was nice of her," I allowed.

"Sure," he said unsurely. "Teaching was something I always wanted to do, and she was pulling all-nighters to climb the ladder of her firm. One of us had to be around for Ramona at dinnertime, right? Her desire for me to have a better work-life balance wasn't entirely altruistic."

I nodded. "Nothing ever is."

"I don't mean to sound ungrateful. Quitting that job was the best thing I ever did," he went on. "Teaching is pretty cool. And math is beautiful. Plus, now I have time to spend with Ramona and I never miss my hockey league. A cappella nights are all right too." He gave me a small smile. I was on my second glass of wine now and felt my cheeks warming. Gabe took another bite of bread.

"This is fucking tremendous," he said.

"It's a good recipe," I said modestly, but I could feel myself grinning with pride.

"Let's hear more about this magic memo," he said, all but cackling. "What would it tell you?"

"I don't know." I looked up at the pub's tin ceiling. "I guess that's the problem. I always believed that I had time to explore and figure out what I was going to become ever since that whole culinary wunderkind thing went up in flames."

Gabe made a sympathetic expression. "It didn't go anywhere." He pointed to the crumbs on the table.

"Gabe." I met his eye. "It did. I set a UNESCO World Heritage Site on fire. As I may have mentioned."

"Only about a hundred times."

No matter how many years had passed since my "accident," as those who loved me encouraged me to call my five-alarm fuck-up, I could never snuff that fire from my memories. I'd shown up in Italy convinced that my apprenticeship at a historic, Michelin-starred bakery was a "life-altering opportunity." It sure had been after that fateful Wednesday afternoon when I'd idiotically ran home early to grab a pair of earrings that I wanted to wear on a date with Massimo, my summer fling. I was so excited I forgot to finish cleaning the oven, which resulted in a stray towel catching on fire and the entire place going down. The reconstruction took close to a year. It was almost two years before I could bring myself to bake so much as a loaf of banana bread.

"Did I ever tell you that when I came back from Italy, I had an opportunity to work at a promising culinary start-up, but I was too traumatized and withdrew my application?"

"Am I missing something?" Gabe asked.

"That start-up is now Cup Queen, the cupcake chain you see on every corner in every major city."

"They make an excellent red velvet, not gonna lie," Gabe said. "You should have taken the gig."

"Thanks." I wrinkled my nose. "Remember my last job in New York, at the public radio station? I'm not sure I ever shared the full story of what happened there."

Gabe nodded for me to go on.

"Well, during one of the pledge drives, they had me come on air—it was a chance for me to convince the top brass that I could potentially host a show. At the moment I should have summoned my charm and winning personality, I had a brain freeze and totally messed up. I named the anonymous donor who'd offered to double people's contributions that day."

"Oops!" I could tell Gabe was trying to contain his laughter.

"It gets better. The anonymous donor," I went on, "turned out to be this old lady who was the matriarch of this borderline fascist political family, which led to a *New York Times* exposé about the ties between dark money and public radio."

I could tell by Gabe's face that my story was losing its funny factor, but I continued, "And when I heard about Alice's foundation, of course I jumped at the chance to work with her—I had no other options. But I didn't know what a phony she was. And here I am on the edge of thirty-six with no clue—"

"Listen," Gabe interrupted. "You're not 'cursed.' And you're still young."

I raised my eyebrows.

"You're not over the hill."

"You really know how to make a girl feel special," I said.

Gabe took another sip and leaned back in his chair, causing his messenger bag to fall, its contents scattering across the floor. I reached down to help him gather his belongings.

"What the. . .?" My eyes fixed on one of the books that had tumbled out. A paperback copy of *Stacey Plunkett Gets a Life* by T. S. Almond. It had the same cover as the version I'd taken out of my middle-school library in the 1990s, a cheesy rendition of Stacey, her hair in a crimped side ponytail, sitting on a park bench with her frozen yogurt.

"You okay?" Gabe asked. "You look like you just saw a ghost."

"That used to be my favorite book when I was a kid! I've looked for it online, but I've never been able to find it anywhere." I started flipping through the pages.

"It was left over from the school library sale," Gabe said. "I thought I'd give it to Ramona."

"This is crazy!" I felt a rush of excitement. "I asked my mother about it the other day, and she couldn't remember the book. She said it was a figment of my overly active imagination."

"It's all yours," Gabe said, handing it to me. "I'll find another way to tempt Ramona off her video games."

IT WAS A CLEAR WARM NIGHT, AND I DECIDED TO WALK HOME. I TEXTED Hal to let him know my ETA, then walked another twenty minutes or so, when my phone buzzed. Hal probably remembered something he wanted me to pick up from the deli, some new kind of plant milk he'd just learned about. But the text was from a non-phone number: 000–000. I never should have let Sophie talk me into signing up for her marketing alerts from the Aurora Foundation. Then I saw the text.

> Jenny Green, you're correct. You never got the
> Memo. Download the app now.

There was some bit.ly mumbo jumbo, an abbreviated link to a website. What on earth?

I looked up and down the street, as if the engineer of this interruption could be lingering under a lamppost in a fedora, silhouetted by moonlight. I had just shared my memo theory with Gabe tonight. But he was good at old-school math, not new-fangled tech.

Geeta was always sending me early editions of her products—imperfect versions with glitches to be identified and worked out. She had just sent me that embodied-self image—maybe this was related? But then I remembered something. Preying on my insecurities wasn't her thing. Plus, I hadn't even mentioned my memo theory to her. Had I shared it with Sophie? It didn't matter. She wouldn't do something like this. She was all about empowerment.

I turned the corner onto my block and tried to come up with an explanation. Whatever it was, I did not click on the link. When I looked at my phone again, the message was gone. It didn't matter. I didn't need anyone else out there to confirm what was painfully obvious. That I, Jenny Green, never got the Memo.

4
. .

ABE?" HAL CALLED FROM THE BEDROOM WHEN I WALKED THROUGH the door. The way he said it, it sounded more like "Baaaabe." I guessed I should have been ready for another mating call, given the "yum" text he'd misfired. He was never horny for me in the evening. But he now had to pretend he was to cover his tracks. Otherwise, I'd know for sure that he had meant to send that intimate photo to the sexy closet organizer down the hall.

"Baaaabe?" Hal repeated.

I tiptoed toward our room and found Hal on top of the covers, wearing boxers and a navy pocket T-shirt. "Come here." He reached his arms out. The magazine he'd been reading fell to the ground. I relented and let him pull me down and roll on top of me. The weight of his body made me feel safe, and then he whispered in my ear what he was about to do to me which made me forget my rage and feel . . . other things.

Here was the problem: no matter what horrible thing Hal did, no matter how neglected I felt, I couldn't not be attracted to him. Hal was more tender and passionate than usual. Afterward, I snuggled against his chest and tried to collect my thoughts.

"Wow," I said. "That was—"

He tousled my hair and grinned.

I rolled onto my back, awash in pleasure. Maybe I could stop asking questions and enjoy the parts of my life that were working.

"Watch out, class of 2007. The heat is going to be radiating off us this weekend," I said, then immediately felt like an idiot. The *heat*? Really? But the overall point still held up. I closed my eyes and imagined entering the welcome dinner with Hal at my side. Eat your heart out, fellow grads. You here may be the SVP of some global bank, and you over there may drive a car that can also fly, but I've got this living god *and* I make the world's best olive focaccia from scratch. And I can sing.

Hal cleared his throat. "This weekend?"

"Are you kidding me?" I looked up at him. "My college reunion."

I could feel his body stiffen beside me. "I forgot. Or maybe I blocked it out."

"You're coming," I told him, but it came out more as a question.

"I have a lot of work." Hal folded his hands behind his head.

"You said you would." I pushed the pillow into his face. "It's on the weekend. You don't work on weekends." He barely worked during the week.

"I have work on Fridays."

"For just four hours," I reminded him. "That's your half day. I'm sure somebody else can cover for you."

"It's not that easy."

"What do you guys do on Friday anyway, besides talk about your weekend plans?"

"What the hell, Jenny?" Hal flung the pillow to the floor. "Way to be condescending. And my job isn't my only work. I'm writing a book, as you might recall."

"You've been writing a book for seven years!"

He changed his tack. "You didn't come to my reunion."

"You didn't *go* to your reunion!"

Hal scoffed. "I won't even know anyone there."

"You know Geeta and Leigh."

"Oh yeah, the illuminati! Your famous friends who you constantly complain about."

"Everyone complains about their friends," I said. "And I don't complain about *them*. It's just that their success can be . . . challenging for me. Which is even more reason it would be really nice if you joined me, for moral support if nothing else." I stared up at the ceiling. If only I could turn back time. Only a year ago, when we'd first moved here, things had been better. Hal and I would go on hours-long urban hikes, exploring the parks, gorgeous bridges, and abandoned steel lots. It had felt like a renewal of our relationship, and, for a second, a renewal of my life.

We lay there in silence. Something had shifted. The space between our bodies felt bigger than an ocean.

"Hey, you know that picture you texted me yesterday?" I finally asked, blinking back tears. "Was it even meant for me?"

"Of course," Hal said too quickly. I glanced at him. His eyes told me everything. Now the tears were spilling down my cheeks.

"Is this even about the reunion?" he asked. "If it's so important to you, I'll come."

"*If* it's so important to me?"

"It *is* so important to you?" He sounded pathetic.

"Well, I didn't go to the last one because we weren't getting along, and I would have been the only single person there," I said.

"By now, half the class will be divorced, so you won't have that problem." I wasn't in the mood for his jokes.

"You know how I get social anxiety in these situations. I thought the least you could do was come and be my body man, give me some support."

"You don't *really* want me to be there," he said. "You just want people to see me there, so that they don't think you're alone."

"Is that so bad?" I was burning up with anger. "I . . . I love you. I said I'd marry you when you asked!"

"Oh now you're going to bring that up. How is that relevant?"

"I know you said you needed more time and it had nothing to do with me," I said, backpedaling. "I believed you."

"And I was telling the truth—unlike you with this reunion. You don't need me there! If I go, you'll barely even talk to me, and I'll be stuck making chitchat with Geeta's conspiracy-theorist husband."

"When was making chitchat ever difficult for you? You're the king of chitchat!" I was tired of convincing him. "Forget it!" I stormed out of bed and threw on my robe. "You know what? After so much togetherness, maybe we could use some time apart. I'll tell Geeta I have space in my bedroom in case she wants to use it to rehearse her next TED talk."

I grabbed my bag off the floor and pulled out my phone. There was a new text from ooo—ooo.

> Don't worry about him. Just come and get your Memo.

I shrieked.

"Jesus, you don't have to be so dramatic," Hal said.

"I have every reason to be dramatic," I said.

At last. Somebody out there in the universe understood. My fingers were practically flying as I typed in my reply:

> Fine. Tell me how.

5
• •

I T WAS A BEAUTIFUL DAY FOR A LONG DRIVE, ALL BLUE SKIES AND FLUFFY
white clouds, a perfect seventy-two degrees—lucky for me, because the air conditioning in my car wasn't functioning properly. I was feeling good in my newly thrifted white T-shirt dress
as I steered my Honda alongside the Allegheny River toward the
highway on-ramp. One eye on the road ahead, I selected Leigh's
Spotify mix, *You Aughts to Know*, a compilation of the greatest hits
from our college days. She had sent it to Geeta and me on that
revitalized text thread, making me wonder if Geeta's optimism
was perhaps warranted.

As Sean Paul sang "Get Busy/Like Glue," I thought about the
wild house parties we used to have. We used to be so tight, the
three of us. There was even a moment right after college, when
Geeta was working around the clock at an elite consulting firm,
that Leigh and I were the two closest members of our friendship
triangle. Back then, she was a low-level gallery assistant. She
didn't talk about all the cool people she was "collab-ing" with,
the way she did now. We used to take field trips to the Korean bath
house in Flushing, where we'd get massages and then go out for
dim sum.

Things changed around the time Leigh's mom died. That was
when she moved to LA to be closer to Seattle, where the rest of her
family was based, and to enroll in art school. It was time to get

serious, she told me. She had a plan and was sticking to it. Leigh started taking longer to return my calls. For a while I wondered what I had done to put her off, but then it occurred to me that I hadn't done anything. She was transitioning to a new phase of life and I simply didn't make the cut.

My wrist started vibrating. It was my watch, informing me that my mother was calling. I fumbled my "decline," then accidentally picked up. Suddenly, the nostalgic melody gave way to Ann Green in surround sound.

"What's doin', Jen?" my mom asked.

"I'm in the car," I said. "On my way to my college reunion."

"You're talking on the phone when you are driving?" She was suddenly in full-on panic mode. "I'll hang up. I'll go."

"Mom, it's fine. Miracle of Bluetooth! What's up?"

"Is *he* with you?"

I let off a sigh of frustration. Ten seconds into the call, and we were on to the only thing on her agenda these days. "Hal?" I said. Ever since this past winter, when he'd shelved our very short-lived engagement, my mom couldn't even say his name. Come to think of it, I hadn't said his name in a little while. Hal and I had barely made eye contact in the days following his great reunion flake-out, but I was not about to tell my mother that she was right about him. I thought about lying and telling her he was with me, but then remembered I was a grown woman and ought to stand in my truth.

"No, Mom. Hal is not with me today." I tried to speak firmly, enunciating my *t*s. My former therapist, Joyce, a caftan-loving woman I'd stopped seeing when I lost my radio job and the health insurance that came with it, had told me that I needed to set better boundaries with my mother.

"Why not?"

"He had work to do."

"What is he working on?"

"His book."

"How's it coming?"

I wasn't about to engage in this line of inquiry. Plus, I didn't know the answer to her question. "It's *my* reunion," I reminded her. "He didn't even go to Coleman."

"Well, maybe you'll meet somebody at the reunion," she said.

"I'm not going there to meet somebody," I said, gritting my teeth. "I'm going to spend quality time with the people I already know."

"Is Geeta going to be there?"

"Of course. We're staying together in our old place."

"She's such a nice girl. So brilliant!" My mom's opinion of my best friend had skyrocketed in recent years, in direct proportion with Geeta's fame and success. "And Leigh? Is she still a—?"

"A lesbian?"

"No," said my mother, even though I was sure that was exactly what she meant to say. "I meant, is she still an artist?"

"Of course she is still an artist," I said robotically. "As Leigh likes to say, art isn't something you do, it's who you are."

"Isn't that nice," she said in a tone that indicated that she didn't find Leigh's success nice at all. She was a practical woman with a considerable amount of skepticism for pursuing careers in the arts. "I saw her picture in the *Times* a little while ago. She looked . . . different. I always thought she was cute, but now she's quite striking." There was a moment of silence as my mother's meaning set in. "Striking" was another way of saying "pin thin." My mother had an unhealthy fixation on my friends' body mass indexes.

"I'd prefer if we didn't comment on other people's appearances," I said, trying to put Joyce's advice to use once again.

"I can't say that someone is striking anymore?" my mom asked with genuine bewilderment. "Is that a new banned word?"

"Forget it. I'll them you send your regards," I said.

My mom sighed. "Your father and I were talking, and we just want you to know that we love you."

"Thanks," I said, waiting for the next blow.

"We know there are better days ahead."

"Okay, thanks for the unsolicited fortune-telling session," I said. "You know, next time you call, you can ask how I'm doing."

"Jen, that's not fair. I wish you'd ever tell me."

The second I hung up, I regretted my knee-jerk defensive attitude. My mom and I might not have been as close as we once were, but she still cared about me. She just had a terrible way of showing it.

My former celebrity crush was singing about girls who become lovers turning into mothers. I couldn't believe how I failed to notice the misogyny in this lyric when I first heard it. Did he mean that they turn into mothers in general or that they turn into *their* mothers? Was I turning into Ann Green without even realizing it? No, no, no, not if Hal could help it. I wouldn't be turning into a mother at all, let alone my own mother. I cranked up the volume and kept right on driving down the ribbon of highway.

6.

A FEW HOURS LATER, THE ROLLING HILLS OF SEQUOIA FALLS CAME into view. I could feel my spirits lift; I hadn't visited this gorgeous place since I'd graduated, which was stupid. There was no law saying I could come up only for reunion weekends. This campus in the middle of farm country in upstate New York was where I'd met the people who meant the most to me, who saw me at my best and worst. I remembered the wooded lakes where my friends and I had gone skinny-dipping on brisk May weekends. The vineyards where I'd tasted my first good Riesling and learned that terroir wasn't just for wine snobs. The farmers market where I encountered that sourdough bread I still dreamed about.

I wouldn't be who I was without my time at Coleman—four perfect years talking about books and ideas with the two people who could make me laugh harder than anyone. Geeta, Leigh, and I knew each other from living in the same freshman dorm, but our friendship didn't expand beyond small talk until our second semester, when we all took the same medieval studies class. Tiny and beautiful, Geeta had been as focused as a ninja. She was quiet in my Thursday afternoon discussion section—taught by a gorgeous and brilliant TA named Tanya whom I was always angling to impress, and whom we still talked about today as if she were a celebrity. Geeta was always ready with the most insightful thing to say when called upon. Leigh, by contrast, was loud and opinionated, always trying to bring something provocative to the table.

Back in the day, I thought I was a pretty cool customer in my white leggings and vintage cowboy boots, smoking clove cigarettes on the side of Baron Hall after class. My friends were even cooler. People gravitated toward us. Mostly, though, we just loved being with each other. The three of us used to borrow 1980s comedy DVDs from the media-center library and hold Friday night film festivals in the thick-carpeted screening rooms while our classmates were congregating at some ridiculous frat party. That scene was never for us. Starting sophomore year, we coordinated our class schedules and, when the weather was good, we ate lunch under an oak tree in the arts quad, surrounded by hippies playing frisbee.

I took the exit off Route 90 and headed down the side roads, past fields of grazing cattle and dilapidated houses. I was feeling something close to happiness, alone with my thoughts and the tray of cherry almond muffins at my side. I couldn't wait for Geeta to utter her signature compliment upon taking a bite: "This, my love, is transcendent!"

A sense of anticipation came over me as I pulled up in front of 25 Spruce Street, the same address where we had all lived together our senior year. When Geeta had discovered the three-bedroom apartment was now an Airbnb property, she'd pounced on renting it for the reunion. "We can't *not* do it!" she'd said in an email to Leigh and me then privately messaged me to say that she'd already put down the deposit. The deal was done.

Steeling myself for the nostalgia trip that awaited me, I parked in front of our former home and made my way up the steps to the porch where we used to put kegs when we threw parties. The door was unlocked, so I let myself in, carefully balancing the tray of muffins in one hand and dragging my luggage with the other.

The apartment had been renovated beyond recognition. The kitchen countertops, once made of cheap Formica in a hideous geometric pattern, were now cream-colored marble. A huge butcher block island not dissimilar from the one in my Pittsburgh apartment replaced the wall that used to divide the kitchen and the living area, opening up the space. Clustered around the island were my friends, dressed up and posed before a stand of ring lights.

I had unwittingly entered a high-fashion photo shoot. Leigh and Geeta were both wearing gowns and jean jackets, their faces caked in foundation. A trio of makeup artists and hairstylists hung back, drinking espresso from paper coffee cups and talking among themselves about their favorite moisturizer. Did any of them even see me? I quietly deposited my baked goods next to the sink in the hopes that maybe someone would at least notice my muffins, then headed back toward the sofa, waving to people and mouthing "Hiiiii" so as not to disrupt whatever it was that they were doing.

"Jenny!" Geeta cried out. "We're just wrapping up this silly thing!"

"Almost there," Geeta's husband, Matt, said as he clicked away on a professional-looking camera. Matt managed some kind of family fund with his brother, but he spent most of his life worming his way into everything his wife was doing. Today he was the royal photographer. Two digital cameras—one massive, one extra massive—hung from his neck. He crouched down to get the perfect shot. In between clicks, Leigh looked my way.

"Hey, girl!" she said. "You made it."

"I did," I said, pumping my fist in victory.

"Third time's the charm, I guess." She had to twist the knife about my bailing on the last one—and the one before that.

"I was worried that you'd sue me if I didn't." I watched the corners of Leigh's mouth turn up. She looked like a model, with her superhuman bone structure and strawberry blonde waves. She also happened to be close to six feet tall. She was a skyscraper next to Geeta, who was as petite as a reedy schoolboy despite having given birth to twins just months earlier.

"Cute 'fit," Leigh muttered. I looked up to make sure she was talking to me. Her compliment made more sense when she completed her thought. "Kristen wore one of those to the gym last week."

I wasn't going to take the bait and ask which Kristen she was talking about. Stewart? Bell? Scott Thomas? Good to know I was wearing what other people considered to be exercise clothes.

"Jenny, could you actually move over there?" Matt asked. "You're blocking the light."

That Geeta married Matt never ceased to astonish me. She could do so much better than this guy. Ever since the birth of the twins, Matt fixated on his daughters' supposed maladies, taking them for allergy tests as often as most people went to the grocery store. But Geeta never complained about him, or anyone, or anything. She moved through life like a sharp knife through soft butter.

I hung off to the non-light-disrupting side while Leigh's new girlfriend, a Swedish singer named Inge, introduced herself and offered me a cold seltzer. When I thanked her, she smiled, revealing a gold tooth. Leigh was so committed to living on the vanguard that even her girlfriends doubled as cutting-edge fashion accessories. I told Inge I loved her last single, which was true.

"How do you and Leigh know each other?" Inge asked. I glanced at Leigh, whose dress appeared to be made of paper flowers. It hurt that she hadn't even bothered to mention me to Inge, a person about whom she was sufficiently serious to bring to our reunion.

"We met here. In college," I explained to Inge, avoiding using the word "obviously." "But we don't really know each other that well—not anymore." Inge was no longer paying attention as she picked at her cuticles.

Then Geeta's real ride or die, Dasha, the indomitable nanny who had been part of the family since before the birth of the twins, entered the room and settled on the couch with the babies, Luna and Maya. My heart swelled at the sight of my goddaughters—or, as Geeta non-denominationally called them, guide daughters, insofar that I was their designated guide mother. I rushed over and busied myself bouncing them on my knees. I tried to tune out all the chaos around me and take in that glorious fresh baby scent.

Something primal came over me when I held Geeta's babies in my arms—and then, a sinking feeling. Hal didn't want kids. And my biological clock was running out of batteries rapidly. Here I was, another girl becoming a lover but not a mother. For all her talk about leveling the gender gap, Alice didn't feel it was necessary to cover even a portion of egg freezing for her female employees. And I sure couldn't afford it.

"Is that a wrap?" Geeta said.

"Not yet," Matt said. "Just a few more."

"Sorry, Jen. It's this silly thing for a magazine," Geeta called out.

"It's not silly!" Matt shot back. "You're making change!"

"Which magazine is this for?" I asked.

"*Moment*," Geeta said. "They have this thing called the Changemakers List."

I froze. The same Changemakers package that Alice had been hounding me about.

This year, Alice told me she *must* be among the chosen Changemakers. She had been overlooked for too long. I didn't want to be the one to explain to her why she'd never get her wish—she hated "Debbie Downers" and believed in the power of positive thinking—so I'd just made some performative outreach to somebody at the magazine, a shoe-closet assistant named Jade, one of Hal's friends who had dated for a week. Then I told Alice I was in talks with someone on staff, that things were looking promising for her.

I wandered over to the kitchen sink and refilled my glass, then ripped off the top of a cherry muffin and shoved it into my mouth. I tried not to think about how furious Alice was going to be with me when the *Moment* piece came out. It was one thing if she wasn't on the list. It was another if she wasn't on it and the closest friends of the person who had promised, in a moment of unbridled positivity, to get her on it, were.

"You're having the best time ever!" Matt shouted. "Nobody is having a better time than the two of you!" My friends fake-laughed and threw their heads back so hard I feared for their necks. When Matt was done scurrying around them and snapping pictures, their faces went back to their natural—and even more beautiful—states.

"So you both got on the Changemakers List?" I said in as gentle a tone as I could manage. "That's a pretty sweet coincidence."

"I know," said Leigh. "It was cute the way they notified us at the same time, on a conference call, because they knew we were best friends and wanted us to be featured together—a celebration of women lifting each other up." Leigh tapped Geeta on the nose. "Boop!" Leigh cooed.

I tried to smile, the words "best friends" echoing in my head. Geeta looked at the floor. She always could tell when I was uncomfortable.

"I love this for you," I managed, tiptoeing a little closer to the two of them. Maybe some self-deprecation would save the day. "You're both having your *Moment* moment, while I'm in Pittsburgh, hearing that I didn't get the Memo."

Leigh and Geeta's arms were still wrapped around each other from the last pose. They looked like they'd been stun-gunned while performing an avant-garde dance routine.

"What did you say?" Leigh asked, her aquamarine eyes widening as she disentangled from her fellow Changemaker.

"Forget it." I shrugged. I didn't want to make this about me.

"No, really. What did you say? You didn't get what?" There was something fishy about Leigh's tone.

"What? Do you happen to be familiar with these mystery texts? About how I never got the Memo? Was it you?"

Geeta and Leigh's eyes met but neither of them said anything.

"So that's it." I was genuinely shocked. "Very funny, guys. Thanks for that. I really needed a reminder."

"No, it wasn't," Geeta said. "But . . . those texts. Could you show them to us?"

"Forget it, never mind," I said, regretting having brought it up. I believed Geeta, and wanted to talk about anything else. "They deleted themselves. Who knows? Maybe I imagined the whole thing."

I didn't want to drag out this embarrassing episode. I was here to have fun with my friends, not shine a spotlight on the differences between us. They were the ones who got the Memo. I was the one who didn't. It was plain as day. I didn't need a text message to prove it.

"That is some freaky shit," Matt said, which reminded me that he was there. "Do you think they're coming from Russia? I heard they do that."

"Who are *they*?" I asked. "The KGB?"

"The FSB. I hope you didn't click on anything," he said.

I stared at Matt, wondering what Geeta saw in this conspiracy theorist. There must have been something I was missing, some hidden quality that made Matt worth keeping around all these years. Geeta was usually so smart about other people. She saw things the rest of us missed. While I was shocked when Leigh came out to us our sophomore year, Geeta didn't even blink. She'd known all along, but kept her inklings to herself out of respect for Leigh. That was nothing compared to the time the following year when Geeta had magically sensed something was wrong at the precise moment a drunk upperclassman had wandered into my dorm room and proceeded to rip off his rugby shirt and chant like an ogre. I had been certain he was about to kill me when Geeta appeared and managed to subdue him with a self-defense technique, then dragged his ass to the campus security outpost.

"I think we got the shots," Matt said as the makeup artists and stylists pulled together their equipment. One of them grabbed a couple of my muffins on her way out.

Geeta clapped her hands loudly. "Thanks, everybody. I'm going to go wash my face. I can feel my pores clogging with all this makeup." The next thing I knew, Leigh had vanished too.

I ducked into my old bedroom. It had changed less than the rest of the apartment. The bed was still against the back wall. The late afternoon sun filtered through what appeared to me to be the same curtains, with the same gray stains by the bottom, from fifteen years ago. The entire house had been improved except for the area that I had occupied. Imagine that. I sat on the bed and felt the lifeless air begin to settle on me. I needed to get outside.

"Guys," I called out, coming out of the bedroom, "I think I'm going to take a little walk."

Geeta's door opened. I could see she was now in deep multi-tasking mode, nursing a baby while wearing a sheet face mask, a book in the crook of her arm. The words "Win While You Sleep" ran across the back cover. Geeta used to gobble up nineteenth-century Spanish literature, but I guessed that pursuit no longer helped her maximize her waking—and sleeping—hours.

"Don't judge me," she said as if reading my thoughts. "Everyone in the industry keeps bringing it up and I need to do my homework. It's by this big-deal thought leader." She rolled her eyes. I shrugged and headed toward the door. "But Jen, hold up!" she called out. "Where are you going?"

"Just a quick stroll around the old neighborhood."

"The welcome dinner's barely in an hour," she said.

Her baby's leg wiggled adorably. I turned around and planted a kiss on the sole of her foot. "I'll be back before you know it. Promise." Then I kissed Geeta's cheek.

7
. .

GEETA'S IDEA TO TRACK DOWN OUR OLD PLACE HAD BEEN CUTE. THE practical reality of being back here, though, was a bit too much for me to take, with or without the Changemaker photo shoot.

I was a few blocks away from the apartment when my phone vibrated. A call was coming in from Gabe's number. Up until this moment, he and I had stuck to texts.

"Gabe? Everything okay?" I said.

"Just checking in," he told me. I could hear the din of children in the background. "I know you were anxious about today, and I guess I was just thinking of you. How's the reunion?" He was just thinking of me? I tried to pretend this was totally normal.

"Oh cool, thanks. You still at school?" I asked.

"I'm at the playground, for a birthday party," he told me. "You know, 'tis the season that all the summer babies celebrate at once. Next Friday there are two parties at the same time and as far across town from each other as can be."

"That's what you get for having a popular daughter."

"Hard to keep up with her." I could tell by Gabe's tone that he was smiling. "Anyway, you good?"

"I think so?"

"How'd the muffins come out?"

"Just great," I said, wondering how pathetic I must have

seemed at our last post-a-cappella pub session to warrant this sympathy call. "A perfect batch." The children in the background were screaming. "Sounds busy. You want me to call you back later maybe?"

"No, the kids are watching some magician pull a gerbil out of a suitcase. Hold on, I'm going to move to a quieter spot." I heard Gabe tell somebody that he'd be right back, then what sounded like a gate opening and closing. When Gabe spoke again, it was in a quieter voice. "This party is not for me."

"I've always found magicians kind of creepy," I told him.

"You should see his gerbil. Not a hair on its sorry body. And then . . ."

"And then . . . ?"

"I'm the only dad here, which, to be honest, can be . . . a challenge."

"I thought you were a 'fearless feminist father.' You have the Aurora Foundation T-shirt to prove it!"

He laughed. "I don't have any problem with being the only dad. But let's just say that single moms can be a little, uh, intense."

"Gotcha." I'd never stopped to think about this aspect of parenting for Gabe. He might have been a bit on the awkward side, but he also had more hair on his head than that poor gerbil, which must have made him a rare commodity among the moms of north Pittsburgh. The realization that I was serving, essentially, as my a cappella friend's beard—a long-distance talisman to ward off horny moms—made me smile.

"I'm just going to sit on this bench for a minute if you don't mind. Catch me up, will you?" His voice sounded serious. "Real talk. Is it as bad as you thought?"

"Well, I've barely been here an hour and I'm already taking a walk to clear my head if that is any indication," I told him. I was strolling along the south side of town, alongside the rows of fixer-uppers where the undergraduates and young professors lived. The light was dimming and the air smelled ripe and sweet.

"Why? Did something happen?" he asked.

"When I showed up, my friends were already in the apartment. You'll never guess what they were doing!"

"Sending weird texts about somebody not getting the Memo?"

"Very funny. No. They were doing a photoshoot. With hairstylists, fashion wranglers, and Geeta's husband doing his best Richard Avedon impression. Nobody even really noticed me—or my awesome muffins—except for a makeup artist, who grabbed a handful and took them to go."

"Your muffins deserve better."

"I don't want to point fingers. The timing was bad when I walked in. I must have been a little early. Or late, I don't know. But I just couldn't stand there in what used to be my own home watching them throwing their heads back and forth like tipsy giraffes. And then when it was over, I got weird and asked them about the Memo and . . ."

"Lemme guess, they all got weird too?" he asked softly.

"Bingo. I was hoping it would be different, and that I'd been silly not to want to come. But the second I said 'the Memo,' they got quiet and then denied knowing anything about the texts. Anyway, the big kick-off dinner is soon. And if this is how I react when I see my actual friends . . . I'm not sure I can handle a cocktail hour with my entire class."

"One foot in front of the other," Gabe said. "You'll have a better time when you start running into the random people you forgot about. Trust me, there will be at least one surprise encounter that makes it all worth it."

I could feel my anxiety dissipating. "How can you be so sure?"

"That's what reunions are for. I've been to even more of them than you have."

"I haven't been to any. I hope you're right," I said, remembering how my mother also said that maybe I would meet someone there.

"And you can call me anytime you need to. Oh shit." Gabe's voice tensed. "It's cake time."

"Tell the MILFs I send my regards."

I hung up and continued to walk down the streets of Sequoia Falls, moving farther and farther away from my old apartment. Soon enough, I came to the town center. The main drag was much as I'd remembered, trapped in time: The same pizza joint, the same mom-and-pop drugstore, the same aura of benign neglect. The hippie clothing boutique where I used to buy hemp hoodies had yet to acknowledge the existence of contemporary fashion. Its sidewalk racks heaved with flowy garments that still looked perfect for the sixty-something flute-teacher set. There was a lone woman browsing the goods, but she looked more like a Fortune 500 executive than a Sequoia Falls music teacher. She was wearing a crisp pantsuit in a deep eggplant, a leather satchel slung over her shoulder.

When she turned around, I froze. It had been an adult lifetime since I'd laid eyes on her, but the woman was unquestionably Desiree LeBlanc, the independent career counselor I had met shortly before I graduated. Gabe had just assured me that a surprise encounter was right around the corner, but I doubted this run-in around the literal corner was what he had in mind. My hands felt tingly.

Desiree tilted her head and gave a fishy smile. "I've been waiting for you, Jenny."

"Who, me?" The words came out like a croak.

"Are you ready for your Memo?"

"That's . . . you?" I asked, my heart speeding as my mind connected the dots. It was all clicking into place. The strange text messages traced back to Desiree. But how?

I hadn't seen Desiree LeBlanc since that one meeting my senior year, although I had a distinct memory of our interaction. She'd advised me to drop out of school, which had seemed unorthodox for a career counselor. But I should have expected the unexpected. The whole point of Desiree was that she was different.

I'd gone to visit her office at the urging of Leigh, who used to talk about Desiree as if she were the messiah. This was all before the whole life-coach boom. Desiree was a trailblazer, the only New York–based employee of Consortium Associates, an enterprise dedicated to "unlocking hidden potential," according to her business card.

What this meant in practice was that she told confused college students what to do, in no uncertain terms. Her methods were alarmingly specific. She had advised Leigh to drop her landscape theory classes and to also drop Emily, her first girlfriend.

Geeta had also made abrupt changes after she started seeing Desiree. She chopped her long hair into a bob and started wearing monochromatic outfits in earth tones. When I asked her what precipitated the makeover, she told me that Desiree said it was important to adopt a signature look.

Desiree had her own signature look, exuding competence with her perfectly tailored silk suits and pristine leather accessories. She still wore her red hair in a neat, shiny bob as well as the same potent perfume, a scent that reminded me of a forest at dawn.

"Desiree?" I was speaking in a near whisper. *"You're* the one? Those texts are coming from you?"

"I'm just the medium." She beamed. "The universe is the message. Come on." She stepped away from the rack and motioned for me to follow her. I swallowed hard and did as told.

"The past has a way of catching up with you, Jenny," Desiree said, taking slow, deliberate strides. "If you had listened to me the first time, you wouldn't be in this predicament. Your life is a terrible mess because you didn't follow my advice."

How did she know about my messy life? And how was she so sure she had the answers? "If I'd followed your advice, I technically wouldn't even be part of the class of 2007," I said, referring to Desiree's bizarre edict that I needed to ditch college right before finals week and go to the Maldives. She'd even offered to buy me the plane ticket. "I wouldn't be here."

"Exactly." Desiree proceeded to stare at me as if she were looking right through me. "I tried to steer you onto your best course. You wouldn't listen. But guess what? You're in luck, thanks to new developments in the study of the soul."

"The study of the soul? You've got to be kidding me."

"I could not be more serious. We are offering you the once-in-a-lifetime opportunity to reconsider before it's too late."

"We?" I said apprehensively. "Who is 'we'?"

Her green eyes were blazing. "Time is not on your side," she said, ducking my question. "Geeta and Leigh stuck with their programs, and look at how well they are doing."

I felt nauseous. Could this be why my friends had behaved so weirdly when I'd mentioned the mysterious texts about not getting the Memo? Had they gotten literal Memos and failed to mention them to me?

"It's not too late," Desiree said. We were now at the village square, in front of the college bookstore. Desiree took a seat on an empty bench, removed a notebook from her satchel and scribbled something in the pages. "I guess you could say that you're the one who got away, Jenny Green. And we want to help you. We're going to bring you back into the fold."

"Why do you keep saying 'we'?" I pressed. "Are you in cahoots with my friends?"

"The 'we' of which I speak is the Consortium."

"Oh right." I gave a light laugh. "That 'we.'"

"It's not funny. We could have helped you a long time ago, had you followed our advice. It's been hard for us to see how much you've struggled. We've been watching you."

"That's . . . kind of creepy," I said. But Desiree just nodded, as if this observation made her proud. I was suddenly overcome by an impulse to get away from her. "Listen, I appreciate your interest and concern. But there are people in this world who are really struggling. Go help them."

"We are helping all types of people, but none of them have been blessed with your untapped potential. And when you factor everything in, technically you are our biggest failure yet! We use a complicated formula to uncover your DMs."

"You're hacking into my direct messages?"

"Please. I am talking about the Disparity Metrics. This is scientific, quantum-quantifiable proof. We review an array of things like your social skills, likability, and your upbringing as well as natural advantages such as body type and BMI. We also look at your economic class and your attendant privileges, and we evaluate your cognitive abilities and self-awareness. And then by exploring your life's various branch points—your mistakes, your regrets, your paths not taken, and so on and so forth—we can determine the size of the gap, or in your case, the *gulf* between your potential and your actual achievement in the game of life. Your failure is of majestic proportions!"

It's not as if this last fact hadn't occurred to me before, but I was still surprised to hear it articulated by a near-stranger.

Desiree reached into the inside pocket of her blazer and pulled out a black device that looked like a cross between a remote control and a digital thermometer. Without asking, she aimed it at my head and tapped a green button.

I glanced around to see if anyone was watching us. The only person on the commons was an older man feeding pigeons. He was totally uninterested in us.

"Are you taking my temperature or something?"

"In a sense," Desiree said. "Hold still."

The contraption started smoking and throwing off sparks. One singed my forehead.

"Ouch!" I cried.

"You broke it!" Desiree cried out. "You broke the Disparity Meter! You broke the technology!"

"I'm sorry!" I said, reflexively, although she was the one who should have been apologizing.

"Sorry? It's phenomenal! The rift between your potential and your reality is off the charts! This is the proof!"

"Of what?"

"That you really are the world's biggest failure!" she said triumphantly.

"So you've mentioned," I said. "If you're going to be a failure, you might as well fail big."

"This is your problem, Jenny," Desiree replied. "You make a joke about everything. There is nothing funny about your situation."

I felt as if I was about to faint.

"What do I get?" I said at last. "A medal?"

Desiree grabbed my hand and squeezed it as she spoke. "I am here to help you out of this muck. Don't be too disheartened. You haven't made the *worst* decisions. I'd say you've hardly made any decisions at all. You've bounced around in your life like a ping-pong ball in a wind tunnel, allowing forces around you to dictate your movements. You have to take ownership of your future. But you need a trustworthy guide. You can't be expected to find the path on your own. It's too damn confusing! That's why you must follow the Memo."

My mind reeled back to that time before graduation, a moment I hadn't thought about in years, when I told Geeta that Desiree's methods didn't resonate with me. She told me that I didn't need this type of thing, that she was 100 percent certain that my career would fall into place with or without outside intervention. Plus, Geeta found the specifics of Desiree's advice to me highly objectionable. She didn't want me to drop out of school and leave our shared house on Spruce Street. Graduation was right around the corner. We still had too much to do together.

"If you have a bad feeling about Desiree's advice, listen to your gut," Geeta had said. "Her methodology is not for everyone."

So I listened—to my gut, and to Geeta. Not that it was a difficult decision. I didn't need some all-knowing life coach–guru telling me she knew what was best for me. Drop out of school and go to the Maldives by myself because some weird lady in a suit told me to? Sorry, no.

I looked at the device smoking on the bench and thought back to that former version of myself: free and self-assured. Where had she gone? Maybe bumping into Desiree was the wake-up call I needed. But I could handle the rest on my own.

"It was great running into you, Desiree, but I think I'm okay," I said, rising to my feet.

She looked at me, her eyes glowing like green lanterns, and cackled as I took off.

8

I HUSTLED BACK TO THE SPRUCE STREET AIRBNB AS FAST AS MY LEGS could carry me. Much as I tried to think about anything but Desiree, my mind reeled to our first—and only—meeting, fifteen years earlier.

Desiree's home office was in a thatched cottage improbably located in the middle of a suburban cul-de-sac. I'd shown up open to a session of self-discovery. I'd visited acupuncturists, herbalists, and psychics at Geeta and Leigh's recommendation. I figured I might as well give this esteemed career counselor a shot too. Her reputation preceded her.

But I could tell something was off right away. First, Desiree buzzed me in, then made me wait for what felt like an eternity in what she referred to in an important tone of voice over the intercom as the "corridor." It was an unseasonably cold, windowless space that was slightly below ground. I sat in the waiting area's only chair, shivering and wondering what this woman had against sunlight. I was on the verge of hightailing it out of there when I heard a door creak open.

Desiree had finally come to fetch me, in her signature look—a snazzy pantsuit, not a copper hair out of place. We walked through the corridor and up a few stairs, which led directly into her living room. Her workplace was a monument to minimalism, all gleaming planes and uncluttered surfaces, nothing like the

Coleman College career center, a wood-paneled office lined with
binders filled with the contact information of various alumni.

She gestured for me to take a seat on a compact sofa. When
she'd settled into the chair across from me and asked me why I'd
booked an appointment with her, I'd told her the truth: I'd heard
my friends talking about her and wanted to see what the fuss was
all about. To be sure, Geeta kept saying I probably didn't need
Desiree's services. Despite my so-so study habits, I maintained a
high GPA. Geeta, on the other hand, had more Bs than As, and
no idea what she wanted to do after college. Her parents, already
devastated that she had abandoned her plans—*their* plans, to be
precise—to pursue medicine, were calling her every night, asking if she had "any news."

When Desiree asked me at that first meeting what I was most
worried about, I'd told her my biggest concern for the future was
that I wouldn't be able to figure out a way to make a living doing
what I loved. All the job opportunities I ever heard about involved
sitting around in air-conditioned offices crunching numbers. Un-
realistic as it may have been, I simply wanted to bake. I'd discovered my passion when I worked at a bakery the summer before my
senior year of high school. I was supposed to oversee the cash register, but by August, I was hauling loaves of sundried tomato bread
out of the industrial oven, as happy as I was sweat-slicked. From
that point on, the smell of a bakery always felt like home to me.

During the course of our initial conversation, Desiree kept
interrupting me. She acted like she already knew exactly what I
wanted, which she told me was "to be high—net worth and high
visibility." Beyond being untrue, her read on me was presump-
tuous. "I don't really care about that stuff. I just want to be successful enough to get by," I said. "Pay the bills, hang out with my
friends. I'm not seeking world domination."

"You need to think bigger," she said, rising from her seat to stand over me and placed her hands on the crown of my head. "Your potential is tremendous. I can feel it." She started kneading my scalp, as if she were giving me a treatment at a salon shampoo station.

Desiree returned to her chair and proceeded to ask me a series of strange questions about whether there were people in my life who aroused excessive jealousy (no one) and which historical figures I would like to have brunch with (Julia Child?). She then recited an assortment of sounds, asking me whether hearing them made me "expand" or "contract."

Finally, Desiree took a seat behind the desk in the corner of the room and typed her conclusions into a computer. After a few minutes, she printed out a banner-length graph. This, she told me, was a projection of my potential.

Her major prescription was that I drop out of school immediately.

"Now?" I asked. It was almost April. My last final exams were in a few weeks, and if I could maintain my past performance, it was likely that I'd graduate *summa cum laude*.

"Immediately," she replied.

"You're kidding, right? What kind of career counselor—"

"College is holding you back. It's imperative." Desiree began citing names of visionaries whose cachet at the start of their careers was that they weren't college graduates: Bill Gates, Steve Jobs, Oprah Winfrey. "It's a point of differentiation that will make your biography infinitely more interesting. Trust me." She told me I should head to the Maldives, where my destiny awaited.

"Why the Maldives?" I asked.

"When you work with a member of Consortium Associates, you don't need to ask questions. You follow your plan and you watch as the world falls at your feet," she said.

But all I could do was spring to my feet and mutter my half-hearted thanks. I'd had enough. Before the allotted fifty minutes were up, I was running like hell to the nearest bus stop.

When I got home, I told my friends about the strange session with their anointed guru. "Can you believe this?" I asked them, still out of breath.

Leigh was stone-faced. She said she thought that what Desiree had said made a certain kind of sense. "What will it hurt? You've already learned most of what you will here, right?"

It was one thing for a random woo-woo career counselor to tell me to quit my studies and take a solo vacation on the other side of the world just weeks before graduation, but I expected more support from one of my closest friends. Then again, Leigh always had a competitive streak, and I wondered if she may have had ulterior motives. Everyone knew that Coleman only gave out fifty *summa*s. Without me in the mix, she stood a stronger chance.

"I am not dropping out," I said. "That's insane."

"Yeah, she's not doing that," Geeta chimed in, bless her. "Not happening."

"I don't understand how this woman can help you two," I said earnestly.

"I'm not saying her advice is the only advice I listen to. But, you know, I'm keeping an open mind," was Geeta's reply.

"I'd be careful," I said, looking at one friend and then the other. "That woman gives me a bad feeling." It was one thing to keep an open mind. It was another to let your brain fall out of your head.

Over the following weeks, I ignored Desiree's phone calls. Eventually, they stopped. Finally, I was done with her. But evidently, she wasn't done with me.

9

THE CAMPUS CLOCKTOWER WAS IN FULL SILHOUETTE AGAINST THE setting sun, casting a long shadow across the main quad. In this light, the Coleman grounds looked like a photo accompanying an Encyclopedia Britannica entry for "college." Watching fellow alumni filter out of stately columned buildings, with my friends close at hand, I remembered what it felt like to scamper across the green at this time of day, ambling toward the library, my head exploding with new ideas, my heart flush with whatever crush was consuming me that week. Back in the day, the whole world felt like it was for me, for us. I took out my phone and snapped a photo of the landscape.

Things are looking up, I texted Gabe. Thx for before.

Anytime, Gabe replied. He attached a photo of Ramona standing next to a magician and the near-hairless gerbil. I acknowledged receipt with a cry-laugh emoji.

Geeta had parked in the lot near the engineering quad, intentionally far away from the site of the dinner event. This way we could take the scenic route, enjoying a stroll down memory lane. Mercifully, Matt had decided to sit out tonight because he was concerned that the twins were sick. Neither one had a fever per se, but he sensed that Luna was developing one. "I don't think it's right to leave them with Dasha," he'd said gravely as we gathered our belongings on our way out. "What if they need to go to the ER?" Geeta agreed that it would be best if he kept a watchful eye on the girls, but I couldn't help suspecting she was just happy to attend the dinner unencumbered.

I was grateful not to have to listen to Matt on his latest Reddit board discoveries or answer any more of his questions about the provenance of those mysterious texts. Walking around campus with Leigh and Geeta took me back to the days when I had nothing to feel ashamed of, other than perhaps the previous weekend's antics.

I smiled at my two dates. We were back together again somehow, and it felt miraculous. Geeta, her onyx hair in a perfectly messy updo, was wearing a low-cut, camel-colored wrap dress that accentuated her post-pregnancy boobs—all these years later she was still on the monochromatic kick. Leigh had put on a fitted silver jumpsuit, which made her look like liquid mercury. One half of her head was shaved and she had a beautiful diamond ear cuff. Inge hung off to the side, vaping.

Arm in arm, we walked up the hill toward the open fields where geneticists from the life sciences school experimented with hardier, tastier versions of garden-variety fruits and vegetables. "There's where the magic happened," I reminded them, as if they needed to be reminded, "when we drank hallucinogenic mushroom tea."

Leigh gave a crooked grin. "The tea ceremony where you found a 'rescue dog' on a leash," she said, her fingers making quote marks.

"The dog that turned out to be an everything bagel tied to a string," Geeta said. We all burst out laughing. Of course she remembered the baked good I had hallucinated as a pet when I was tripping.

"And you wonderful women guided me back to sanity," I said, tightening the link of our arms to draw them closer. The memory filled me with warmth, and I was tempted for a moment to tell them about my run-in with Desiree. But bringing up my encounter meant bringing up all that she stood for and all the decisions that drove a wedge between my friends and me, between their trajectories and mine. Because they both got the Memo. And I didn't want to talk about it.

So I kept mum as we strolled past the art library, where we used to pull books from the stacks and search for the most flagrant nudes to prop open on the reading carrels where coffee-addled graduate students pulled their all-nighters. We cut across the main green and floated past the freshman dining hall, the science center, and the provost's office. Everything was immaculately maintained, untouched by time.

I didn't spot any evidence of the fifteen years that had passed until we came upon the soccer field. A hulking modernist building now occupied the far edge of the green. It shimmered like an enormous black crystal. With its aerodynamic construction and cantilevered glass wings, the structure looked nothing like the nineteenth-century Gothic revival architecture that proliferated on campus.

I glanced at my friends, who did not seem to find this new member of Coleman College's real-estate holdings half as odd as I did.

"There it is. The Simcott Center for the Study of the Soul," Leigh read aloud. I froze for a moment as I thought about what Desiree had said to me earlier, something about "new developments in the study of the soul." Could it have something to do with this place?

"Is this, like, a divinity school?" I asked.

"You haven't read about it?" Geeta asked, her eyes squinting incredulously. "It's the S.C.S.S. Pronounced 'success.'"

"Sorry, I don't always read the alumni magazine," I said.

"It was in the *New York Times Magazine*," Geeta said in a teasing tone.

"Even *I* know about this building, and I live in bloody Stockholm," Inge intoned from a half step behind, vapor rising from the side of her mouth. "The architect designed our opera house, too."

Leigh proceeded to fill me in. The S.C.S.S. was funded by an anonymous donor to honor a professor named Juliet Simcott, an eccentric theoretical physicist-turned-philosopher who embraced the counterculture in the late 1960s, then resigned from Coleman's faculty and fell completely off the grid. Her whereabouts were still a source of Internet intrigue. Her book, *Time Wounds All Heels*, was now out of print. Copies, if they could even be found, sold for thousands of dollars on eBay.

"So it's not a divinity school. More like a physics lab?" I asked, marveling at the building.

"Not really," Geeta said. "It's more about spiritual studies. Finding answers to all the unanswerable questions."

"Good luck with that," I said.

THE REUNION DINNER WAS INSIDE A HUGE CANVAS TENT. THE AESTHETIC was shabby-chic, with natural linen table runners and hemptied bouquets of local, seasonal flowers for centerpieces. My classmates swarmed around long picnic tables, mingling at full velocity, holding plates of tiny delicacies that had probably taken hours to create, only to be consumed in one quick bite.

I accepted a cocktail from a fresh-faced server who looked like an undergraduate and did my best to circulate with the slew of Class of '07 luminaries. I felt a surge of joy when I spotted Keisha Phillips, my freshman year roommate, the one who inadvertently led me back to Hal. And there was a balder version of David Smalls, the soccer player—now hedge-fund manager—who Geeta was once so in love with that she threw up out of nervousness when he unexpectedly showed up at one of our house parties.

But now Dave was staring at Geeta, and she didn't even notice he was there. She was busy holding court in front of a small group, talking about how her venture-backed company was on track to generate $100 million in revenue in the second half of the year, a prediction I found to be highly optimistic given what she had told me in our more candid private conversations, during which she often fretted about making payroll. I'd once congratulated her on having an entire country using her app as a pilot program, as I'd read in *Company* magazine. She'd confessed that the article had contained a bit of an exaggeration. "Princess Francine of Luxembourg told me that her friends use it, so my PR team said I could say that in the interview," she'd said. "I was skeptical at first, but the VCs said I should think of it like a manifestation." Oh yes, the venture capitalists and their positive thinking. Now, perhaps because of that story, Luxembourg was one of the company's fastest-growing markets. I had to hand it to Geeta. She turned faking it until you make it into an art form.

I came closer to Geeta and placed my chin on her shoulder. Without turning toward me, she reached up and gave my cheek a little pinch.

I looked to my right and saw Leigh turning her back on her ex, Emily, to chat with Lyndsey Bogatsky, the former poet who now worked as a rocket scientist at SpaceFisch. Emily tried to approach them as Lyndsey regaled Leigh with stories of boardroom humiliation at the hands of the company's cantankerous founder, Levi Fischer. Leigh pretended not to notice Emily's attempts to interject as she made some charming but obvious jokes about art not being rocket science.

Emily had been Leigh's first love, the one Desiree had insisted that she ditch back in college. Watching Emily try so desperately to get her attention and Leigh trying equally hard to ignore her, I felt ashamed for both of them. I wondered if I should go hang out with Emily, but dropped that thought when I noticed who Geeta was talking to.

Here was Lonnie Berger, who'd been in our medieval studies class. Lonnie was always good at raising his hand and starting his question with his trademark opener, "Not to be whatever, but . . ." By which he meant "Not to make this all about me," right before making his question all about him. Every moment in medieval literary history was an opportunity for Lonnie to reflect on his own personal issues rather than the assigned reading material.

I smiled at Lonnie and said hello. He seemed happy to see me and proceeded to recall with astonishing detail my feminist insights on Grendel's mother in *Beowulf*, which was flattering even though it slightly weirded me out. I could barely remember reading *Beowulf*, let alone what I thought about one of the character's mothers.

"Lonnie!" Leigh cried, darting over to us. "What are you up to? Not to be whatever . . ." It was slightly cruel, but I couldn't help but laugh a little, along with my friends. I was giggling not so much at him, but at the memory of us all being together and unable to contain ourselves.

Lonnie looked confused. "Are you all okay?"

"Don't mind us," I said. "The cocktails are strong. So, Lonnie, seriously, what have you been up to?"

"Emerging market bonds," he said. "I live in Park Slope with my wife, who works in beauty PR. She stayed home to watch our two kids so I could come here and reflect on the good old days before everything got so . . . you know."

"So . . . what?" I prodded. He played with the dried-fruit garnish on his drink.

"You know, so adult and . . . stuck in the routine." He paused for a second and laughed. "Sorry, this is supposed to be small talk," he said.

"No, it's okay," I said. Lonnie always was into talking about his issues. Finally, we were in a venue where it was appropriate. We drifted a few steps to the right so that we were suddenly alone. "I hear you," I said. "Everyone's sort of killing it here, right?" I glanced down at my scuffed-up clogs.

"I'll say." He whistled. "What about you? I see that purple hair is no longer your thing."

"That was only for a few months during our freshman year," I said, surprised that he remembered that, too. "My mother begged me to dye it back to my natural color. So I did it for her birthday."

"I saw your video," he said, changing the subject. "You moved to Pittsburgh?" I thought for a minute about the pathetic video that I made before Sophie helped me reframe my current situation in a better light, and with better lighting.

"I moved there about a year ago. It's been . . . a new adventure. Not a lot of Coleman people there, other than my boss." I wrinkled my nose at the thought of Alice.

"Cool. I remember you hosted the best wine and cheese parties—I always thought they were the height of sophistication," Lonnie said. "You even baked your own crackers! Who does that?"

"I still do," I told him. I'd just brought a batch to a Memorial Day barbecue at Sophie's parents' house. That was how I learned that her mom was fatally allergic to sesame seeds, luckily before any real damage was done.

"Those were the days," Lonnie said wistfully. "What else? Married? Kids?"

Deflation was rising in me. "I have a boyfriend but he couldn't make it. And, as I mentioned in my video, I work at a feminist non-profit, in fundraising."

"Did someone say 'fundraiser'? I am so over them! Why can't parties just be parties?" This came from a poofy-haired, overly made-up woman in a floral one-shoulder dress. I realized this was our class president, Allie Dourous—now known as Alessandra D'Ourous, the highly decorated film producer. Geeta and Leigh were suddenly both on the scene, as if pulled in by the exploding floral scent of Alessandra.

"We were just talking about your MoMA fiesta," Leigh said, enveloping Alessandra in a theatrical embrace. "We are so there." By "we" she clearly meant herself and Geeta because, not so shockingly, I had not been invited. By the way Alessandra glanced at me and then quickly looked away, I could tell that she didn't remember who I was.

"Hi, Allie, it's me, Jenny," I said, a little too eagerly. "We were in Sociology 201 together."

"I go by 'Alessandra' now," she reminded me. "Wow, Jenny! You look so different."

"Thanks," I said. "I've been working on it."

"Cool," she said with a pursed smile. Silence hung between us. She couldn't be bothered to even come up with something for us to continue conversing about. Then again, neither could I. The awkwardness led to my blurting out the question running through my brain.

"So, what is this party of yours?" I asked, surprising myself with my boldness.

"It's our summer solstice gala at the Museum of Modern Art," Alessandra explained in a drawl. "For young patrons. I'm the chair."

"Wow, how'd you—"

"The solstice is on the twenty-first, and nobody is going to be in town then, so we bumped it up to the seventeenth. This way it can be more of a prelude to summer, a *curtain raiser.*"

"The seventeenth is my birthday," I said dumbly, turning to Geeta and Leigh. "I guess you guys can call me from the party."

Alessandra smiled politely. "I'll let you know if we have any last-minute cancellations."

My gaze moved from Leigh to Geeta and back again. Neither of them seemed to share my sense of injury. They were going to this party and there was nothing that I could do about it. I hated myself for being offended by something so ridiculous. It sounded like a big, fun event; of course, they wanted to attend. What did it matter that it fell on my birthday? It wasn't like I was having a party. Did I expect Geeta to come to Pittsburgh and take me to Desmond's Tavern for mozzarella sticks? Or . . . did I? I felt a lump in my throat. I needed to get out of there before I embarrassed myself any more than I already had.

"I have to make a call," I muttered. As I walked toward the edge of the crowd, I decided to take Gabe up on his offer. This counted as a time of need, did it not?

It turned out not to matter. My call went straight to voicemail. Maybe one of the MILFs had already captured his heart. The thought filled me with a strange sense of dejection. I kept walking away from the party. I wasn't ready to return to mingling. Next I tried Sophie, who'd surely have some words of wisdom. The phone rang and rang; then I remembered she didn't do calls. Voice memos were more her jam, another of our intergenerational differences. I started to record one, but changed my mind.

I needed support, in real time. Which was how I found myself FaceTiming Hal. Much to my surprise, he picked up. He looked so cool—perfect stubble, tendrils coming loose from his golden manbun. For a moment, when I saw those hazel eyes focused on me, I was glad I had called him to check in. He was just so nice to look at. Another thing that I really loved about Hal was how allergic he was to try-hard phonies like Alessandra. His instincts not to come to this event, it turned out, had been sound. Talking to him about what just happened would calm me down.

"Hi from the reunion!" I said, a little too desperately.

"Hey, hey. How's it going?"

"It's, well, a little harder than I expected it to be," I said. "What's happening over there?"

"Uh, not much, all good," he said in that antsy way that indicated he was ready to wrap up the conversation before it even started. "You good, bruh?"

Bruh? He never called me that. Was he trying to pretend he was on the phone with a guy?

I told him about the solstice party, but Hal seemed to be only half listening. "I told you it was going to be annoying," he said as he stepped into our bathroom. "Who wants to hang out with a bunch of insufferable tools anyway?"

"Yeah," I said, noticing that across the lawn, Geeta, Leigh, and Alessandra were taking selfies together.

"All right, well… want to call me later?"

"Just stay with me for a minute?" My tone was vaguely pleading. The lump in my throat wasn't going anywhere. "You don't have to say anything. Just be with me, okay?"

He nodded and set his lips together, and in that moment of quiet, I heard the unmistakable yap of a dog.

"What was that?" I asked. "Am I disturbing something? Bruh?"

Hal started to sputter something about how the toilet had been acting up.

"Right," I said stonily. "The toilet."

"Hey, I—" he faltered.

"Whatever you do, don't let that animal make a mess on the rug—the one you brought back from Costa Rica. Where we met all those years ago. So many years, Hal." I tried to blink back the tears stinging my eyes and hung up.

I wasn't in the mood to eat, but after taking a breather under a tree, I returned to my table. Dinner was about to begin. Thankfully, I was seated next to Keisha. She was always so wonderful to be around, and I hadn't seen her in at least a decade. The last time we hung out was at her barbecue in Brooklyn, before she moved to Delaware, of all places. Keisha used to be so bookish and serious, studying to be a veterinarian.

She and I fell out of touch soon after she moved out of the city to take a job at a Wilmington-based pharmaceutical company. It had never made sense to me, Keisha's dropping out of vet school to be a suit. She was still working at the same company, now as chief scientist. Her face was so bloated with fillers that it barely moved anymore. It was hard to tell, but she seemed truly happy to see me and ignored everyone else over the salad course.

"You know what I still think about a lot?" Keisha said. "The time in our junior year when you bought a last-minute ticket to Caracas and flew down there for spring break." I had almost forgotten that I did.

"I wanted to practice my Spanish," I said.

Keisha knit her brow. "Your Spanish was *terrible.*"

"Which was why it was brilliant to go."

"Without a room booked or anything?"

I felt a tug of sadness. I used to have my own appetite for adventure. Maybe I'd given Hal too much credit for forcing me out of my comfort zone.

Keisha shook her head and rolled her eyes. "I was so sure you were going to get killed."

"I almost was," I said. "By my mother. She was expecting me to come home for the break."

"I *definitely* would have killed you if I were her." Keisha laughed. "Hey, speaking of your south of the border escapades, do you still talk to that handsome guy you met in Costa Rica? The one who randomly became my neighbor?"

"Sometimes we talk," I said, smirking. "We live together, if you can believe it." Keisha's eyes went wide. "So I guess the answer to your question is no, not really."

"What? Wow!" Keisha craned her neck and looked around the table. "Is he here?"

"He couldn't make it." I violently buttered my roll. "He appears to be hanging out with a dog." Keisha looked at me with confusion. I took a big, buttery bite. "I don't really want to get into it. Hey, do you have a dog? You always said you were going to have at least five."

"Yes and no," Keisha said with a resigned sigh. "They're so much work. I'm on the board of a rescue shelter, but it's in Maine, so I never have a chance to go out there."

"That makes me sad," I said. "Keish, can I ask you something?"

"Of course."

"Why did you drop out of vet school?"

She paused, then shrugged. "Sometimes, you know what you need to do, you know? It was just in the stars, I guess."

"Right," I said meekly. Another one who got the Memo.

As the servers cleared our salad plates, I excused myself and headed to the bank of luxe porta-potties. On my way over, I saw Emily standing alone, blowing her nose as she observed Leigh huddling with Alessandra by a picnic table. Alessandra slipped Leigh what appeared to be a wad of cash, then Leigh extracted a small bag from her jumpsuit and passed it to her. Alessandra did a little dance move. Oh my god. It appeared Leigh dealt in more than just art.

Did I really know anybody? Had I *ever* known anybody?

Fifteen years ago, I was living my best life in this very same place, dancing and drinking and having midnight conversations about Greek mythology and ancient farming systems, and not feeling embarrassed about my thirst for knowledge. I had a passion and I had a plan: bake it until you make it! I was going to make a living by creating beautiful, delectable objects of substance in a world driven increasingly by bits and bytes. But here I was, surrounded by people in thrall to a woman with a fake name and a fake Italian accent, while my boyfriend carried on at home with a closet organizer named after a stinky cheese.

I unlatched the porta-potty's plastic door. Once inside, I lowered onto the toilet seat, fully clothed, and allowed myself to cry. It felt so good, to let my emotions out. I stayed seated until there was nothing left inside my tear ducts, then moved over to the makeshift sink. I was working on reapplying my eye makeup in the mirror, using a Q-tip hack that Sophie had taught me, when the door creaked open. What the hell? I was sure I'd locked it.

"I'm in here!" I shouted, but it was too late. Desiree had found me.

"Don't you worry, Jenny," she said in a breezy voice. "It's not too late."

10
· · · ·

GETTING THE MEMO WAS NO MERE COLLOQUIALISM. THE MEMO was an actual, tangible, Upper-Case-Letter thing. And, for that matter, there wasn't just *a* Memo. There were thousands of Memos, reams of life-enhancing prescriptions handed out to countless Coleman alumni ever since the school went coed in 1954. As Desiree steered me away from the reunion tent, she rattled off the names of our college's most notable female graduates. It was mind-blowing, but it also made so much sense. They all got the Memo.

"So basically every successful Coleman woman I've ever heard of has the Memo?"

"Not *all*," Desiree said. "Those born into families of great means don't need our help. We're here to level the playing field."

"I see," I said. "I had no idea Sequoia Falls was such a sphere of influence."

"The Consortium has opened bureaus all over the country, though we are headquartered here. This is where Dr. Simcott made her initial discovery and where our work is concentrated."

Ah yes, Dr. Simcott, of the Success Center. The one who studied the soul.

As we continued walking, weaving our way past stragglers from various reunion events, I flipped through my mental Rolodex of notable alumni. Was it possible they all held keys to Desiree's club? Was it possible any of them didn't? As preposterous as it sounded—a document that would guide you to perfection—the existence of a world of Memo holders and Memo-less people did explain a lot. One didn't need to have a PhD in soul studies to understand Occam's razor: the simplest, most elegant explanation is usually the best one. For example: everyone got the Memo except me.

"By the way, it was so nice to lay eyes on Keisha." Desiree said in a tone that indicated she was dropping something heavy and important.

"I gather you two are close. And your Memo is why she's working at that horrible-sounding pharmaceutical company instead of being the small-town veterinarian of her dreams?"

"It's not my Memo, it's *her* Memo," Desiree tutted. "And Keisha isn't merely working at that company, she's *thriving* at that company. She's very happy!"

"What makes you so sure?"

"I haven't heard any complaints from her. Look at her annual Christmas card."

The green stone of Desiree's ring flashed as she worked at the clasp of her satchel. She rummaged around for a moment, then her hand emerged brandishing Keisha's holiday card as if it were an exhibit in a trial. The card showed my old friend standing by a New England lighthouse with her handsome husband and their five children—not the five dogs she'd always said she was going to have. Close enough, I guessed. They were all wearing matching nautical outfits, smiling with gleaming perfect teeth. I was once on her Christmas-card list, back when Keisha had just one kid, but somehow I'd dropped off. This was just one of the sad realities of getting older, I'd thought. Only now did I realize our lives had gone in opposite directions for other reasons. I felt a tightness in my chest. Up ahead, the Simcott Center for the Study of the Soul glowed in the twilight.

"Beautiful, isn't she?" Desiree sounded like she was talking about a magnificent ship. "I've been doing a lot of important work there, both policy based and archival."

"So that's where the magic happens?"

"Not all of it, but yes. I've moved my office there, which has been terrific. So many changes are afoot, all groundbreaking. And now we have you!"

"You *have* me?" I repeated. "Why are you so interested in me? Aren't I the biggest failure?"

"We've never been able to pull off a blitz-track like the one we have in mind for you, and a great deal is riding on how it goes. Think of yourself as a human beta test, advancing scientific innovation while optimizing your own existence. But don't worry, the methodology has been vetted by the sharpest minds in physics and metaphysics. And the Consortium reviewed your medical records to make sure you can handle it."

"You looked through my medical records?" I stopped in my tracks. "That's totally unethical!"

"Cool your jets. It's going to be tremendous, Jenny." Desiree pulled me by my wrist and we were back to walking down the path. "I know how you feel about pop feminism, the sort of hashtag hokum that you peddle at your foundation. But trust me, this is feminism at its finest. The Consortium is helping women everywhere mastermind the game of life."

I wished what she said sounded better to me. My dream was to live with integrity, to work with my hands, to make bread—the staff of life, not the game of life! Was that too much to ask? More important, I wanted to have good friends, a significant other, maybe a kid or two, provided I could find a suitable partner. I always fantasized about having time to travel, to eat wonderful foods, to read great books, to soak up the company of the people I loved. The career piece of it, for me, was the means to that end.

"It's going to happen, Jenny," Desiree assured me.

"What, I'm going to finally be happy?"

Desiree brayed like a donkey. "You're about to be a household name! This is the best deal you'll ever make."

"You know that I'm in no position to buy anything, right? I could barely cover what our introductory session cost back in the day. And you should see my credit score now."

"We're much more equitable now, thanks to the success of some of our early clients. There's no need to pay anything up-front. We simply collect a small sliver of a client's earnings at the end of every fiscal year."

"Like tithing?" Medieval history class had been good for something after all.

"It's ridiculous we didn't work this out sooner. Given our commitment to equalizing the playing field. Fairness is our North Star." Desiree was practically exploding with energy. We were only a few yards away from the building's entrance, but Desiree stopped in her tracks.

"Now, Jenny, your potential"—there she went with that word again—"is so great, your future so bright, that you're poised to help so many future lost souls. Your journey—and the profits of that journey, let's be honest—will go toward helping countless other women optimize their own existences. You are setting in motion a magic flywheel of magnificence."

This was, as my grandmother would say, totally *fakakta*, yet my curiosity was getting the best of me. If I was really the biggest failure on earth, if my potential was truly monumental, maybe I should give it a shot. What, really, did I have to lose?

"How do you think Zia Bradzitski, the architect of this

stunning edifice, made it out of a pitiful commune and wound up designing this masterpiece?" Desiree tilted her chin at the gleaming glass structure. "She got the Memo." She said the word practically at a whisper. "And who was the anonymous donor who funded this building, with its world-class research laboratory exclusively for women studying the intersection of astrophysics and metaphysics?"

"Another Memo person?"

"Don't say it too loud."

"What's going to happen if I do? Is Beetlejuice going to pop out and drag me to the underworld?"

Desiree grabbed me by the arm. "This isn't a joke. We operate in the utmost secrecy."

"Okay." I laughed. "I'll take it easy."

"Look, I don't mean to cast aspersions on Alice Hustad and her Aurora Borealis foundation," Desiree said. "But if you really care about obliterating the gender gap, you need look no further."

"Does Alice have a Memo?" I checked.

Desiree shook her head. "No Memos for nepos. They're up there with the men."

"What men?"

"The men who don't have Memos. Which is all of them." Desiree sighed. "Men do not need this kind of support. Even after admitting some of us into their ranks, they still dominate the Fortune 500, Skull and Bones, and the power structures of Washington, DC, do they not? This is about women supporting women! Feminism as it was intended." Desiree stepped up to the door and entered a security code, then briskly motioned for me to follow her inside.

11
• • •

WITH EACH STEP, THE CRISP SOUND OF DESIREE'S HEELS ECHOED
off the walls in sharp contrast to the thump of my clogs.
We passed through an immaculate lobby and walked up a flight of
marble stairs that led to a long, high-ceilinged hallway. Desiree
had upgraded in the corridor department. Finally, we came to a
stop in front of an eye scanner that verified Desiree's iris before a
steel pocket door noiselessly slid open.

Now we were in her office, a container that could only be described as maximally minimalist, whistle-clean. There was a
coffee table featuring a tableau of business magazines, each with
a different woman on the cover. Presumably, they were all clients. The table was situated opposite an onyx fireplace. In addition to a love seat at a right angle to the fireplace, there were two
white, egg-shaped chairs suspended from the ceiling in the center of the room. I hopped into one. As I lightly swung back and
forth, I noticed the design of the rug: a pile of bones in the shape
of a triangle.

"Can I get you anything?" Desiree asked. She was kneeling
in front of a mini fridge in the corner of the room. "Diet Coke?"

"I'm fine," I said. "I'm pretty keyed up as it is—and I should
probably get back to the reunion dinner soon. So, I'll just have
my Memo, thanks!" I smiled uncomfortably. "Seriously, can I
have it?"

"You already do." Desiree turned to stare at me.

"I definitely don't."

"Didn't you download it?"

I thought back to those strange texts. "Do you think I'm a total idiot?" I asked. "It could have been from the KGB," I said, echoing Matt's theory.

"The FSB," she said.

"Whatever. I don't download random junk from strangers."

Desiree plunked down onto the love seat, pulled back the tab of her can, and watched me as the soda hissed. "I'm not a random stranger. Check your phone."

I reached under my swinging chair for my bag and pulled out my phone. Sure enough, there was another text message:

Congratulations, Jenny Green. You got the Memo!

"How about that," I said. This time I clicked on the link. My phone's screen flashed white for a moment. Then a graphic materialized, a strange cosmic cube, the sides of which fell back to reveal the words "The Memo" floating over a pile of bones in the shape of a triangle. Then a dialog box popped up.

The text was in a barely legible font, full of boring clauses that appeared to be intended to induce migraines.

Donor Party will guide Recipient through influential branch points utilizing manufactured fuel to traverse the unstable portal. This Recipient agrees she cannot breach covenants pertaining hereto. Parties hereby agree to BlitztrackBeta™ program.

I'd always had an allergy to legalese. My brain turned off at the sight of it. This was why I couldn't bring myself to take the

LSAT after my culinary dreams went up in smoke. ("Life is boring, Jen. A decent income helps," my mother had said.)

Desiree came to sit in the love seat. We were nearly at eye level, and she was close enough that I could smell her perfume. "If you want to have a lawyer review your NDA, I have a list of vetted attorneys you can hire." Exhaustion colored her voice. "But really, your thirty-sixth birthday is in what . . . a week?"

"Next Friday," I confirmed. "Why? What does that have to do with anything?"

"Our technology can no longer help you reclaim your optimized self after thirty-six. You will become locked in. Fully cooked. Geriatric."

I blew my cheeks out. "Way to make a girl feel good about the aging process."

"This isn't about fine lines and all that jazz," Desiree said, leaning back in her seat. "Thirty-six is when a woman comes into her full flowering. It's when the story is already written." She paused. "Do you know how old Marilyn Monroe and Princess Diana were when they both died?"

"I think I can guess."

"Cleopatra was thirty-nine when she killed herself, but she spent three years plotting that snake bite."

"This all sounds highly scientific," I said.

"You want science? You might have forgotten that thirty-six has the distinction of being both a square and a triangular number. And do you know the number of degrees in the interior angle of each tip of a pentagram?"

"Gonna go out on a limb and say I do."

Desiree clucked. "I could go on about how in the Jewish tradition, the sun shone for thirty-six hours on the first day of creation, or how the Egyptians believed in thirty-six gods watching over the zodiac. The best hip-hop album of all time was—"

"*Enter the Wu-Tang Clan (36 Chambers)*, obviously."

Desiree stared at me. "We don't have all day."

The phone in my hands felt hot. I eyed the screen and checked the box.

"Okay, it's done. I have agreed to follow your Memo," I said, in slight disbelief. "And at long last, I can say I got the fucking Memo!"

"How is this not getting across to you, Jenny? Don't cry it out like that. It's not something you want to be in the business of doing. The one thing you can never do is talk about the Memo," Desiree whispered.

"We're in the privacy of your office," I reminded her. "And you're talking about it."

"I'm not you. And you need to develop clean habits. That breach would have far-reaching implications. The first rule of the Memo is that there is no Memo."

Geeta's and Leigh's strange behavior was starting to make a whole lot more sense. Why Leigh got tattoos only on the left side of her body, or how Geeta insisted on going to the same bar every Wednesday night and order an Old Fashioned with two orange slices, nothing more. The times she suddenly had to leave a party when things were starting to get fun because she just "had a feeling."

"Look at your phone again," Desiree instructed. The agreement had vanished; in its place were two little boxes at the bottom of my screen, a red one labeled Pathetic and a green one labeled Kinetic.

"We've discovered a portal to the past, but it is wildly unstable," Desiree explained. "So you need these things, what we call negative energy shock waves—literally jealousy and regret, which thankfully you have in spades—to make the path temporarily traversable. You just tap the Pathetic button to see reminders of all your missteps and all the amazing things happening without you.

And then, when you're sufficiently fired up, you enter the date of interest into the Kinetic tab. Your dark feelings will be so powerful that we believe it will have the ability to propel you backward and fix your life!"

I couldn't help but laugh. "You've gotta be kidding me," I said.

Desiree just stared at me, slowly shaking her head.

At a loss for what to say, I drew a deep breaths and checked out the Kinetic section. At the top of the screen was a wheel where I could scroll to any date from the past. Once I selected one, a directive would pop up, my digital Memo. The Memos looked more like grocery lists than carefully calibrated strategies for self-betterment. The July 6, 2008, suggestion, for instance, read:

> Go to Barney Greengrass and purchase a half pound
> of smoked mackerel.

"I have so many questions," I said, feeling dizzy.

"Good thing I'm here to guide you." Desiree smiled. "Did you know that the term 'getting the memo' can be etymologically traced back to the 1960s? That was Juliet's time, following the publication of her landmark book."

"Juliet," I repeated. "The study of the soul lady?"

"Yes, Juliet Simcott, the physicist philosopher. She is the patron saint of Memos. Though she didn't invent the form, obviously." Desiree rubbed her hands together and leaned forward. "Let's get you oriented."

Memos, Desiree proceeded to explain, dated back to the late nineteenth century, along with the birth of corporate management science. When commands were written in memo format, people tended to follow them.

"The official memo style made them stand out, leading workers to prioritize and focus on their objectives," she said. "It made organizing large groups much easier, helping them to achieve shared goals, thus leading businesses to greatness. As Juliet was to discover, the same could be applied to individuals.

"Before there was a Consortium," Desiree went on, "there was the Savard Company. Headquartered in Sequoia Falls, Savard was a manufacturer of rubber gloves that eventually expanded into making all sorts of consumer products. When Juliet was a teenager, she dropped out of high school and took a job as a bookkeeper at Savard so she could help her widower father make the rent. She hated the job but loved the employee library, where she would lose herself in books about theoretical physics and relativistic quantum mechanics. She often ran around the office, delivering memos from one division to another, but lost in thought about black holes and alternative universes.

"Juliet wasn't only thinking about the things she'd read in books," Desiree went on. "Visions had started to come to her during her reading sessions, all of which concerned her female colleagues. And so in the evenings, she'd write Memos to the subjects of her reveries. The first person to receive one such Memo was a receptionist named Wanda Millman."

TO: WANDA MILLMAN
From: Juliet Simcott
Date: January 10, 1955
Subject: Walking

Please be advised that it has been determined that your route from your desk to Manufacturing is suboptimal. It may seem inconvenient, but if you take the freight elevator located at the northwest corner of the building, you will soon notice a great improvement in your circumstances.

According to Desiree, on the following day, January 11, 1955, Wanda Millman took the freight elevator when she went to deliver a stack of receipts to the Manufacturing Department. She tripped on a piece of compressor equipment, slicing open her leg. The injury required no fewer than forty-one stitches.

"Juliet felt terrible. But the accident turned out to be a miracle," Desiree said. "Wanda completely recovered, got a handsome settlement from the company and used it to pay for law school at Coleman. A tremendously rewarding career followed." Desiree craned her body forward. "You see?"

I swallowed and nodded. "Wanda got the Memo."

"It was just the beginning," Desiree said, and continued telling me the story:

Her head swimming with visions, Juliet wrote Memo after Memo, urging her coworkers to arrive at work three minutes early, to use two not three tablespoons of cream in their coffee, to wear shoes one size too big, to put their pants on backward, to study German, and so on. The Memos, when followed, catapulted dozens of women to untold levels of success. Many of them left the Savard company to pursue their passions.

Eventually, and perhaps inevitably, Juliet's boss discovered one of her Memos. Juliet tried to explain the nature of her visions, her obligation to help womankind improve their lives. Her boss was unmoved. He felt Juliet was consumed with hysteria. He fired her.

"Which was for the best, because Juliet had always wanted to write a book," Desiree said. The words poured out of Juliet as if she was channeling a gift from another dimension through her fingers. The result was a humorous treatise on time travel and career achievement for women called *Time Wounds All Heels*. It wasn't a huge success financially, but Juliet's innovative ideas garnered critical acclaim, which led to a professorship at Coleman. All the while, she developed the Consortium, a group of women who had benefited from her visions. They recruited others to join the cause.

"So it's sort of like a multilevel marketing scheme," I said.

Desiree scowled. "Are you even listening? The timing and place were fortuitous, for now it was the 1960s, and Juliet had noticed her female students were becoming overwhelmed with career options and societal expectations."

"Good old having-it-all syndrome," I said.

"Correct. There were so many choices that needed to be attended to, with consequences that needed to be better understood. Juliet couldn't single-handedly manage the project. She needed to scale her operation."

"Scale." I shuddered. "I hate that word." Geeta was perpetually stressing about the requirement to scale. Alice, too. It always annoyed me that a business couldn't just exist without seeking to destroy the competition and maximize market share.

"It doesn't hate you," Desiree replied. "Not anymore. To wrap up the story, Juliet's initial adventures in scaling were shaky. The Consortium's methods were imprecise at first. More blunt instrument than scalpel." As a result, Memos were as short as the messages contained inside a fortune cookie. Juliet, or Professor Simcott as she was called by then, could see immediate changes that needed to be executed to lead to a subject's optimal existence, seemingly small tweaks like booking a long weekend in Cape Cod or avoiding bus travel on Tuesdays.

But as time went on and technology improved, the Consortium was able to leverage the marvels of computing power to explore almost every possibility for a given woman's life, and determine the series of smaller decisions required to reach cumulative success.

"And voilà!" The great emissary of the S.C.S.S. raised her

arms high above her head. "The Memo as we know it was born. Life was never the same after that."

"But what's with all the secrecy?" I asked.

"It wasn't always so secret. Juliet used to talk openly—to anyone who would listen—about her discovery, but many were unable to understand what she was trying to say. They thought she was crazy." Desiree's eyes went cloudy. "So she went off the grid. Disappeared. I don't blame her. And she left her research to us."

"Is she dead?"

Desiree gave a placid smile. "The heart might give out, but the soul can live on. We can use her visions when we need to." Desiree rose from the love seat to take another can of soda out of the mini fridge. "Now that you've had your crash course, you can have a good look at the app."

I went back into my Memo and began scrolling through dates.

December 19, 2010: Attend the 8:10 p.m. screening of *Black Swan* at AMC Union Square.

November 27, 2013: Purchase a Green Thumbs membership at the New York Botanical Garden.

April 7, 2015: Seek out the second car of the N train.

"Pretty incredible, huh?" Desiree glanced at me. "By this time next week, you'll be the best version of yourself imaginable."

"And what is your definition of 'best version'?"

"Jenny, we're not here for a philosophical symposium. I fought tooth and nail to get all the necessary sign-offs. There's still quite a bit of trepidation around blitz-tracking."

"Blitz-tracking?"

"It's an experimental technique for retroactive Memo implementation," Desiree muttered, sipping from her aluminum can.

"Normally, the Memo works in real time, but owing to our scientific advancements, you will be able to rewind to the essential moments. It isn't going to be easy, but it will be well worth it."

"I can just spin the wheel and rewind to the moments in my life where I screwed up?"

"Correct. Your case is a highly targeted last-chance dance, if you will."

"You know I'm not the best dancer," I told her. Swooping back and forth through time seemed risky, particularly for a klutz like me. What if I set another fine culinary establishment on fire?

"You're plenty nimble," Desiree assured me. "And our technology is fairly foolproof."

"Fairly?" I asked.

"Consider it your duty. For womankind."

Ducking my head down, I flipped around my electronic file.

April 23, 2008: Sing Rod Stewart's "Da Ya Think I'm Sexy?" at karaoke night.

May 6, 2009: Attend Keisha's book club meeting for *One Hundred Years of Solitude*.

July 25, 2009: Put on your cameo earrings at 6:07 a.m.

I went cold at the sight of that date. July 25, 2009. The day of the fire at the bakery in Italy. The day my life went up in flames.

"See something you like?" Desiree asked.

"I'm not sure I'd say I *like* it. But here's the moment when everything started to go terribly wrong," I said, pointing to the date on the screen. "Not that I am proud, but I was distracted by a date I had that night and left work early to put on my cameo earrings and get ready for it. I started a fire in the bakery kitchen, got kicked out of my fellowship, and fell into a depression that lasted more than a year."

Desiree raised an eyebrow. "I wouldn't put too high a premium on a single mistake. There are myriad downward junctures along your trajectory—not to mention the unfortunate tendrils, like when you decided to ignore my advice about dropping out of school—but you are correct. This is the moment you really started to go off course. Wearing your cameo earrings for Massimo was the right impulse, but you should have put them on in the morning before you left for work. As your Memo would have told you."

I still couldn't believe she knew all about the earrings. I was speechless.

"There's no way for you to fix all your past mistakes in the time we have." Brutal as Desiree's words were, her voice was eerily calm. "You'll focus on a few key incidents, which, thanks to the Consortium, have now been identified. Righto. Time for your preview."

12
. . .

DESIREE LED ME INTO A ROOM DOWN THE HALL FROM HER OFFICE, where she would show me some sort of special presentation. The room was much like the lecture halls I remembered from college, with rows of seats and whiteboards at the front of the room. The side walls brimmed with portraits of women that looked like they had been painted in the past half-century. She gestured for me to take a seat in the front row, raised a remote at a projection screen and clicked a button.

And thus I was treated to a montage starring a slightly more attractive version of myself—a version of myself that looked eerily like the AI-generated image that Geeta had sent to me. There I was, me but not me, doing a handstand in a field of pale pink wildflowers, sunlight refracting in gorgeous diagonals. Wearing a sleek pantsuit, not unlike Desiree's getup, accepting an award in the ornate townhouse I recognized as the James Beard Foundation. Seated front row at a fashion show in a sheer dress with over-the-knee boots showing through, working my angles as the paparazzi shouted my name.

The next scene featured a version of myself with toned abs and intricate silk lingerie, astride a dark-haired man who most certainly was not Hal. The man took off my bra and lobbed it across the room like a cowboy spinning a lasso.

Desiree tittered. "Alex is such a character!"

"Who is Alex? Besides being incredibly good looking?"

She ignored my question, and kept staring ahead at the montage. Now I was at some kind of gala dressed in a slinky ballgown. I was laughing with Keisha and Leigh. The three of us were the picture of fulfillment and joy. Instead of hopelessness and insecurity, I radiated confidence. An arm swung into the image. I saw the limb didn't belong to Geeta but to Alessandra, whom I double-kissed with the ease of a lifelong jetsetter.

The trailer of my alternate life faded to black.

"Where's Geeta?" I asked.

"*That's* what you have to say?" Desiree's face flooded with irritation. "This is *your* story, Jenny. When are you going to be Player A?"

Her question reminded me of something Geeta was fond of saying: Every relationship has a Player A and a Player B. A leader and a follower, a first in command and a second banana. But I'd always thought she was talking about romantic relationships—like hers and Matt's, for example—not the two of us. We were never in a race.

"You are the driver here," Desiree intoned. "I am just giving you the keys. You understand?"

"Sure," I said, even though I didn't.

"Feel free to open the app and fuel up. You'll want to tap the Pathetic button first."

I scrabbled for my phone and pressed the red button labeled Pathetic. Now I was treated to a series of photos of Geeta and Leigh hanging out without me. There was Geeta embracing Leigh at a clambake event sponsored by a luxury handbag maker. I stiffened and scrolled down. There they were, laughing at Leigh's gallery opening, the one I had missed because I couldn't afford a ticket to LA and was too proud to accept another handout from Geeta. There was Alice seated in the front row at the Bruce Springsteen show on Broadway, the tickets to which cost $20,000, money that undoubtedly came from the foundation's coffers. Oh, and there was Hal with the flowing long hair he'd had a few years ago. He was making out with someone who was not me—and not Brie either. My breath went short.

"Those are all real," Desiree told me. "Things you've lived through without realizing they were happening."

"What the hell? How did you dig all this up?"

"Everyone's a little different but we've discovered that for you, self-loathing is your very own flux capacitor," she said, not answering my question. "These images will precipitate feelings that will hasten your journey."

I shifted uncomfortably in my seat as my phone started making a strange noise, like a plane about to take off.

"We're leading you to states of self-doubt, jealousy, regret," Desiree rattled off, her voice vibrating with excitement. "They are infused with the energy that will allow you to traverse the wormhole and rewrite your past. All you need to do is keep looking at those pictures. Harness your fuel, like a sailor help-ing herself to the wind! And when you're ready, head over to Ki-netic."

I was marinating in more bad feelings than I could stand. I tapped the Kinetic button. A message flashed:

> Your outrage levels are sufficient to propel you
> back in time.

"Well done," said Desiree. "Now flip to the bakery fire."
I hesitated.
"Just think of how happy and smug your supposed friends

are," Desiree said, egging me on. "And how two-faced and self-ish! It's high time you took care of yourself."

So I did as told, and scrolled toward that fateful date from the summer of 2009. The phone emitted a flash of light, and my hands began to tremble.

The last thing I remembered was leaning forward and burying my head between my knees. I felt sicker than I ever had in my entire suboptimal life.

PART II

. . . .

MEMO-MADE

13

• • •

PIENZA, ITALY
JULY 25, 2009
AGE: 23

CRANED MY NECK, EXAMINING MY SURROUNDINGS. THIS WAS UNBE-
lievable. I was back in my studio apartment in Pienza. My living
quarters looked the same as they had during my truncated stay in
the summer of 2009, down to the loft bed and the Italian graffiti
on the ceiling beams. Sun streamed in from the window and il-
luminated a patch on the rug. I saw three postcards with Geeta's
loopy hearts affixed to the kitchen backsplash.

Sending each other postcards was a tradition that had begun
when I was here and continued even when we were living in the
same city. Geeta said there was something about letter writing
that kept her grounded. I was always plenty close to the ground,
but I loved having our own special language, an analog commu-
nication style that survived despite the Internet revolution.

I was seated on top of the studio bed. My diary was splayed
open across my thighs, probably bare due to the lack of air conditioning. My diary confirmed it was July 25, 2009, the day I made
a huge mistake—the first of many—that would flip my life belly
up. I studied the entry in my journal. It was about Massimo. Of
course it was. He was the only thing on my mind that summer.

I would have blushed at the words if my head weren't going so foggy. I'd experienced déjà vu before, but this was different. This was . . . time travel. Literal time travel. Desiree wasn't kidding around. I was really here. I could feel the breeze on my skin and my heart thumping against my ribs. I put down my diary and padded over to the postcard gallery. As I read Geeta's messages, even more came rushing back.

In the summer of 2009 Geeta was toiling away at a management consulting firm, working for a man who kept confusing her for the other brown-skinned woman on her team. I told her that she needed to get out of there immediately. But Geeta stayed put, determined to push through for reasons I could never fully comprehend. She acted out in other ways, though. She sold her collection of vintage jewelry as a single lot on eBay as if she hadn't spent her entire life amassing it. There'd been the Saturday she flew to Dallas to buy a red cowboy hat that was only available for purchase at the original Neiman Marcus, she'd told me. These were actions that I chalked up to misplaced stress, but now wondered if they'd been Memo mandates.

I scanned the notes taped to the wall. "I can't quit, Jen, you don't understand," she'd written in a card dated June 23. "I'm not like you. I wish I was. But it's too late to do anything about it."

Now I got it. She wasn't like me because she was following the Memo. She didn't have free will, not in the way I did. My initial pity was followed by a stab of resentment. If it was fine for her, why had Geeta gone out of her way to prevent me from getting my Memo? Was she afraid I would outshine her? But this was Geeta, who had an unfailing belief in me. Perhaps she thought that I didn't need any extra help.

I could see why she would believe that. I mean, look where I'd ended up without a set of instructions! I had this amazing fellowship. And look where her Memo got her! Trapped in a skyscraper for twenty hours a day, working with people she often felt like murdering.

It suddenly occurred to me to look in the mirror. I ran to the bathroom. Lo and behold, there was my wasted youth staring right back at me! I leaned in to examine my reflection. My prominent nose was set off by the girlish glow of my cheeks. Gone were the circles under my eyes and the ever-deepening creases on my forehead.

Something even stranger happened when I returned to the postcard wall. I saw that Geeta's same card was there, except the last part had somehow transformed. Now there was no mention of her not being like me. Those words had vanished, like a magic ink trick. The postcard now read: "I can't quit, Jen. You understand."

Yup, I sure did. In this configuration of history, we both had Memos.

The church bell chimed, signaling it was seven a.m. Time to head out to work. I showered, threw on jeans and a T-shirt, and put on the delicate cameo earrings just as the Memo had instructed. Properly accessorized, perfectly Memo-assisted. It was time to undo the worst day of my life.

As I walked through town to the bakery, Pienza street life playing out around me, my whole body thrummed with excitement. My potential was unlimited. I was on a mission. I took a deep breath, inhaling faint notes of citrus and fresh dirt.

Old women sat on the benches that dotted the cobblestone street, and a band of young mothers chased after their kids. A pair of teenage girls walked arm in arm, giggling and talking rapidly. One of them looked like an Italian Sophie, and I reflexively smiled at her. She scowled at me in response, but I didn't care. I was really here, fully present in this moment, and everything was glorious.

Remembering the village map perfectly, I turned down an alleyway and entered the arched doorway of Forno Amadeo as if it were a totally normal day. I grabbed my work coat off the hook and joined Rosa and Giovanna, my mentors, at the kneading station. They were humming as they worked. A Vespa-driving single mother of two, Rosa had a beautiful zest for life. Giovanna was in her fifties, with a pixie haircut and five young grandchildren who lived in the neighborhood.

My co-bakers murmured hellos to me in Italian. It took every ounce of self-discipline not to clobber them with hugs and then spend the rest of the morning ogling them with disbelief. As far as they knew, they'd seen me the day before, and I was just some young American girl who had no idea how good she had it, not the moron who had messed up their lives by burning down their workplace. I had to keep it together.

As the recipient of the Gabrielli Foundation Fellowship—the Foodie Fulbright, as it was known—I was only expected to be in the kitchen for six hours a day, from 7:30 a.m. to 1:30 p.m. I was supposed to spend the rest of my time soaking up the culture and researching and writing the paper that I would deliver as a speech at the end of my fellowship to hundreds of program alumni. My research was going to center on gifts of bread in medieval folklore and how baked goods defied traditional notions of commodification. After delivering a summary of my findings, the foundation's luminary alumni would guide me to my next position in the food world—or they would have, had I not gotten thrown out of the program in ash-covered disgrace.

Now hovering over the eerily familiar centuries-old farmers' table, I was trying to summon all the recipes I used to know by heart. As I poured some flour into a giant metal bowl for my olive ciabatta, I wondered where we kept the *biga*, the wet prefermented mixture. Looking around, I saw a bowl sitting atop a wooden shelf covered in a cotton dish towel. My heart hitched. Was that the towel that I had set on fire? I must have gasped because Rosa looked at me skeptically and asked something in Italian.

It had been a long time. My grasp of the language was rusty.

She laughed and pointed at my earrings. "Che bella!"

"Grazie, grazie," I said, smiling.

We worked in silence until Rosa and Giovanna started tidying up. It was time for them to head home for lunch. I, the promising young baker from America, was trusted to remain in the kitchen a bit longer to mind the shop and bake the day's final loaves.

I'd just removed a batch of bread and loaded up the oven when a disarmingly handsome man with wavy brown hair appeared at the back door. The sight of him made me go weak in the knees. *Massimo!* It was startling to see him again, with his brooding brown eyes and six-foot-four stature. He was just as gorgeous as I'd remembered. Maybe even more gorgeous.

"*Non vedo l'ora*"—"I can't wait"—he told me and made a puppy-dog face. I went over and playfully pushed him out the door. He finally disappeared, but not without planting a soft kiss on my neck. I could still feel the warmth of his touch after he'd slunk off.

At first there was only a tiny crackling noise. The sound was almost cozy, and so was the aroma, a woodsy tinge that reminded me of winter. My heart sped up when I saw the flames playing on the edges of the towel near the oven. The smoke had not yet gone beyond the confines of the room, and I was able to staunch the fire with the help of the oversize water bottle that Giovanna kept at her station.

And now, the massive conflagration that had once been my fault, the fire that had brought ruin to the centuries-old kitchen, as well as my lifelong dreams, was extinguished. I was shaking, finally crying the tears of joy I had suppressed in front of Rosa and Giovanna earlier. It was so simple and yet so tremendous. I had the Memo, and the Memo had my back.

This time, I supposed I would remain in Italy until my intended date of departure. If Geeta ended up coming, it would be for a fun visit, not to talk me through my pain and regret. And tonight, I would get to have my date, which, by whatever perverse logic, made me feel like I was somehow getting even with Hal.

After tidying up, I took off my apron, excitedly applied some fresh lip gloss, and headed to Massimo's house, which, his being a true Italian, was also his parents' house. I spent the rest of the afternoon reading in the garden hammock, curled up next to him, our fingers grazing. Finally, Massimo and I had a delicious dinner with his family. We drank a gorgeous chianti, then slipped upstairs when the elders were busy watching a dubbed western on television. It was almost too perfect.

Massimo's room was crammed with simple furniture that looked hundreds of years old, and a poster on the wall for the Antonioni movie *L'Avventura*, which Hal and I had recently watched at a drive-in. I laid beside him on the bed, and we laughed awkwardly before we started kissing. Massimo took care to remove my shirt, taking his time rolling it over my head while he kissed my rib cage. He took care with everything that followed too.

As I lay in bed afterward, Massimo by my side, I felt delirious, and spent. I caught sight of my face in a small mirror hanging on Massimo's wall. I raised my chin to confirm that once upon a time, I had a jawline. I stretched my arms and legs out, grateful for my tight young body and all the things it could do and feel. I closed my eyes, full of carbs and contentment, on the verge of sleeping soundly. Then I fell off the bed and tumbled headfirst onto the hardwood floor.

14

····

SEQUOIA FALLS, NEW YORK
JUNE 10, 2022
AGE: 35

I SAT UP ON THE LOVE SEAT AND GLANCED AROUND MY SURROUNDINGS. I was back in Desiree's office, feeling more than a little groggy. It was as if I was experiencing the gnarliest hangover of my life. I raised my hand to the spot on my head that had hit Massimo's floor, but there was no bump. Internally, though, I was a scrambled mess.

"Scone?" Desiree was over in the corner kitchenette. "We suspected that blitz-tracking would make a subject quite ravenous." She said it as if I'd just driven up from Connecticut, not dived back in from the depths of a parallel universe. At any rate, she wasn't wrong. I *was* starving.

"Thank you," I said. The scone she proffered was a bit chewy—the secret to a crumbly scone is to handle the dough as little as possible—but I kept my opinion to myself. Now was not the time for baking advice.

The scone wasn't the half of it, anyway. My Italian sex god was gone, as was my optimized self. Come to think of it, this was far worse than any hangover.

"How did I get back here?" I asked, wiping sweat from my forehead.

"You never really left." Desiree sounded matter of fact. "Your consciousness went through the alternate pathway, where you reunited with your old self—your *true* self, in our opinion—and changed course. And then you fell off the hunk's bed." There was a note of amusement in her voice. "Don't worry. Your klutziness will be coming in handy this week."

Just then, my phone buzzed. I momentarily panicked, wondering who was looking for me, but saw it was a notification from my Memo app: an icon with a female firefighter emoji. Two words flashed on the screen.

"Level up?" I read the message aloud. "Who am I, Super Mario?"

"In a sense," Desiree said and then proceeded to explain that my up-leveling had occurred in an entirely separate track, the alternate path I would be bolstering by making these incremental changes. "It will all stand you in good stead for your permanent leap," Desiree said. "In the meantime, I'm glad you enjoyed yourself back in Pienza."

I blushed at the memory of the way Massimo had taken off his gold chain and dangled it over the ticklish skin on my inner thighs. Desiree gave a knowing smile.

"You didn't . . . see all of that stuff with Massimo, did you?"

"It is my job to know everything," she replied. "I witnessed you erase disaster from your personal history. In its place was an evening night with Massimo. A pretty unforgettable one."

I could feel myself blush. "Will I be seeing him again?"

"Jenny," Desiree tut-tutted, lowering herself in the spot next to me. "A man in his thirties whose mother still irons his underwear?"

"She does?" I suddenly remembered the stack of folded waffle towels by his bedside, and the thimble of mouthwash by his bathroom sink, at the ready for bedtime ablutions.

Desiree leaned over to grab my phone and scrolled to November 9 of that same year, when I would have been back in New York.

She read the Memo aloud: Do not respond to Massimo's emails—ever.

Desiree then raised her eyebrows at me. "Capiche? Your summer fling was just that. You must stay focused on the Memo, no distractions."

"Fine," I said, chastened. "So what else happens in Italy?"

"Happened," she corrected me.

"Did Geeta still visit me?"

"Did you need her to? You didn't send an SOS, like you did after your disastrous fire. In your optimized track, you were too busy focusing on your research—and having fun on your off time with that car mechanic. Geeta was busy climbing the corporate ladder. She met you at the airport when you returned in October. On the third, to be precise."

I smiled. "So I really didn't get kicked out of the program."

"Of course not. You excelled. Your final paper about the bread and the exchange economy was a tour de force. Now we need to move on to your next big blunder. The one that landed you with Hopeless Hal."

"That wasn't until years later," I told her. "I met him at Andrew's wedding. My charming brother." I didn't bother to temper the sarcasm in my voice.

"I know who Andrew is," Desiree said. "He got married in 2011. The Massimo adventure was in 2009. Don't think I don't know my stuff. Ready to blitz-track some more?"

"Wait! Slow down. Tell me more about that summer. I never moved back in with my parents?" This whole reconfiguration of my personal history was shocking.

"Jenny," Desiree said with a sigh. "We can't get bogged down.

We only have a few days. We must move with purpose and intention."

But if there was an alternative reality, one where I didn't spend my early twenties boarding with my parents and attempting to process my trauma and rise above my shame—while earning minimum wage and answering the phone at the family accounting firm—I needed to experience it.

"Can I please go back to 2009? Just to get a tiny taste of how it all wraps up? It will be so healing." Maybe I'd even be able to say goodbye to Massimo. In bed.

Desiree shook her head and rose to her feet. "I need a Diet Coke," she muttered. "Why must you be so unstrategic? This kind of behavior is exactly what led you nowhere."

She had a point. I needed to get away from myself, the one whose instincts took her nowhere. But the temptation was real. Too real. And so, when Desiree was halfway to her mini fridge, I discreetly opened the app and started feasting on images to trigger the feelings of regret and jealousy to power my next leap. I scrolled through some photos of Hal and Brie playing catch with her dog. I looked at an image of myself nodding off in a Monday morning work meeting at the radio station. The shame was overwhelming. "What are you doing?" Desiree cried out, sensing I was up to something. "Put down the phone! That's enough!"

But I was loading up on bad juju, like a kid grabbing at the sugary contents of a piñata. I was already properly amped up, so I tapped Kinetic and scrolled to the precise date that I wanted—no, *needed*—to revisit.

15
• • •

NEW YORK CITY
OCTOBER 3, 2009
AGE: 23

WAS DRAGGING MY WHEELIE SUITCASE PAST AN AIRPORT NEWSSTAND. The gossip magazines all seemed to be focused on facts about Michael Jackson's death. The refrigerator at the back of the shop was stocked with Vault, the disgusting energy drink I used to love before it was discontinued. In the distance I spotted a bouquet of balloons featuring the letter J, a heart, and a Mylar slice of pepperoni pizza. The sight of my mini entourage made my heart swell.

Geeta squealed during our hug, and Leigh joined her, our athletic young bodies nearly toppling over each other in baggage claim. Geeta's hair was slightly longer than I was used to, and she hadn't yet taken the plunge and gotten the micro-bangs that would later become her trademark. Leigh looked healthy and baby-faced, a little chubbier than she would be in her mid-thirties. I ran my hand through my hair—so long and thick!—and as my friends and I pulled apart I glanced down at my nonexistent gut, which surprised me, given where I had just come from. The Memo version of me had a supermodel metabolism. I jumped up and down, unable to contain my energy.

"I'm so psyched to see you guys!" I cried out. "Let's call an Uber and get out of here."

"A what?" My friends said. Whoops. In 2009, Uber was a tiny start-up in San Francisco that nobody had ever heard of, not the colossus providing ride-sharing services in dozens of countries.

"Oh, it's just Italian slang for a cab," I ad-libbed.

My crew guided me outside and packed me into a yellow cab, the old-school kind, with stiff fake leather seats and a meter. Geeta and Leigh were so excited, I could hardly get a word in as the car hurtled through traffic.

It was a beautiful fall day. The trees brimmed with reds and yellows and there was a golden cast to the air. This was life as things had been intended, no disastrous fire, no premature return flight, and no need to let feelings of shame and regret get the best of me and make me want to avoid the people I loved most.

"You must be so jet-lagged," Geeta said.

"Not at all." I felt like my heart was going to burst out of my chest. *Reel it in*, I told myself. *And do not mention the Memo. They're going to catch on if you keep acting weird.*

This became slightly more challenging when I looked out the window and my eyes fixed on a trio of guys crossing the street. One of them was a dead ringer for Gabe—not the Gabe I knew from the Looney Tunes, but a much younger one, without that world weariness in his eyes. He was wearing a brown fleece jacket with red pockets, the same garment that I recognized from our a cappella sessions. But now it looked brand new. What the hell?

Just as he was about to step up onto the curb, young Gabe paused and turned toward the traffic. I rolled down the window all the way. Our eyes met and time stood still. And then his body slipped out of sight. Down a sewer grate it went, first his Converse-clad feet, then his fleece-clad torso, until everything was wiped out. It was as if he was pulled underground by an invisible force. Strangest of all: his companions kept walking, as if he had never even been there.

Neither of my friends appeared to have registered what I'd just seen. They were busy admiring a gold bracelet on Leigh's wrist. Maybe I had hallucinated?

Geeta looked up and smiled at me. "You look way too stunning for someone who just flew across the Atlantic," she said. "Did you rest? I thought you never slept on planes."

"A little," I lied, my voice shaky. "I don't know. Maybe."

"What's up, Jenny?" Leigh asked. "You sound weird."

I felt a hitch in my chest. *I just saw somebody, a real friend I know from the future, get swallowed by a sewer grate in front of my eyes.* What would the point be? My mind was playing tricks on me, and I wasn't going to risk my own ejection from this realm. I glanced out of the window, trying to think fast. We were passing a movie theater. Reading from the marquee to change the topic, I blurted out, "*500 Days of Summer.* It's not out in Italy yet. Did you see it?"

"Yeah, it's your typical heteronormative emo whatever." Leigh gave a knowing chuckle. "You didn't miss much."

"I'll see it with you, Jenny," Geeta promised me. We always loved going to the movies together. Even the terrible ones were fun with Geeta at my side.

We finally pulled up to the apartment building where the two of them lived and walked to the elevator. I pressed the button for the fifth floor, proud of myself for remembering.

Geeta opened the door to their enormous loft apartment, the likes of which no twenty-something could afford in present-day Manhattan without serious family help. But this was a previous decade, a time in the not-too-distant past when recent college grads could still occasionally manage to inhabit a two-bedroom in SoHo and didn't even need magic Memos to win the real-estate lottery. Or maybe I was wrong. Was it possible that their Memos, not just dumb luck, had guided them to this prime address?

"You can stay here until your new place is ready," Geeta said, ushering me inside.

My new place?

Geeta and Leigh had offered to let me shack up with them before. Back then, I had been too ashamed to take them up on it. I remembered feeling like such a loser for getting kicked out of my prestigious program. I'd hightailed it to my childhood home, not wanting to be a burden on my friends. But now, with the clarity that only time travel affords, I had the confidence to see their offer for what it was: a gesture of friendship, not pity. "Thank you," I said. "About that new place—"

"The one you sent me to suss out?" Geeta started laughing. "Leave it to you to find a perfect one bedroom overlooking Tompkins Square Park when you're living your European dream."

"Don't forget the roof deck. Or that it's rent-controlled," Leigh said in a mock groan. "I don't know how you pulled that off."

"I guess I got the . . . apartment magic," I said. I so badly wanted to tell them the truth, that I, too, got the Memo, that we were all part of the same club now, following these Consortium-mandated edicts to live our best lives. There was so much else I wanted to tell them, so many questions I wanted to ask. Did they have words of advice about living according to a set of seemingly arbitrary instructions? Had the Memo ever asked them to do something they really didn't want to do?

Instead, I took a shower and changed into a daisy-print dress that I remembered from my twenties, then found a spot on Geeta and Leigh's velvet living room sofa, directly beneath a dramatic green chandelier that inhabited the open space like a perfect punctuation mark. The walls were painted a beautiful cream. The parquet floors gleamed with polish.

"Gross, I know," Leigh said when she caught me staring at the Band-Aids and blisters all over her feet. I now remembered the high heels she used to wear to her front desk job at the art gallery. They were nothing short of instruments of torture. Leigh wiggled her toes and sighed. "You, on the other hand, look amazing from head to toe."

"It's true," Geeta said, coming over with my coffee. "The Italian experience was definitely good for you."

"The bakery fellowship lifestyle is good and all, but . . . have you ever had sex with a gorgeous Italian car mechanic?"

"Mercifully, no," Leigh said with a laugh.

"The Italian stallion you mentioned in your last postcard?" Geeta said. "You've said arrivederci, I assume."

"Yes, but he was just so—" I said.

"He lives with his extended family," Geeta reminded me.

"Let's be real," Leigh interjected. "You're in a city filled with eligible bank accounts." She theatrically covered her mouth with her hands. "Oops, did I say that? Eligible *bachelors*."

Geeta gave Leigh a playful shove. "It's not about the money, Jen. It's about finding an equal. You had your summer fun and now you need a guy whose drive matches your own. Look at you, about to start working at Daniel for that amazing new pastry chef, what's his name?" She picked a postcard off the coffee table. It had been written by me, I saw. "Oh, Dominique Ansel—"

"The cronut guy?" I asked.

"Cro-*huh*?" said Geeta.

"Never mind," I said, realizing that the advent of the hybrid "it" pastry that would cause the entire city to lose its mind was still a few years in the future. "It's this experimental thing he's working on. A cross between a croissant and a donut. You'll see." I put my index finger to my lips to indicate I was letting them in on a secret.

"A croissant crossed with a donut? That sounds disgusting," Geeta said.

"Well, tell that to the people who are going to line up around the block just for a taste," I said with a laugh.

"I can't believe he's making you start tomorrow," said Leigh.

"Neither can I!" I said, earnestly. "I am really working for Dominique Ansel? It's like, too good to be true!"

"Girl, always remember: he's the lucky one," said Geeta.

"Thank you," I said.

"The really good news is that we have just enough time to have a little fun with each other before we all dive back into the grind," Geeta said.

They'd planned a welcome-back party for me, Leigh said.

"Tonight?" I said.

Geeta nodded. "We have some people we'd like you to meet."

"By people she means a person," Leigh clarified. "There's this guy, Alex, who is perfect for you." My ears perked up at the name that Desiree had mentioned. He was the hunk I was hooking up with in my little preview. "He's up to here"—Leigh raised her hand a couple of inches above her own towering body, which indicated that this man was quite possibly a Sasquatch. "And he's a big shot biotech patent lawyer. Plus he has excellent taste. He just bought a Hockney from my boss."

I suppressed the impulse to tell Leigh that she didn't need to meddle with my love life to climb to the top of the art world. Soon she would have no boss, and she would do just fine on her own. Instead, I laughed. "He bought a Hockney? How old is this person?"

"He's twenty-eight or twenty-nine, super successful," said Leigh. "He's a character. He told me he sleeps with his laptop open next to his pillow so he can write down all the messages that come to him in his dreams. When his subconscious is properly inspired, he says he stays up all night long ideating."

"Sounds like a super chill guy," I said.

"Seriously, Jenny," Geeta said. "Have you ever even hooked up with a real man with a real job?"

I shrugged. I thought I had but I guessed, according to their definition of what a real man was, I hadn't. Even thirty-five-year-old me still hadn't. Now Leigh was the one who shook her head and smiled. "Alex is going to love you. I bet he's never met a genius college dropout."

I felt my shoulders tighten. So I had dropped out of school after all. And, evidently, I'd still managed to get the fellowship of my dreams. I supposed that Desiree had been right. A Coleman diploma was not necessary to get me where I needed to be.

"I really think it's meant to be," Leigh said.

"The world has a plan for you, Jenny," Geeta said, "and you need to follow the signs."

I cocked my head at her. Was she alluding to the Memo? Did she know I had one?

"You okay?" Geeta asked.

"Yeah, I'm just going to call my parents and let them know I arrived safe."

"You better not be calling that Italian guy," Geeta said, rolling her eyes.

I went to Geeta's room and located my phone. I didn't want to call anyone though. Instead, I scrolled for today's date to see what the Memo told me to do.

Wear something red.

Plain and simple. So I took off the daisy-print dress and threw on a crimson number with spaghetti straps—the only red item of clothing in my suitcase—while my friends chatted in the living room. When I emerged, Geeta whistled at me like a construction worker, poured us each a few inches of sparkling rosé, and raised her glass.

"Love you, Jenny!" Geeta and Leigh said in unison.

"Love you more," I shot back.

I was halfway through my glass when I noticed something across the apartment. A woman was walking out of the bathroom in a towel. It took me a second to place her face. Leigh's former flame, Karenna Michaelson, an established artist who had a major cocaine problem, and who, I now realized, must have passed that charming hobby onto Leigh.

"Hi, Karenna!" I called out.

Her face flooded with confusion, and I realized we probably hadn't yet met in this realm.

"I'm Jenny!" I clarified. "I've heard all about you." I hoped that Leigh had at least told me about her.

"Right. Hi." She raised her hand in a wave. "I'm just going to finish getting ready."

"Take your time, babe!" Leigh called out. "We'll be here all night."

I always thought Karenna seemed so old. But now she looked much younger than I remembered, and I suddenly realized she was younger than my true, thirty-five-year-old self.

As Geeta topped off my glass, I rubbed my trusty cameo earrings and thought about how bizarrely easy it had been with the help of the Consortium. Much as I tried to keep cool, I couldn't stop smiling, particularly when I looked at Geeta, so young and adorable. Where would we go from here now that we were both Player As? In this world, Hal was a complete nonentity, and Gabe had been banished to the underworld. Massimo was likely pining for me, but I'd forget about him soon enough. This time I was going to make the right choices.

"Why so quiet?" Geeta asked.

"Just thinking," I said, crossing my legs and taking another sip. "This is all so amazing. I missed you."

"I'm proud of you," she said softly. I didn't know how to respond. As the bubbles went to my head, I felt my commitment to the Consortium's NDA slipping away. I wanted to share my good news with her, the "covenants pertaining thereto" be damned. I looked into Geeta's loving brown eyes. I couldn't stand it anymore.

"Geeta, we've never had any secrets, right?" I asked.

"Not that I know of."

"I should tell you something," I said. My hands and feet started to feel numb. "I'm here today because I got the—"

Before I could finish what I was saying, there was a crunch of metal from above. In a split second, the chandelier detached from the ceiling and sliced through the air, coming straight for my head.

16

● ● ●

DESIREE WAS GRIPPING MY SHOULDERS AND SHAKING ME. "WHAT the hell is wrong with you?"

She'd changed into a suit in a pale stone hue. Everything behind her was a blur. "Just because you got the Memo doesn't mean you need to flaunt it! You signed a legally binding document. Breaking it has cosmic, cataclysmic consequences."

"Sorry." I rubbed my eyes. I was back in her office, on the good old love seat. The space was coming into focus. How my head hurt. "I was . . . in my feelings. It's hard for me to conceal anything from Geeta. I probably shouldn't drink anymore when I'm blitz-tracking."

"I could give a toss what you imbibe." Desiree clenched her jaw, sat down next to me, and put her hands on my shoulders. "I *specifically* told you not to go back to 2009. Your work there was already done. But you were determined, so off you went. When Valerie gets wind of this violation . . ." Desiree let go of me and began pacing back and forth across the office, hand to her head.

I felt a vibration and looked down at my phone. A sad-face

emoji was flashing on my home screen. Valerie, whoever she was, wasn't the only one disappointed with me.

"What a fool I was, letting you waste our time and have your little champagne toast. And you thanked me, how? First, you had to bring that weird man into your optimized life."

I remembered watching Gabe's body slip down the sewer grate and felt a wave of worry. "What happened to Gabe? Did I hurt him?"

"You invited him in, and he had to be disinvited," she murmured.

"I didn't invite him anywhere!"

"You didn't?" Desiree's voice pulsed with accusation as she looked down at me. "*I* sure didn't! Get with the program. He is not part of the program. Leave him well enough alone—in Pittsburgh. And then, to make matters worse, you went back, opened your big trap, and nearly ruined everything. Do you have any idea what such a revelation would have done?" Desiree was now inhaling and exhaling heavily, as if she were in labor.

"I was only trying to—"

"Look at you, trying to outwit the physical universe. The reason we had you sign the NDA is not because we at the Consortium are vindictive. It's because we know things about the ways energy pathways interact. This is theoretical physics in action, Jenny! It's no longer just theoretical! If you reveal too much information about the future in your past, it disrupts the flow, which could seriously impact our research." She glared at me.

"You do realize I am a human being, not a guinea pig?"

"If only. Guinea pigs are cute creatures that can't talk. I'll put it another way: if you were to reveal to your friends that you had the Memo, you would be altering the course of human history."

"Geeta and Leigh are just two people," I reminded her. "It's not like I went on the nightly news."

"You need to get in line. It might be a lot to juggle in your little head, but remember, this is all temporary. On your thirty-sixth birthday, you will permanently latch on to your new life and you will never have to worry about anything ever again. You understand?"

"Yes," I said. "I'll be a good soldier. Promise."

"You're not a soldier. You're an *explorer*. Somewhere, out there, you're meeting Alex. And you're also opening your first storefront! And you're at a squash tournament in Boston. You play doubles. You're making the semifinals."

"I play squash?" I was truly puzzled. "And I'm playing it as we speak?"

Desiree leaned against the fireplace. "Haven't you ever heard of things happening in tandem? Or looked at a star and stopped to think how long it takes for the light to travel to earth and that what you are really seeing is that star in a past state, millions of years ago?"

"Sure, I think about that all the time," I deadpanned.

"You, Jenny, are that star. You're still burning, then and now. With all the additional information we've introduced to your reality, you're in a very delicate state, spinning a chrysalis that could come undone if you're not careful. Valerie, my supervisor, can explain it better. She wanted to have a word with you. She didn't take kindly to your slipup."

"How many of you were watching me?" I asked in horror.

"Just me, but I report everything to Valerie," she said. "What was I supposed to do? I needed her help to get you the hell out of harm's way. Only she knows how to do that chandelier trick." Desiree motioned for me to get up.

Fear set in as Desiree and I trudged up a flight of stairs to Valerie's office. Desiree had me wait outside at first, so I pulled an old magazine out of my bag, trying and failing to focus on a story about a pirate ship that had recently been discovered at the bottom of the Indian Ocean. There was a muffled altercation on the other side of the door. I tried to tune it out.

Desiree's head finally poked out the doorway, cuckoo-clock style. "She's ready."

Valerie's office was lined with plane windows that overlooked the quad. It featured its own science lab, with a fume hood, Bunsen burners, and test tubes arranged in an orderly fashion.

Valerie's onyx-colored hair was styled in a bowl cut—the look was similar to Desiree's but slicked in such a way that she resembled a Lego figure. She was sorting vials and mumbling to herself, something about "stupid ideas" and "geriatric wanderer."

Heat rushed to my face.

"Just to be clear, you do understand that a nondisclosure means you *don't* disclose, right?" Valerie said by way of greeting. "I know the directions can present challenges to those who have issues with authority."

"I understand," I said quietly.

"So you were simply doing as you pleased because you thought having a little heart-to-heart with your girlfriends before party time was more important than keeping the entire fucking universe aligned?"

I froze, too stunned to defend myself. "I'm really sorry," I said. "I lost sight of the rules."

"Evidently." Valerie pressed her lips together. "You put all of us in grave jeopardy when you don't abide by the terms. The Consortium, yourself, Geeta too. I'm not overstating the facts. Do it for Geeta if nothing else. Do you want to hurt her?"

She let her final words hang in the air. My insides went cold. Of course I didn't want to hurt Geeta. That would be the last thing I ever wanted to do.

"I hear you," I said.

"It's not that hard," Valerie said. "Mouth shut, mind open. If you can't hack it, now's your chance to delete the app and go back to that sorry Pittsburgh existence of yours."

"I can hack it," I said. It surprised me how much I wanted to return to my alternate life.

Valerie stared at me, as if she was determining whether I was worth any extra breath. "I'll see you at your ceremony," she said, and walked out of the room.

"I know she can be a bit brusque," Desiree said a moment later. "Don't judge her too harshly. Valerie has been dealing with some terrible back pain."

I wasn't sure Valerie deserved any of Desiree's excuses, but I knew better than to speak ill of her. Instead, I asked, "What is this ceremony she was talking about?"

"*Your* ceremony. It's in a week."

"So it's my birthday party?"

"Of sorts. Until then, you will be zigzagging between two lives. And, at the end of this journey, you will accept your destiny. Everything will click into place and you will soar." She pressed her palms together. "Every ending is also a beginning."

Again, the questions began to swirl in my mind.

"And when I click into my new life, what happens to the old Jenny Green? The one in Pittsburgh, with Hal and Alice? Does that Jenny . . . die a violent death or . . ."

Desiree waved her hand in the air, her movements soft as smoke. "She transitions to her new, better life. There will be no trace of Jenny Green in Pittsburgh."

"So I erase myself, effectively?" I said.

"You don't *erase*, you *adjust the dials*. The pieces of your life will rearrange accordingly. That crew of yours will all still be there; they'll just be there without you. They'll have no memories to bog them down. You'll be gone without a trace."

"And what about Geeta?" I spluttered.

"Geeta? She's got the Memo early in life, so you don't have to worry about her branch points." Desiree cocked her head, waiting for me to understand. "There's only one Geeta who accepted her Memo when she was supposed to. We expect that she's fully equipped to handle either version of you. Make sense?"

"You want me to be honest here?" I mumbled, but she either didn't hear me or didn't care.

"We'll be running some tests on you between trips to check your vitals and quantify the impact, yada yada. This is an important data set. You may be the first, but remember there are others who we will be blitz-tracking after you. You're our pioneer."

"No pressure or anything."

"Oh and one more thing: after the next blitz-track, you'll need to return to Pittsburgh."

"And do what?" I wondered how I would act upon seeing Hal now that I knew for sure that he had been cheating on me this entire time.

"You'll go home and live your old life. Pretend nothing's happened. Your prior existence should be more or less the same. There may be some QB disjunctions given the trouble you already got yourself into, but don't mind them."

"QB whatsits?"

"Qubit disjunctions. But let's not dwell on them. The objective is to minimize them."

"Minimize what?"

"The disjunctions!"

I felt like we were Abbott and Costello, doing a metaphysical "Who's on First?" bit.

"But how can I minimize them if I don't know what they are?"

Desiree fixed her gaze on the window. "When you jump between lives, you want to create as few disturbances as possible. If you don't follow the laws, however, there will likely be some ripple effects. So I'd expect them if I were you. Just act like everything is normal. Where's your phone? I need you to pull up the Pathetic tab."

I did as told. "This is all real footage, mind you," Desiree said as I cringed at the sight of a video of my best friends getting side-by-side massages at a tropical resort. The Turkish eye tattoo on Leigh's left shoulder, which I had recently learned about via social media, told me this scene had taken place sometime in the last year. There was audio this time.

"She's doing her own thing," I heard Geeta say.

"But does she have to do it so slowly and so annoyingly?" asked Leigh. "She's exhausting."

"Cut her some slack," Geeta said. "She's had a lot of microtraumas."

Microtraumas?

My heart went heavy as I scrolled down. There was a clip of Yelena, my former intern at the radio station, winning a Guggenheim Fellowship in Poetry. How had I not heard about that? Next up was Alice delivering an address about women's empowerment at what looked like some fancy private club. "In our fast-paced, achievement-obsessed society, self-doubt runs rampant," Alice said in the video. "There's a woman I know, a woman I have tried to mentor, who once had everything going for her but might as well wear a sandwich board that says: 'I Am So Lost I Don't Even Realize I'm Wearing a Sandwich Board.' It's heartbreaking."

"Is it working?" Desiree asked. I could barely nod in response. My hurt and envy levels were off the charts. "Good. Now pick a date. Anytime will do, just as long as it's after your last journey." I scrolled the dial to a random date, tapped the button on my flashing screen, and waited for the gates to my other life to swing open.

17

• • •

I WAS STILL WOOZY, AND MY BODY FELT LEADEN. I WAS SINKING INTO A padded movie theater seat. The scent of artificial butter infused the air. On the screen, Meryl Streep was screaming at the actor who played her husband. I remembered this movie from my twenties. Geeta was sitting next to me, her unmistakable profile, that arrow-sharp chin and perky nose, clear in the dark. I felt a stab of gratitude. Of all the places and times I could have spun the wheel to, I was at Geeta's side.

After the closing credits ran, I followed Geeta out of the theater and onto Twenty-Third Street. New York City was bustling, and it was still bright out, not too hot. I noticed I had on form-fitting jeans and a cropped vest. My midriff was jacked.

"Well, that was fun," Geeta said to me as we lingered underneath the marquee. She shifted her weight on her feet a bit awkwardly. "I can't believe how long it's been since we've seen each other."

I was mystified. How long could it possibly have been? We were in our twenties, an age when best friends still saw each other all the time.

"It hasn't been *that* long," I said, hoping she'd provide an explanation.

"I guess. What is time anyway?" Geeta forced a laugh.

I wanted to tell her that time was my magic carpet, and that I had just traveled through it to see a summer matinee with her, but I held my tongue. It wasn't easy. I had so many questions. What had happened to us between the time I'd apprenticed with the cronut genius and now? What had happened at that party? Did I meet Alex? And what the hell was going on between Geeta and me? When we lived in the same city, Geeta and I never let a week pass without a hang.

Geeta drifted toward the curb and I could see her eyes scanning traffic for a taxi. I didn't want her to go.

"Wait," I said. "It's such a beautiful day. Want to grab a drink?"

"You're the one who said you only had time for a quick movie—the perfect way to avoid talking about anything of substance." She was trying to sound sarcastic but I could detect a note of hurt. "Besides, I have a dinner party tonight."

"It's still the afternoon."

"I'm hosting," she said. I stopped short. It was clear I wasn't on the guest list.

"Can I come?" I asked.

"You're not serious, are you?" She cocked her head. "You told me that your weeks are ruled by your job, and your weekends are also ruled by your job, so I didn't invite you. You know how small my table is."

"I really said that?" I asked, dumbfounded. I couldn't imagine ever saying something so idiotic.

"Yes, you did," Geeta said. "Besides, speaking of your job, don't you have to go to Florence's cocktail thing tonight?"

"Florence will get over it," I said, even though I had no idea who Florence was.

"Are you crazy? It's not every weekend you get invited to your boss's home." Geeta put her hand on my shoulder, a tender concession. "Let's get something on the calendar soon," she added brightly. "I still haven't seen your new apartment."

"Me neither." The words slipped out. "I mean, me too! I'd really like that." But much more than that, I wanted to know how it was possible that my best friend hadn't seen my home and was hosting a dinner party to which I was not invited because I had an obligation to brown-nose a boss named Florence.

Geeta raised her hand to flag down a cab and gave me a hug before getting in. Her embrace was listless, but I held her tight.

"Seriously, let's not let five months go by again without catching up," she said, shutting the door and blowing me a kiss from the back seat.

"Five months?" I mumbled as the cab drove away. It had been almost half a year?

I walked west, feeling melancholy and lost. I wasn't sure what, exactly, I was supposed to be doing here. I needed my Memo mandate. I was still digging around in my bag for my phone when I stepped off the curb and onto the street. A runner who was hurtling up Seventh Avenue crashed into me.

"Watch it!" I cried out in alarm.

The runner was intent on keeping pace, so he barely glanced over his shoulder. "*You* don't have the light!" he told me.

My jaw dropped.

"Gabe?" I cried out before I could think better of it.

He looked at me expectantly. Crap. What was I going to say? *You don't exactly know who I am, but I've blitzed here from the future. I know that you are going to become a lovelorn single dad and join Pittsburgh's scrappiest a cappella entourage.*

He resumed his run. I gasped as he ran straight into an oncoming bus and collapsed onto the pavement. Then the bus continued rolling along. I stood there watching the cars go by and staring at the site where Gabe's body had just fallen. He was gone, though. He'd completely vanished. There was nothing on the ground but a couple of pigeons nosing around for a snack. Stranger still, nobody appeared to have seen this accident happen but me.

"Goodness, your imagination has quite a violent bent," came a familiar voice. Desiree was heading my way. She linked her skinny arm with mine and led me to the opposite side of the street.

"What the hell was that?" I asked.

"That little 'run in,' if you will, was another one of your strange fantasies." Desiree's voice was as smooth as cream. "If you want to hang out with your a cappella buddy, you're free to stay in Pittsburgh. You can't keep summoning Gabe from your subconscious. Got it?"

"No, I don't get it at all. Why does this keep happening?"

"Forget about him. We need to go to your apartment. It's fabulous."

"What are you doing here?" I asked. This was our first encounter in my alternate life.

"You think we are going to take another risk with you? Trust must be earned."

Desiree didn't let go of my arm as she led me down the busted-up steps of the subway station, then brandished a Metro-Card and swiped us both through the turnstile. A man on the platform was playing "El Cóndor Pasa" on a one-string instrument.

"So, how was your little movie date with the old BFF?" Desiree inquired as we made our way onto one of the last cars of the downtown 1 train.

"Weird," I said, looking down at my feet. My chunky-heeled patent leather loafers looked very expensive.

"They're Prada," Desiree supplied. "Now, you were saying?"

I looked back up at her. "On the one hand, it was great seeing her. On the other, how is it possible that she and I are too busy to get together anymore?"

"You both need to focus on your careers right now," Desiree said.

"But that seems so . . . sad."

"Listen, your friends will either be there in the end, or they won't. You need to take care of yourself."

By that point, the train doors opened at Christopher Street, which was my stop apparently. I was living in the West Village? *Not bad.*

"Dare I ask, what am I doing now, in this phase of my perfect life?" I said. "And who, exactly, is Florence?"

Desiree rubbed her hands together. "Now *these are* the right questions to be asking! You're hustling nonstop, but you love it. You're working at Demeter Editions, a top-notch publishing house run by Florence McIntosh. You are the marketing liaison, always coming up with creative ways for the chefs on their roster to promote their books. The job is a steppingstone, but you do excellent work and you schmooze like nobody's business. You live in a gorgeous apartment that, thanks to an intro from Florence, one of Demeter's authors rented to you while she travels in Asia researching ancient spices. She'll fall in love with a trekking expert and be gone for ages so you'll be set here for a long while."

"Not Anya Sturgeon?" I could feel my eyes widening. I remembered reading an essay she'd written about re-learning how to cook in the mountains of Burma. I had bought her book *Spice Trail* the second it came out. I had it to thank for the online curry shopping habit I'd developed. "I'm subletting from her?"

"More than that—you're her protégé," Desiree said, smiling. "As I said, good things await on the other side." We turned onto

Barrow Street, which was always one of my favorites, with its cute cafes and brownstones decked out with colorful flowerpots. We walked up the steps of one such building.

"Okay. Wow. Anya Sturgeon is my mentor and I am living in her townhouse," I said.

"The keys are in your pocket," Desiree said. I dug in and there they were, attached to a leather keychain embossed with that familiar triangular pile of bones.

"Thanks for the Consortium swag," I said. "I should probably go inside and settle in. Gotta get ready for the boss's cocktail party and see what the Memo has in store."

Desiree lifted her finger in the air. "Today's something of an orientation day. It's tomorrow that really matters."

"Obviously," I said.

"You should swing by Florence's tonight, of course. And before you go to bed, I want you to set the dial for September 8, 2013. Can you remember that date?" I nodded. "In 2013, you'll be on a kickboxing streak. The training session will be memorable. We'll fine-tune your career—and your . . ."

"My what?" I prodded.

Desiree ignored my question and informed me that I was to report to the Uppercut Gym first thing the next morning. "And take it easy on the cocktails. It's going to be a doozy of a workout."

18

. . . .

I T WAS STILL DARK OUT WHEN THE ALARM WENT OFF. I FLIPPED ON THE
lamp and fumbled for the magazine on the nightstand, an issue
of *The Manhattan Review* dated August 2013. The address label
confirmed that I was still on Barrow Street. I took an inventory of
my surroundings. Past the foot of my bed, there was a brick fireplace. Unlike the cracked ceilings of my Pittsburgh sublet, the
one over my head had ornate moldings.

I got out of bed and walked over to the dresser. The drawers
were filled with clothing in size small, tags still attached to many
of the garments. I threw on a shimmery workout ensemble and
didn't have to decide what to do with any extraneous rolls of flesh.
My body was in fighting form.

The city was quiet except for the sounds of garbage being
loaded into trucks when I walked over to the Uppercut Gym. I
opened the building's heavy iron door and clomped up to the
fourth floor. The halls smelled like ripe sweat, and the studio
door was painted with that familiar pyramid-shaped configuration of bones.

The silver-haired woman who opened the door defied all

laws of aging with her slim physique and paper-smooth complexion. She wore a black, crocodile-textured bodysuit. "Come on in, Jenny," she said in a hoarse voice.

The studio was stocked with punching bags, heavy-duty jump ropes, and kettlebells. The walls were covered in lush plants. Groups of boxers, all women, sparred with each other in this urban rainforest while Nicki Minaj's voice pumped through the air.

"This is for you, Jenny." The silver-haired woman handed me a waiver on a white clipboard. I figured it was the typical we-have-no-liabilities-if-you-die-while-gasping-for-breath type of thing that I'd filled out so many times before braving hot yoga classes. But no, this was different. I had to initial each item on a list of Core Values:

> Today's excellence is tomorrow's mediocrity.
> Intelligence without ambition is a bird without wings.
> Success is a process, not an event.

If that's what it took to have this banging body, far be it for me to question these mantras. I initialed everything as quickly as possible and handed the clipboard back to the gorgeous raspy-voiced woman of indeterminate age.

"Thank you, Jenny," she said, bowing her head slightly.

She gestured to the back of the room, where Desiree awaited. My Svengali was wearing a gold track suit.

"We meet again," I said.

"We'll be working together this morning," Desiree told me as she handed me a pair of silver boxing gloves and led me to a white mat at the back corner of the studio. Here she demonstrated the art of the jab, twisting her forearm as her fist made contact with the punching bag. I was reminded of the boutique Thai kickboxing studio Sophie once dragged me to. The following day, my quads were so sore I could barely move.

Desiree adjusted my stance. "Your turn."

I gave it a try. It was harder than it looked. But I kept at it, stepping one foot solidly forward and throwing all my weight into the punch. I repeated this over and over until Desiree was satisfied with my speed, power, and accuracy.

"There you go," she said, her green eyes twinkling with evident satisfaction. "Now I'm going to show you a cobra roundabout."

This move involved crouching into a tight ball, then springing up into the air and hissing while landing a punch. The white-cushioned pillar in front of me now revealed its second function. Not only was it a punching bag, it doubled as a projection screen.

"You and your Consortium sure are into screen time," I murmured.

"Let's go, tiger."

As I crouched, leaped, and punched, images of characters from my life flickered before my eyes.

First there was Hal. *Punch.* Then Alice Hustad. *Punch.* There was a series of guys who never called me after our first dates, guys whose names I barely remembered. *Punch.* Brie and her perky nose. *Punch.* But when I saw Geeta's face projected on the bag, the violent impulse drained away.

"Come on, Jenny!" Desiree sounded frustrated. "Get her hard!"

"But why?" I wiped the sweat off my forehead.

"To prove that you are willing to do what's necessary," she said. "You're not going to hurt her—it's just an image."

"Let go of your inhibitions," the silver-haired woman said,

coming over to join us. "Why are you so gentle with the one who convinced you not to get with the program in the first place?"

"Seriously, Jenny, how's that been going for you?" Desiree egged me on. "She didn't even invite you to her dinner party. And when you asked, she couldn't be bothered to make an extra space at the table. Puhlease."

Desiree really had my number. My eyes darted between my two coaches. I resented their complicity, but they had a point. Geeta was the reason I didn't accept the Memo in the first place. I would have listened to anything she said. And she'd urged me to stay away from Desiree, to steer clear of a life that was better than the one I'd idiotically clung to for so many years.

I threw a punch but it didn't land. My glove grazed the edge of the bag and I lost my balance, toppling to the floor. Before I could get a word out, the silver-haired woman crouched down and drove her fist into the middle of my face. The pain that followed was liquid and pulverizing. Everything went as white as snow.

Once I came to, Desiree was tending to me in the reception area, applying an ice pack to my nose. She had changed back into one of her boardroom outfits.

"You did great," she said tenderly. "We didn't want to tell you what was coming in advance."

"You *planned* this?" I cried out. I grabbed the ice pack with my bloody hand and brought it to my face. I felt a new stab of pain.

"Although it might not feel that way now, this was a gift," my silver-haired attacker said. "I'll see you both later." I looked up and watched her body transform to smoke. The silvery shape-shifter was gone.

"What the hell?" I asked.

"The body is just the vessel," Desiree said, and escorted me out of the exercise studio and onto the street. The sun had risen high in the sky, and morning commuters were bustling to and fro. "Let's take a walk."

"To a hospital? I think I broke my nose."

"You did. In two places, in fact." Desiree's tone was plucky. "So you're going to get it fixed. Just keep the ice in place for now."

"Are you serious?"

"You must learn how to cope with physical pain."

My head throbbed as we walked westward. "Do you have any Tylenol at least?"

Desiree sat down on a bench facing the Hudson River and pulled me into the spot next to her. I was losing sensation in my fingers, so I switched the ice pack from my right hand to my left.

"You're perfectly fine," she told me. "You haven't really lived until you've been punched in the face. Especially if you're Jenny Green. This is all part of the plan. So what if your sense of smell is slightly compromised?"

"What? I thought I was supposed to become a culinary superstar," I reminded her. "How can I do that if my sense of smell is compromised?"

"One woman's 'compromised' is another's 'optimized.' You'll start blogging about baking your way back to taste, one smoked-feta crumpet and passion-fruit éclair at a time. This is exactly as we intended. Juliet has excellent aim."

"Hold up," I said. "That lady who beat me up and turned into smoke was Juliet—*the* Juliet Simcott?"

"The one and only." Desiree stared straight ahead, a small smile playing out on her lips.

"And the Consortium purposely knocked out my sense of smell? But I *need* to smell. I can't cook without it. It would be like painting blind."

"Exactly. People are captivated by journeys of attractive women overcoming adversity and, quite frankly, you weren't conventionally attractive enough. Which brings us to our two-in-one solution. Ninety-nine percent of the women you see on television have had rhinoplasty." I thought about how Desiree had said she was going to fine-tune my career and something else. By something else, she'd meant my . . . face?

"This is about building a narrative," she went on. "Your fan base will broaden far beyond the food world now that you have an interesting story to tell, the story of a scrappy fighter. And you'll have a perfect profile to match," she said with increasing enthusiasm. "Don't you see? Your story is getting richer and more compelling. First you dropped out of college to follow your passion, then you came up against adversity and you persevered!"

I sniffled. "The adversity that you and that risen-from-the-dead lady engineered? People will believe that I got in a fight with . . . a ghost?"

"A little struggle will look very good on you. There's no over-estimating the importance of relatability in your line of work."

"Relatability has never been my problem. And I don't really follow how being taken out by a kickboxing instructor who appears to be made of vapor is a particularly relatable narrative."

Desiree laughed. "We're talking about aspirational relatability. Not snoring-boring relatability. In your blog, you will share with your followers that you were attacked by a disgusting man on your way to the gym. He ran off without a trace, leaving you to lick your wounds and double your therapy visits because of your lingering PTSD. But there will be an upside to your assault. Thanks to this incident, you have something to recount in chilling detail on multiple platforms. The only person who might get sick of it is you." Desiree gave my back a gentle pat.

I felt something dislodge from my nostril and watched a clump of blood drop down on my shiny yoga pants. I began to wonder if perhaps this whole thing was not the best idea.

19

● ● ●

WAS DOWN ON THE GROUND. MY BODY WAS SPRAWLED OUT ACROSS A blanket so flimsy that I could feel the hard floor beneath me. I tried to speak but was only capable of grunting noises. The room was pitch dark. Was I dead? A voice cut through the silence, indicating that I was not.

"You were overheating so I brought you down here," Desiree said. She was silhouetted against a doorframe across the room.

The officious sound of Desiree's pumps echoed through the space as she walked over to me and pulled me up to my feet. "Your friends are looking for you. It's time to go back to them," she said, leading me through the darkness to the stairwell. I held tightly to the banister and made my way up to the ground floor. Right. My friends. How long had I been gone?

"We'll see each other soon enough," Desiree said, all but pushing me out the door.

Dawn was breaking as I stumbled out of the Simcott Center's side entrance. I darted down the Ellison lawn and broke through the campus gates, reaching the town square. The familiarity of the scene comforted me. Vendors were setting up the Sequoia

Falls Farmers Market, my old favorite. The scents of peppermint and tarragon shot through the early summer air. I could smell again! I stroked my nose and felt the familiar little bump on the bridge.

I looked down at my phone. Sure enough, the Memo app featured another achievement badge: a pair of boxing gloves rotating 360 degrees around a disembodied nose. I felt a stupid prick of pride. I'd done something right.

Much as I hated to admit it, Desiree had a point. All my heroes had their own tales of adversity. Julia Child was awkward and past her prime when she started to master the culinary arts. Nigella Lawson didn't become a celebrated home cook until she was tending to her husband who was dying of throat cancer. There was that mother-daughter duo from Texas who used to be unhoused and now had a Michelin-starred restaurant with a two-year waiting list. My backstory, if you could call it that, had always been so boring: a girl from Long Island whose parents were still married and whose greatest claim to fame was setting a bakery on fire. I supposed I could use a spicy narrative of my own, even if it was entirely fabricated.

I stopped at the table of a pepper farm. The teenage girl running the stand handed me a sliver of bread drenched in chili-infused oil. The flavor made my mouth pucker. It was just like old times, when I used to come here every weekend, talking to vendors and tasting everything on offer. I inhaled another sample.

This market was up there with the best things about college. If it hadn't been for the farmers market, after all, it's unlikely I would have had my meet-cute with Yuri, the culinary student whom I dated for a few months. For all his talents, Yuri had also turned out to be a pathological liar, a fact I learned when Geeta had investigated his supposed stint with the Mossad. He'd spent his years between college and culinary school living in Tel Aviv with his eighteen-year-old fianceé and indulging an online poker habit. Geeta had assured me that I'd get over him in a heartbeat, calling him a "stupid starter boyfriend." He'd given me my first sourdough starter. That was worth something, wasn't it?

I wondered where Yuri had ended up as I admired a pyramid of apricots. I bought a couple as well as a loaf of sourdough bread. I ripped off a handful. The crust had integrity but the interior could have used a little more bite.

As I headed back uphill toward the Spruce Street house, I wondered how I was going to explain my extended absence to my friends. I cobbled together a story in my head. Hopefully, they'd understand how Alessandra had driven me away from the dinner. That was my explanation: her talk of the party on my birthday that I wasn't invited to put me in a terrible mood, and I didn't want to ruin their big night by being such a sad sack so I'd split. A defensible alibi.

As I turned right off Sedona Street, I spotted my beat-up Honda, one block down from where I remembered parking it. Geeta must have moved it for me. She used to do that for me in college, too, since she had a better handle on the strange local parking rules. As I neared the car, I noticed a dent on the rear left door. My rear-view mirror was also cracked and hanging by a wire. Someone must have slammed into my car and sped off. I kicked the ground and cursed.

I was still fuming when I walked up to our Airbnb. I tried to open the door with my key, but it didn't budge, so I rang the doorbell. A disheveled guy came to the door in his Coleman College Class of 2023 shirt. He looked vaguely familiar. I wondered if one of the student waiters working the reunion dinner had come back to party with my friends.

"Hey." He sounded tentative. "Can I help you?"

"I'm staying here," I said. "I actually lived here when I was a senior."

"Cool," he said flatly.

"Are Geeta and Leigh sleeping?"

He furrowed his brow. "Who?"

"Geeta. And Leigh."

"The only person who *was* sleeping is my girlfriend, who isn't sleeping now that you've been ringing the doorbell," he said.

A wash of confusion came over me. "But this is my Airbnb."

"Hate to break it to you, but this is my home. It's not an Airbnb."

"I'm sure this is the right address: 25 Spruce. I used to live here. It used to be my address when I went to school here."

"That must have been a long time ago," he said.

I craned my neck and looked past him into the apartment. All the renovations I had seen the previous day were gone. The place was in the same state of disrepair as it had been when we lived there fifteen years ago. I felt my palms slick with sweat. "Can I just see something?" I said, shoving past him before he even had a chance to answer. All the furniture was different—used, beat-up, college-student stuff; none of the marble finishes or pristine light sconces from the previous day were there.

First the car, now this. Something must have changed when I was flying through the wormhole. Was this related to those disjunctions that Desiree had warned me about?

"This is so weird, I'm sorry," I told the guy, stepping back outside. "I had a rough night. I think I got . . . mixed up on my way over. I didn't mean to disturb you."

"Whatever," he grunted and shut the door in my face.

My hands were shaking as I texted Geeta:

Hey, I got a little turned around. Could you tell me
the address of the house where we are staying?

My phone rang immediately. "What the hell, Jenny?" Geeta
barked. "You totally ghosted us last night. If we didn't hear from
you in an hour we were going to call the police."

"It's a long story," I said. "I'm trying to find my way back to
you. Where are you guys again?"

"I think I'm the one who should be asking that question," she
said. "We are exactly where we're staying. At the house."

"Right, right. I thought it was 25 Spruce Street, but it seems I
have amnesia?"

Geeta went silent for a moment, then said, "Did something
happen to you?"

*I've been time-traveling and just got punched in the nose by a
mercurial elderly physicist who asked me to assault a projection of
you, which I was unable to do . . . but now I'm back.*

"I just had a crazy night. Like, really crazy. I need some rest.
Remind me of the address?"

Now I heard Leigh in the background. "Lemme talk to her,"
she said. I could hear the two tussling over the phone. "Be nice,"
Geeta whispered right before Leigh came on.

"Jesus, Jenny," Leigh said. "We stayed up all night searching
for you."

"I'm so sorry." My mind was blank. "Alessandra was being
such a jerk and I lost my cool and just needed a little alone time,
and . . . I should have called."

"You don't say." Leigh let off a huffing sound. "Are you *ever*
going to start thinking about how your actions impact other people?"

"I'm really sorry," I repeated.

"That's all you ever are these days." She took a deep breath. "For years, actually."

"Leigh, are we really still stuck on your art show?" I squeezed my eyes shut. "I thought I explained to you that I couldn't afford it."

"After the fact you did. This too-little-too-late thing is becoming your specialty."

"And taking my problems as personal insults is yours," I said. "It wasn't about you."

"Oh, I know," Leigh agreed. "It was about you. That's all it ever is." Leigh handed the phone back to Geeta without even saying goodbye.

The address Geeta had provided, 17 Poplar Street, was two blocks away from the Spruce Street house. The apartment had the identical layout as the one on Spruce Street, and Matt's photo equipment was in the kitchen, just as I'd remembered. The equipment, that is, but not the kitchen. The room was painted melon and was crammed with vintage cooking devices. There was no way I wouldn't have remembered being here, and yet, I supposedly had been. I felt queasy. Keep it together, I told myself.

Geeta came down the hall. Her arms were folded across her chest.

"I'm so sorry," I said.

"What happened?"

I tried to reconstruct the night's events in a way that was understandable. "Alessandra was so rude to me, and I got upset and made the mistake of calling Hal from the dinner, which felt right at first but then was all wrong. It was obvious that Brie was there with him—"

Geeta shuddered. "The dog-hair girl?"

"The one and only. At least her dog was. I heard a bark."

"Did you confront him?"

"Yeah. Sort of. I mean, no," I said.

Geeta frowned. "Well, which is it?"

"I guess I was tipsier than I thought and just went to a dark place," I said.

"But, where did you go? Literally?" Geeta pressed. "Where did you sleep? We were so worried."

"I . . . wandered around. I was feeling really off . . . and by the time I'd cooled off, I couldn't remember our address. So I rested on campus."

Geeta squinted. "Like . . . you broke into a dorm?"

"There was a basement in that beautiful building we saw last night," I said, as if that explained anything. "It wasn't so bad."

"You slept in the basement of the Success building?" Geeta's eyes were bulging. "I am really concerned about your mental health."

Leigh headed into the hallway to join us. "Why the fuck didn't you text us? What is wrong with you?"

"I don't know . . . I was just in a state." I gave Geeta my best hangdog look. "I didn't want to ruin your night."

"Guess what, genius?" Leigh said, practically spitting out her words. "That's exactly what you did."

"I'm sorry," I said, for the millionth time. "I really wasn't thinking straight."

"You look horrible," Geeta said, reaching out to stroke my hair. "Sleep it off. We'll talk more later."

I wandered to the back of the apartment and lay on my bed, memories swarming my head. Crazily enough, the older recollections felt infinitely fresher. I could picture the boxing gym far more clearly than the workout room in my own apartment building (granted, I rarely exercised in Pittsburgh).

Through the walls, I could hear Geeta's babies crying and Dasha's soothing voice. Geeta, meanwhile, was running through lines, reciting what sounded like her next keynote speech.

"Nothing in my training could have prepared me for this," she said. "I was so burned out that my doctor told me, 'You're going to need medication.' And I said, 'How about meditation?'"

I lay there, emotions pressing in on me. I was so ashamed—and also so hurt.

My friends had been essentially lying to me for our entire adult lives, letting me obsess over my lame dramas like a dog with a chew toy while they followed their Memos and focused on their legitimate triumphs. I'd been so naive about them, even more so than I had been with Hal. Chasing after a perky closet organizer was one thing. What Geeta had done was next level. Leaving your best friend out in the cold so you can have all the riches for yourself? It was almost too much to comprehend. And still, I couldn't even punch a projection of her face when asked to.

I sat up with a jolt and stuffed my junk in my bag. I should have listened to Desiree back in the day or at least listened to my gut and blown off the reunion. This was a huge mistake. I'd had enough of everybody.

20

● ● ● ●

U.S. ROUTE 22 WEST
JUNE 11, 2022
AGE: 35

A S SOON AS I CROSSED THE NEW YORK BORDER INTO PENNSYLVANIA, I stopped at a Starbucks drive-through and got a latte to keep myself from falling asleep at the wheel. I was moving a cluster of random receipts aside to make room in the cup holder when my phone started to ring. The number 000–000 flashed on my watch. I picked up and a voice filled my car.

"You can't just peel out of town like that," Desiree said. "Not without telling me."

"You're the one who said I had to go back to Pittsburgh!"

"You sure love to point fingers."

"I didn't want to screw things up more than I already did—plus my friends don't need me around. They are crazy pissed at me, and all I can think about is how betrayed I feel that they never told me they got the Memo. But that's the one thing I cannot say!"

"There you go again, blaming others for your own shortcomings."

"Are you kidding me? They're furious at me for ditching them at dinner. And your friends are pissed at me too. Juliet or Valerie, or whoever in your consortium sits at the magic control panel, is pulling the levers to mess with me. My car was all busted up when I found it. My Spruce Street house was occupied by an angry undergrad. The kitchen in the house where I supposedly lived in college was painted this ugly orange!"

"I told you there would be some disjunctions."

I gritted my teeth and glanced out my side window. The mirror was hanging on, but barely, thanks to the packing tape I'd just purchased at the Sequoia Falls Drugstore.

"You're experiencing the consequences of your actions," Desiree said. "But at least you're taking action. Finally."

"Let's just hope I don't need to make any left turns on the ride home," I said, stepping on the gas.

"It's good to know your blind spots. You only have six days to correct a lifetime of—"

I was relieved when a double beep interrupted our conversation.

"I have to jump," I told Desiree. "I have another call." I switched over before Desiree could put up a fight.

"What the fuck?" Alice's voice rang throughout the car. What a lovely weekend surprise.

"Morning, Alice!"

"How did you drop the ball like that?"

"The Father's Day parade is on track," I lied. "We have an incredible roster of rad dads."

"I'm not talking about the parade. The List. The *List*." She pronounced the *t* at the end of the word so sharply it sliced through the air.

"The Changemakers' names are out on *Moment*'s Instagram page. I don't see my name there. How did you manage to mess that up? You said you had a connection."

"I tried," I replied. "I made your case." I didn't see any reason to tell Alice my connection was a closet assistant at the magazine.

"Am I a maker?" she asked.

"Yes," I said.

"Do I care about change?"

I gripped the steering wheel so hard my knuckles turned white. I had been so naive. Barely a year ago, I'd allowed myself to believe that Alice was the real thing, a Rust-Belt Robin Hood who cared about the plight of womankind. But there was only one woman Alice cared about.

"So . . . do I care about change?" she repeated.

"Of course you do. You've devoted your life to challenging social norms," I said in my most sycophantic voice. I felt sick to my stomach for not telling her the truth: she was a narcissist who hadn't changed a thing and never would.

"This is an insult to you too, Jenny. No disrespect to your friends' chanting apps and vulva sculptures, but our foundation is what belongs on that list! We're the ones promoting the cause of women."

"I am not going to disagree with that," I said.

"What are you going to do about it?"

"How about I go back to the magazine and try to see if they can squeeze you in—maybe there's some kind of sidebar about up-and-comers?" I sounded like a restaurant hostess craning her neck as she looked around the room for an extra table.

"You're not getting it," Alice said. "You're supposed to know about these things before they happen. And look where this leaves me. Who is going to shine a light on the foundation if nobody ever hears about us? I'm not sure the damage can be undone."

I so badly wanted to tell her that I *did* have the power to undo things!

Suddenly, the car gave a startling hiccup. There was a loud clunk and then a scraping sound.

"Alice, we can talk about this later," I said. "My side mirror just fell off, and I have to focus on the road."

"You really need to think about getting a new car," she said.

"I'll get right on that," I said before hanging up.

AS I ENTERED PITTSBURGH CITY LIMITS, ROLLING PAST THE OLD WARE-houses, a sensation of relief came over me. This city was starting to feel familiar. Funny how that worked. When I first arrived here, I was convinced this place would never feel like home. Geeta had given me a pep talk, reminding me it was "the original epicenter of American disruptors," the place where railroad barons and steel magnates envisioned the future and molded it to their convictions. Little by little, I had found my own landmarks, the independent movie theater where Sophie and I enjoyed our Saturday matinees, and a baking supply shop that had everything I needed. I even had an ob-gyn I liked. And I had Gabe, who knew how to make me laugh when I needed it most.

When I finally reached my building, I parked the car in a public lot across the street, then walked a lap around my block, trying to keep some shred of composure, envisioning what I'd like to say to Hal even though I knew I couldn't say it. *No picking fights about his obvious affair*, I told myself. *Just keep it cool for six more days and you'll be in the clear.*

I rode the elevator to the seventh floor and entered our apartment. Architectural renderings, partially-assembled shelving units, and papers with graphs were strewn about the floor. Did I even live here? Was this the result of more disjunctions?

"Hello?" I called out unsurely.

Hal emerged from our bedroom. His cheeks were flushed and he was holding an electric drill. "I thought you were coming back on Sunday?"

"A little bit of nostalgia goes a long way," I said with a sigh. "What's going on here?"

"I'm finally getting organized," he said. "Just like you always wanted."

It was true. I was constantly telling him to clean up after himself. This chaotic tableau starring my soon-to-be-ex boyfriend as Mr. Fix-It was indeed a step in the right direction.

"I tried calling you after we got disconnected, but your phone—"

"I know, I know," I said. "Straight to voicemail."

"Hey," Hal said in a pouty tone. "I missed you. Let's not fight."

"I didn't realize we were fighting."

"We don't have to if you don't want to." He put the drill down on the kitchen table and came toward me. So like Desiree, he just wanted me to let everything go, pretend it was normal? I turned away before he could give me a kiss. He ended up nuzzling the back of my neck.

"I've been traveling all day. I need to shower." I wriggled free from Hal and dropped my stuff on our bedroom floor alongside his tools.

He'd really transformed the room. There was a beautiful new shelf on the wall featuring framed pictures mostly from back in the days when we were co-adventurers. There was a photo of us enjoying a Japanese tea ceremony on our trip to Kyoto. A selfie of us looking happy on a park bench in Prague. Then there was one of me reading the newspaper at our tiny kitchen table in our old apartment in Brooklyn. I remembered that day so well. It was the day Hal and I had decided to move to Pittsburgh together. The job that Alice had offered me had sounded important and exciting. I'd convinced myself it would be better than the public radio station gig, where I'd spent three years going nowhere before getting fired. Pittsburgh might be the fresh start that would save us.

And now, just as I was about to depart this universe and finally go somewhere, Hal had created a shrine to our relationship. A welcome gesture, but way too late.

"You like the picture shelf?" Hal stared at me in that hopeful way that he did when I acted uninterested.

"Yeah," I said, fingering the smooth wood and averting my eyes from the pictures. My sadness was building. I opened the hallway closet door and saw the contents were arranged by color. Six trash bags were lined up on the floor, ready to be disposed of. He pointed to our bedroom closet. The door was back on its hinges.

I ripped off my shirt and rolled on an exercise bra. I had to get out of here—and fast.

"Actually, I'm going to go for a run," I said.

"Now? Are you still mad at me?" He looked a little scared.

"Should I be?" I asked, playing dumb. "I just need to move my body. I've been driving all day."

"All right." Hal shrugged and turned away. I was grateful that he did because I was about to start crying.

I ran for twenty-five minutes, two miles and change, more ground than I had covered in my running shoes in a year. Before I'd made it down three blocks, I was wheezing. After another few blocks, my lungs were hurting. But my head felt clearer. That was something.

When I returned home, I hopped in the shower, as peaceful a place as I could find. *One foot in front of the other*, I told myself as I adjusted the water temperature. *Just get through this with as little drama as possible*. After I dried off, I changed into a clean T-shirt and jeans and lay down on top of the covers. I tried to read an old issue of *The Manhattan Review*. It put me right to sleep.

When I woke up from my nap, there was a text from Hal saying he'd gone out to pick up gluten-free vegan pierogi for dinner. Either he was feeling caring or he needed an excuse to go see Brie. Whatever.

The only thing I wanted to do was call Geeta. Things would never be okay until we could be fully honest with each other. But that was the only thing that would make my life more of a mess. Then I remembered something my former therapist used to suggest: to write letters that I had no plan of sending to clarify my thoughts. I found a blank postcard in my bureau drawer.

> *Geeta,*
>
> *I've always sensed there was something off and I couldn't put my finger on it. Now I get it. I know the truth.*
>
> *I should be mad at you, and I am mad at you, like really made at you, but I am stupidly hopeful for us too. I miss you, G. I got the Memo and I'll be joining you soon. Maybe things will be better that way. How could they not? See you on the other side of 36.*
>
> *Jenny*

I folded the postcard in quarters and tightened my fist around it. I knew I probably wasn't going to mail it, but it was something to hold on to when everything else was slipping through my fingers.

21

PITTSBURGH
JUNE 13, 2022
AGE: 35

HUMAN NATURE IS SO PREDICTABLE. JUST AS YOU ALWAYS WANT THE thing you can't have, you only appreciate the thing you do have when you're about to lose it. Or, as Pittsburgh's golden boy Andy Warhol put it, "As soon as you stop wanting something, you get it." Now that my days in Pittsburgh were numbered, I was starting to see my life in a new light. This might have explained the bounce in my step as I approached SteelHaus for one of the last times ever.

My optimism instantly vanished when I spotted Deck pecking away on his laptop, pretending to be working, hours before he usually showed up at the office. This could only mean one thing: Alice was on the scene. So much for enjoying a long lunch with Sophie at the Mexican spot that handed out unlimited guacamole. I noticed Deck had on a polo shirt and loafers with braided tassels. He always attempted to up his game when his ex-wife-boss popped by the office. He grunted to acknowledge that he saw me, but didn't do anything drastic like say hello.

Then I saw Sophie charging across the workspace with a cardboard box in her arms. She scurried past the freelance event planners, art directors, and computer coders who toiled away in the common area. As she came toward me, I grasped the full picture. The neck of her goose lamp stuck out of the box, and mascara was running down her cheeks.

"What's going on?" I asked her.

"We're going bankrupt," Sophie said. "And suddenly it's all my fault."

"But we've always been going bankrupt," I said. "We're a nonprofit."

"Well, she's 'seeing patterns,' is what she said."

It was hard to make out exactly what had transpired from the jumble of expletives and gasps that tumbled out of Sophie's mouth, but it seemed that Alice showed up at the office unexpectedly that morning and picked a fight with Sophie, probably because she was still angry about not being celebrated as a Changemaker. She berated Sophie for not reporting one of Alice's social media impersonators to the Instagram authorities last week. Sophie told me that Alice got it in her head that a vaguely fat-shaming caption on the imposter's grid was the reason *Moment* left her off the Changemakers List. I started to feel guilty. Could it be possible that this was my fault, some misstep that I wasn't even aware of making? After all, Sophie had always been Alice's favorite. I was supposed to be the office punching bag.

"She said she's the victim of cancel culture," Sophie said. "And that I let her down."

"So she canceled *you*? Nice."

Sophie sniffled.

"Seriously, Soph. You're the only one around here who gets anything done these days. How could she fire you?"

"I have some dignity, thank you very much," Sophie replied. "She told me I was a useless, entitled moron. Maybe I am, but I still have some self-respect. So I quit."

"Does she not remember that I was the one who was supposed to get her on that list? That's not your job," I said.

"What can I say?" she said. "Rage is blind."

"And stupid is stupid." I sighed. Alice was always freaking out about perceived slights on social media. When a local mayonnaise brand had posted something about women's empowerment, she'd made Sophie write to request that they tag Alice, as if our fearless leader held the trademark to first-, second-, third-, and fourth-wave feminist thought. When Sophie pointed out that a #MindTheGap hashtag was inspiring British subway riders, not American gender-equity activists, she blamed Sophie even though the campaign had been Alice's idea.

"Alice has no memory. She'll get over it," I assured her, thinking of all the times she had threatened to fire me before forgetting about it. "Please. Don't do this. We need you. I need you."

The idea of a workplace without a friend was too much to bear. Then I remembered that I was going to be here only another few days. The quality of my work life wasn't the priority. Sophie's well-being was what mattered.

Sophie started for the door. "This was probably meant to be. The law firm where I used to work is opening a Philadelphia office, and I've been low-key talking to them about a marketing position."

I grabbed Sophie by the arm. "Hold up. The law firm where your ex works? Roger?"

The last story Sophie had told me about Roger involved him reading all her emails and getting mad about every correspondent who was male, including her second cousin and a gay friend from college.

"You're kidding me, right? The guy who wouldn't let you wear lipstick if it wasn't nude?" I stared at her. "You're not seeing him again, are you?"

Sophie looked down and tucked a stray tendril behind her ear.

"We've been talking. He's been doing a lot of teletherapy. People can change, right?"

I took a deep breath and stood there, looking at this rosy-cheeked sweetheart in cropped clothing, and wishing I could step in and undo the mistakes she was about to make. I'd heard enough about Roger to know he was very bad news, and always would be.

"Sophie," I said. "Please reconsider. Stick around a little while. I'll take the blame. Alice will forget everything by cocktail hour."

She gave me a glassy-eyed stare. "I appreciate your mom-splaining. But if I was going to stick around somewhere, I'm not sure this would be the place. I don't think you get how toxic it is here." She snuggled the box to her chest. "I'll be in touch."

My heart ached as I watched Sophie walk out of SteelHaus. I did get how toxic it was to remain at the foundation, but everything's relative. Even I, the biggest failure in history, could tell that working with Roger was a bad idea for Sophie. Maybe I could take her case up with the Consortium. If Desiree could make an exception for me fifteen years too late, surely she could help a deserving non-Coleman grad.

Fired up, I barreled down the hall to Alice's office, imagining how to begin this conversation without lashing out in red-hot anger.

There she was, Pittsburgh's golden girl. Her flaxen hair was blown out in barrel curls and her enhanced lips were coated in pixie gloss. She gestured for me to come in. My boss was in the middle of a call, little surprise there. Talking on the phone was pretty much the only work Alice ever did.

I took a seat on one of her floral-pattern poufs and looked at my phone, pretending I was not engrossed in the conversation she was having.

"Are you coming to Ibiza?" a man's voice sailed out of her phone's speaker. He sounded American, but he pronounced "Ibiza" as if he were Castilian.

"Of course, babe," she said. "I wouldn't miss DJ Mikael's listening party for the world."

"You should fly with me," he said. "There's always space on my Gulfstream."

"I would love to—you are such a stinking cutie!"

Alice's life was like this, flitting from one event to another, draining her trust fund, and the foundation's coffers, in the process. She loved to lord it all over me, but while I envied the ease with which she moved through the world, I didn't aspire to be the type of person who bopped over to "Ibitha."

Alice looked up and gave me the blah-blah hand gesture, her thumb and forefingers opening and closing like a bird beak, and looked at me wide-eyed, as if she couldn't wait for this guy to shut up. But it was obvious she didn't want him to shut up at all. He was shamelessly flirting with her, asking her about who she was dating, and bragging about his open relationship with a woman who worked "not exactly in but adjacent to" his office, whatever that meant.

"You're going to have to slow down one of these days." Alice's tone was indulgent.

"I know, I know. I'll reform. Soon."

"Who's the lucky lady?"

"Just this wellness maven. A total MILF. We're doing some business together. I'm flying her to the Bermuda compound for a meeting."

"Nobody closes a deal like you," Alice said, forcing a laugh.

"She's a rising entrepreneur of color. A bona fide changemaker. You should align with one of them yourself. Easy way to get some good press," he said.

His repulsive words ricocheted around my head. MILF changemaker. Wellness maven. And the tokenizing cherry on top, the "of color" bit. It couldn't be Geeta, could it? Anything was possible.

"I'll take any press." Alice gave me a pointed look. I seethed with rage.

"I'm all about diversifying my portfolio." He managed to say "diversifying my portfolio" in a way that sounded positively pornographic.

"Don't forget, there's always an export tax," Alice said. "Ciao."

"Who was that?" I asked as she got off the call.

"An old friend, Levi Fischer," she said.

"The SpaceFisch guy?" I asked.

"The one and only. As wild as his reputation. Maybe even wilder." I thought about that pretty poetry major from Coleman, Lyndsey Bogatsky, regaling Leigh with stories about how Levi screamed at people in big meetings to humiliate them into submission. I wondered if she had a Memo. If I was wondering, I basically had my answer.

"A woman I know from college works at his company," I said. *And another woman I know from college might be headed to his Bermuda compound*, I thought to myself.

I tried to steady my breathing and talk myself down. I was jumping to wild conclusions. There were hundreds of MILF-y tech entrepreneurs of color, possibly thousands. The chances of the person he was talking about being Geeta were small, but not zero. No matter the answer, the tone of the conversation still revolted me. That Alice considered herself to be a warrior for women was truly laughable.

"So, did you ever hear back from *Moment*?" she asked. She was now flipping through a magazine. "There's got to be a way to fix their oversight."

I told Alice that Jade, the editorial assistant, had answered me. This was not a lie; Jade had, in fact, finally written. She wanted to know who'd given me her email address. "She said she's seeing what she can do. There might be some wiggle room," I added, picturing Jade wiggling around the bottom of a shoe rack. "I wanted to talk to you about Sophie, though."

She rolled her eyes. "These Gen Z-ers are cute but they're so entitled. They aren't tough like us."

The word "us" made my insides clench. I did not want to be lumped into any category whatsoever with Alice.

"Is it true you called her a 'useless, entitled moron'?" I waited for Alice to deny this, but she just laughed. "She seems to think you're pinning the foundation's entire financial health on her ability to police all of Instagram."

Alice leveled her gaze at me. "Jenny, a word of advice. Have you heard of the Law of Attraction? Everything is connected. The energy you put out will be returned to you. We're on a downward spiral. And Sophie's clearly got other priorities. Her energy isn't exactly helping us."

"But I always thought you loved Sophie's energy," I said.

"Past tense."

"She needs some guidance. A mentor! Feminism starts at home, right?" My voice was getting louder, and I felt an unfamiliar spike of courage. I had to stand up for Sophie. "Alice, can I let you in on a secret? Sophie's ex-boyfriend was a really, really bad guy."

"And." Alice didn't say it like a question.

"He was super-controlling. He only let her go out with friends one night a week and he gave her a curfew." I waited for her reaction, but there was none. "He wants her to come work for him again."

"That doesn't sound like a brilliant idea." Alice frowned.

"And neither does meddling. Jenny, why don't you focus on fixing your own problems?"

"If only she knew."

Alice pulled a face. "Remind me not to order venti-size anything. I've had to pee all morning. Stay where you are."

A moment after she slipped out the door, I heard a chirp, then saw that a text message had popped up on the phone Alice had left on her desk. It was from Levi.

> P.S. I dreamed you and I were swimming in a fish tank. Naked.

I wanted to throw up. I sprang away from Alice's device and repositioned myself on the pouf just in time for her return.

"On the plus side," Alice said as the glass door to her office swung shut behind her. "Sophie quit so we don't have to give her any severance. You know as well as anyone how we're doing on funds."

"But I'm on track to surpass last quarter," I shot back.

"Our expenses have increased substantially." Mine certainly hadn't increased. The few receipts I had amassed were stuffed in the back of the utensil drawer in my kitchen. Maybe Deck was threatening to sue Alice again for child support. He was such an idiot for signing that prenup.

"Why don't I set up a call with Levi Fischer?" I blurted out. "Sounds like he has more than enough money sloshing around?"

"That doesn't mean he's generous. I've tried."

"You may have tried but I haven't," I said. "If I can get the funds, you will convince Sophie to come back, okay?"

Alice frowned. At least she wasn't saying no.

22

••••

GABE AVOIDED MY GAZE ALL THROUGH A CAPPELLA PRACTICE, EVEN during "A Long December," one of our favorites. The other Gabe—Gabriel Winkhorn, a retired podiatrist who was partial to sixties girl-group songs—made a thumbs up when he caught me glancing down the row. But Gabe, my Gabe, wasn't up for acknowledging my existence.

It made no sense. We'd spent so much time at Desmond's Tavern bonding over our shared love of the Counting Crows. We'd even seen them on the same tour, and we both had the concert T-shirts to prove it. And now we were singing lyrics about hospitals and oysters that I never really understood but that always made me well up with emotion.

I belted out about a day up in the canyons for the third and last time, an ache rising in my chest. This would be my last day losing myself in song with the Looney Tunes.

Gabe's hands were balled up into fists and his face was in an agonized expression. This made me feel both better and worse. On the one hand, I wasn't the only one getting carried away here. On the other hand, I had no idea what Gabe was going through. I

thought about the times I'd seen him in my alternate life, falling
through a subway grate and getting rubbed out by a bus. Could he
know about those events on some unconscious level and be punishing me?

It wasn't just the song I wanted to share with him. I so badly
wanted to tell him about everything that had transpired since
we'd last spoken. My hurtling back and forth between realms, my
trying out my could-have-been perfect life where he kept popping up and getting popped down like a prop in a cosmic game
of Whac-A-Mole. I wanted to look into his sympathetic eyes
and describe the premature nostalgia that filled me now that my
Rust-Belt life was coming to an end. I wanted to tell him about
Sophie, and how worried I was about her. Most of all, though, I
just missed the guy and his weird observations about life.

I rushed over to Gabe after the session. I caught him by the
exit door.

"You were right," I said as we made our way out of the main
auditorium. "The reunion had its bright spots."

"Great," he said. "I'd love to hear about it sometime." He was
looking over my shoulder.

"I guess tonight is not a good 'sometime'?" I was trying to in-
fuse my voice with lightness.

Gabe cocked his head. "We didn't have a plan, did we?"

"Not officially." I felt confused. Gabe and I never made
plans. We just got drinks. Every time.

"Right, right, sorry," he said. "I just have to be somewhere . . ."
I now noticed he was wearing brand-new white Converse sneakers
with a red cartoon heart—the signature of a famous designer—
not the slush-splattered ones that I was used to. "I'm supposed to
meet up with someone."

Something felt different. "One of the moms in Ramona's
class?"

"Sort of." He winced, then coughed.

"It's kind of a yes or no question." I forced a laugh.

"It's her mom."

Now I coughed. "Ramona's mom?"

He nodded. "Thea. My wife."

"I thought she was . . . your ex-wife."

Gabe ran his hand through his hair and kicked at something invisible on the floor. "Not officially. Thea and I had dinner with Ramona this weekend, and it was nice . . . and we ended up . . ."

"Oh!" I took a tiny step back, my head spinning. My first conclusion was that Gabe's news had something to do with my Memo, that this was the result of some disjunction, but that wasn't necessarily the case. All relationships had their ups and downs. Theirs was certainly not for me to judge, I thought as I kept judging.

"That's great," I spluttered. "I'm really happy for you."

"It's a little stressful. I'm not sure what I am doing." Gabe was looking everywhere except at my face. "Which is why we should probably . . . hold off on that next drink? For a while."

My heart sank.

"Thea saw your number in my call records and was asking questions." Gabe's cheeks were turning red. "She wanted to know who you were."

"Did you tell her that I'm a friend? And that you're the one who suggested I call you if I needed to talk?" I sounded a bit intense.

"I tried to, but you know how she is."

"I don't know how she is," I said. "All I know is what I've heard about from you, and well—"

I was about to say I didn't think he should be pursuing getting back together with someone who cheated on him, but given who I was still living with, I was in no position to weigh in.

"I've probably said some stupid things to you about her that I shouldn't have. In fact, I'm sure I did. I'm afraid I'm making a mess for everyone, and that's the last thing I want to do. Especially for Ramona's sake."

"Of course," I said. "I understand. I mean—I don't understand, but I wouldn't ever want to mess things up for you guys."

"Jenny." Gabe said my name so tenderly I wanted to cry. His mouth opened, but nothing further came out. It looked like whatever he had to get off his chest was physically hurting him.

"I know, relationships are complicated," I said. It was the same thing I had told him at Desmond's Tavern when he first showed me that he wasn't wearing his wedding ring. The ring that, I now noticed, he was wearing again. "I wish you all the good things, Gabe." I leaned over and kissed Gabe on the cheek. It was the closest our bodies had ever come together.

We lingered in place an extra beat. There were no words. Then Gabe walked down the veteran hall steps and onto Liberty Street. "See ya, Jenny." He turned to look back at me and smiled. I waved and forced my lips not to tremble. He deserved his space if that was what he needed. He was one of the good ones.

Besides, I had to be honest with myself. Sitting across from Gabe at Desmond's for upwards of an hour and trying to pass myself off as same old Jenny, the same old struggling soul without a Memo, would have been nearly impossible. I'd inevitably let it all come tumbling out, including how I somehow kept summoning him into my alternate reality, only to witness his demise again and again. I watched him cross the street. I was about to depart this world, and I had to let him move on.

What now? I didn't particularly feel like going home to Hal. Maybe I'd ask another Looney Tune if they wanted to grab a drink. I was still standing by the bulletin board at the entrance, waiting to see who else was going to stream out of the practice room, when Gabe's impeccably dressed understudy presented herself.

"They serve Vienna lager at your little watering hole?"

Minutes later, Desiree and I were sitting in a wooden booth at Desmond's Tavern. She ordered a tasting flight and opened a tab on her corporate Amex Platinum card. I got my regular glass of German wine. But I barely touched it. Sophie was probably with Roger. Hal was probably with Brie. And Gabe was definitely with Thea.

"Enough with the self-pity," Desiree said, reading my mind.

I forced myself to sit up straighter and mumbled an apology.

"Gabe is a math teacher who gets emotional when he watches nature documentaries," Desiree told me.

I smiled. "He's become a very good friend, one in a million."

"But he's not a millionaire. You need a winner—a gorgeous entrepreneur who happens to also have a preternatural gift for real estate. And you've got one: Alex!"

There was that name again, Alex. The lawyer—art buyer Leigh had set me up with, the one I'd glimpsed myself fooling around with in my preview.

"Now *he's* the kind of guy who finds a second home in Tuscany. The kind you always wanted." Desiree went on. "A marvelous semi-abandoned convent on a hilltop, with a fantastic vegetable garden."

"Semi-abandoned? Is that like semidetached?"

"Semi-abandoned. Just a few elderly nuns who can be relocated, no big deal. The rocket is to die for. Arugula, I'm talking about, but you'll call it rocket there. All the expats in your circle do."

I was going to be part of an expat circle? In Italy? But only after displacing some old nuns from their home?

It had always been a dream of mine to own a place in Italy. I used to send Geeta real-estate listings and ask her if she knew who I had to fuck, marry, or kill to own whatever piece of earth was being showcased on the slideshow. I hadn't meant it literally, but here we were. At least I didn't have to kill anybody—just push out some nuns.

Desiree's eyes bore into me. "You know what to do."

Barely two seconds later, I was staring at my phone, watching Gabe and a woman who had to be Thea having drinks in a booth at a bar whose walls were covered with hummingbird print wallpaper. I was pretty sure I recognized the setting as Grape Expectations, a natural wine bar across town. Thea looked like an early-career Nicole Kidman, with her shiny auburn hair and peachy cheeks. I hated her.

"This is all live stream," Desiree told me. "It's happening in real time."

"I know what a live stream is."

I watched Gabe, his adorable face twisted in what looked like hopefulness. Thea was playing with her ginger hair, a coy smile on her lips. I didn't know what they were talking about but they clearly weren't plotting their divorce. Sadness swelled up in me.

"Quite the manipulator, that woman." Desiree rolled her eyes. "Now do you need to see what Hal is up to?"

"Can we not?" I was upset enough already, ready to shoot through the wormhole. "I think I get the idea."

"August 5, 2014," Desiree instructed. "And away she goes."

23
• • • •

BRASILITO, COSTA RICA
AUGUST 5, 2014
AGE: 28

SPIT OUT A MOUTHFUL OF SAND AND WIPED MY EYES. I WAS AT THE
beach, laying out in the sun in front of the bluest water I'd ever
seen. The scenery was bananas. My body was even more bananas, like off the charts ripped. How often did I work out in this
alternate life? And what exactly was I supposed to do now? Luckily, my phone was at my side. I scrolled to the date Desiree had
just directed me to, then found the matching instruction. It was
far more rambling than the ones I was used to.

> Walk to the ocean. Pass the lifeguard chair on your
> left, after which you shall walk twenty paces, ap-
> proaching a family of four. Pick up a piece of aqua-
> marine sea glass. Hold it up to the sun and admire
> its curved edges.

I gave myself another minute to gather my bearings. It was
2014, which meant it was eight years ago. Which meant I was
twenty-eight, that supposedly perfect age when every cool re-
tailer and entertainment company is trying to seduce you with

their marketing messages—and, going by my sick gingham bikini, I was readily receiving them.

I gazed at the ocean. Waves rose and curled into ribbons of sea foam. Surfers played in the water, and small children with plastic buckets and shovels dotted the shoreline. It was hot, but the ocean breeze made everything feel perfect. My sense of zen was disrupted by a sound coming from my left side.

"Can you pass me the sunblock?" My mother was splayed out behind me, her slim body clad in a floral skirted swimsuit. Who better to put a damper on my tropical relaxation than Ann Green?

"Mom!" I said.

"Is that so scandalous?" she said. "You should probably re-apply too."

"Here you go." I picked up the bottle of sunblock next to me and handed it over.

I was in such a hurry to get out of Pittsburgh that I hadn't even considered where I was going. But the Pura Vida Ecolodge key card poking out of my mother's shoe told me we were at my brother's destination wedding in Costa Rica. Another historic moment in my life: meeting Hal, an encounter that led me straight to nowhere. I guessed correcting my Italian oven debacle hadn't sufficiently altered my destiny to steer me away from Hal's corner of paradise, because here I was. Again.

My eyes scanned farther down the beach. I spotted the craggy bluff where exotic birds and reptiles roamed. And a little farther, the funky treehouse of my sexual awakening, the birthplace of my eventual undoing. The sight of it made me blush.

When we'd met, Hal had been sowing his oats in Costa Rica before returning to New York to complete his PhD at NYU— "Jungian Archetypes in American Folk Music (1961–1969)" was the title of his dissertation—while working as an assistant to conceptual artist Ezra Lightfoot, the one whose neon sculpture Alice had in her office. Throughout our years together, Hal had amassed an impressive collection of books about music, poetry, and psychology, books intended to fuel his research. These volumes were presently sitting on a shelf in our Pittsburgh sublet, collecting dust.

"This is so nice, Jen," my mom said, rolling onto her back and letting off a sigh. She sounded relaxed and content.

"Yeah," I said a little unsurely. "It is nice to be back here."

"When were you here before?" she asked me.

"Oh, I just mean on this exact spot of the beach. I was right here yesterday."

"You certainly have a knack for real estate." My mother chuckled and slathered cream on her shoulders. "So, back to what I was just saying. If you notice Aunt Eileen acting funny around Uncle Russell, now you know why. You heard nothing from me."

Was my mother sharing a family secret with me? She hadn't told me anything juicy since I'd accidentally let slip to my brother, many years earlier, that she and my dad were helping me financially. "That was supposed to be between us," she'd said at the time, and griped that he was requesting a loan to finance a new car, even though he was gainfully employed. "Thanks to you."

Now, though, we were delighting in what appeared to be family gossip. "Don't you dare say a word, not even to your father or Andrew. Eileen would kill me!"

"Your secrets are safe with me."

My mom grabbed my hand and kissed it. "I'm having so much fun," she said. "We should do this more often. I love you, my sweet baby girl."

"I love you too, Mom," I replied, stunned by all this affection. My mom resumed spilling the beans on her sister's new love interest. Previously, I hadn't known the ins and outs until years after Andrew's wedding. The reason behind Uncle Russell and Aunt Eileen's split presented itself when Hal and I had run into my aunt on the Fire Island ferry. There she was, holding hands with another woman. It turned out Eileen had fallen for the young female massage therapist she began seeing after a foot injury.

"Who knew plantar fasciitis could be so romantic?" my mom tittered. She started stroking my hair.

"You used to do this at bedtime," I murmured, luxuriating in the soothing sensation. "Remember how you used to massage my head and I was afraid to sleep over at my friends' houses because I thought I needed my mom to help me fall asleep?"

"You did need me back then. But you've blossomed into such an independent woman."

I felt something catch in my throat. "I could use a snack," I said abruptly.

"I'll get it. How 'bout those shrimp skewers?"

"Maybe just some fruit?" I wasn't hungry.

"You know, you don't have to starve yourself," my mom said. I tried not to look surprised. In my other life, she was constantly reminding me that salad was my friend and that bread was my enemy. "Straight from the lips to the hips" was her mantra. "You can afford the extra calories. Don't think I didn't notice your dress was falling off you at the last fitting. You can't let your heartbreak keep you from eating."

Heartbreak? Who—me?

She wiped sand off her thighs. "I know it's hard, seeing your brother get married, and Sean not being here . . ."

I gave her a smile, trying to cover up the fact that I had no idea who Sean was. He must have been someone that the Memo had told me to date.

"You have so much going on, honey. How many people at the wedding do you think were written about in *Bon Appétit*?"

"I was?" My mom gave me a funny look. "I mean, which article are you talking about? There've been a couple."

My mom grinned. "You've always been so driven. Your dad and I sure did something right."

I wasn't sure what was weirder—that I'd achieved anything before my thirtieth birthday or that my mother wasn't oh-so-unsubtly reminding me that I needed to get my act together by yesterday. I was successful here, and instead of blaming themselves for my failings, they felt like good parents. My success was their success.

"It means a lot to me to hear you say that." The words came tumbling out before I could think better of it.

My mom cupped my chin in her hand and looked at me intensely. "Look at you. The doctor did such a great job after you were so savagely attacked, poor baby," she said. I raised my hand to my face. The bridge of my nose did feel unfamiliarly smooth. In the months since Juliet had punched me in the face, I clearly had seen a cosmetic surgeon.

"It's very subtle," my mom went on. "Only your mother would notice any difference. And the way you've bounced back, sharing your journey with others, has been nothing short of inspiring. I'm just so proud."

As she tromped down the sand toward the snack hut, I thought back to my instructions. Not bothering to pull on a tunic, I stood up and walked past the lifeguard chair, feeling the eyes of the young man following me. I counted twenty steps, trying not to make them too big or too small, for fear that I would miss my target. Sure enough, there was a family of four wearing color-coordinated swimsuits and speaking to each other in Italian as they sculpted a turtle out of sand. The father was big and burly, and reminded me of Massimo. My jaw went slack when the mother play-slapped him and cried out, "Massi!" This *was* Massimo, my unambitious Italian lover. I was amazed that barely five years after our fling, he had a wife, two children and the means to travel to a luxury resort in Costa Rica. Cutting the cord had clearly been for the best on both of our accounts. Not wanting him to recognize me, I turned my face away and continued my march.

Sure enough, twenty steps in, the shard of sea glass was sticking straight up in the sand. It was gleaming in the sun, calling for me. I picked it up and held it up to the light. It was a stunning object, a rare hue, which I took as a sign of good luck.

I took the long way back to my beach blanket, walking along the shore. As the waves crashed around my feet, I admired the sea glass's curved edges, which were almost soft to the touch.

When I returned to our spot, my mother was back, holding two cocktails and talking to a tall guy. He had a mess of dark hair and a short beard. There was something familiar about him, too. I wondered if I'd known him when we were kids. He was probably one of my brother's friends. Then it hit me: He was the handsome man I'd glimpsed in Desiree's preview of my perfect life. The man I had been riding. My cheeks went hot.

"Oh there she is!" my mother called out. "Jenny, meet Alex."

"Alex!" He was even better looking close up. Before I could fully process what was happening, Alex smiled and extended his hand. I went to shake it, forgetting for a moment that I had the sea glass in my palm. My treasure fell to the ground.

"You dropped something there." Alex bent over and picked it up. "It's beautiful." He squinted at the glass, and then right into my eyes.

"Hi. Thanks. How do you two know each other?" I asked, looking at him and then my mother.

"I'm not allowed to talk to a handsome guy walking on the beach?" my mom said, giggling like a teenager. She wasn't unattractive, and men tended to eat up this sort of flirtation. "Alex is Andy's longtime lawyer."

"I had no idea that Andrew had a longtime lawyer," I said in a light tone. "I should have figured he'd need one eventually."

Alex laughed. "And I had no idea that Andrew had a sister." His eyes lingered on me. They were a deep blue.

"Well, we're not that close." Disappointment flickered across my mother's face.

"I was just telling Alex that you broke up with your boyfriend and are attending the wedding without a date," she said.

"Mom!" I looked at Alex. "I'm so sorry," I said to him. "She's out of control."

But he didn't seem to mind. He was rubbing his stubble, making the motions of thinking hard about something. "This is so random, but were you by any chance living with Geeta Brara and Leigh Sullivan a while back?"

It seemed like just a few days ago—because it was, sort of—that I'd been in that apartment dipping my toe into an alternate life. The one where Geeta and Leigh were trying to sell me on some big shot lawyer–art collector named Alex under the calamitous chandelier. And here he was, standing before me, in a pair of board shorts. He had the body of a champion swimmer. Why hadn't they mentioned that part?

"Yes!" I said. "You're the guy who bought the Hockney from Leigh's gallery!"

"I thought you looked familiar," he said with a laugh. "What are the chances?"

"Geeta and Leigh were actually supposed to be here, but my mom wouldn't let me invite them." I gave a half-teasing eye roll.

My mother was always suspicious of Geeta and Leigh's influence on me. Things came to a head when she stumbled upon a postcard that Geeta had written to me shortly after I'd come back from Italy and had a blowout fight with my parents, who couldn't handle the idea that I wanted to live in the city like a normal young adult. They wanted me to stay with them forever, because— according to Geeta—if I stayed at home, they could pretend that they weren't empty nesters, that they still had at least one kid who still needed them for sustenance. "Failure to launch," she'd said in her postcard, "is a two-way street."

"What are you talking about, Jenny?" my mom asked. "The girls are up by the pool." She pointed past the beach. I craned my neck and saw Geeta and Leigh horizontally arranged on lounge chairs. My head swam with confusion. The last time I'd seen Geeta in my alternate existence, she had acted like we were vague acquaintances, not best friends. A few years had passed, though. Maybe we were back on a friendship upswing. Maybe our laser focus on our careers had paid off sufficiently to afford us some leisure time. Or perhaps it was something else I'd done to fix things. Whatever the reason, my spirits brightened at the sight of the two of them lying there, soaking up vitamin D in their bikinis.

"It's all coming back," Alex said. "They had a party for you when you came home from Spain, right?"

"Italy," I told him, resisting the temptation to tell him that my Italian boyfriend was a few yards down the beach and not only that, but Alex and I were destined to displace a flock of Italian nuns so we could occupy their former convent.

"You can't blame me for getting it wrong. You would barely talk to me that night."

I had blown this guy off? I must have been too focused on Massimo back then. But what was wrong with me? Alex was a total catch.

"Don't mind me, I think I'm going to take a dip in the pool. Take this, Jenny!" My mother passed me the drink she'd been cradling in her hand and ran off.

"Mind if I join you?" Alex sat down onto the beach blanket before I could answer.

My stomach was fluttering. I kept my straw in my mouth and let him do most of the talking. I was afraid I was going to say something that would once again upset the balance of the universe.

Alex was charmingly self-deprecating, referring to himself as a failed lawyer and "professionally lazy" before I got it out of him that he'd resigned from his partner-track job at a law firm to focus on his writing career, which was going "terribly" until suddenly, it wasn't. "The book I wrote kind of took on a life of its own." He sounded bashful.

"Meaning . . . it was a bestseller?"

"It did all right. I'm shocked your brother didn't tell you about any of this," he said in a teasing tone. "He's in the acknowledgments."

"Not only did I not know that Andrew had a lawyer, I had no idea he read books, let alone that he was friends with superstar authors."

Alex raised his eyebrows. "I wouldn't call myself an 'author.'"

"So what would you call yourself?"

"I don't know, a guy who got lucky with a single idea he turned into a very short book? It was basically a pamphlet when I first wrote it, so my publisher had to make the type big."

"I just set the margins extra wide when I need to."

We were both laughing now. "I'll tell you a secret. Writing is my least favorite activity. Thankfully, the book has led to a lot of speaking engagements, team-building gigs, management consulting, et cetera—that's the stuff I'm good at," he said.

"I'll have to check it out."

"I can explain it right here, and save you the twenty-four dollars. If you want me to?"

"Of course," I said, smiling at his consideration. Hal never asked for my consent before delving into one of his mini lectures.

"It's based on this amazingly simple theory that I came up with one night. It came to me while I was dreaming, which is sort of the point."

I was focusing on Alex's eyes. They were Disney-prince blue. He was the type of guy who could give a lecture and make everyone in the auditorium feel like he was talking only to them.

He went on, "You can get all your work done in four flashes of inspiration each day. Even if they occur when you're sleeping."

"You wrote *that* book? I think Geeta was reading that!" I now realized that she wouldn't touch it for another seven years, when she brought it to our college reunion to catch up with the thought-leader zeitgeist, but I let it lie. "You wrote *Flash: Win While You Sleep.* That's so cool."

"Guilty as charged," Alex said.

"And you don't even like writing?"

"I like the writing life. I was just in Japan for three weeks. I could have done it in two, but I'm . . . it's not like anybody needs me to stick around." He grinned and looked embarrassed. "That was me clumsily signaling that I am single. Really subtle, huh?"

I laughed.

"I'm glad we're meeting—again," he finally said. "And that you deigned to talk to me this time."

I cast my gaze down toward the sea glass. It was refracting the sun in dazzling shards of light. This felt so good. The Memo was coming through for me. "I'm really sorry if I was a jerk that first time," I murmured.

"No ifs about it." Alex's eyes shone with what looked like amusement. "I think I'll finally be able to get over it."

I could feel the smile stretching across my face. "I think so too."

24
. . . .

WAS HEADING BACK TO MY ROOM WHEN I SPOTTED MY PARENTS BY THE
pool, reading and drinking Piña Coladas. My dad was in one of
his signature Hawaiian shirts. My mom put down her magazine
and waved me over.

"So?" she cawed.

"So what?" I asked.

"You spent a long time chatting with Alex Stone. You must
tell me everything!"

My mom and dad had nicknamed me "the CIA operative" and
given up on me proffering any information about my romantic
life long ago. But things were different here and now. My mom
was behaving as if we were best friends with no secrets between
us. It felt weird, but also nice. I could just share what was on my
mind. It was so much easier than editing out any details that she
might use against me.

"He's incredibly cute," I told her.

"'Handsome' is the word I'd use," my mom said.

"And I hear he's not broke," my dad chimed in without looking up from his thriller.

"Dad!" I said.

"Well, Sean wasn't broke either," my mother said.

"She has a type," my dad said.

I had a type? And it was . . . rich guys?

"Find a fellow I can jam with, Jenny," said my dad. He'd taken up guitar a few years before my brother's wedding and had since amassed an impressive collection of instruments, both acoustic and electric.

"I don't know if Alex plays guitar, but he was very sweet, for a friend of Andrew's," I said, trailing off when I noticed another man in a Hawaiian shirt walking past the pool. I squinted, trying to get a better view. Was the sun in my eyes playing tricks on me? Nope. It was Gabe again. Why did my subconscious keep doing this?

"You all right?" my mom asked.

"I think I know that guy," I said, reaching for my sunglasses. "He looks exactly like an old friend."

"Emphasis on *old*." This was coming from my father.

Only five years older than me—and a musician. Maybe Gabe was the jam partner of my dad's dreams. I said nothing.

"Not only is he old, but he's married," said my mother, pointing toward a strawberry blonde sprawled in a hammock and flirting with a surfing instructor. She was the Nicole Kidman look-alike I'd seen in the Pathetic section of my Memo app.

"How do *you* know that?" I asked.

"Your mother knows everybody at this hotel already, even the people who aren't involved in her wedding," my dad said.

"Andrew's wedding," I corrected him.

"If you saw the bill you'd think it's fair to say it's ours." My dad snorted.

"I'll be right back," I said. There had to be a reason why Gabe kept dropping into my do-overs. I needed to talk to him—and before his next death.

I chased after him down an immaculately landscaped path to the front entrance of the hotel. I was huffing and puffing by the time I reached a van painted with giant green leaves and macaws. It was idling in front of a sign that read Cloud Forest Hike. I could see Gabe's back as he entered the vehicle.

"Gabe!" I shouted. He turned around, looking confused.

"Hi," I said breathlessly. Moving slowly so as not to scare him off, I came a bit closer. "Remember me?"

The corners of his mouth twitched. "Maybe? Did you once audition as a vocalist for my band?"

I shook my head. "Well, I do sing, but that's not it."

For a split second his eyes clicked into mine. But then the vehicle honked, and he looked half-relieved. "I gotta go . . . I didn't catch your name."

"Jenny," I told him.

"Jenny," the younger, thicker-haired Gabe repeated with a smile. "To be continued," he said, then climbed onboard. I stared as the van wheeled away. It didn't make the turn at the end of the road. Instead, it sliced through a thicket of vegetation and plummeted off a cliff. This was followed by an ear-splitting explosive sound. A cloud of smoke wafted over the horizon.

"There she goes again," a voice called from overhead. Desiree was perched in a tree. "What is wrong with you, Jenny? Didn't you just meet Alex?"

"Yes, but . . . what the hell just happened to Gabe? Is he okay?"

"That was all a mirage, a manifestation of your own making. He's living his best life back in Pittsburgh, making sweet, sweet love to his cheating wife. You need to stop with the Gabe nonsense. Get going. You have a wedding to get ready for."

ANDREW'S WEDDING WAS A PERFECT SUNSET-ON-THE-BEACH AFFAIR. The bride, Jacqueline, was a slender vision in a column gown with a delicate rosette on the back, her hair in a loose chignon. My mom sobbed at the end of the ceremony, her cries drowning out the melodies of the string quartet. This time, I was the one who caught the bouquet—not one of my sister-in-law's bridesmaids.

The reception dinner was slightly different than it had been in reality. I wasn't seated with my parents, as I, their falling-through-the-cracks daughter, had been previously. I didn't get to sit with my friends, either, which was a bummer. Then again, it was probably for the best because the signature tamarind cocktails were so delicious that I was on my third; if I were with my friends, I might have slipped up and regaled them with tales from the future. Instead, I shared a table with Jacqueline's bridesmaids—all of whom were her sorority sisters from the University of Arizona—and their dates. The men were talking about golf and skiing and the women were ignoring their crab cakes and debating whether balsamic vinegar was too sugary to be considered healthy.

When it was time for me to give a toast, I spoke far more graciously than at Andrew's other wedding. In my non-Memo life, I'd congratulated "Jacko" on marrying "a prince—and I mean that in a Machiavellian way," which had failed to generate the laughter I had been hoping for. I didn't understand this couple, and it showed.

Now, though, I was a veritable toastmaster. "You are one lucky guy," I said, locking eyes with my brother. "The first time I met your new girlfriend, and learned that this beautiful, brilliant, athletic creature also liked golfing and spearfishing, I thought there was no way you'd manage to keep her. The next time I saw you, I remember learning that she shared your fondness for blue-cheese sauce on pizza—which, ladies and gentlemen, we all can admit is disgusting." The crowd broke into howls now even though what I was saying was not very funny. But now I was the type of person who didn't have to even be funny to get people to laugh. Such was the power of popularity.

When I picked up again, my tone took a more serious turn. "Like blue-cheese sauce on pizza, this pairing was admittedly one I didn't understand at first." I paused. "It seemed scary, too good to be true. I feared for your eventual heartbreak, Andrew. Here was the perfect woman for you, and it terrified me. I remember how your voice cracked when you told me how much you loved her." I took another beat, so everyone could make the appropriate cooing sounds. As if on cue, a single tear streamed down my cheek.

I caught sight of Alex seated at a table with my brother's friends. We exchanged a smile, and I almost forgot that I was in the middle of a speech. "Andrew," I went on, "you've changed as a brother and as a man. You are a responsible, kind adult. You no longer leave the toilet seat up. You even have a lawyer!" I watched Alex double over in laughter. "I am so proud of you, Andy. And I'm even more proud to call you my sister-in-law, Jacqueline."

As I walked off the stage, the air filled with applause and dog whistles. One of the sorority sisters was crying when I came back to the table. I touched her hand and glanced across the room at my real friends, but they were too busy talking to their tablemates, a bunch of Andrew's friends from business school. I tried not to let myself feel too disappointed. I brightened a few minutes later when I saw Alex making his approach. He looked so gorgeous in his tuxedo, like a modern-day Paul Newman.

"You sure clean up nice," I said.

"I haven't been able to take my eyes off you all night," he replied. "You're not going to go back to giving me the brush-off, like you did back in New York?"

"Never in a million years." I let him pull me by the arm onto the dance floor. Alex proceeded to surprise me with his moves.

He was energetic and fun. We were still dancing well after midnight, only now he was holding me close and barely moving at all.

"Meant to be," Leigh whispered into my ear as she glided by in a sleek pink tuxedo.

When the wedding party left, Alex invited me for a drink at Sol 311, the only bar in town. Of course I said yes. He was too good to be true—as opposed to the guy who I saw seated down the bar. There he was, a younger version of Hal chatting up Bevin, the chief balsamic vinegar skeptic. She appeared to be quite wasted, which was not surprising given that I didn't see her consume anything the entire evening except for Vodka Sodas. Hal was tilting his head ever so slightly and pretending to listen to his conversation partner before going on one of his monologues. It's funny how qualities you once found charming in a person can become horribly annoying with the passage—or, in this case, the reversal—of time.

Alex, meanwhile, was truly listening to me. I found myself telling him things about my relationship with my brother I wasn't sure I'd ever said aloud before.

"We've had a lot of ups and downs. My parents used to favor him, and he never threw me a lifeline when I was in trouble."

Alex looked concerned. "What kind of trouble are we talking about?"

"Oh, nothing important. All stuff that happened a lifetime ago," I said, waving my hand in the air. After all, the trouble I was referring to didn't occur a lifetime ago, but in a completely different lifetime. "It's really on me to get over it," I told him. "I should warn you. I can be very petty."

Alex rested his hand on my arm. "You're not petty. You're pretty."

His words hit me hard. "You know what? So are you."

Just when I thought he was about to kiss me, I realized I needed to use the bathroom, and excused myself. I couldn't resist drifting within earshot of Hal. He was railing against "the aesthetic imbalance," whatever that meant.

"You're enjoying yourself?" asked the woman in line behind me at the door to the ladies room. Her again. I turned to face Desiree.

"You climbed out of your tree?" I replied.

She smiled conspiratorially, then pointed at Hal and Bevin. "That could be you, Jenny, fawning over a future Pittsburgh pauper."

A gaggle of women spilled out of the bathroom, and Desiree stepped in alongside me. The reflection in the mirror was shocking. My clavicle was jutting out from my blush-colored one-shoulder dress. Jacqueline's sorority sisters and I could have been quadruplets.

"You stuck with the kickboxing," Desiree said approvingly. "And yoga and a new fitness thing called Scream, where you run around in circles naked in a 110-degree room. Absolute hell, but it does wonders for the lymphatic system."

"Do I still . . . bake?" I asked.

"Sometimes, when you're on camera. Truth be told, you've been gluten-free since 2012! On the down-low, of course. You're more likeable when you're cramming a baguette into that adorable face." She squeezed my cheeks a little too hard.

"If you say so," I muttered as I dipped into the stall. I tried to remember the last thing I'd baked back in my real life. Cheddar and dill scones. They'd been perfectly flaky, with a kick of pepper. Strangely, my mouth wasn't watering at the memory of them.

"You no longer need to eat your feelings," Desiree called out to me. "Tastes marvelous, doesn't it? Now go back out there and sit next to the right guy."

"I wasn't planning on running away," I said. "Trust me."

When I returned to the bar, Alex pulled out the stool next to him. "It's getting cooler," he told me and draped his jacket over my shoulders. "While I was waiting for you, I had a vision."

"One of your famous flashes?" I teased him.

"More like a feeling. I know we practically just met, but I have a strong sense this night is going to be consequential. For us both." Alex smiled at me and leaned in a little closer. "I have something for you." He reached into the pocket of the jacket and pulled out a piece of ruby-red sea glass. "I found it on the beach, right after we met."

"It's stunning," I told him. "Thank you."

"Not yet," he said, pulling it away as I reached for it. "I'm going to hold on to it and give it to you another time. To make sure I see you again."

And then he kissed me ever so gently. His lips were soft as petals. I pulled him in closer, my body lighting up with desire. The pressure of Alex's lips on mine intensified. This guy sure knew what he was doing.

"Do you want to get out of here?" Alex asked. I nodded, breathless.

We got up and headed for the exit. I was trailing slightly behind him. Before we reached the door, Desiree emerged and yanked me off course. "Good work, Jenny."

"Please let me go," I said, trying to shake free. "I'm not done here."

"Oh yes you are. This is headed exactly where you imagine it is. We need to leapfrog ahead. That's a requirement, not a request."

Alex turned around to scan the room. His expression was hopeful, a little vulnerable. "Please, please? Can I just see this night through?" I asked Desiree. "Your timing here could be a whole lot better."

"Exactly. It's time to visit 2016. Don't worry, petunia. Alex Stone isn't going anywhere."

25
. . . .

WAS COCOONED IN A HEAVY DUVET, A PILLOW BENEATH MY HEAD. AS
soundlessly as possible, I slipped out from under the covers and
fumbled my way through the dark to the window. When I slid the
curtain slightly to the side, early morning light filtered into the
room. Something resembling relief filled my body when I spotted Alex. Even in the dim light, I could make out his eyelashes,
thick as spokes. He let off a groan and rolled onto his other side.
I moved to close the curtain before the light woke him up, but
the view stopped me in my tracks. Fanned out in front of me was
a stunning cityscape, all water towers and skyscrapers. A yellow
ferry chugged along the surface of the river below.

The ruby-red sea glass that Alex had found on the beach was
shining up at me from my ring finger. Now encased in a thick gold
setting, the glass was surrounded by a sunburst of diamonds. I
let off a gasp. The noise roused Alex. He blinked in confusion at
the empty spot in the bed.

"Over here," I said quietly.

His expression softened when he saw me standing by the

window. "Hey, you." His voice was deep and groggy, almost musical.

"Sleep well?" I asked.

"I think so?" Alex sat up and brought his hand to his temple. That's when I noticed he had a gold band on his ring finger. I was married! *We* were married.

Then he removed something from behind his ear, a patch studded with little sensors. Alex picked up the phone on his bedside table. "Signs are looking promising," he said, turning the screen toward me. There was a squiggly line. "87 percent—not bad," he said. "Let's see how you did."

I lifted my hand to my hairline and confirmed that a foreign object was affixed behind my ear as well. "What are we going to do with you, Jenny?" Alex said tenderly, still looking at his phone.

"What's the matter?" I asked.

"Your REM sleep was disrupted four times, baby."

"No way," I replied as if I knew the significance of this number.

"This will not be good for your creativity today."

I crawled back in bed and snuggled up next to Alex, my husband who was worried about how my lack of sleep would affect my creativity. His body was warm and he smelled like fresh laundry. He pulled me in and I planted my face in his neck. Maybe we could pick up where we left off in Costa Rica. That would be good for my creativity.

"Your REM hasn't been this choppy since last October," Alex muttered. "What's going on?"

Oh nothing, just blasting through the space-time continuum.

"I'm fine, babe," I assured him, kissing his collarbone. "I'm great."

"Sure you are. I saw your nose doing that bunny-twitch thing. The way it does when you're anxious." He stroked my back and I lay still, enjoying the sensation and wondering if I did this bunny twitch in the other realm, too. Hal had never said anything about it. But then again, Hal didn't even notice the time I got bangs. Now I had a man who loved me so much he had an elaborate interpretation for my every twitch. Here was a guy who paid attention, who read my body as if it was a mysterious code to be deciphered. Speaking of bodies, this husband of mine had a spectacular one. Time to enjoy what the Memo had handed me.

Twenty minutes later, our legs tangled up in a Jenga-like pile, a goofy smile played across my face as Alex stared at the ceiling and stroked my hair. "How are we going to get in sync?" he mused.

"Um, I'd say we're pretty in sync."

"I'm talking about our sleep cycles. Our patterns could stand to be more aligned." Alex chuckled and kissed my forehead. "Maybe you should call Dr. Janklow?"

"Wouldn't hurt," I agreed, slipping out of bed. Alex's body properly explored, I decided it was time to look around my new home.

Alex's apartment—*our* apartment—was a spotless shrine to perfectionism, with a supplement-stocked medicine pantry, a massive self-help library complete with copies of *Flash: Win While You Sleep* in twenty languages, and a mini-gym outfitted with colorful spiky balls and machines.

The only element that was in short supply was food. There were plenty of jars and packages, but they didn't contain anything I'd consider to be a comestible. I scoured the cabinets, then the freezer. I found dehydrated chia seeds, frozen kale, tubes of infused slurries. There was a mason jar filled with a pink, undulating mass labeled "sea-moss gel." I helped myself to the most appetizing item I could locate, a blood-red smoothie. I took a glug. It tasted vaguely like dirt.

"Are you taking a day off, hon?" Alex said as he came out of the bedroom. He'd put on a workout outfit.

"Not to my knowledge," I faltered.

"It's not even seven, Jen. What are you doing eating this early? Did you skip dinner last night?"

Hold up. Were we one of those intermittent-fasting couples? He was looking at me expectantly.

"Sadly, yes," I said, wiping the liquid from my upper lip. "I was so crazed with work, I didn't have a chance to eat until it was too late." As if I'd ever be one of those people too busy to eat.

"You're nearly at the finish line. Things will calm down soon enough." Alex now lowered to his knees and began a series of stretches on the rug. I stood there and watched him. He was a vision to behold, simultaneously the sculptor and the sculpture.

He noticed me staring and paused mid-hamstring stretch. "What?"

"Nothing," I lied, and told myself to snap out of it. But it was hard to act normal when there was so much information to process. My new habitat, my new habits. My new husband. A man who was as gorgeous as Hal—but without all the self-indulgence and commitment-phobia. He was a man who considered all his options, used available data, and made smart choices. Craziest of all, I, Jenny Green, had been one of those smart choices.

"You'd better not be too busy to eat tonight." Alex was working his calves over a foam roller. "Seven p.m. at Le Lapin Vert. Don't forget."

"Le *what what*?"

"You're the one who got us the reservations. That new vegan place."

"Are we—" I almost asked if we were vegan, but then I remembered the contents of our refrigerator. Of course we were.

"It's been ages since we've seen Matt and Geeta," Alex said.

"Geeta!" I could barely suppress my joy. "And Matt," I added, less enthusiastically.

"I knew you'd come around," Alex said. "Every time you see her, you end up having a good time. It doesn't always have to be so complicated."

Alex's words rattled me. I wanted to know what complication he was referring to, but refrained from asking any questions.

"Just try not to think about what happened last time," Alex said. "She'll be over it by now."

"That silly thing? It's all history, water under the bridge," I said quickly. "I don't even remember it."

He flashed me a smile and rose to his feet. "I know you're crazed at work, but please don't be late."

I sighed. "Promise."

"Off for my morning run." Alex gave me a goodbye kiss and bounded out of our apartment.

After the door closed, I resumed my exploration. Big pieces of abstract art hung on the walls. A hallway was a gallery of personal artifacts, with magazine profiles of Alex and me as well as business-y think pieces with our bylines hanging on the walls. I noticed a framed photo of Alex and my mom laughing together at an outdoor cafe table in what looked like a European city. Weird. In all my years with Hal, I was pretty sure there was no photographic evidence of him and Ann Green spending time with one another, let alone traveling together.

And onto my *New York Times* wedding announcement. According to the article, we met in the Maldives when I was traveling solo after dropping out of college with just a few weeks left. Then we met again in New York, at a party my friends threw for me when I returned from Italy, although no one, including us, realized at the time that we had already met before. But I still wasn't ready to commit. The article quoted Geeta Brara, maid of honor: "The third time was the charm," she said, referring to the moment when Alex and I reconnected on the beach before my brother's wedding.

Geeta found a postcard from me, describing the "perfect guy" I had briefly encountered at a bar in the middle of the Indian Ocean, and gave it to us as part of her wedding gift. It was now framed and affixed to the wall next to the *Times* article.

It was so strange, recognizing details from my life embedded in a life that was entirely new to me. I found my phone in our bedroom and located the date on the home screen—November 20, 2016—then hit up the Memo. I was desperate for my instructions. Today's missive was just as wordy as the one in Costa Rica.

> Take the full course of Dr. Janklow's Splindar vitamin program before jumping in the ice bath. Remain in place for two minutes. Enjoy a ten-minute sauna, then write down your newsletter ideas when you emerge. Do facial yoga from 7:15 to 7:30 a.m. Do not answer the phone when it rings while you are in the middle of "bulldog face." Put on your seersucker suit and arrive at the office at exactly 8:16 a.m.

My Memo left little room for error. I nosed around the apartment until I located a ribbon of blister packs on the kitchen countertop with the word "Splindar" and my name printed on each one. I popped the daily allotment into my mouth and gulped them down with the remainder of the smoothie. Positively overwhelming.

Next, I headed into the bathroom, where I leaped into an ice bath that Alex must have prepared for me before he left. My mind went blank as the violent chill set in. The experience was like a full-body ice-cream headache. Two minutes felt like an eternity. I was certain I was going to die of hypothermia. I got out of the water quickly, shivering as I jumped into the sauna. The scent of lavender and cedar filled the air as I began to thaw out. I closed my eyes and tried to access a state of calm, but the heat coupled with the aftertaste of the smoothie was making me nauseated. But then, just as suddenly, I felt better, simultaneously energized and at peace. The Memo knew its stuff.

Time for the next task. I threw on my robe and waited for newsletter inspiration to strike while I cleaned my face with cashew milk foam and attempted some facial yoga moves. What exactly was "bulldog face?" I was sticking out my lower lip and frowning when my phone started ringing, as the Memo had predicted. I didn't pick up. That's when it came to me: cedar-roasted quinoa salad with cashew cream. Not the type of fare I typically went for, but I'd give it a try.

A phone notification told me that my car was five minutes away. I had no idea where it was going to ferry me, but I'd find out soon enough. I ran into the closet and threw on the ordained pink seersucker suit—so not me, yet undeniably cute.

A half hour later, the vehicle pulled up next to a Long Island City building covered with a mural of unicorns and stars. The words "Jentle Lentil" were spray-painted in puffy enormous letters. Weird, as lentils were never my favorite, I'd named my company after them?

My personal corporate headquarters featured an open pen filled with furniture in dusty pinks and creams. Being in the space felt like being inside an enormous grapefruit. The office swarmed with young women who offered ingratiating smiles but seemed skittish around me.

My office had a white leather wraparound sofa and a chrome

desk. It was piled with papers with scribblings in unfamiliar handwriting, which indicated that other people here did all the work for me. There was a mockup of a promotional pamphlet for a luxury and wellness cruise through the Red Sea, with food provided by my company. There were sample aprons from an athletic apparel brand I was doing a collaboration with; they featured a slogan on the front pocket in that geometric sans serif typeface that every Millennial brand was using, as if able-pocketed customers were unable to read text in any other font.

I'd barely been in my seat a minute when a brigade of employees—or should I say *my* employees—began showing up at my door with all sorts of urgent business. A young woman with lettuce-leaf sleeve tattoos wanted to know if I had seen the summer promotional codes, located in a binder with color-coded tabs. A petite redhead, her hair styled in beautiful twists, came to inform me about pushback from commercial landlords on the compost stations.

Then came a group of middle-aged men wearing gray suits with designer sneakers and carrying laptop cases that looked more expensive than the devices they contained.

"Do you have a minute, Jenny?" one of them said. "We need to go over the strategies."

"We had a very interesting call with Monsanto," added another.

Like I knew anything about strategy. I tried to think of something that a boss might say.

"I don't have time right now," I said. "Just think about the pillars of our brand, look toward our North Star, and go for it." Would they fall for my Alice impersonation?

"Got it. But you're still up for the synthetic currency swap to hedge our risk in emerging markets?" asked a third suit.

"And the equity waterfall looks okay?" said Monsanto man.

"Guys," I said in a sterner voice. I channeled more Alice: "I really don't have the bandwidth. Let's game it out and reassess tomorrow." The only thing crazier than the fact that these words were coming out of my mouth was that they appeared to be working.

Once I was alone, I checked out my company website. Jentle Lentil was sending ready-made meals to subscribers all over the country. We had partnerships with all the top yoga studios, fitness apps, and makers of smart appliances, like a company that made a wi-fi connected blender that tracked users' fruit consumption. My company, "the taste of start-up," as our tagline described it, specialized in dehydrated, spiralized, and reconstructed vegan, gluten-free meals topped with edible flowers.

As I browsed our menu—zoodles this, lentil-chickpea flats that—I began to feel not just hungry, but hangry. There wasn't a single carbohydrate on offer. If I was going to be a well-known figure in the food world, why couldn't I be known for my bread, the one thing I could make better than anyone? Did the world really need lavender sweet pea lasagne?

My sense of disorientation only intensified when I checked my voicemail. There was a message from Ann Green. "Hiya, Jen. It's Mom. I know you told me to stop saying thank you but the transfer went through and . . . *thank you*! Just think, our own pied-à-terre! Oh—and I'm making reservations for that spa getaway, but I need to run dates by you."

A spa getaway? With my *mom*? Look at me, finally the golden daughter, making all the right moves, buying real estate and getting hot-stone massages with Ann Green. "Give a call when you can," my mom chirped. "Love you to the moon, baby girl!"

26

• • • •

A T SOME POINT IN THE LATE AUGHTS, GEETA AND I STOPPED INVIT-
ing our significant others to our hangouts. We'd tried doing the whole double-date thing many times, but it never quite
worked. Geeta made Hal nervous in a way that no one else did. He
acted like a fool around her, going on endlessly about his ob-
scure obsessions or—even worse—resorting to sarcasm that bordered on outright mockery. He didn't want to be outside the orbit
of his art-world friends. And I was never crazy about Matt, who
mistook conversation as an opportunity to panic about vaccines
and hidden plastics.

After one too many unsuccessful attempts, Geeta and I had
an awkward but necessary talk. Enough was enough, we agreed.
We loved each other and that was all that mattered. No big
deal, right? We agreed on a solution: If we couldn't change the
dynamic, we could change the format. We would stick with girls
nights, going forward. At least it meant more one-on-one time
with Geeta, was what I told myself. Until life intervened—her babies, my move to another city—making it increasingly harder for

us to get together in person. And then I started wondering if I'd have seen more of Geeta if we'd functioned as a quartet.

Now with Alex as my date, I found myself feeling short-changed for all those nights that could have been. Conversation flowed easily around the beautifully set table at the Michelin-starred vegan restaurant where I'd managed to snag a reservation. Sure, I never loved hanging out with Matt—we weren't even up to the appetizers and he'd already brought up the secret city that supposedly lurked beneath the Denver airport. But he was being slightly less insufferable than I remembered. The tension that normally buzzed between us was magically gone. It felt so good to be part of a group again and to see my new husband make the effort with my friends that Hal never cared to do.

A waitress—tall, blonde, her hair pulled back in a neat ballerina bun—brought us an amuse-bouche: a tiny brown gelatinous cube nestled in a spoon. It came with a clear, sparkling cocktail with a glass straw and what appeared to be dried algae clinging to the side of the glass for dear life.

"This is from chef." Our server had the voice of a guided meditation instructor. "It's faux gras, made from chanterelles gathered upstate at his biodynamic farm, paired with a celery spritz."

"Gorgeous," Geeta said. The waitress bowed her head and asked if there was anything else we needed.

"Could I see a wine list?" I asked.

Everyone froze and looked at me. Geeta finally broke into laughter.

"We're an alcohol-free establishment," our server said, sotto voce. "We do, however, have a water list."

"That's what I meant!" I said, wondering if I should make a joke about turning water into wine, but deciding against it. Geeta fixed her eyes on me and took a sip of her elixir. "Please, can we see the water list?" I asked. Our server bowed her head again and slipped away.

By the time our next course arrived, spirulina caviar in a fried sea moss nest, everyone seemed to have forgotten my faux pas.

"Amazing, right?" Matt said, tucking in.

"Beyond," I told him. "It's giving haute-couture mermaid."

Geeta rolled her eyes at me. "You, of all people, should appreciate the art that is coming out of this kitchen. This is culinary storytelling." She pointed to the open area in the back where white-aproned line cooks attended to their stations with military precision.

"No, I get it. I appreciate the effort involved. It's impressive."

Geeta's face relaxed. "Thank you for pulling whatever strings you had to pull to get us a table." With that, she raised her water tumbler (Greek, sparkling, 2005). "To Jenny Green."

As I lifted my glass, I wondered how much of our previous dynamic had to do with my own failings to come to the table as an equal? Maybe Hal wasn't the only one whose company Matt and Geeta collectively objected to. Maybe I was the problem.

Alex and Geeta started reminiscing about a retreat they had both been on, some getaway in the mountains of Idaho. Apparently there were tents outfitted with king-size beds and personal chefs who could fulfill any dietary request.

"They even managed to satisfy my spontaneous sushi craving up there in the mountains, hundreds of miles away from the ocean," Geeta said. "They said it was all local fish sourced from the Snake River. I didn't realize that sea urchin was available in Idaho."

"That's because it's not," I said, laughing.

"Did you get to talk to the shaman?" Alex asked. "She had such a wild story." He began to fill us in on the spiritual guide's backstory, which included an unfortunate accident involving circus parents and a baby elephant stepping on her big toe.

Alex shined in the company of others. He was an excellent raconteur. It was more than a great talent—it was a gift to me. I could lean back and not worry about Geeta shooting me the are-you-seriously-with-this-guy look that Hal used to inspire whenever he went off on one of his philosophical sermons. Most people were impressed by Hal's breadth of arcane knowledge, but not Geeta. She could see right through him.

"You did the reishi mushroom experience, right?" Geeta asked. It took me a second to realize she was addressing me. Which meant that I had apparently been on this amazing retreat, too. I straightened my back.

"It's such a crazy story," Alex said, leaning over to rub my arm. "I can't believe you haven't told her, babe."

"Jenny!" Geeta cried out. "Tell us what happened."

"What happened," I said unsteadily, "is something you will not believe." I paused, unsure whether reishi mushrooms were hallucinogenic. "She and I made beautiful music on a bongo drum." The group looked at me expectantly. "And then I took off my clothes and tried to do back walkovers."

Alex's brow furrowed. "You didn't tell me that part."

"You did naked gymnastics on a retreat with the Canadian prime minister?" Geeta snorted. "Are you sure you aren't *still* tripping?"

"Might as well be," Alex said, now rubbing my back. "The upcoming sale is making Jenny act all kinds of crazy."

An upcoming sale explained all those suits back at my office who were desperate to talk to me about deal points. "The sale, yes. It has been very stressful," I confirmed. I turned to my husband and twitched my nose.

"See?" Alex said. "She's a nervous wreck."

"The deal sounds bananas!" Geeta said. "I want to hear everything."

"You don't want to hear all the specifics," I said. "Equity waterfalls, stock swaps, it all gives me a headache."

Alex smiled at me like I was a prize. "Jenny doesn't like giving up control," he told our friends.

"Oh yes, we know that about her," said Geeta. I stiffened at this characterization. When was I ever a control freak?

"Which is why," Alex continued, "she's decided to only sell a 49 percent stake—"

Just then our server came up from behind Geeta, bearing a breadbasket. I spotted olive sticks, my favorite. But Geeta held up her hand. "We're fine," she said.

The despondency must have shown on my face. "Sorry, Jenny," Geeta said. "We don't all have your discipline. The big party is only two weeks away and my new Victoria Beckham dress is not being my friend."

"What big party?" I asked in a light tone.

"Uh . . . my engagement party?" Geeta said.

"The one that you and Alex are co-hosting," Matt reminded me.

"Duh. I was just kidding," I said unconvincingly. "It's the sale. I am losing my mind."

"Jenny." Geeta angled her head toward the back of the dining room. I saw more than a hint of exasperation on her face. "Can you come with me? Now."

The ladies lounge featured a wall-to-wall sink made of pebbles and enormous vases of hibiscus arrangements. The flowers were gorgeous, and I felt sorry for forcing my meal-delivery customers to ingest tiny versions of them.

"Are you sure you're okay?" Geeta said.

"Yeah, I told you, I'm great," I said. "I'm just overwhelmed."

"It's not that. I know we don't get to see each other that often, but I can still tell when you're not, um, yourself. I thought you were on the edge of a nervous breakdown, but I'm starting to wonder if you're in the midst of one."

"I'm just go, go, go all the time. You know how it is."

"I do know how it is. Sometimes I feel like I know too much." Geeta pressed her lips together and stared at me. "Look," she whispered. "You can still change your mind."

Was she talking about the Memo?

"Change my mind about what? Selling my business?"

Geeta gave a shake of the head. "I just want you to take care of yourself. There's more than one way to keep moving forward." Her eyes moved side to side, as if she was scanning the restroom for spies. "I know you're not a quitter, but you can say no. Rules aren't always meant to be followed. You know you can still write your own. The way you used to."

"But you're the one who always said you had to do certain things to get where you needed to go. I'm doing the same thing, following my . . . path. I want to be a disruptor!"

She cocked her head. "Back in college, you were an OG disruptor."

"I'm an OG disruptor now," I corrected her. "In college I was just OG."

"You were happier."

"Isn't that for me to say? I feel pretty happy right now."

Her brown eyes bore into me. "I'm only saying this because I love you, Jenny. You don't need all of this."

There was little doubt what Geeta was trying to tell me. Memos were for people like her, not me. In her view, I wasn't cut out for the fast lane. Desiree and her silver-haired associate had warned me about this. There was only enough room for so many winners, according to Geeta.

"The thing is, I like this," I told her with more force. "I really do."

"You were doing great, without the . . ."

"Without the . . . ?" I kept staring at her, waiting for her to utter the forbidden word. Geeta tilted her gaze down to the ground.

"Why do you keep doing this?" I pressed.

Geeta had talked me out of taking my Memo at college, and now here she was, in a luxe powder room of an exclusive restaurant where we could both finally afford to dine, trying to convince me to get out of her way. Geeta loved me, but never as much as when she was the top banana. She preferred the nights we went out to dinner by ourselves, her treat. Now I was on her level, with an amazing man and a skyrocketing career, able to get a table at Le Lapin Vert and pay the tab, and she didn't seem thrilled by it. Deep down, she wanted a best friend who was stuffing her face with buttered bread and despairing about the mess of her life.

Geeta's phone buzzed and her expression changed when she glanced at the screen. She broke out into the kind of smile I had only seen her give her daughters—daughters who weren't born yet. I knew it couldn't be Matt texting her since he was sitting at the table bonding with Alex. Plus, she never looked at Matt that way.

I watched Geeta as her fingers flew over the screen. "We should probably get back to the boys," she said at last, stuffing her phone back in her bag. "But, first—I have to pee." With that, she placed her purse on the edge of the sink and headed into a stall. I waited a beat, then helped myself to the phone sticking out of the bag pocket. The phone was locked but that didn't matter, I knew the code: 2543, the last four digits of our college apartment landline.

The most recent text was from somebody named Sharon.

> I dreamed you and I were skinny-dipping in a fish
> tank.

Geeta had replied with a fish emoji and a blushing face.

I felt a wave of revulsion. Levi Fischer had sent the same text to Alice. Apart from that drunken New Year's Eve in college when she kissed a gorgeous transfer student named Chiara, Geeta was pretty far on the straight side of the Kinsey scale. I clicked on the "info" button to see if "Sharon" was who I suspected "she" was. The email address that came up was levi@space.fisch.

What a loser. Levi couldn't even be bothered to come up with new material. Geeta was the woman he'd been bragging about, the one with whom he had been "diversifying his portfolio." I felt none of the satisfaction that usually came with being right.

How did their relationship date back this far? After all, we were currently in 2016, so Levi and Geeta had been engaged in some kind of escalating flirtation for what . . . six-plus years? And she hadn't told me about any of it? I seethed with anger. I always told Geeta everything. But there was so much she had been hiding from me.

I returned the phone to her bag just in time for Geeta to emerge from the stall. She couldn't resist checking her texts one last time.

"What's going on?" I asked, watching her cheeks flush.

"It's just this friend I met in Deer Valley . . . Sharon. She's hilarious. You'd love her."

"You should invite her to the engagement party," I said chirpily, concealing my wounded ego.

"She's pretty busy, but yeah—good idea," Geeta muttered as she strode out of the bathroom.

Alex and Matt were having so much fun they barely acknowledged our return. Matt was slapping his thigh while Alex spoke in a wheezing voice, doing an impersonation of a winded old man. "You're outta your element, Donny," Matt said.

Geeta rolled her eyes at me and smiled warmly, as if nothing had happened on our bathroom break. "And to think, we almost missed the *Big Lebowski* appreciation segment of the evening," I said. Now it was Matt's turn to send Alex into a fit of laughter. I'd never noticed how deep my husband's dimples were.

"Oh my god, this is transcendent," Geeta said. "Try it, Jenny."

I saw the tasting spoon in front of me. Nestled in it was a pea-colored blob studded with what appeared to be razor-thin radishes.

It was subtle at best, bordering on tasteless. But I wasn't going to give Geeta any more cause for concern. If I was going to abide by the Memo, I had to prove that I could play along too.

"Damn, that's exquisite," I said, widening my eyes. "We are so coming back here."

After the meal was over, the rest of the group waited outside while I fumbled in my pockets for my coat-check ticket. "Jenny, Jenny, Jenny," the attendant said, stepping out of the shadows.

"Desiree," I said, only half surprised to see her here. "I was wondering when we'd bump into each other."

"Pittsburgh beckons you." Desiree grabbed me by the wrist and yanked toward her. My body banged against the closet divider, hard enough to bruise my hip bone. Not that I'd ever know for sure.

27
• • • •

I WOKE UP IN MY USUAL BED, IN MY USUAL NEIGHBORHOOD, NEXT TO MY usual boyfriend snoring his usual snore. And yet I felt completely unusual—strangely well rested and energized, although I had no biometric data to prove it. I lifted the covers and crept toward the bedroom door, careful not to wake Hal.

In the kitchen, I considered my plan for my remaining time in Pittsburgh. Not just the logistics of the Father's Day parade or finding a last-minute benefactor to save the foundation—and keep Sophie from sliding back into the clutches of her rotten ex-boyfriend—but all the other things I wanted to do while I was still here. I'd always meant to go to a Pirates game, and what better way to deliver the fancy farewell date that Sophie and I deserved? Or maybe I'd take her to that chic seafood place in the converted theater in the Strip District. And then there was Hal. How would we mark our last days together?

So many options, so little time. I needed to calm down. I heated a cup of water in a copper pot on the stove, then emptied a packet of yeast into it. I could feel my body relax as the earthy aroma rose from the liquid's surface. I looked out the window at the brightening Pittsburgh sky.

I waited until the last possible minute to throw on a clean button-down and soft-wash jeans and head out the door. A sense of nostalgia filled me as I made my way to work. I'd hardly given this city a chance and I was already ditching it. I resolved to come back. I could open a Jentle Lentil outpost near SteelHaus, and keep an eye on Sophie. First, though, I had to ensure she'd still be working out of SteelHaus. Thankfully, according to my calendar, I had a call scheduled with the one and only Levi Fischer. This was my chance to save Sophie's job and make everything right.

I should have been used to video calls by now. They were part of modern business life, but I still hated them and the way people wasted no time getting down to business on them. Alice insisted that Levi was a highly visual person, so audio-only, my typical go-to, was not an option. Knowing what I did about him, I doubted it was charts and projections that he liked to look at. And I more than doubted he really had any interest in investing in a concern whose purported mission was to empower women. But I could persuade him. I was doing this for Sophie, I reminded myself.

When the pop-up reminder on my laptop told me it was time for the call, I went into Alice's office for privacy. My heart was racing as I clicked "join" and waited to be let into Levi's virtual room.

Suddenly, there he was, the grossest entrepreneur-turned-investor to roam the earth. I inhaled deeply to brace myself. I was always my most inarticulate at the beginning of these calls; small talk was not meant to be conducted on a small screen.

Levi looked relaxed in that way only very rich men can. He had a bandana tied around his neck and he was at an outdoor table, the sea sparkling in the background. I wondered if he was already in "Ibitha."

"Hello," Levi said in his arrogant drawl. "Did you just wake up from a nap or something?"

I looked at myself in the tiny window on the screen and confirmed that there was a slight bedhead situation going on. I'd been so stressed all morning preparing the presentation I'd forgotten to freshen up before the call.

"The opposite," I said briskly, smoothing down my hair. "Hard at work over here. I'm juggling a few initiatives, trying to keep Alice happy."

This made him laugh derisively. "Best of luck to anyone who tries to crack that nut. I bet Alice is riding you hard." He made a gesture with his hand that I imagined signaled a whip.

"You know Alice," I said. "Entropy is the enemy."

He chuckled and leaned back, kicking his feet up next to his computer. "She's intense. Always plotting something new. But you should know that we go way back, so any friend of Alice's is a friend of mine." He made slow, undulating nods.

"Well, thanks again for your interest in the Aurora Foundation. Why don't we look at the slides I prepared," I said nervously. I shared my screen and showed him the animated presentation I'd built around the foundation's work on gender equity. I'd made it as far as the bar graph tracking big banking's failure to fund women-owned businesses over the past decade when Levi cut me off. "I don't need to see some PowerPoint presentation," he said. "Just gimme the real deal. Open the kimono, am I right?" He said the last words in a fake cockney accent. I was probably expected to laugh.

Had my best friend really fallen for this guy? It seemed completely out of character for Geeta, who always went for men who were accommodating to the point of being subservient. But Levi had gotten his hooks into her. Even if Geeta wasn't entirely operating out of free will, I'd seen that blush when she read the text from "Sharon."

I tried to push Geeta out of my mind as I delivered my spiel about how we at the Aurora Foundation believed that getting men involved in the gender-equity conversation was critical to making the change we wanted to see in the world.

"What's your flying car?" Levi asked, interrupting me.

"My car's at the shop. It got sideswiped at my college reunion."

"You know what I mean. Uber didn't just dispatch taxis; they developed flying cars. Airbnb opened a film studio. WeWork elevated people's consciousness—until it didn't," he said with a laugh. "But at least they had ambition. How are *you* changing the world?"

I cleared my throat and started with a line I had delivered hundreds of times. "We're committed to achieving a more gender-equal society across communities by raising barrier aware—"

Levi made a horn noise. I could see his eyes sliding somewhere below the camera. He was probably looking at his phone. "The problem with non-profit chicks like you is that you don't get business. There's an important question you're not answering: Where's my perk?"

"Your perk would be aligning with an organization that's committed to—"

"You're not hearing me, babe. I don't have time for bullshit."

"I'm not sure how fighting for gender justice is bullshit," I said.

"I'm investing in Ashton's clean-energy initiatives because I am getting hammered in the press for my enthusiasm for crypto, which is supposedly bad for the environment." Levi smiled, as if impressed by his own power to contribute to global destruction. "You follow, Jessie?"

"It's Jenny," I reminded him. Levi's expression told me that he didn't like to be corrected.

"The point is that Alice put you up to this because she needs funding for her cute little philanthropic venture that she uses to write off her vacations, and I, in turn, have a little bitty problem with women. Just come out and say it." He folded his hands behind his head and a smirk hovered at the corners of his lips. "It's okay. I won't bite. Unless you want me to. If I'm going to bail you out, Key Relationship Officer, you and I would be having our own special key relationship, you know?"

"I'm sure we'd be in regular contact." I sat up straighter and forced a smile. "Levi, this would be in both of our interests. We could use a chairman-level commitment of $100,000 for the year and it would greatly benefit you in light of your situa—"

"Hold up, hold up," he interrupted me and picked up his phone. "Hey, sweets," he said to the lucky caller. "No, no, I'm not doing anything important . . . Yeah, I can hear them. You're not nursing them both at once are you?"

I went rigid with anger.

"God, it's so hot when you do that." He made a little grunt. "You can show me some of that on my new flying machine."

"Um, hello, Levi?" I said loudly, half-hoping Geeta would recognize my voice in the background. "Are we still doing this?"

Levi faced me. "That's my latest investment. Business with me is three-hundred-and-sixty degree. When you're in my circle, you're all in."

The thought of being "in" with anything involving this cretin made me physically ill.

"You know what," I said. "I just can't."

"You can't . . . what?"

"Do this. With you."

"Oh really?" Levi looked surprised. "Let me call you back, baby," he said, putting away his phone. Then he looked back at me and gave an impish smile. "Alice didn't tell me you were such a little tease. You're perfectly fine looking, but you act like you're a ten. Don't take that the wrong way. I find self-respect incredibly erotic." There was that grin again. "I own a hotel, you know. We could meet there and—"

My mouth fell open. This guy was psychotic.

"Just keep your money." I slammed my laptop shut. And then, a moment later, I remembered my mission. Sophie. My head dropped into my hands.

I'd messed up royally, as the text from 000–000 that appeared on my phone was keen to remind me. It came with a loud, high-pitched sound, like a flash-flood warning.

Stop before you create any more damage. Go to July 8, 2017. Immediately.

I wasn't looking forward to a dressing down from Desiree but at least here was an opportunity to escape this moment before I heard from Alice.

I opened the Memo app and scrolled through the trove of Pathetic video clips. Leigh on the *Colbert Report*, talking about her new exhibition. Geeta on a stage, leading a meditation session at the G7. And then I came upon Gabe and Thea, sitting by a fireplace in what looked like the lobby of a lodge. They were wearing matching fleece Snuggies and cuddling.

That did it. I tapped on the Kinetic button and made my exit.

28
• • • •

COLD WATER SPLASHED THE UNDERSIDES OF MY THIGHS. I WAS sitting on a heated toilet in the spacious bathroom that I recognized from my previous Memo-assisted visit to this apartment. Evidently, Alex and I had sprung for a little renovation since the last time I'd dropped in. Glazed tiles gleamed behind the his-and-hers sinks, and then there was this yacht of toilet-bidet combos on which I was now perched. When I got up to wash my hands, I noticed a note taped to the mirror.

HAVE A GREAT WEEKEND, MY SWEET DESTINY. SEE YOU ON SUNDAY. A.

My sweet destiny? I almost missed Hal's laid-back "bruh."

I picked up the phone charging on the counter and read my instructions for today:

Say yes to Sebastian.

It made a certain sense. I was home alone for the weekend. Everybody else seemed to have their own little secret flings going on. Why not me?

I took half a step back and studied my reflection in the mirror.

I was wearing a dress made of white linen—a color and fabric I never normally trusted myself to go near. Yet the garment looked miraculously stain-free and unwrinkled. I angled my head to the side. I liked what I saw. So would Sebastian, whoever he was.

I gave a little jump when I came out of the bathroom. Geeta was in the living room, seated at a small table and puzzling over tiny slips of paper. She moved a rectangle from one end of the cluster to the other. She paused, then let her face fall into her hands. "I am never going to get this right, am I? How on earth did you survive wedding planning?"

"I'm sure that whatever it is you're doing, you're doing it perfectly," I told her.

"At least Matt isn't here to tell me why we can't seat his Aunt Deb with anybody who is pro-fracking or who eats tree nuts. He's even more neurotic about this crap than I am if you can believe it."

"I can believe pretty much anything," I said, taking a seat on the sectional couch in the middle of the room. There were two purses on the coffee table, Geeta's Goyard tote and one I didn't recognize, made of blue suede and gold hardware. My own, I assumed. I rummaged through the bag's contents, examining my belongings. The Jenny Green who could be trusted to wear the color white had a quilted Chanel wallet that contained more than five hundred dollars in cash and membership cards to no fewer than four private clubs.

"I put your contraband in the fridge," Geeta said.

"My what?"

"The iced oat-milk latte. It was starting to look sad. I know how much you hate condensation."

"Thank you," I said, tucking the wallet back into my bag.

"And . . ." she went on, "I ordered sushi. Stress makes me so fucking hungry. I hope you don't mind."

"Why on earth would I mind?" I asked.

"Because the operating philosophy of your business is 'No Animals Ever'?"

"Ah whatever, nobody'll know," I said.

Geeta raised her eyebrow and resumed playing with the cards laid out before her. She made a little whimper. "I wish you didn't have to be at my table. I mean, of course I want you at my table, but I feel like you could handle Aunt Deb better than pretty much anyone. I really can't see another way out of this."

"Do whatever you need to do," I said. "You know I'm here for you."

"You say that now." Geeta pursed her mouth.

"What do you mean? Of course I am here for you, no matter what," I said defensively.

"Sure you are," Geeta said. "If there's one thing we all know, it's that Jenny Green does not take kindly to being seated in Siberia."

Was that so? Maybe this was how this being a winner thing was done. Respect only came to those who demanded it.

"Fine," I said. "Don't put me in Siberia. Or Moscow, or even Pittsburgh."

"Pittsburgh?" Geeta cackled. "How random. Where'd you pull that from?"

"It's actually pretty nice there," I said.

"Yeah, sure, as if you've ever been within a hundred miles of Pittsburgh." Geeta squinted while she worked, as if she was playing a high-stakes poker game. "I'm almost done, promise," she said. "And then we will watch all the rom-coms we can stand."

Now that sounded incredible. As I moved through the room to get my iced latte, I wondered why Geeta had called the drink "contraband." Was I against caffeine, or was Alex? Whatever the answer, I mentally thanked the Consortium for giving me this latte and this moment with Geeta, devoid of Silicon Valley cowboys and meetings about topics I wasn't up to speed about. I was just doing the thing I was best at in any and all realms, hanging out with my best friend, planning and plotting, ordering takeout sushi, gearing up for a junky movie marathon. The Memo was my friend.

"I'm so excited for your wedding," I called out from the kitchen. "You and Matt are my favorite couple ever."

Better than you and Levi, I resisted adding.

"You talking about the actual wedding, or the full week of pre-wedding activities?" Geeta groaned. "I thought the whole point of having a destination wedding was that you could keep it small, not that you had to become a travel agent writing personalized itineraries for 317 people. I am so sick of worrying about hurting other people's feelings!"

"If anyone can pull this off, it's you," I told her, stirring my drink.

"How did I become a bridezilla?"

"I don't think bridezillas call themselves bridezillas," I assured Geeta, taking the seat next to her. "Don't fall apart over this, sweet Geet. Can't your wedding planner help here?"

"She doesn't know the personalities involved. When I saw her seating chart, I had to overhaul the whole thing," Geeta explained, fluttering her lips as she exhaled. Geeta was always described in the press as an extremely hands-on manager. If you wanted anything done right the first time, you had to do it yourself, was her attitude.

"Jen, I'm losing my mind," she said. "This is going to seem so silly, but remember that meditation retreat we went to in the Berkshires?"

"Yes, of course," I lied.

"Let's do that thing we learned there."

I leaned in closer and waited for her to fill in the specifics.

"You know, the Infinity Mirror. The thing where you listen to what I say and echo it back to me?" She took my hands in hers and looked me squarely in the eyes.

"The thing where you listen to what I say and echo it back to me," I replied.

Geeta gave me a playful kick on the shin. "Ready?"

"Ready."

"My worries and fears are just noise in my head."

"Your worries and fears are just noise in your head," I told her.

"The anxiety is not me."

"The anxiety is not you," I whispered back.

We continued in this vein until a buzzer blasted through the apartment.

"Your delivery is here, Ms. Green," a voice informed me from a speaker overhead. A second later, there was a knock at the door. A uniformed doorman handed me the delivery bags.

"I already feel so much better," Geeta said when we'd tucked into lunch. "Seriously, what am I so worried about? I'm going to crush that fucking seating chart."

"You are going to crush that fucking seating chart," I said in a meditation-master voice.

"I don't know how you planned your wedding without checking into a mental asylum," she told me.

"Me neither," I muttered, helping myself to the salted edamame. "It's like I blacked it out."

"You should see Matt, with his tweezer set and glue palette, building his own centerpieces. Each one is supposed to represent a different stage in our relationship."

"You can't say he's not obsessed with you," I said.

"Or just obsessive, period," she said through bites of spicy tuna roll.

"He's sweet," I said. "And he knows how lucky he is. He's never going to do wrong by you." I stole a glance at her face and wondered if she was thinking about Levi. Then I stuffed a slab of salmon in my mouth. "This is so, so good."

"Your secret is safe with me," she said. "I never saw you touch the latte either."

Just then my phone buzzed. It was an email alert. The sender: Sebastian Shapiro, editor in chief of *The Manhattan Review*. The subject line said "Jenny, please say yes!" My guess was that it was an offer for a discounted subscription.

Geeta glanced at my device and raised an eyebrow. "You going to open that?"

"As if Sebastian Shapiro is emailing me personally. It's got to be spam."

"Open it. Now." She sounded serious.

I gasped when I saw that it was a personal note from New York's most powerful media titan. Sebastian Shapiro was writing to Jenny Green in a groveling tone.

> Jenny, how can you say no? The magazine needs you. Your fans need you.

"What the hell?" I muttered, scanning the thread below. I'd been asked to appear at *The Manhattan Review* Festival opposite a Basque chef who made "steak" out of beluga lentils. Hal and I had once tried, and failed, to get a reservation at his pop-up in Bushwick. The event to which I was invited was on a Saturday, set to occur after a Women of *Saturday Night Live* roundtable. Both panels would be held at Carnegie Hall, followed by an intimate dinner with "Amy and Tina." I was being begged to break bread—or lentils—with my comedy heroes Amy Poehler and Tina Fey? Sebastian signed it with an *xo*.

Why had I been so slow on the uptake? This was Sebastian of say-yes-to-Sebastian Memo fame. It seemed like a no-brainer, saying yes to Sebastian. I wasn't sure why this was my Memo mandate—as if anybody would ever need some coven to push them to accept this invitation. Perhaps I was so smashingly successful I could afford to blow off *The Manhattan Review*? Maybe I'd thought saying no to Sebastian added to my mystique or something? I wrote back to Sebastian:

> Yes—if you insist. You'd better seat me next to Tina. xo, J.

"That was weird," I muttered, tossing my phone back onto the table.

Geeta's expression was strangely flat.

"Sebastian Shapiro signs his emails '*xo*.'"

"And what was he writing to you about today?"

"He wanted me to do a panel and then have dinner with Tina Fey," I told her. "As if I'd need any arm twisting."

"So you said yes?"

"As opposed to . . . ?"

"Jenny, are you fucking kidding me? You caved?" Now I saw her expression wasn't flat. It was her nothing face, the one that came before a storm broke out.

"You changed your mind?" Geeta shook her head. "Are you out of your mind? Just because I'm bitching about my wedding doesn't mean you don't have to come to it!"

I was too startled to speak. The date of *The Manhattan Review* Festival was the same Saturday as Geeta's wedding. That was why I had originally declined.

Geeta pushed her chair out from the table and stood up abruptly. "I should have known you were going to do it the first time you brought it up. You didn't care about what I thought at all. You just wanted to feel me out, and when you determined I'd kill you if you missed my wedding, you waited for our intimate one-on-one hang to spring the news on me." Her tone was barbed but her eyes were brimming with tears. "Priceless."

"That's not what—" I started.

"You're so fucked up, Jenny. I should have known when you asked me to have a 'cozy old school day' together that you had an ulterior motive. Though I guess 'old school' was correct. Putting yourself first has been your MO since forever."

"Geeta, please believe me! I totally blanked and forgot it was the same day! Look—I'm going to write to him and say I can't make it."

"You already told me you wanted to go. It's too late. Own your truth, Jenny. You are who you are."

"What's *that* supposed to mean?"

"You don't care about anybody but yourself. Do you know what I missed to go to your wedding? Do you even remember?" She waited for me to answer. If only I had a clue. "You don't get it."

"I do, Geeta, I really do," I said. She wouldn't meet my eye.

"But I was happy to be there. And I showed up, with a big-ass smile and a Mabel Katz bowl under my arm." She tensed her jaw and glanced into the kitchen. "At least you'll always have a souvenir of our friendship."

I followed her gaze and spotted the piece she was talking about. I'd been obsessed with Mabel Katz ever since I took art history class sophomore year. The bowl was a masterpiece, with its riot of orange, pink, and yellow glazes and an organic rounded triangular shape like a half of a clamshell. Shame engulfed me.

Geeta shimmied into her sandals and grabbed her bag. "I

can't believe I was looking forward to spending time with you today."

"Geeta!" Desperation shot through my voice. "I don't care about the stupid festival. I'm not going. I'm coming to your wedding."

"Too late," Geeta said, reaching for the doorknob. "You're no longer invited."

29

. . . .

THE SOUND OF THE DOOR SLAMMING BEHIND GEETA STILL RANG IN my ears as I studied my new surroundings. The rooftop herb garden at SteelHaus. I pulled out a basil leaf and took a good long sniff, then made my way to one of the deck chairs.

I closed my eyes and let the sun beat down on me, trying to process what had just transpired in my alternate life, when my phone buzzed. The Consortium had posted a new success badge for me, an emoji brain, signifying my status as a thought leader. Of course, the Consortium was happy with me. I'd managed to step on Geeta as instructed, accepting my invitation to speak at a high-profile conference that wasn't nearly as important as her wedding. And I hadn't even summoned Gabe into my alternate life in a little while. Desiree must have been thrilled.

The same could not be said for Alice, whose name now flashed on my phone. As soon as I answered, she switched to FaceTime. My chest tightened when I saw the SteelHaus logo in the background. She was on the premises.

"Where are you?" she hissed. "I've been looking everywhere."

I'd barely said I was up on the roof when she burst through

the door and charged at me. "You didn't wear *that* for your call with Levi, did you?"

I looked down and took note of my outfit: the button-down shirt and soft-wash jeans I'd worn on my call.

"Funny you should ask," I said. "He seemed to want me to not be wearing anything at all."

Alice scoffed. "No offense, Jenny, but you're not his type."

"He's not my type either."

"I'll tell you what he is," Alice hissed. "Furious. What exactly did you say to him?"

"We dodged a bullet," I told Alice, my head spinning as I tried to line up my words. "The foundation—your foundation— definitely doesn't want to be involved with somebody like that. From a crisis comms perspective, it's very high risk."

"As high risk as running out of money?" she asked.

"It was a terrible idea, and I'm so sorry I ever suggested it," I said, hoping that a dollop of self-flagellation might warm her heart. "Levi represents everything we stand against. How are we going to be shifting the paradigm if we're taking funding from the protectors of the status quo?"

Alice laughed as if this was the funniest thing she'd ever heard. "It must be nice to be so principled, Jenny."

"You make it sound like there's something wrong with having principles."

"All they are is an excuse for you to sit back and do nothing except stare with contempt at everyone who does the work. Don't think I don't know what you're thinking behind that smug face."

"You barely see my face. You're never around!"

"Damn right. I'm out there, doing the work. And there's another thing you judge me for: my ambition."

Now I was the one laughing. I couldn't put on a front anymore.

"Oh look at you," Alice said. "Waiting for an opportunity to knock so you'll have another thing to say yes to without putting yourself out there, without owning your choices and standing in your truth." Alice was beginning to sound a lot like Desiree.

"But I did put myself out there. I moved here to work for you!" I said. "That took some courage, right?"

"You can believe what you want." Alice scoffed. "The only reason you're here is because I emailed you out of nowhere and persuaded you to join me."

It was true that Alice had emailed me out of nowhere and that I hadn't needed much persuading. But that wasn't the whole story. I'd loved what she told me about the foundation. I'd believed in the mission. "The reason I moved my life to Pittsburgh was that I thought the foundation was doing important work," I told her.

"Correction. The reason you said yes was because you needed a job."

"You told me you were starting a movement. You said you'd heard about me and my work at the radio station . . ."

The corners of her lips twitched. "Do you think I heard about a low-level associate fundraiser who'd been canned for making a huge mess on live radio and thought: 'I need a piece of *that* disaster artist'?" My stomach dropped. "Do you not even know why you're here?" Alice waited. "Why you're still here? It's because Hal wanted you to be here."

There was a buzzing in my ears. It was as if I could hear her and not hear her at once.

"Hal?" I repeated. "He was supportive of the move, sure. Lots of space, cheap rent, a cool arts scene."

"You're not getting it, Jenny." Alice's voice dropped to a lower register. "I did it as a favor to Hal."

"But you didn't know Hal." She was watching me, waiting for me to put it all together. "Did you . . . know Hal?" I sputtered, remembering the first time I'd introduced Hal to my boss at our annual gala. Now it was dawning on me that they already knew each other, and from the gleam in Alice's eyes I suspected it might have been in the biblical sense.

"Are you and Hal—" I made an awkward gesture with my hand.

"Past tense."

Oh my God. This couldn't be happening. Alice had slept with my boyfriend. "How did you two even meet?"

"Ezra Lightfoot introduced us," she said. "His old mentor."

"I know who Ezra is," I shot back.

"Ezra loved Hal and thought I could help him, so I called in a favor to the gallery. I think he said you were finding your feet and could use a little help," she said.

"Why didn't he just tell me he'd pulled some strings?"

"I guess he thought you needed an ego boost. He felt bad about the radio disaster, and the trauma from your famous oven fuck-up, not to mention his calling off the engagement."

"You . . . know about all that?" I could feel my cheeks burning.

"He was convinced that if you could get a cool job, you'd be happy again. And then he'd fall back in love with you."

"He told you he'd fallen out of love with me?" I could barely get the words out.

"He really cared about you, Jenny."

"Cared." I rubbed my eyes. "Oh sure, he really cared so much that he cheated on me, lied to me to get me to move to this city with him, just so he could do it all over again! I'm so through with him!"

A grin broke out on Alice's face. "There you go, cowgirl. There's life in you yet. Now bring that energy to fixing this Levi mess. Apologize to him and get that money. Otherwise . . . we should have another talk. A more serious talk."

I swallowed hard. "Is that a threat?"

"It shouldn't have to be," Alice said in a heartless tone. "I'm sure you'll figure your way out of this."

Stress made me hungry. I exited the building and headed toward my favorite deli, Papa Joe's, for a cheesy egg sandwich. It might be my last one before locking into the Memo diet plan. Sophie had introduced me to the world of Papa Joe's back when I was new at the foundation and still starry-eyed about our mission. One day I'd worked through lunch and Sophie had surprised me with a black cherry seltzer and a fluffy egg sandwich. From that first bite, I'd understood Sophie was more than just a coworker. She knew the path to my heart.

As I approached Mellon Square Park, I saw a couple walking their dog, their hands entwined through the leash handle, having a carefree moment on a clear summer day. A pair of girls sat on a bench giggling. I felt so alone and stupid. I entered the park and sat down on the bench opposite the girls. The despair was overwhelming. I put my head in my hands and let myself cry.

I was a joke to Hal. Alice had slept with him. I was about to get fired. And Levi was about to fly a beautiful entrepreneur to Bermuda to seal some kind of deal. I blew my nose and made a call.

"Geeta," I said after the beep. "You need to listen to me. I know Bermuda is beautiful. But please, please wait until you can go with me. Don't do this Levi thing. Please don't. He's bad news. Trust me. We'll make it a girls trip."

I still couldn't believe she was involved with Levi. Even if their relationship was the result of the Memo, how could she not know he was so vile? Had she been so blinded by ambition that she couldn't see the obvious?

"Hey, are you all right?" one of the girls asked from her bench. She had a purple streak in her hair, just like I once did in college.

"Don't worry about me. I'm good. I'm going to be great. My

thirty-sixth birthday is in two days and everything's going to change."

"Really?" the other said uncomfortably. "You don't look that old."

"Thanks." I stood up and typed Gabe's name into my phone. He'd told me he needed his space from me because Thea was getting suspicious about our relationship, but this was close to an emergency. He'd been so helpful when I called him from the reunion. I could use some more of that this time.

Hey, I texted as I walked to the park entrance. I'm in a rough spot. You up for a hump-day drink?

My heart lifted when I saw the three dots indicating he was composing a response. Then the dots disappeared. No message. I guessed he was holding firm.

I turned onto Carnegie Street and saw the line emerging from Papa Joe's—all moms and strollers. I'd hit the after-school rush. As I took my place at the end of the line, my phone buzzed. It was Gabe.

> Sorry to be rude but . . . I don't have this number in my phone. Who is this?

How could he not know? He was so good with numbers that he had memorized mine the first time I said it.

> It's Jenny, I wrote.

> Jenny . . . ?

> Jenny Green.

No reply.

Are you kidding me? Your BFF from a cappella.

Had he gone so far as to delete me from his phone?

How can I help you? he wrote.

I'm sort of having a crisis. Can we pls grab a drink?

The dots emerged again and then vanished. My phone rang. Thank god.

"Gabe!" I said.

"Jenny Green?" he sounded confused. "Are you looking for me? Or are you trying to reach Gabriel Winkhorn?"

"Ha, very funny," I said. "Much as I love retired podiatrists."

He paused. "You're asking me out for a drink?"

"I know it's early in the day," I said. "Maybe later on?"

"Sorry to sound so surprised . . . We've never really had a chance to . . . you know, really speak before. But, hey, you know what? I'm open to meeting new people," he said, which was exactly what he blurted out when we first went out by ourselves.

I was too shocked to say anything at first. I wanted to curse the Consortium—and the entire cosmos—so loud. Their funny little apartment swaps and car scratches were one thing. But now they were snatching Gabe away from me?

What were they punishing me for? I'd done everything I'd been told to do. I'd put on the seersucker suit. I'd stopped to pick up the sea glass. I'd taken the nauseating vitamins, done the facial yoga, and said yes to Sebastian. Maybe I wasn't supposed to ruffle feathers in Pittsburgh like I did on my call with Levi, but I'd finally found my backbone, just like Desiree always wanted me to.

"Hello?" Gabe's voice sounded so far away it was almost like an echo. It made me miss him so much.

"I'm here," I said. "I didn't mean to startle you. It was just a friendly thought."

"But you said you're having a crisis?" he checked.

"Oh, just the old garden-variety existential crisis we're all having." I forced a laugh.

"All too familiar with that one," he said. "I'm with my daughter for the next few nights, but how about I check my calendar and send you some dates? Maybe we can open it up to a few other members of the group?"

Gabe didn't want to be alone with me. Why would he? I was certifiably insane.

"Sure," I said. "That's a great idea. Tell Gabriel Winkhorn to join us too."

Gabe chuckled. "Okay . . . so, I'll see you soon?" I wondered if he was going to skip the next Looney Tunes meet-up to avoid me. By then, I'd be living my optimized life far away from here, so why did it even matter?

A hollowness grew in the pit of my stomach. I was such a disaster. No wonder I needed a Memo. In only a handful of days, look at what I'd done without one. I'd alienated Gabe. I was failing Sophie. Alice was ready to hand me my severance. Enough already!

My fingers trembling, I tapped the Pathetic button. I glimpsed Alice talking to a redhead on the SteelHaus rooftop. "We're looking for a real go-getter," she was saying. "The last thing I want is another self-destructive complainer." She was interviewing somebody for a job. My job, no doubt. I was toast. I let the hopelessness rise in me and launch me up, up, and away.

30

• • • •

'D KNOW WHERE I WAS EVEN WITHOUT THE PLAQUE BEHIND THE front desk. Just the smell of the place—eucalyptus mixed with disinfectant—told me I was in the waiting room of the J. T. Harris Clinic, one of Manhattan's finest fertility centers. I used to come here with Geeta when she was struggling to conceive with Matt. There were no signs of my best friend now, but everything else was the same, from the potted orchids to the soothing white noise pumping out of the air vents.

"Jenny Green?"

I looked up and saw a woman in a crisp lab coat and white clogs. The attendant waved her clipboard, motioning for me to join her. I froze for a split second when I saw that I was on the cover of the magazine in my hands: I was wearing a macramé bikini and leaping over what appeared to be hot coals on a beach. The headline read, "How #GirlBoss Jenny Green Traded Gluten for Gorgeousness."

I put the magazine down and followed the woman into a consultation room. "The doctor will be right with you," she said as she closed the door behind her. I slipped into the hospital gown that was folded on the table.

At last, Dr. Rosequist—the same physician who'd presided over Geeta's treatment—strode into the room. "Yes, chef!" He had a booming voice. "Fantastic to see you again," he said, easing into the seat across from me. His tone turned more serious as he rifled through a set of papers. Then he guided me into a small consultation room, where I lay down on a patient's table covered with a sheet of examination paper. He commenced a pelvic examination, sussing out my ovaries with the help of an ultrasound wand and a loud casualness that made me uncomfortable. "Your hormone levels are looking very promising," he said. "And we have seventeen excellent follicles!" He looked at me expectantly. "My bet is we'll be cooking up a baby in no time."

A baby in no time. My breathing went short. I'd always wanted to become a mother, but I'd barely spent a collective twenty-four hours in this strange world, and now I was going to oversee another person's entry into it?

"I'm going to be a mother," I said in disbelief.

"Not quite yet—we need to do the fertilization first. But all signs are a go," he said. "It's a lot to take in, I know. Alex is going to be over the moon when he hears how well everything is going."

Right. Alex. It would have been nice of him to come with me to this appointment. Or nice if anybody had. Matt always said that he was worried about the clinic's gamma-ray levels, and so he kept his distance. But I never let Geeta come here alone.

The doctor told me to put my clothes back on and led me back into his office.

I took a seat in the chair opposite him. He spun in his seat to face the bookshelf behind him. He turned back around to show me his copy of *Flash* by Alex Stone. "I tracked down a first edition," he said. "I was hoping he'd sign it for me."

"I'm sure he will happily sign it," I told Alex's fanboy, taking the book from his hands. "I'll bring it back for our next appointment."

"Tell him he can't skip the fertilization. Doctor's orders."

"He'll be here," I said. "For your library's sake if not mine."

"Very funny, Jenny," Dr. Rosequist said, running his hand through his salt-and-pepper hair. "Life is complicated for young, driven couples like you two."

"You have no idea," I agreed.

"As you said when we first met, 'It's hard to have a baby when you're not in the same city more than half the time.' But you know what they say about absence." He smiled, as if he'd personally come up with the maxim. I nodded, indicating that yes, I knew that absence made the heart grow fonder. Yet, Alex's absence from this particular moment was just making my heart sink. "Make an appointment with Loretta for the fertilization, and I'll see you tomorrow. I'd tell you to get plenty of rest and stay hydrated, but knowing you, none of that will be necessary."

"I can assure you that I am really, really into hydration," I said.

The doctor laughed. "You know I'm not supposed to have favorite patients, but . . ."

"And I'm probably not supposed to have favorite doctors."

"Oh, there's no law against that," he said, with a wink.

As I came out of the office, the doctor's assistant gave me a warm smile. I struggled to return it. My mind was racing as I thought about what the doctor had just told me. Seventeen viable follicles in my body. Seventeen miniature Jenny Greens. Or seventeen miniature Alex Stones. I pictured tiny versions of my husband swimming around a milky fluid.

"I'm excited for you," the assistant said quietly. "Oh, by the way—your friend came."

"She did?" I said, my spirits lifting. I guessed Geeta and I had made up after the say-yes-to-Sebastian debacle. All hope was not lost!

And then I spotted Desiree in the corner of the waiting room. She was wearing a tailored yellow suit, her hair pulled back in a neat, tiny chignon. "I'm so happy for you, Jenny," she said, rising to hug me. I stiffened in her embrace.

"You look less than thrilled," Desiree said on the elevator ride down. "What's going on?"

What wasn't going on? Geeta was excised from my life. And I'd just learned I was on my way to becoming a mother, and soon.

"I am not entirely sure about this baby thing," I said. We were now heading toward Fifth Avenue. "I've always thought I'd wind up having a family, but to have the news sprung on me like that? Seventeen follicles? It's just a lot to take in."

"Don't get all twisted up," Desiree replied. "Do you think anybody is ever completely ready for motherhood? Besides, you don't have to be sure about anything. It's all written out for you. You don't need to overthink, or think at all."

"But . . . with Alex?" I lowered my voice.

"Only one woman gets to be married to Alex Stone. You're welcome." Desiree grinned.

"We barely know each other. How is that fair to my child?"

"Children," Desiree corrected me. "You'll have two. Two at once!"

"We're having *twins*?" I gulped.

"Twins are a must for people of your caliber. Get the baby making out of the way. Look at Geeta and how well she did. Don't worry, you'll have all the childcare you need."

"Are you even listening to me? It's not the childcare I'm worried about."

"Having kids will give you more credibility when you become an icon for mompreneurs," she said. "They are essential for your brand."

I felt a spike of dread. "Look," I said, trying a different tack. "Isn't mother-baby bonding incredibly important? All that imprinting, attachment, and whatnot?"

"The imprinting will happen," she said in a tone that suggested that I was boring her.

"What about the memories? If I have babies 'now,' and then I blink and it's 2022 somewhere, I'd effectively miss the first few years of my own babies' lives! How is that fair?"

"The kids will be fine. They won't remember any of this, and you'll have a superb relationship with them. Your memories will eventually be full of joyful moments, indistinguishable from your actual experiences. And your live-in nanny, Hazel, could not be more nurturing." She sighed. "I cannot say the same for your night nurse, but you'll cross that bridge when you come to it. Goodness, I'm starving," Desiree said, and made a beeline to a hot dog stand on the corner. "It's been such a busy, busy day. I was just at a meeting with the Consortium, reviewing your case."

"What did they say?" I asked earnestly. She held up a finger, a sign for me to be quiet, and ordered extra sauerkraut from the vendor.

A few minutes later, Desiree had her lunch in hand, and we resumed our walk, heading down Fifth Avenue toward Central Park. "Despite your fumbles, the team remains impressed with your work and your dedication to the cause." Desiree wiped a dollop of mustard from her mouth with a paper napkin. "We've never seen anything quite like this before. If you can successfully lock in, we will be rolling out the beta in the next quarter. Oh—that reminds me." She popped the final bit of hotdog in her mouth, wiped her hands with a fresh napkin, and tossed it in a nearby trash can. Then she opened her briefcase, from which she extracted a wandlike device.

"We can do this right here," she said, leading me to a green wood bench abutting the park, and inserted the instrument into my mouth.

It beeped a moment later. She snatched it back. "Your temperature has gone up three-tenths of a point! This is terrific! It means your energy levels are heightened." She yanked me to my feet and resumed walking. "This will make your transition through the portal easier."

"Right," I said, keeping up pace with her. "The portal."

As we entered Central Park, I noted the birdsong rising above the city noises. A horse-drawn carriage clomped by, with a couple of tourists—a man and his very pregnant wife—on board. I stared at the woman's swollen belly as she rode past. Desiree noticed me notice it.

"Don't you remember how hard it was for Geeta to conceive?"

Of course I did. It was painful to think about. So many false starts, every month a tragedy. She'd gotten into experimental treatments too—both normal, like acupuncture, and strange, like eating Jordanian poppy seeds and placing healing crystals in strategic locations in her bedroom. I'd assumed Geeta had read about these therapies on the Internet. But maybe her Memo had been their true wellspring?

"I remember all too well," I said.

"You're going to get pregnant on your first try," Desiree said as casually as if she were making an observation about the weather.

"It was nice of you to come to the clinic . . ."

"But?" Desiree eyed me warily.

"If I'm being real with you, I'd be feeling a lot better now if Geeta had been there for me."

"But she's not there for you," Desiree said, twisting the knife. "She's on her path and you're on yours. Far better that way. Believe me."

I didn't know what to believe anymore. Maybe it was true that such a world didn't have room for both of us to be at our most successful or that we wouldn't have time to "waste" on our friendship. Maybe I'd move on.

"Where is Alex, anyway?" I asked.

"Never close at hand," Desiree said with a laugh. "Which suits you fine. You have nobody's needs and desires to tend to but your own. You can barely keep up with yourself!"

"I'm not going to argue with that."

"You speak Mandarin. You are on the board of seven highly regarded nonprofits, one of which you co-founded with that Coppola girl. You know *everyone*. You are on a first-name basis with the governor. It beats baking breadsticks and singing a cappella versions of Maroon Five tunes before drowning your sorrows in cheap Riesling." She gave me a pitying look.

"Do Alex and I love each other?" I asked quietly.

"You are a great team." Desiree watched me intently. "Oh, Jenny. This doubt, it will fade away." Desiree pulled a lollipop out of her purse. "Eat this. The sugar will help."

I bit down on the candy. "I think I need to sit down again for a second." I walked over to a bench. From my seat I watched the passing joggers. A little girl in unicorn leggings and rainbow roller skates was playing with a white puppy.

"Ramona!" a man's voice called out.

Come again?

Sure, there were girls named Ramona, but not *that* many. This girl appeared to be around five. When I saw who was calling her, my heart lifted. There was Gabe once again—or some disjunction-mediated manifestation of him—wearing shorts, a Wayne Gretsky T-shirt, and in-line skates. His legs looked surprisingly muscular but his expression was one of pure sweetness and devotion. I couldn't help thinking that *this* was a guy who would show up for his wife's fertility appointments.

"Mo-Mo, wait up," Gabe shouted, gliding toward his daughter. I wanted to run over to him, but Desiree held me back, her arm cutting across me like a tight seatbelt.

"What is *he* doing here?" Desiree said through gritted teeth, then mumbled something about QB disjunctions. Just as I thought Gabe was about to skate off, he pulled a U-turn and started back our way. I saw Ramona running into the arms of a woman with strawberry blond hair, her mother, as Gabe came toward us.

"You're going against the flow of foot traffic!" Desiree called out to him in a shrill tone. "Turn back around!"

Gabe gave no indication of having heard her, and kept gliding against the stream of joggers and cyclists. He passed a groundskeeper slicing a branch off an enormous tree that looked to be hundreds of years old. The tree was surrounded by barriers and hazard tape, but Gabe didn't change course. I had a feeling about what would come next. Within seconds, the tree branch fell to the ground and Gabe vanished in a cloud of smoke. I looked over at Ramona. She was playing with her mother as if nothing had even happened.

"Good one," I said to Desiree. "Very cinematic."

"We thought you would have learned by now. We need to get you out of here." Desiree tugged me to a standing position and frog-marched me toward a park exit. Did she really believe I'd intentionally brought Gabe into this realm? The same Gabe who didn't even want to be my friend in the other one?

Just as we were reaching the street, my phone rang. It was Alex.

"Hey babe," I said to my husband, trying my best to play the part.

"Ciao bella! Such good news."

There wasn't an iota of ambivalence in Alex's voice, which made me feel more than a tug of guilt. "Big news, that's for sure," I said. "How did you find out?"

"The transfer went through to Banca d'Italia, and the lawyer said that because of the size of the purchase, we are on the express path to dual citizenship if we want it," he said, and launched excitedly into an update. I now understood Alex wasn't celebrating my doctor's appointment but the Italian home, the convent that Desiree had mentioned to me before, the one with the rocket, and the displaced nuns. He moved on to talking about a group of community protesters. "Not that I have anything against the old nuns, but come on, did we really sign on for this?"

"Thank god you'll be able to handle it in your sleep," I told him.

Alex chuckled. "I've got my team on the case. The neighbors will love us in no time. The only real downside, as far as I can see, is if we're going to have to start taking long weekends to oversee the reno. I know what a freak you are when it comes to tiles. Can you handle being away from work for three-nighters?"

"I guess. I mean, what are they going to do, fire me?" I said. "Hey, while I have you, the doctors said they'll do the, uh, insemination tomorrow." I waited for him to reply. "Evidently, I have seventeen viable follicles."

"Always an overachiever," he said.

Why was I not surprised that his response was to do with achievement?

"Well, it's not a done deal yet. Dr. Rosequist recommended

that we have sex today and tomorrow, which I suppose is out of the question since you are away."

"Oh man," Alex said in a wistful tone. "And I'm stacked with meetings. You know what? I am going to try to take the red-eye tomorrow night. But in case I can't be there, I'll just send my, uh, seed, by FedEx. They do that now, on dry ice! Health insurance even pays for it."

"Wow," I said. "You've got everything covered."

"No, darling," he corrected me. "*We* do."

Neither of us said "I love you" before hanging up. I needed to gather my bearings. There was one thing that always worked. I reached for my phone and scrolled through the names in it. There were hundreds of G names in my address book—Greta, Greta Assistant, Greta West Coast, Gal Gadot, two Gyllenhaals—but no Geeta. Good thing I knew my best friend's number by heart.

Desiree's expression turned stern. "Who are you calling?"

It was now my turn to hold up a finger. I smiled at the sound of Geeta's raspy voice, even if it was just a recorded message. "Hey you, if you know me, you know I never check my voicemail. Just text me." I was then informed that the mailbox was full.

I hung up and texted. The response came immediately:

This message was not delivered.

My heart hitched. She'd *blocked* me?

"Better to have been loved and blocked than to never have loved at all," Desiree said briskly.

"Lost," I corrected her. "Loved and lost. Are you saying I lost my best friend?"

"I am sure you will patch things up eventually," she said.

"Is this still about my saying yes to Sebastian and not coming to her wedding?"

"Does it matter what the trigger was? The trigger is never the issue. She needed her space so she could shine, and she needed a reason to pin it onto," Desiree said.

"I didn't need to make it so easy for her," I said.

"We must stay focused on your objectives, our eyes on the prize. You did the right thing, going to that panel. One must have priorities. She's being ridiculous."

"Then why do I feel so awful?" I was clenching my fists so tightly I could feel my fingernails digging into my palms. "Look, I need you to help me fix things with Geeta," I said stonily. "She's my best friend."

"Your *best fwend?*" Desiree said, mocking me in a baby voice. "How old are you, eight?" I wanted to smack her briefcase over her head. "Speaking of your *fwends*, are these young ladies pals of yours or just adoring fans?"

I now saw a trio of young women gawking at me. One of them, with long ombré hair and wearing a mock turtleneck crop top, was eerily familiar. Her abdominal muscles were so defined they made their own hashtag. I realized whose stomach it was. Brie! She stared at me for a moment before speaking. "Jenny Green of Jentle Lentil?"

What was going on here? Brie should be in Pittsburgh. She was a bit player in my garbage life. God help me if my destiny was also tied up with Brie's.

Desiree pretended not to notice my discomfort while Brie gave a jump in her puffy sneakers. "I knew it! I love your overnight gluten-free oats! The berry carob ones are so yum! And my boyfriend stans the red lentil shakes."

I felt a tightening in my chest. "Hal?" I ventured.

"How did you know his name?" Brie looked taken aback.

I glanced at Desiree, who was shaking her head in disapproval. I'd overstepped. "Hell!" I said jumpily. "Hell yes! Those shakes are *so* good, right?"

The confusion clouding Brie's face faded. "Not to be weird," she said, "but would you take a selfie with me? We're just so *obsessed.*"

Brie cooed as I arranged my face next to hers. "We're platinum subscribers, four meals a week," she said. "We'd do more if it were an option."

"That's what I like to hear!" Desiree said, a note of triumph in her voice. "As I was just saying to Jenny here, why dabble when you can go all the way?"

31

. . .

JENNY? YOU OKAY?" HAL WAS RAKING MY HAIR BACK FROM MY FORE-head. "I think you were having a nightmare."

My body spasmed as I returned to the present. "What was I saying?"

"It was hard to understand, but something to do with having a baby. You sounded terrified, so I guess we're on the same page." Hal laughed uncomfortably.

I gave a moan as August 6, 2019, came flooding back. The follicles. The babies. The phone number that was missing from my contacts. The "This message was not delivered." I bolted up in bed and tugged on the lamp chain. Hal and I were on top of the covers. He was wearing a ratty U2 T-shirt and boxer briefs, his legs haphazardly splayed.

"Thursday, right?" I said.

"What?" Hal replied groggily.

"I mean, today is Thursday?"

"Yes, I think so. Very early on Thursday." Hal reached across my side of the bed to turn the light off. "Why?"

I didn't respond. Only one day to my birthday. Only one day

to make the leap into the new realm of possibility. How could I sleep? I turned the light back on.

Our bedroom, I saw, was an even more orderly paradise than the last time. While I was journeying through the contrafactual universe, Hal had apparently finished his organization project. My phone flashed a new badge: a pregnant-woman emoji. I turned the screen away from Hal.

"What's going on with you?" He sounded concerned.

"I'm overwhelmed," I said. "One day to go till the big three-six."

"Saying goodbye to your misspent youth?"

"Terribly misspent," I said.

Hal rubbed his eyes. "Come on. Are you going to do this again?"

"Do what?"

"Wallow in the past?"

"No!" I said indignantly. "It's just that thirty-six seems like the moment when you . . .lock into adulting." I felt proud of myself for finding a way to tell the truth without violating the terms of my deal.

"Uh . . . okay. I didn't realize it was so monumental," Hal mumbled. "I thought I'd make a reservation at the Falcon's Nest."

The Falcon's Nest was the new gastropub I'd been wanting to try for the past few months. It was a hot table. Of course Hal hadn't even bothered to make a reservation yet. Knowing him, though, he'd figure out a way to make it happen. Just as I was about to say something about it, I noticed a paperback on his bedside table *Flash II: Dream When Awake* by Alex Stone.

I reached over and picked it up in disbelief. "Are you reading this, Hal?"

"I'm sleeping, not reading," Hal said, pulling the sheet over his face. I pushed it down and put the book in front of his face.

"Is this yours?" I asked again.

"You think I would subscribe to this pop-psychology business guru bullshit?" Hal snorted. "Your mother sent it to you for your birthday. I was in a hurry and I opened the package by accident. Sorry."

I flipped the book over and studied Alex Stone's author photograph. It took up the whole back cover. Sitting cross-legged on the ground, his ramrod-straight back against a tree trunk, Alex had the good looks of a Roman gladiator. His feet were bare, his linen shirt artfully unbuttoned. He appeared to be intelligent, thoughtful. Someone my mother would be into.

Something about the image made me feel uneasy, though. Alex was attentive, rich, and handsome—modern-day Cinderella bait—but why couldn't my Memo husband be someone I enjoyed spending time with? If I did Memo life long enough, maybe I'd get to remarry eventually. That was probably the case.

"Look at that clown," Hal said, taking the book and pointing at Alex. "'Oh, look at me, I am a ridiculous thought leader, come listen to my TED Talk and plan your next billion-dollar business in your sleep. For an extra grand, I'll show you how to stick wires up your butt to monitor your every fart.'"

I suppressed a laugh. I tried to remember a single time Alex had made me laugh—not just an eager-to-please bark, but a real belly laugh. Then I remembered to be insulted on Alex's behalf. How dare my boyfriend insult my husband from another universe!

"Well, he's very successful and people seem to like what he is saying," I said defensively, grabbing the book out of Hal's hands and putting it on my nightstand. "This is mine, not yours," I said.

"I shouldn't have opened your birthday present from your mom," Hal said. "I wasn't paying attention."

There's a shocker. I said nothing, though. What was the point?

I'd already made enough trouble for two lifetimes. Hal would be somebody else's problem soon enough.

"Come on. Let's have breakfast."

Hal seemed to be having different thoughts, though.

"You're only going to be thirty-five for one more day. We might as well make the most of it," he said.

He tugged my T-shirt, and one thing led to another. Neither of us said a word the whole while. It was eerily intense. Lucky Brie.

Afterward, a feeling of warmth and gratitude for Hal came over me. I reached out and held his hand. There were parts of him I was really going to miss. Like his calves. And his sex. His sense of humor. And his make-up sex.

"Hey," I said. "Can you make me one last smoothie?"

Hal gave me a funny look. "Are you dying or something?"

"My last smoothie as a thirty-five-year-old," I rushed to say.

"Uh, sure," he said, shaking his head bemusedly. Hal got up and got to work mixing powders and nut milks, frozen fruit chunks, and juices. The result was jade-colored, and I detected pineapple. It was much better than the dirt-flavored smoothie that I'd chugged in that gleaming apartment Alex and I shared.

A half an hour later, I was just about ready for work when someone started banging on our apartment door and shouting my name. It was a woman's voice, shrill and speedy. It sounded a lot like Alice.

I looked through the peephole and got my confirmation. A few months had passed since the last time my boss, foaming at the mouth about some total nonemergency, had shown up at my home, I still wasn't completely dressed and opened the door warily.

"Jenny." Alice was out of breath. "I've been calling and calling. Where have you been?"

"Right here, getting ready for you," I told Alice. I guessed I hadn't heard my phone vibrating while Hal and I were getting busy for what would undoubtedly be the last time ever.

"We need to talk about Levi Fischer," she said, barging into my living room.

"I know, I'm on it."

"Bloody hell," Alice said.

She grabbed the remote off the coffee table and turned on CNN. The chyron said: "Coast Guard Searches for Missing Gulfstream Owned by Billionaire Tech Investor." The screen showed a picture of Levi Fischer.

"His plane took off in Bermuda and was headed to New York," Alice said, trembling. "The newscaster said something about unidentified passengers."

I felt the blood drain from my face. "Wait—who was he with?" I turned to Hal, who was lingering by the fridge, then back to face Alice. "When we were on our call I heard him talk to somebody about flying to Bermuda. I think it was—" I couldn't even say Geeta's name. It would make it all too real. I was hyperventilating now. "I think he was with Geeta," I said at last. "Geeta Brara."

"He had a lot of little unicorns," Alice said dryly.

"She is not a little unicorn," I replied. "She's my best friend."

"That's really tender and special," Alice said. It was obvious that she didn't care if Geeta was dead or alive. In fact, the former might have been preferable to her because it would open up a slot on the Changemakers List.

"Breaking news: the coastguard is now looking at this as a retrieval, not a rescue," the anchor said. I stared at the television, completely dumbstruck.

"Just tell me the transfer is on track," Alice said. It's all locked in place? We need this. And it's why I hired you.

I couldn't even process what she was asking me. This man—a horrible man, but still a human being—had apparently died in a tragic accident and all she cared about was whether she was in possession of some of his cash. "You got a commitment? Tell me you got a commitment." Alice was practically growling.

"Is that really what you're here to ask me—if a dead guy said he'd write you a check? Wasn't he your friend? What is wrong with you, Alice?"

I grabbed my phone and ran into our tiny bathroom, locking the door behind me. Crouched down on the floor, I searched for Geeta's number. I was relieved to see it was still at the top of my favorites list. When she picked up, her voice sounded muted, thin.

"You're okay, you're okay," I incanted. "Thank god. You weren't on the plane."

She was silent for a moment, and I heard a door close on her end. I pictured her finding refuge in a corner of her own.

"How did you know I was supposed to be on that plane?" she asked me.

"I just had a feeling." I leaned my back against the wall.

"We were planning to go to Bermuda, for a working mini-vacation. The girls, Matt, and me. Levi wanted me to come, to give me the term sheet for my company's next round of financing."

"Oh my god. The girls," I said. She was going to bring the girls.

Geeta sniffled. "I got your voice message when I was in San Francisco," she said quietly. "It made no sense, but I listened. It occurred to me that sometimes plans are meant to be broken. Even the opportunities you think you can't say no to . . . you can, as long as you're ready to face the consequences."

She didn't need to say the rest. I understood: She'd gone

against her Memo. "You didn't sound like your normal self," she went on, swallowing audibly. "And I wanted to come see you for your birthday. So I had Matt head home with the girls and I booked a flight to Pittsburgh instead. I'm taking the red-eye."

"You're coming here? I asked, shocked. "But what about Alessandra's summer solstice party? The one you all were pumped up about at the reunion."

"Please. Why go to a gala where Beyoncé is performing when you can fly across the country and back to see your bestie? I thought I could take a cue from you for once. You know, do the unexpected thing. I was really upset by how she treated you at the reunion. It wasn't cool. I should have said something earlier." A warm sensation spread over me as Geeta kept talking.

"Remember that American history seminar we took our junior year? How we were supposed to write a research paper on how Enlightenment philosophers influenced the farmers, and you handed in a historical romance?"

"Dimly," I said, though I knew exactly what she was talking about. I'd gotten so carried away during my research that I'd ended up writing a novella from the point of view of an innkeeper's wife.

"Which one of us got an A?" she asked.

"You got an A, too," I said.

"A minus," she said. "Believe me, I remember these things. And Leigh—she was so pissed."

"What does this have to do with anything?"

"It's everything, Jenny! I've always wanted to be more like you. Only one of us marches to her own rhythms."

"Rhythms that cause me to walk into walls . . ."

"Only when you stop listening to yourself." A moment of silence followed. "You told me to trust you in your voicemail . . . God, I can't believe Levi's . . ." She was crying again.

I squeezed my eyes shut. It was all too much. Geeta's faith in me had saved her life. Which, essentially, saved mine. Because I couldn't fathom a world without Geeta.

The next realization hit me like a thud. I remembered the preview that Desiree had shown me when she was trying to lure me into an adventure in blitz-tracking back at the S.C.S.S. Center. I'd seen Leigh, Keisha, and even Alex. But Geeta wasn't in the picture. When I'd questioned her absence, Desiree told me not to dwell on it. Now I knew why: In an alternate world where I got the Memo, there'd be no Geeta. In that world, where we were ex-friends at best, she was sticking to the script. The one that told her to board Levi's stupid plane.

In the world where she'd been vanishing from my life bit by bit, she was about to vanish from everyone's lives for good. But maybe, just maybe, I could save her there too.

32

• • • •

I'D MADE MYSELF A CUP OF PEPPERMINT TEA TO CALM MY NERVES. BUT there was more banging on the door. It had to be Alice again, back to toss out another absurd demand that she had previously forgotten to mention. When I slid the latch to the side and opened the door, I saw Desiree, looking super pissed off.

"Who's there?" Hal called from the shower.

"Just Alice again," I shouted back quickly. "She forgot her bag!"

"You're coming with me," Desiree said.

I could tell I was in big trouble. This time, though, I really didn't know what I had done. Or rather, I didn't know which of my mistakes had set her off. There were too many to count.

"Is this about Geeta?" I asked.

Desiree waited until we were on the elevator to reply. "Among many other things. You can't just start having *opinions* at the eleventh hour. Why are you challenging Alice about her foundation's *philosophy*? Why are you interfering with other people's choices? I told you not to make waves here."

"Are you kidding?" I said, breathing hard. "I saved some-body's life. Do you even care about that?"

"What I care about is you. More than I think you grasp." She almost sounded hurt. "You don't bring information from one realm into the next, do you understand? You must maintain the space between your two worlds. You do things over in your do-over life. Not here. There are bigger needs at play than your own."

"Whose needs are you talking about now?" I asked as we emerged from the elevator and exited my apartment complex.

"God, you really can be so self-absorbed." Desiree clenched her jaw. "No more disjunctions before the ceremony. You need to suspend all action, full stop."

"Wait—but what about Sophie?" I asked. "I still need to make things right for her." I realized I still didn't have the solution, but I could try to talk to Alice again once she calmed down. "That has nothing to do with what I learned from your Memo."

"How is Sophie your problem? Why are you so hung up on somebody you hardly know?"

"I *do* know her!" I insisted. "She's not just some random per-son from work. She's my *friend*. And she deserves a chance to fig-ure out her life on her own. That's not going to be easy if she's clinging to some guy who makes her feel small and sad."

"I fail to see how any of this is relevant to your trajectory," Desiree said as she continued her brisk walk past our apartment complex's garden. Chubby bumblebees buzzed through the air and a couple of residents, women in their twenties, were enjoying a breakfast picnic on a blanket laid out on the grass. They were laughing; they looked so happy and unburdened. I wanted to run over and tell them to appreciate what they had, to warn them to never let anything come between them.

"Do you recall what happened toward the end of February 2020?" Desiree said.

"When a deadly virus began making its way around the world?"

"Something else. More personal."

I tried to think of what else had transpired around that time. It was all a bit of a blur, our retreat into full-time domesticity. I supposed I'd been sinking deeper into codependency with Hal, struggling to help the radio station in New York raise money for its investigative reporting unit.

"Where's your phone?" Desiree said impatiently. "February 21, 2020. Don't just stand there."

I found my Memo app and opened the Pathetic tab, my reliable all-you-can-eat buffet of jealousy and rage. This time, I was treated to a montage of Leigh dancing at a party with a couple of matinee idols who were clutching gleaming Oscar statuettes, followed by Geeta and Levi on a tropical island. Their faces were coming together for a kiss. Panic and disgust ripped through me. I needed to find her on the other side.

"You ready, Jenny Green?" Desiree asked.

I was too worked up to give her an answer.

33

....

CAN I GET YOU ANYTHING ELSE?" CAME A VOICE.

I looked up and saw a young woman staring at me. She was wearing a striped wrap dress and flats, office attire. We were back in Jentle Lentil HQ. "Edith packed your bags, which are up by reception. I called you a black car," she reported. "Flight 695 to LAX. All the details of your itinerary are printed out for you here." She handed me a pink branded folder.

"Thank you," I said. "Did you check what Edith packed?" I asked, digging for intel. I had no idea who Edith was, or why I was going to Los Angeles. "Is it all appropriate for the trip?"

She gave a cursory nod. "The gallery scene there is a little different from the one here, so she found a couple of your more romantic pieces, like the ones you wore for your *Fortune* shoot. Edith uploaded the styling board on Pinterest so you can review the looks on your iPad on the flight. All the accessories are labeled with your color-coded index system, don't worry. You're going to really light the art world on fire with your style."

"I think I've lit enough fires in my life," I said wearily.

It was clicking into place. I was going to the Leigh Sullivan exhibition that I'd failed to attend, a decision that had cemented our split three years ago.

"Your prenatal vitamins are all packed," she said. I glanced down at my torso and realized with a whopping start that I was massively with child—no doubt the result of my visits to Dr. Rosequist's clinic and Alex's understanding of FedEx's dry-ice shipping capabilities.

"I'm pregnant," I said.

"Don't worry. I have your doctor's note to travel," the woman added. "We booked you at the Chateau. There's just one thing." She looked away, and I could tell she was extremely anxious as she blurted out the next part. "Your preferred room wasn't available."

My preferred room at the Chateau Marmont? A hotel I'd only seen in *Us Weekly*? This seemed like the least of my problems. I glanced down at my midsection again. My belly button was poking through my stretch T-shirt like a Thanksgiving turkey thermometer. Whatever was inside me was almost fully cooked.

"I'm so pregnant!" I blurted, once again.

The young woman looked like she was girding herself for an act of physical violence. "I know. I know," she said, still cringing. "The room should be very comfortable given your, um, situation. I know how you feel about your hotels. I know I should have booked this sooner. If you want me to resign, I'd understand completely," she said, tears welling up in her eyes. "But I want you to know that this job has been the opportunity of a lifetime and I have learned so much from you. You inspire me every day. You have a vision and you're never afraid to demand what you want."

"Thank you," I said. "It is not that big of a deal, the hotel thing. Sometimes a change of scenery is good."

Her chin trembled as she mumbled thank you. She was overcome with disbelief. "Your car is outside and ready when you are," she said. "We'll get everything sorted out by the time you land. It will be better than your last visit, I promise."

"I'm sure it will," I told her.

I did my detective work on the car ride to the airport, reading my emails. It was confirmed: I was flying out to the opening of Leigh's solo exhibition, *Over the Influence*, the same show I'd been too broke to attend in my real life. I'd told Geeta the truth, that in addition to being broke, I was on the fence. My ambivalence came from all of Leigh's partying and star fucking. Geeta had agreed with me that Leigh's behavior was getting increasingly insufferable, but urged me to reconsider.

"Think of this like it's her wedding," I remembered Geeta saying. "You *can't* RSVP no. It's really important to her." I didn't RSVP no; I spent weeks debating whether I should go and then just didn't RSVP at all. I didn't go either. Over the following few months I remained in a shame spiral, afraid of what Leigh would say to me. But she never said anything. She didn't reach out once. It was as if she had never invited me at all.

At the time, I'd told myself Leigh's nonreaction was further proof that she didn't care about me anymore. But she must have known the truth: as tight as money had been, I could have swung it. Hal and I had traveled to a wedding on the Oregon coast a few months after her show and I'd posted photos of the event online, which no doubt upset her. A wave of nausea hit me, and I doubted that it was just because I was a pregnant woman in the back of a speeding car.

THE AIRPORT'S FIRST-CLASS LOUNGE WAS FILLED WITH AN ARRAY OF free cocktails and tidy rows of snacks, nothing like my typical experience of eating Panda Express out of a Styrofoam box. At the buffet bar, I reached for a neatly packed box of sushi, then remembered I probably should stick to the vegetarian rolls. I added some baguette slices and jam to my plate and started eating greedily, fueling up for whatever lay ahead. My phone interrupted me with a buzz. It was a message from ooo—ooo.

> Cut the carbs. You must stay in a permanent state of ketosis—even in pregnancy.

After my fourth seaweed salad, I made my way to the gate, sat down, and studied the gallery website. Leigh's show was a series of multimedia sculptures that "interrogate the dialectic of influencer culture, exposing post-modernism's aesthetic detachment," which was a fancy way of saying that the exhibition was a collaboration between Leigh and Zach Houston. Zach was a social-media personality known to his tens of millions of fans for signature apology videos that he created every time he offended an oppressed group of people, which was quite often. His defenders argued that he wasn't racist, sexist, or homophobic, calling his detractors a bunch of woke snowflakes trying to silence a voice of truth. Partnering with Leigh seemed to me a blatant effort to cozy up to the LGBTQ+ community. I wasn't sure what she gained from it, though, other than an army of annoying Instagram followers.

Maybe I would benefit from Leigh's art in ways I hadn't given her credit for. I could stand to learn a thing or two about apologies. I'd failed to extend one to Leigh after I failed to show up for her big debut. She'd been under the impression that I was coming, saving a spot for me at the dinner after the opening. In all the photos that she posted that night, there was an empty seat that stuck out like a missing tooth.

Leigh and I didn't speak for almost a year after my no-show, not until Geeta's stunning Hudson Valley birthday party weekend, where I had tried in my half-hearted way to make amends. When I brought it up, Leigh said she was over it, all was forgiven. She didn't want to talk about it. But I could tell I was more or less dead to her, beyond redemption.

Just then, a text came in—from Leigh. It was a selfie in which she was standing next to what looked like a gargantuan tube of lipstick festooned with mirrors. See you soon, baby!!!!

Boarding now. I'll be there in no time, I wrote, adding a lipstick emoji as I got up to stand in the boarding line.

My smile evaporated as I considered what was happening. This was supposed to be my final fix, the decision that would supposedly set me on the right path. And it was geared at righting all that went wrong with . . . Leigh? I'd always loved her, but how could attending this event possibly matter in the grand scheme of the universe—a universe where Geeta still wouldn't speak to me, and where she was in grave danger.

As I inched forward in the boarding line, I sent Geeta a text. Damn it. Still blocked. And where the hell was Alex? The answer was in my text messages. Make that answers.

Babe, I'm at 42nd and 3rd.

Don't be mad. I am going to make it. On the Belt Parkway.

The driver is gunning it.

I love you so much I feel badly for all the men out there who don't get to love you.

Five minutes from the terminal. I'll meet you at the
gate.

Why won't you respond? Are you mad at me?

You couldn't say Alex wasn't communicative. It was a bit
much, nearing on creepy. But there had to be a reason for him.
There was a reason for everything. My actions in the Memo always seemed small and ridiculous, yet their consequences were
stratospheric. A pair of cameo earrings was all that stood between me and a lifetime of professional excellence. A piece of
sea glass poking out of the sand was what led me to a man most
heterosexual women would kill for. Maybe I had been sent to Los
Angeles so I could go to a party and fix my relationship with Geeta
by also fixing my relationship with Leigh—right? Everything was
connected in strange ways.

Alex shot into the gate just as we were boarding. My husband
looked so tall in the sea of average-size people. He reached out
and gave my belly a warm rub. "How's our little destiny doing?"

Our little destiny? Dear lord.

"I was stuck in an advisory meeting," he said. "I told them
I had a hard out but, my god, they had a fourteen-hour agenda."

"Hard out" was a term that Alice liked to throw around
when she just wanted to cut a meeting short. It occurred to me
that Alex, though, really did have a hard out, and that I was it. He
had arrived at my side in the nick of time. He was so unlike Hal,
who rarely texted me, only showed up when he felt like it, and
had a litany of excuses to weasel out of any obligation. Hal and I
may have been more similar than I'd initially realized. I needed
someone who complemented me, who made me a better person,
someone who wasn't afraid to commit and make babies together.

I stood on my toes and tapped my nose against Alex's.

"So glad you made it," I said, rubbing his back.

"You sure?" he asked. "You seem a little off."

"Off?"

"Your left eyelid is twitching. You're stressed, huh?"

"A little," I said. *Maybe a lot.* The fact that he was analyzing the microscopic movements of my left eyelid seemed to only make things worse. Would he ever stop examining my every twitch? Who cared about my eyelid when there was a chance Geeta would be at the opening? Would she let me talk to her, let alone talk her out of making the worst mistake of her life?

Alex began to massage my shoulders. I felt my body relax as we stepped up to scan our tickets.

I was assigned seat 3A and Alex was in 3C, across the aisle from me. When he asked me why I hadn't gotten him a seat next to me, I just shrugged and blamed Edith. "Typical," he said. "I'm surprised you haven't fired her already. You're only on your second assistant this quarter? Congratulations!"

His words shouldn't have stunned me, but they did. I was one of those monster bosses. The assistant who'd volunteered to resign just because my suite wasn't available at the Chateau hadn't been joking.

A different kind of shock came over me when I saw who was walking down the aisle toward us. In a hoodie and shredded jeans, carrying one of those stupid Supreme bags that cost thousands of dollars, was Levi Fischer. He was smiling at me like we were old friends.

"J-train! *You're* my seatmate?" he said.

"Small realm," I muttered. "Want to swap with Alex?"

"Nope." He gave me a double air kiss before turning to Alex and offering a fist-bump. "I don't normally fly commersh. This will be the last time, if I can help it," he said, easing into the seat next to mine. "Got my pilot's license!"

My stomach pooled with dread.

"That sounds—" I was about to say "idiotic," but instead I had the presence of mind to say "exciting!"

"You're looking good," he told me. "Pregnant women are so *fuego*."

I wished I had a barf bag. Instead, I had a misogynist troll for a seatmate. Picking up my phone, I scrolled through my photos, pretending I was engrossed in something extremely important so I wouldn't have to engage with Levi. I swiped around a reverse chronological timeline of my current existence: selfies with my team at work; wallpaper samples taped to the wall of my Jentle Lentil office; screenshots of Yelp reviews of my company; calling my products "life-changing" and "waist wonders." Then, a 3D sonogram of the two babies growing inside of me. *These were my babies.* They were kind of cute. I looked over at Alex and smiled.

"Hey," I said to my seatmate, staring at the image. "Want to see them?"

"Them?" Levi said. "Let me guess: You don't subscribe to the 'gender binary'?" He used his fingers to make quotation marks.

"There are two of them. *They* are twins," I said, turning the image toward him.

"Oh! No wonder why you're so huge!"

I shot Alex a look. To his credit, he managed to convince Levi to trade seats with him, by warning him that I might throw up. Unfortunately, this new arrangement prompted Levi to speak at even higher volume than when he'd been on the other side of my armrest.

Shouting like a sportscaster at the Super Bowl, Levi proceeded to tell us that he was planning on attending Leigh's party before jetting back to his home base in San Francisco. "I just bought a new pad," he said, describing his six-bedroom town-house. "There's a gorgeous view from the roof garden. You can fire up the grill, prep a Negroni, and see the whole bay before you. It's like you're on the edge of the universe. My friend said it's 'transcendent.' I just call it 'sick.'" He chuckled.

Transcendent. Geeta's favorite word.

"You okay?" Levi squinted at me.

"It's nothing," I said, forcing a smile. "I just get emotional on planes."

"I can attest," Alex said. "You should have seen her bawling through *Eat, Pray, Love* en route to Copenhagen."

"Nice," Levi said, raising what was left of his glass. "You checked out Noma, I assume?"

"Obviously," I said. "What is the point of going to Denmark if you don't check out the one place every rich person brags about checking out?"

"You are hilarious," Levi said. We clinked our bubbly that had just been poured by the flight attendant—I took a tiny sip, then handed my flute to Alex, who promptly drained both of our glasses. Levi finished his, too, then popped some kind of pill and pulled his hood over his head. "Catch you on the flip side."

34
● ● ● ●

A FEW HOURS AFTER LANDING, ALEX AND I PASSED THROUGH A throng of photographers shooting a step and repeat outside the Marks-Orlish Gallery, a rectangular glass building on Robertson Boulevard. The paparazzi shouted our names, exhorting us to look here and there. I was wearing a floral maternity dress whose spaghetti straps showed off my taut biceps and sharp collar bones and a pair of skimpy sandals that, despite a low heel, were extremely uncomfortable. Alex was in a perfectly tailored linen blazer and dress sweatpants that looked surprisingly cool with his vegan Birkenstocks. I was holding my baby bump like I had seen so many A-listers do on red carpets when my heart gave a flutter, a flutter that had nothing to do with the life inside of me.

I noticed a white convertible idling at a red light. Gabe was at the wheel, his face turned up to the clear blue sky. What the hell had brought him to LA? He'd once told me the only part of California he liked was California Pizza Kitchen.

"Smile!" one of the photographers shouted at me. I forced the corners of my mouth upward and braced myself for whatever disaster the Consortium would spring on Gabe's vehicle. Sure enough, a missile hissed down from above and nosed straight into the car, which went up in flames. Well done, Consortium Associates. Traffic continued, vehicles moving around the fire as casually as if avoiding a stalled vehicle.

I was still shaking my head, astonished by the latest display of special-effects work, when Alex and I entered the gallery. It was a massive hangarlike space with poured concrete floors and exposed pipes. Behind a DJ booth, a woman was spinning songs from the 1990s. In the distance, adoring fans encircled the woman of the moment, Leigh Sullivan. She held hands with a blond man-child who looked as if he was dressed for soccer practice, with his mesh shorts and rubber slides. Leigh looked fabulous with green streaks in her hair, wearing a black pantsuit with a lime-green bustier underneath to coordinate with her hair. I scanned the crowd for the person I really wanted to find.

"Can you spot Geeta from up there?" I asked my husband.

"The coast is clear," he said, squeezing my hand. I felt a stab of sadness.

Alex and I made our way through the crowd, waving at strangers who appeared to know us, and who, knowing Leigh, were people I probably should have known about. I barely recognized anyone—I was never that good at keeping abreast of who's who in pop culture. My favorite TV show was a Japanese dating program that involved cooking challenges.

There were young people and old people, both well-dressed and disheveled. The crowd was a real melting pot, save for the fact that everybody looked obscenely rich. While Alex was waylaid by a woman who pronounced herself his biggest fan, Leigh gestured for me to join her circle. "This is my best friend from college," she told her group, pulling me in for a performative mega-embrace. "Thank you for coming all the way out." She sounded genuinely vulnerable, and I looked down at the floor. There was no question it meant a lot to her that I was here, just as there was no question I'd genuinely hurt her when I'd blown off this same event.

"I wouldn't miss it for the world. I've missed you." I felt myself start to tear up.

"I missed you too," she said.

"There's something I should tell you," I said. Leigh looked confused. "I feel like I haven't always been there for you, not the way you needed me to be, and I am so, so sorry about that."

"I'd ask if you're drunk, Jenny, but . . ." She gave my belly a pat and turned to face the others. "Pregnancy is making you emotional. You've always been there for me."

One of Leigh's hangers-on caught my eye and told me she swore by my quinoa harvest salad with cashew cream, the Memo-inspired recipe I came up with in my bathroom while doing facial yoga. "I've eaten it every day for the last six months," she said.

"It came to me in a flash of inspiration," I said, looking at Alex, who was still engrossed in a conversation with his fan.

"Jenny is a tastemaker in all ways, not to mention the closest thing I have to a sister," Leigh said. I forced a smile. I'd never heard Leigh speak of me so effusively.

Her pupils were the size of dimes, which I guessed helped explain the enthusiasm. "And soon, I will be a guide mother two times over!" she said. This filled me with sadness. If Leigh was the twins' guide mother, then what did that make Geeta? Where was Geeta, anyway?

Leigh squeezed my elbow. "So? What do you think of all of this?" She beamed and made a sweeping gesture at the room. I wasn't used to Leigh caring about what I thought of anything she did. I whispered that I was insanely proud of her and gave her a kiss on the cheek.

"I love you sooooo much," she said. Her face was so close I

could feel her breath on my neck. "And you'd better bid on one of my sculptures, bitch."

Now Levi walked over toward us, flanked by two younger women—assistants? girlfriends? The crowd parted as he approached Leigh.

"I have something for you!" I heard her say as she pulled him toward a corner. They were barely discreet about what happened next: He handed her an envelope, and she placed something in the palm of his hand.

Then I understood: Leigh was popular for the real commodity she was selling. Leigh was running a serious business, and I was certain I knew what was behind it all. Desiree and her Consortium didn't seem like the type to aid and abet criminal activity, but if Leigh's dealings were helping fund the S.C.S.S., and the S.C.S.S. was invested in liberating womankind from centuries of oppression, I had a feeling the Consortium's leaders told themselves that Leigh's other line of work was defensible.

Leigh practically twirled around the room, doing more meet and greet. She seemed happy and in her element. The loud, outwardly tough but secretly insecure girl I had met as a sophomore, the one who wasn't sure if her landscapes were any good but nevertheless kept painting because she couldn't stand not to paint, was gone. In her place was an it girl with saucer eyes and a million acquaintances who thought they knew her well. And she thought that I was her best friend. It beat having no friends, I guessed.

I made my way over to the bar and ordered a grapefruit juice. Alex popped up behind me. "I'll have what she's having," he told the bartender.

"Make his with mescal," I clarified.

Then I leaned in closer to Alex and whispered what I had just seen transpire between Leigh and Levi.

Alex didn't seem that concerned. "Whatever gets you through the night, baby," he said with a shrug. "But I just witnessed something you'll find even more interesting. Your nemesis is on the premises."

I whipped my head around and scanned the crowd. At last, I caught a glint of Geeta's glossy bob. She was wearing a cream-colored cropped sweater with matching wide-legged pants and talking to Levi or, rather, listening to him talk ad nauseam, smiling and hanging on his every stupid word. I wondered if she'd already seen me, and had purposely turned her back to me. A slew of thoughts hit me at once: Was she still mad at me for skipping her wedding? What did she see in Levi? Did she ever miss me?

"I have to pee," I told Alex.

"What else is new, mama?" he said with an adoring smile.

I wiggled away from him and drifted toward Geeta. I tried to catch her eye but she looked right through me. She wasn't going to make this easy. I slowed down as I tried to scare up the nerve to make my move.

She was now talking to a woman holding a reporter's notebook, which I realized I could use to my advantage. Geeta was less likely to cause a scene with a witness on hand. She had a reputation to uphold.

"Geeta?" I said a couple of times.

Geeta finally spun around to face me. "Can I help you?" She was speaking to me as if I were a stranger trying to horn in on her conversation. My heart felt so heavy.

"It's me, Jenny," I said, my tone pleading.

The reporter was looking at me. "Jenny Green of Jentle Lentil fame! You two went to college together, right?"

Geeta stared coldly at me. My hands were shaking. "Can we have the quickest of words?" I asked.

The reporter, sensing something serious was going on between these two ballers, excused herself before Geeta could stop her. When it was just the two of us, Geeta looked me directly in the eyes. "Leave me alone, Jenny. I'm serious. I've had enough of you for one lifetime."

"Or two," I muttered. "I get it! I didn't come to your wedding, and you despise me."

"That's all you think this is about?" Geeta crossed her arms, then started to walk away. "It was nice to see you," she called over her shoulder.

"Hey! Come back, please!" I begged. She kept going.

"I'm going to say the word that cannot be said!" I called out, a last-ditch effort. Her gait slowed, then she turned around and begrudgingly returned. "This better be good."

"Look, if you want to be my enemy for some reason that I don't even know about, go ahead," I told her. "But we need to talk. It's serious."

She screwed up her face. "Now you'll talk to me? Last time I tried calling you, you never called me back. I guess you were embarrassed for squeezing me for all my contacts to help build your mobile-delivery platform and not even stopping to say thank you. By the way, congratulations."

"It's just a food company," I said.

"No, on that." She gestured at my belly. My heart dropped in despair. This wasn't how it was supposed to go.

"I was just another body for you to step on as you continued your ascent, right?" she said.

I swallowed hard. "If that happened, that was . . . it is unforgivable."

"*If?*" Geeta let off a cackle. "So now we're operating in some kind of dissociative fugue state?"

"Geeta, you can hate me. You should hate me. But you need to listen to me. If you never speak to me again, which is totally justifiable considering everything that's happened, just please don't forget this one thing. You have to stay away from Levi's—"

"I love to see this," came a deep voice. Lo and behold, as if I'd summoned him, Levi Fischer was bearing down on us. "Are the 'hashtag girl bosses' kissing and making up?"

Geeta laughed and leaned into his body, as if seeking protection. I wasn't sure if she had heard what I said or understood how serious it was. The evidence was not heartening. "This one," she said with contempt, as if I didn't even have a name, "was just offering me a piece of unsolicited advice. It's amazing. We go years without speaking, yet she thinks she has a say in my personal life." People were starting to stare at us, and I felt embarrassed. But this was my last chance to break through to her.

"Just because we're not close anymore doesn't mean I don't care about you," I said. "In fact, I probably care about you more than I ever did. I meant what I said, and you should listen. Because you know how I feel about you deep down."

I could feel something shift in the air between us. I detected a glimmer of hope. Had I reached her?

"Lovely seeing you, Jenny," Geeta said crisply. I guessed I hadn't reached her. "They say motherhood changes you. Maybe you'll turn out all right after all." She turned to Levi. "Ready for takeoff?" And then she looked straight at me, her eyes blazing with defiance.

Unbelievable. Geeta was probably going to jump on his plane just to spite me. I stood there dumbly, my heart racing, as the two of them glided away. I pulled out my phone and composed a text. Please stay away from his plane, Geeta.

But it was in vain. This message was not delivered.

That's when I saw my solution: the pile of postcards on the

gallery's front desk. The glossy side was printed with a triangular pile of bones. Nice branding, I thought. I helped myself to a card and a pen and scrawled out a message.

Geeta, I'm serious. Don't board Levi's plane, ever. Even if I can't save us, I can save you. You must believe me.

Desiree and her friends were going to kill me for attempting to meddle with destiny. So be it. If the situation were reversed, I knew Geeta would try to save me, too.

I folded the card in half, then quarters, and tried to find Geeta. I'd discreetly press the note in her hand before she even knew what was happening. The room had become hotter and noisier, though, and the crowd had swallowed Geeta up. I circled all the rooms. There was no sign of her.

"There you are." Alex was smiling like a maniac. "We got it," he told me. "Zach is coming home with us."

"Us? He is?" My first thought was Alex had arranged a threesome, which might have been better than the truth. My husband led me to a cordoned-off space in the back that was devoted to an enormous replica of Zach Houston. The piece was lit from within, giving off a halo as if he were a figure in a religious sculpture, and not an immature kid who had filmed a man jumping off the Golden Gate Bridge and set it to death metal. I almost wished Alex had bid on one of Leigh Sullivan's signature celebrity vulva sculptures.

Alex wrapped his arm around my waist. "The asking was a bit lower. But I saw Levi was eyeing it and I knew it was a now or never kind of thing, so I just went for it."

"How much did this cost?"

"About a hundo," he said.

"A hundred . . . thousand? Dollars?"

I could have put a down payment on a good apartment in Pittsburgh for that much money. I could have bought myself an electric car and driven the hell away. I could have funded Alice's foundation for another few months and rehired sweet Sophie.

"It's a bargain, I know," Alex said. "The valuation is . . ."

I stopped listening. Geeta swept into the room, arm in arm with Leigh.

"Congratulations, you sexy patrons of the arts!" Leigh squealed.

Geeta hung back when she realized who had just won the auction, but Leigh barreled over to Alex and me, covering us both with kisses. "A million, zillion thank-yous," Leigh cried out. "And I'm so happy that you bid on that piece. It's my favorite." Young and beautiful scenesters streamed into the room, like moths drawn to the glow of Leigh.

"I should be thanking *you*," Alex told Leigh. "I love it."

"Me too," I forced myself to say. "It's so . . ." I squinted into the light emanating from replica Zach's forehead. "Brilliant!"

"I love you," Leigh said, taking me in for a slobbery hug. Oh god. She was absolutely wasted. "You're my best friend," she blubbered. "I wish I was the pregnant one so I could name my twins after you two!"

"Leigh, stop," I said, steadying her on her high heels. I couldn't go so far as to call Leigh my best friend in return. My eyes shot over to Geeta, who'd turned her back to me again. Even if she hated me for all the choices I'd made in this version of my life, the role of best friend was always going to be hers.

One more chance. I attempted to sneak up from behind, but Geeta had a special sense. She could always feel me coming. She turned around and met my eye as I slipped the folded up postcard into a pocket of her pants. She did nothing for a half second. Then she took the note out and let it fall to the ground.

"Will you do me a favor?" Geeta asked.

"Anything." I felt a stupid surge of hope.

"Leave me the fuck alone," she said. With that, she shot out of the room.

I knew how she operated when she was wound up like this. She got stubborn. She was going to stick by Levi's side, because that's what the Memo told her to do. It was so much bigger than me.

A couple of hours later, everybody but Geeta, who'd disappeared long ago, convened in a tent behind the gallery for a dinner in Leigh's honor. I spotted the artist in a cluster of people in the shadows of a trio of palm trees. Their bodies were angled every which way—lots of downward dogs going on. At first I thought they were playing a game of Twister. And I supposed they were, but a very adult version, no game board required. Just an enormous cuddle puddle.

"Jenny!" Leigh cried when she saw me. "Get over here!"

"Shall we, lovey?" Alex said, kicking off his Birks.

"You go ahead," I told him. "My back is hurting."

"Don't be like that," he said. "You can still have a little fun."

"I'm having a blast." I slapped on a smile. "Besides, who wants an enormous pregnant woman in their orgy?"

I watched my husband find a spot next to a familiar pretty face. He started sucking this familiar pretty face. Oh my god. This face wasn't just familiar. It was Brie's. She couldn't stay away from my men in any timeline.

If only I cared. All I could think about was Geeta, and how I'd failed her. Not for lack of trying. The more attempts I'd made, the less my words mattered.

Alex disentangled from his new friend and looked up at me. "Everything okay, Jen?" he called out.

"Yeah," I said hazily. "You have my blessing!"

"That's not what I mean. You're, like, vibrating!"

Now Brie craned her neck to look at me. Her face flooded with alarm. "What the hell is happening to her?" she shrieked.

I glanced down and saw my hands weren't all that was twitching. The rest of my body was quaking. I felt a rattling in my chest, a tremor in my shoulders. Everything was spinning around me. The next thing I knew, I was flying through yet another glorious wormhole.

35
• • • •

THE SUN WAS BEATING DOWN ON ME AND I WAS BUTT ON THE GROUND, my limbs splayed out like a crab. I dug my hands into the dirt, squinting at my surroundings. I had landed on the side of a freeway in a barren desert landscape. Maybe Arizona . . . or Nevada? Cacti sprouted at odd intervals from the ruddy earth.

I looked down to see if I was still pregnant. I was disappointed to see that I was not. I was back in my old life. Soon enough, though, I'd be locked into the new one, the better one. I'd be done with all the hurtling back and forth. I'd have kids, a husband, and a best friend in Leigh Sullivan. The memory of how Geeta had reacted to me at the art opening filled me with a numbness. She was as good as gone in that realm, but not for my lack of trying. My conscience could be clear. I reached into my pocket for my phone, only to discover it wasn't there.

There was a rustling sound from behind. At first I thought I was about to be attacked by a rattlesnake. Then I spotted a patch of red hair poking out from behind a desert plant. Desiree stepped out in an immaculate ivory pantsuit, perfectly tailored to her slight frame. Her knobby fingers were stacked with turquoise rings.

"Happy almost birthday," she said, helping me to my feet. "We have a very special party planned for you." I shielded my face from the blazing sun and Desiree tossed me a baseball cap. "The Big Three Six. Congratulations! According to our calculations, you course-corrected enough to fully self-actualize."

My mouth was so dry it was hard to speak. "I did?"

"Well, 94 percent, but that's better than we expected, if I'm being perfectly honest. Your last trip went well but we had to get you here urgently—we were running out of time," she said quickly. She sounded a little nervous. I wondered if she and her associates were getting sloppy in their accounting. Maybe the fact that Geeta hadn't listened to me meant we could all avoid getting bogged down with more disjunctions and repercussions.

"We'll get you some water and you'll feel more yourself," Desiree assured me.

"Where are we?"

"Near Santa Fe. We try to find conference centers that are equally convenient to most of our Consortium members, which invariably means we settle on a destination that's equally inconvenient to everyone. You were supposed to touch down in your suite at the hotel but there was a glitch in the coordinates as we rushed you out of California. It was getting dicey back there." She eyed me disapprovingly. I knew exactly what she meant. "Geeta was on her way to the after-party," I said.

"Yes, and goodness knows what you would have tried to pull."

Before I could defend myself, a black van rumbled down the desert road and pulled over next to us. My knees felt weak as I followed Desiree into the back of the vehicle.

"I should be more upset with you, but frankly I'm exhausted and relieved. And lucky for us, everything is falling into place. The rest will be a cakewalk," Desiree said. She took two bottles of water from a seat pocket and handed one to me. I chugged and chugged.

"I know what you're wondering. You're now in the liminal state, neither here nor there."

"I thought I was in New Mexico," I replied.

"Barely. Don't get too comfortable," Desiree said. "Tomorrow morning you'll officially be food-world royalty. Happily married to a successful thought leader. With two healthy daughters, and a best friend who loves you to bits."

"My best friend is not speaking to me, last I checked."

"Your best friend is Leigh Sullivan," Desiree supplied. "That other person was always a snake in the grass, keeping you from attaining full empowerment." Desiree let off a melancholic sigh. "Which reminds me. There's been a security breach at the conference center. There was a . . . sighting. Your nemesis is making trouble."

"Geeta showed up here?" I couldn't keep the glee from my voice. She had crashed the conference. And to go by Desiree's expression, it wasn't because a Memo had told her to do it.

"A few of our elder Consortium members saw her lurking by the tennis courts, no doubt looking for the woman of the hour. She ran off before anyone could apprehend her."

I bit down a smile. Even if Geeta didn't want me to have the Memo, she was going out on a limb. At least she cared.

"It's really getting to her," Desiree said. "She just can't stand to see you be celebrated. She's got tall-poppy syndrome. That's when people are psychologically unable to see others grow. They feel compelled to cut them down to shine themselves."

That was one theory for it. I turned to look out the window. A big-beaked bird swooped down frighteningly close to the van. I traced its path with my eyes.

"I understand that it hurts, cookie. But soon it will sink in, and you won't even remember what you saw in her in the first place. I have to say, I never got it."

"Really? You've never had a friend who had your back, ride or die?"

Desiree guffawed. "More like who stabbed you in the back! Tell me this. Who is the one person who did not want you to get your Memo?"

"Geeta," I acknowledged. "And I agree that a lot of her behavior has been upsetting. But up until this week she was also . . . my soulmate."

"Is that what you'd call it? She was there for you provided that you were suffering. Is that a real friend?"

"I wasn't much of a real friend to her either," I said. "I blew off her wedding to go to a stupid panel and then squeezed her for her business connections and never even said thank you."

"Hey, connections are key. And it's not every day you have the opportunity to go mano a mano with Sebastian Shapiro. That conversation led to a *Manhattan Review* profile. Eight pages, with a double-page portrait by Annie Leibovitz. You are your own best friend, Jenny. Finally. If you don't love yourself, how can you expect anyone else to love you?"

I swallowed hard as the van trundled along.

"What a week it's been." Desiree reached out and squeezed my hand.

36

· · · ·

THE CONFERENCE CENTER CONSISTED OF A CLUSTER OF STUCCO buildings. Pink and squat, they reminded me of enormous mushrooms.

"I know what you're thinking," Desiree said as we neared the entrance. "We used to find the most outrageous luxury retreats, but this is better for anonymity. Nobody ever pays attention to what goes on here. As far as they're concerned, we're just a bunch of middle-aged professional women—already teetering on the brink of invisibility—catching up over huevos rancheros and turquoise shopping expeditions." She waggled her fingers at me.

"I saw them," I muttered. "Very nice."

"Welcome, Consortium Members! Celebrating Fifty Years of Excellence" read the bubble letters on the flatscreen that greeted Desiree and me inside the fake-marble-tiled lobby. The women milling about the premises were all slim and neatly put together, dressed in monochromatic business attire accessorized with identical thermoses and lanyards swinging from their necks.

While Desiree consulted with the receptionist, I hung to the side and pretended not to notice that more than a few of her sisters were eyeing me with wonder, subtly pointing and whispering among themselves.

In the cocktail lounge, a pianist was playing, of all songs, Toto's "Africa," which made me think of singing alongside Gabe at our a cappella outings. I started humming to the part about taking the time to do the things we never had.

"You're going to do *all* the things!" Desiree said, popping to my side and handing me a key card. "We'll settle into our rooms, but a few of my colleagues would like to meet you first." She waved over a trio of women. Two of them had matching tortoiseshell hair clips. The third wore a tank dress which showed off a pair of exquisite biceps. I'd recognize those arms anywhere. It was Juliet Simcott, the silver-hued shapeshifter from the boxing gym. I reflexively reached up and felt my nose. The bump was still there.

"We've been waiting for you." Juliet said, cupping my chin in her palm. Then she took her fellow sisters' hands and they broke out into a little incantation, leaving me to smile awkwardly.

"*Vita . . . Forte . . . Melior . . .*" they said.

"Your departure is imminent," Juliet intoned when the chanting was done. "Go relax. You'll need all your energy soon enough."

Desiree and I were staying in rooms opposite each other on the second floor. As we lingered in the hallway, she told me that there were a few things I needed to do before the ceremony. "You'll want to take a hot shower. But no scented toiletries. The residue can clog the portal." Desiree followed me into my room. "If you get peckish, stick to the fruit basket. Steer clear of the junk from the minibar. It will create interference."

Everything in the room was beige and clean. A painting of a desert landscape hung over the queen-size bed. I examined the contents of the bag that had been left for me on the duvet cover. Clean underwear, a water bottle, and a packet of dried fruit. "Your ceremony dress should be in the closet," Desiree told me.

I opened the closet door and found a long white gown hanging from a nonremovable hanger. The dress was ruffled on the bottom and had covered silk buttons up the back, not unlike what a beautiful Victorian ghost might wear to her wedding.

"The ceremony begins shortly before midnight. I'll leave you to get ready," Desiree said. A wistfulness came to her eyes. "Oh, Jenny. I think I'm going to miss you a wee bit."

37

• • • •

I SPENT THE NEXT FEW HOURS FLIPPING THROUGH TELEVISION CHAN-nels, trying to block out my thoughts and feelings. I was terri-fied, excited, and relieved. Finally, Desiree came for me.

"Are you ready to meet your destiny?" she asked when I opened the door. Standing before her in my gauzy white dress, I felt less like a woman seizing her destiny and more like a human sacrifice.

Desiree took me by the hand and led me onto the elevator. "This is it," she said portentously as the doors opened onto the lobby. "The end. And the beginning."

With great concentration, I walked down the diamond-patterned hallway carpet toward the Topaz Ballroom. I hadn't eaten anything more than a banana and a handful of prunes since my arrival in the Southwest. Between the hunger and the nerves, I felt weak, as if a blast of air-conditioning could blow me over.

All but a couple of the ballroom's seats were filled with Con-sortium members. They bowed their heads and rose to their feet when I came in. Desiree motioned with her chin for me to go to the stage. I noticed the beads of sweat on her brow. She was nervous, too.

Countless screens lined the walls of the room. They all displayed the same seven words.

> Resilience
> Enlightenment
> Achievement
> Change
> Happiness
> Unflappability
> Power

The column resulted in the anagram REACH UP. Seven magic values, like the words on a days-of-the-week underwear set. As I made my way toward the stage, I caught sight of a few familiar faces in the crowd. There were some celebrities as well as a few Coleman grads I recognized.

As everyone took their seats, I saw Keisha wipe tears from her eyes. I could feel how happy she was for me. I was finally getting the chance I'd always deserved. She and I would be united once again.

A trio of women wearing coordinating berets waited for me on the stage. They all possessed the proud and mighty posture of the spiritually enlightened.

At the center of the stage was a shiny metal contraption that looked like a miniature Airstream without wheels. Puffs of smoke emerged from one end. The door flung open, and out came Juliet Simcott. Over raucous applause she raised one finger in the air. The audience stood once again and began to hum. When their leader lowered her finger, the group sank back into their seats.

"Lighting, please?" Juliet intoned. The stage lights took on a blinding quality and the smoke emanating from the machine assumed the form of a purple cloud. "We've been waiting for you, Jenny. The one who got away," Juliet said, gazing at me tenderly. "And now I summon forth our soul sister Desiree LeBlanc. Desiree has worked diligently to bring Jenny back into the fold so that she can fulfill her potential."

My cosmic career counselor came to stand next to me with a closeness that was proprietary.

"Thank you," Desiree said, bowing her head to Juliet.

"Jenny Green, we can't tell you how grateful we are for your service," Juliet said. "We've learned so much from your journey, and we can only hope that your new life is as satisfying for you as manifesting it has been for us."

Valerie, Desiree's immediate supervisor, walked out from backstage, her black-helmet hair gleaming under the bright lights. I hadn't seen her since that time she screamed at me in her science lab for almost revealing to my friends that I had received the Memo. She was the one who'd sent a chandelier crashing down on my head to push me back through the wormhole after I almost blew my cover. But now, everything seemed to be copacetic between us. I had fixed my mistakes and was about to become a recurring source of revenue for the Consortium. She lifted her arms overhead and began chanting, the same rhythm and melody from the hotel lobby earlier in the day. The words drifted by like clouds. "*Vita . . . Forte . . . Melior . . .*"

The women in the room continued their chant, layering it in a round with harmonizing. It reminded me of a cappella, minus the lightheartedness. I was starting to feel like the star of a low-budget documentary on cults, but I smiled and went along with everything. On the other side of this ceremony was a dream husband, babies, financial success, and friendships built on strength, not neediness. This was my choice to make, not Geeta's.

"Ladies and gentlewomen," Desiree's voice cut through the ballroom, bringing the chant to an end. "We are here today to honor the thirty-sixth birthday of Jenny Green, who has spent this past week journeying into the possible, testing our theories, implementing our newest blitz-tracking techniques, and learning about the forces that really control the world. The data we have gathered during this trial will forever change the course of our research on the science of the soul."

The crowd applauded. "Friends who were able to join us tonight were wise enough to accept their Memos early in life and have been living by their direction ever since, reaching untold greatness," Desiree said.

"Jenny has been a tricky customer," she went on. "She made the mistake of turning us down back when we first approached her in college, but then—after realizing her mistake, or shall I say *mistakes*—she did something truly daring. Right before her complacency and laziness turned her into the paragon of mediocrity, the biggest failure on earth, she agreed to travel through the portal fueled by her own regret and shame, righting her wrong decisions and propelling herself to where the Memo had always wanted her to go—and just in the nick of time. Let's review, shall we?"

I tensed as a huge screen lowered from the ceiling and covered the wall behind the stage. It began displaying the horror film that was my life.

The first image was a younger me standing in front of a burning bakery, distraught and weeping while hysterical townspeople screamed at me in Italian.

"This moment was our subject's first branch point, the first, but certainly not the last decision that shook her confidence and led her from a life of promise to stunning failure," Desiree said. Ouch.

She clicked her remote, and the ballroom was treated to a succession of clips from my error-filled life. There I was, graduating from college, when I should have been meeting Alex in the Maldives. There I was, looking miserable in a ratty Snoopy T-shirt and ill-fitting shorts, answering the phones at my parents' accounting business. There I was, eating a muffin after it had fallen on the floor in an empty conference room at the radio station. Oh, and look over there, there I was with my then-fiancé Hal, who was explaining to me that he no longer believed in the "marriage industrial complex." The Jenny on the screen fought back tears and told him that she was so grateful to him for his honesty and transparency. Anything not to lose him.

"So given our time constraints," Desiree said, "our first destination naturally would be to fix the site of the subject's biggest disaster, where she would make a seemingly minor choice—putting on a certain pair of earrings in the morning—that would alter her trajectory. This tiny shift would allow her to be inside the bakery when the minor fire started—and extinguish it." Desiree clicked the remote again, and the guests cooed as they watched me put out the fire, the cameo earrings glinting in the Italian sunlight.

"The subject even got a bonus out of it," Desiree said, as a video of me wrapping my toned legs around Massimo's naked torso played out on the screen. This occasioned a great deal of cheering and whistles.

Click.

Now the assembled crowd was watching a late-twenties version of me locate a piece of sea glass on the beach in Costa Rica and look Alex Stone in his blue eyes.

"By contrast, here's how she spent her time at the wedding in the mediocre alternate life she is parting with."

The video showed me rolling around on the uneven floor of

a treehouse with Hal. My hair was flying this way and that and I was grunting like an overtaxed Labrador.

"Can we move it along here?" I asked meekly.

Desiree skipped through slides of Hal cheating on me with various women, many of whom I didn't recognize. Jenny the Pathetic could be seen trudging into work at the radio station and Alice's foundation, looking increasingly pale and drained of life and self-respect. The crowd made sympathetic murmurs. Why did I take so much crap for so long? Never again!

"I don't want to end that portion on a sour note," Desiree said, flipping to a photograph of Alex and me on our wedding day. I was as taut as a rope and leaning into his shoulder. I looked happy. He looked . . . catalogue-model gorgeous. We were perfect. The crowd agreed, to go by their swoons.

"Let's zoom in on the subject's career trajectory," Desiree said, advancing to footage from my festival interview with Sebastian Shapiro. I felt a stab of pride as I watched myself answer his question. Apparently I was helping a UN-appointed international botany group identify new edible flowers native to the Amazon that appeared to speed up metabolism, alleviate stress, and address economic inequity.

I watched my shiny-haired self stretch my arms across the back of the sofa. I looked like I was waiting for two lovers to come over and feed me grapes from either side. "I'm always thinking to myself, 'How can we innovate? What legacy systems can be disrupted here?'" power-posing me said to the celebrity intellectual.

Desiree winked at me. "And again," she addressed the crowd. "Here's what she was doing that same day in her ordinary unfortunate life."

Click.

We were treated to a scene from Geeta and Matt's wedding.

I began to feel ashamed as I watched the scene play out. There was my regular self, with my blah hair and blotchy skin, smiling like a madwoman and dancing the macarena with Geeta—until my heel snagged on a loose floorboard and I fell on my doughy ass.

Juliet smiled and stepped closer to me. "Ten minutes until showtime," she whispered, pointing at the red LED clock at the back of the ballroom. It said 11:50 p.m.

I inhaled deeply. I was about to be someone else, a better version of myself. Juliet wrapped her arms around me, her chin pressing into my shoulder. "Before we send you off," she murmured, "do you have any final words you'd like to share?"

I glanced up at the two hundred or so pairs of expectant eyes and scanned the crowd, some idiotic part of me still searching for Geeta. But of course she hadn't shown up. I was meeting her at her own level, and she couldn't stand it. I'd tried to help her. Now it was my time to shine.

"Sure," I said. Public speaking was never my forte, but there was something about knowing how soon my departure was that made it easier. "First of all, I'd like to thank you all for having me," I said, my voice gaining in volume. "Thanks to Juliet, Valerie, and the rest of Consortium. And"—now I realized I'd omitted the most important player—"especially thanks to the incomparable Desiree LeBlanc, who never gave up on me, and who always knew I had more potential than I'd ever realized.

"As we all know," I continued, "my life has been marked by indecision, often of the paralyzing variety. I long suspected I was a failure. The biggest failure in history, evidently. But I managed, thanks to the Consortium's valiant efforts, to find my way here. I will not be blocked by ambivalence anymore. I will no longer complain that I didn't get the Memo. Because I got my

Memo, and I am ready to follow it. Not just for me, but for the good of womankind!"

Over thunderous applause, Juliet approached the chamber that occupied center stage and opened its door. "Take a moment in there to reflect," she said. "When you are fully ready, you'll pull the lever. We will see you on the other side." She kissed my forehead. Her lips felt like paper.

The contraption was cryogenically cold and pitch dark inside, save for the red lever with a blinking light on top. I sat down on what felt like a velvet cushion—no doubt one of Desiree's decorative touches—and took a deep breath. This was the moment I'd been working toward. It was time to say goodbye. To the bad and the good. To the confusion. But I was still confused.

My old life had been a mess, but it had its pluses, didn't it? That treehouse sex with Hal was, no question, the best sex of my life. I'd loved Geeta, even though she never told me that she was following the Memo and that she didn't want me to follow it for some reason. I loved to sing, despite my musical limitations. I loved to bake, even though the passion had turned me into an inadvertent arsonist.

"Five minutes!" the crowd cried.

I thought about the look of delight on Gabe's face when he ripped off a piece of my focaccia. I thought about the unbridled joy of dancing at Geeta's wedding. Now I was heading to a destination where I couldn't even be bothered to show up for her. My throat tightened. Desiree insisted Geeta's motivation boiled down to her need to keep me from dipping a hand into her treasure chest. But . . . that didn't compute.

"Two minutes!" The crowd was roaring.

What's it going to be, Jenny? I asked myself, pressure building in my chest. *Old me or new me?*

Geeta always liked the old me. Leigh liked the new me, but it had helped that my rich husband bought her ugly art. My mom loved the new me to bits. Gabe liked me as I was, the only me he ever knew. But why did I care? He'd completely forgotten about me. Hal . . . why was I even giving Hal any thought? Our relationship was deader than dead, and I was delaying the inevitable.

On the other hand, there was Alex. The dream man who took note of my every mood swing, who catered to my every need, who looked at me like he'd never seen anything so beautiful. Alex who supported me and saw to it that I had the career and the Italian villa I'd always dreamed of. Then there were the two perfect children who were now waiting for me in my optimized life. Didn't I want to meet them? It was unlikely I'd ever get to be a mom in dead-end Pittsburgh.

Maybe I'd still have Sophie, but she was so young and cute and she'd probably get married, have kids, and become too busy to bother with the likes of me.

The crowd in the ballroom was now counting down seconds. Only sixty to go until I pulled the lever. Fifty-nine. Fifty-eight.

"You have nothing to fear, Jenny!" Desiree called from the outside. "She's hesitating! Fire up the live cam!"

There was a beeping sound. Now another screen revealed itself, unfolding from the ceiling like something out of an old-model airplane. "New York City" read the subtitle beneath a bird's-eye view of a cocktail party. The frame moved in closer. My friends were assembled at Alessandra's summer solstice gala, the one I was not invited to, the sort of event I would never be invited to if I didn't pull the lever.

They were in the MoMA sculpture garden close to midnight, still raging, drinking champagne, and eating what remained of the canapés. Allie was talking to an actress I recognized from an

HBO drama about drug cartels in 1970s Texas. Leigh was thrusting her hips in erotic figure eights, her body balanced on top of what looked like an enormous cast-iron ram. Geeta was standing in a corner and staring into space. She looked so sad. I had to remind myself to snap out of it: Geeta hadn't just lied to me all these years. She didn't want what was good for me, and if Desiree was to be believed, she had come here to try to yank me off the life track that I was due. Our days of codependency were long behind us, which was for the best.

"Ten, nine, eight, seven, six!"

Come on, Jenny, I told myself.

I had to go through with this. I had to go through with *something*. And it wasn't just for me. My collaboration with the Consortium was going to help womankind. I was but a droplet in the sea of possibility. I stood on the shoulders of giants. *Now or never, Jenny.*

I reached for the lever and tightened my grasp around the cold metal handle.

"Five! Four!"

Look, I told myself, *it's not like things are so great. What are you going to miss? You'll get used to your new life. You're popular there. Your mother loves you there!*

"Three!"

This is your chance, Jenny. You can catch up with everybody else. You will make your mom proud every single day for the rest of your life.

"Three! Two!"

A sense of spaciousness was opening inside me. I was crossing over to the other side. Finally.

"One!"

My stomach went light as my hand cramped around the lever and I pulled it toward me. My thoughts evaporated. I was gone.

But when I opened my eyes, the lever was still in neutral position. I was still in the metal chamber. And the screaming outside the contraption had taken a terrible turn.

"She failed to self-propel," I heard Valerie cry. "She overanalyzed and blew the deadline. Just like I told you she would."

My body went rigid. I was a Houdini trick gone terribly wrong. The world's biggest failure had failed again.

"We'll find another, more appropriate, subject," boomed Juliet's voice. "It is possible that our underlying assumptions were flawed. More experimentation is needed." The sounds of mayhem rose as somebody wrenched the door open. Several Consortium members were peering into the chamber, staring at me in abject horror.

"Eject her!" Juliet cried. "It's enough!"

I could feel the floor slide out from under me. I was in free fall, on a fast track to nowhere, grasping that cushion that had once connected me to the ground. Down, down, down I went, through a tunnel of blackness, barreling along like an elevator car plunging toward its destruction.

Then all movement ceased, and I was exactly where I'd started. Flat on my ass on the side of a road, just the tumbleweeds and me.

PART III

· · · · · · · · · · · · ·

MEMO-UNSUBSCRIBED

38

····

MANAGED TO HITCHHIKE TO THE NEAREST BUS STATION, A CORRU-
gated metal shack on the outskirts of Santa Fe. My ceremony
gown was caked in dust. A tote bag dangled limply from my elbow. In it, shockingly, were my wallet and phone. But the Memo
app had vanished. Only one text had come in, from 000–000:

> You're on your own, loser.

I had enough money in my checking account for a one-way
ticket back to Pittsburgh. After dozing on a bench in the bus station for a little over an hour, I boarded the bus and collapsed in a
row near the back. The upholstered seats smelled like stale milk.
I'd call Geeta as soon as I was alone, I strategized, as my eyelids
closed, heavy as weighted blankets.

As the bus wound its way through New Mexico's dark and
pitted flatlands, I drifted in and out of horrifying dreams, occasionally waking as we came to another stop. All I knew was that
I was now thirty-six, locked in my suboptimal existence, and

unable to do anything to rectify the mistakes I had made in the past. I had thrown away my one precious shot.

I drifted off again, only to be woken up by a familiar pinelike scent. I craned my neck back and looked over the rows of other passengers in various states of wakefulness. Now I saw that one passenger, her face covered in a light linen scarf, was coming to join me. She had a massive emerald ring on her middle finger, but the surrounding turquoise was gone. I stifled a gasp as Desiree slid into the seat next to mine. The aroma of her perfume overpowered the stale smell of the bus.

"Have you been here this whole time?" I asked.

She looked like she had aged ten years since I'd seen her gushing about me onstage. "I staked my entire career on you, Jenny." Her jaw was set in a tight lock. "There are consequences for failure, at least in the world I inhabit."

I couldn't tell if she was trying to shame me or just state the facts. Maybe both.

"I was excommunicated from the Consortium because of you."

"I'm sorry. I didn't try to mess things up for you, Desiree. But I couldn't do it. I tried."

"Not hard enough. You didn't want it. We cannot help you anymore, even if we wanted to—which we don't," Desiree said. "Why do I keep saying 'we'? Now it's 'they.'"

"I'm sure they will understand it wasn't your fault, eventually," I said hopefully.

"Oh, but it was. I nominated you," Desiree said. "Next time, if there is a next time, the Consortium will have to pick a subject who isn't quite as hopeless and error-prone."

"But you did get some promising data, right?" I said meekly. "Haven't I advanced the science of the study of the soul?" A woman seated across the aisle gave a dramatic clear of her throat, and I lowered my voice. "Haven't I proven that it is possible to fix your life retroactively?"

"You have proven the opposite," said Desiree. "You are the human embodiment of a null hypothesis."

As much as it stung, I was surprised by how much I didn't regret my decision, the decision I'd made in my heart before my mind even realized I'd made it. "You could have declined the program much earlier if you knew you weren't up to the task," Desiree tutted.

"I thought I was up to the task. I really did."

"You're going to have a lot of work to do, Jenny. You'll be busy enough for a lifetime dealing with all the disjunctions you have caused. Don't say I didn't warn you."

I gritted my teeth and leaned my head against the headrest. Somehow I managed to fall back to sleep. When I woke up again, the bus was still threading through barren landscape and Desiree was still sitting next to me.

"Can I ask you something?" I knew I was pushing my luck but this might be my last chance to get answers. I lowered my voice to a whisper. "You say your Memo is so great. But why did Geeta have to ride Levi's plane? Why was death . . . written for her?"

Desiree exhaled impatiently. "That part wasn't what was written. It was just a side effect."

"I don't follow."

"You know that the mortality rate is 2.6 times higher for the people we help."

"You never told me that."

"It was in the fine print. High rewards require high risks. Haven't you ever watched a documentary about the Kennedys?"

"And this never troubled you? These are your clients whose lives you're supposed to be improving, not destroying," I said. "And you know what else? I think that the 'tall-poppy syndrome' theory is total bullshit by the way." Desiree stiffened in her seat. "You don't believe in it either! Geeta was never threatened by the prospect of my success. You totally lied to me."

"I put my neck out for you," Desiree hissed. "I did everything I could to help you find happiness."

"No you didn't. Geeta did! She just knew that I had to achieve it authentically or I'd be miserable. She came to save me from making a huge mistake. She must have understood that I'd saved her from making one, too. And that's why you wanted her dead. So you could get credit for the Jenny Green experiment. She was your biggest obstacle."

"The two of you." Desiree shook her head. "You have no idea what you've both unleashed. No idea!"

I had no words. The bus wheezed to a stop in a rural town called Custer Springs. "This is me," Desiree said, rising in her pumps. "The first of many transfers to Sequoia Falls. It's not exactly a world-class destination, ergo not a highly traveled route. It's been tremendous reconnecting with you, Jenny." She shot a fake smile at me. "Enjoy the rest of your suboptimal life."

The driver announced that we'd be taking a ten-minute rest stop. His words roused most of my fellow bus riders, but I stayed put, and stared straight ahead. Finally, the remaining passengers returned to our vehicle and the front door heaved closed. Only when we inched toward the freeway did I allow myself to fully exhale. I turned toward the window. There was Desiree, standing stock still by the side of the road. Our eyes met, and she raised her middle finger mightily, her emerald ring glinting off the vehicle's rear beams.

39

MY NEW SEATMATE, AN ELDERLY MAN WHOSE NOSE WAS COVERED in crater-like pores, was trying to shift my head off his shoulder with his forehead. I bolted upright and looked out the window. A sour taste lingered in my mouth.

"I'm so sorry," I said.

I glanced at the rows behind me. There was no sign of Desiree. The bus was back to its stale smell.

"St. Louis," the driver announced as the vehicle headed onto an offramp. "We will depart thirty minutes after we park."

This time I got off the bus and went to a vending machine, where I bought a dry croissant and a cup of coffee that may as well have been petroleum. I was so ravenous I'd hardly snarfed my breakfast when I bought another disgusting croissant. An inauspicious start to my forever life.

An older woman with a peroxide pixie approached me.

"I don't want to intrude," she said in a baby whisper. "But I've been watching you. Are you escaping from a cult?"

I looked down. I was still wearing that ridiculous white dress, now covered in grime, a runaway bride.

I straightened my back. "No," I said, then realized her story would go down easier than the truth. "Well . . . yes. But I'm going to be okay, I think."

She nodded knowingly. "If you ever need to talk, or need any help," she said. "I'm up in the third row." She gave me a sad smile and walked away. It was a small kindness, a reminder that there were people in the world who really did care.

I leaned against the vending machine and thought back to that day in my senior year of college when Desiree advised me to drop out. The idea had seemed preposterous at the time, but now I knew that it was anything but. Dropping out of school and following the Memo would have led me down a different path, with unending days of travel, no worries about money or time lost to commuting or waiting on bosses. In that life, there were only beautiful homes, charmed friends, a perfect body.

But who cared? I was on the side where I belonged. The one where I didn't need to lose Geeta or Gabe, or sacrifice the earthly delights of a warm loaf of bread. Now I could eat all the gluten I desired. I could stop listening to my mom and all the other people who wanted me to be an airbrushed version of myself. I could focus on the things and the people worth my time, the people who saw me for who I really was. I could stop being so mean to myself.

I reached for my phone to call Geeta and was so relieved when her number showed up in my contacts. I wasn't blocked! But my call went right to voicemail, and her mailbox was full. I took a bracing breath and reminded myself we had all the time in the world.

As I walked back toward the gate, it occurred to me that I should check in with Hal. He was probably worried, since I had disappeared on my birthday and all. I tried to call him. Strangely, his number was no longer in my phone. Maybe it wasn't so strange. Desiree had warned me that the disjunctions stemming from my obstinacy were going to be off the charts.

I scrolled through my contacts like a cosmic explorer looking for new life forms on an alien planet. No Alice. No Leigh. And, of course, no Gabe. There were untold unfamiliar names, along with my parents and my brother. I spotted Sophie's name and felt a rush of relief. I called her. She didn't answer her phone either, but her energetic voice was on the recording.

"Hey Soph, it's me Jenny. I'm on a Greyhound bus—long story—but I should be back in Pittsburgh tomorrow. Give me a call when you can and I'll try to explain. Let's just say that my college reunion led me down an unusual path. Hope everything's all right with you."

I climbed onto the bus and took my seat again. The sky was dotted with cottony clouds, and the plains stretched out before me, vast and open.

40

PITTSBURGH
JUNE 17, 2022, 8:49 A.M.
AGE: 36

BY THE TIME WE PULLED INTO PITTSBURGH, I HAD A BETTER SENSE OF the life that awaited me. My phone reception had gone in and out over the course of the journey, and thanks to the Internet, I'd been able to more or less piece together where things stood in this new and final universe.

Geeta was here but not here. More specifically, she was at the Clinton Hills Correctional Facility for Women. A *Washington Post* article with the headline "Geeta Brara: From Silicon Valley Darling to Disgraced CEO" had filled me in. Now I knew more than I wanted to. My most recent actions had altered the cosmic equation, and so had hers.

Desiree had been right about one thing: Geeta had tried to interfere with my optimization. She hadn't wanted me to cross over, but for reasons that I could only imagine were good. Now Geeta was paying the price for messing with the all-mighty Memo.

According to the newspaper coverage, Geeta had been pressured by investors to fudge her company's numbers and to give the impression that she had contracts with some of the biggest firms in the country when, in fact, the contracts had yet to be signed. She lied about having 100 percent penetration in the Luxembourg market. She lied about having a deal with the American Psychiatric Association. She lied about having a PhD from Stanford.

Silicon Valley was bloated with grifters, but my best friend was the one who was going to take the fall for the outsized expectations of an entire industry. To make matters worse, her affair with the late Levi Fischer was all over the tabloids for the world to see.

Matt filed for divorce, and his close friends gave an interview to a gossip rag stating that he was "shocked" and "heartbroken." Matt blamed a covert influence campaign from a shady consortium of illuminati for his ex-wife's crimes. In this one instance, he wasn't wrong.

A Reddit board was devoted to Geeta Brara Halloween costumes (clip-on baby bangs, monochromatic earth-toned ensembles, and Gen-Zen branded water bottles). Some pundits wondered why a woman should have to be the fall gal when so many men behaved even more badly. Others felt that hers was just the first of a wave of similar cases that would bring equality and justice for all.

Geeta was held up as a symbol of the hypocrisy of wellness and hustle culture. But what Geeta had to go through was anything but symbolic. She'd pleaded guilty to one count of fraud, and her company filed for bankruptcy. She no longer had Levi to distract her or Matt to indulge her every whim. Suddenly, she was a single mother of baby twins and had huge fines to pay. It seemed she was midway through serving what had been described in the press as an "unusually lenient" four-month sentence at a state prison located less than an hour from our alma mater.

I walked from the station back to my building, my heart heavy as I pictured Geeta locked in a cell.

Pittsburgh was eerily quiet at this time of day. Fog hung over the rolling hills. I thought about Geeta's twins. Luna and Maya were too young to understand what was going on, but they'd know that their mother wasn't with them. What would happen when they got older and learned about her crimes? I'd have to talk to Matt, get to New York, and work extra hard to help get them through this difficult period, if Geeta still wanted me to be the girls' guide mother, that is. Who knew anything anymore?

I passed by a day care center and a mom-and-pop hardware store, then an empty bodega with a note in the window that looked like it was composed in a rush: "To our loyal customers: After 25 years in Pittsburgh, we're moving to California to live near our grandchildren." That seemed as good a reason as any. Something compelled me to press my forehead against the plate glass. As my eyes adjusted to the darkness, I marveled at the tin ceiling and the black-and-white hexagonal floor tiles. The shop was too charming a space to sit empty for long, I thought with a swell of hopefulness. And then I kept walking.

Soon enough, I was back at my apartment complex. I got into the elevator, rode up to the seventh floor and put my key into the door. It didn't work. I tried to wiggle it, but it didn't fit. I tried again. No dice. Was I locked out? Was this a repeat of what happened on Spruce Street, a function of the many disjunctions I had unleashed? I knocked furiously on the door. "Hal!" I cried out. "Hal?"

I was relieved when I saw his sleepy face. But he wasn't at my door. He was coming out of Brie's apartment. Behind him came a bed-headed Brie, followed by her dog, who gave a yapping bark.

"Is everything okay?" Brie draped her arm over her head and stood there in slinky silk shorts and a camisole. "We've never really had a chance to talk. I'm Brie."

"Nice to, uh, meet you," I said. "Jenny."

"I know, obviously," she said, looking at Hal.

Her awkward body language seemed to indicate that I was a random woman who happened to live in the compound but wasn't a part of their lives. I was part of Hal's past, now a neighbor they tried their best to avoid. An odd feeling washed over me.

"I'm so sorry for bothering you," I said, feeling the blood drain from my cheeks. "I got confused. Late night."

"Are you all right, Jen?" Hal asked. "You look like you're coming down from some awful kind of trip. No judgment but—"

"I'm just, you know, adjusting to our new reality," I said.

"If you need your key, the doorman keeps extras," Brie said.

"Right." I was unable to move my feet. It was dawning on me what had happened: Our paths kept crossing—when she saw me in the city after my doctor's appointment, and then again at the party in San Francisco. We were somehow destined to be in each other's worlds. Now we had been cosmically swapped—a karmic punishment from the Consortium that turned out to be a gift I never knew I needed.

Ten minutes later, my spare key obtained from the doorman, I opened the door to Hal's and my old apartment—now my apartment. I saw the same half dozen hooks still hung on the wall by the buzzer, and in the kitchen, the same butcher block island and the same beautiful oven.

The biggest difference was the sleeping bag smack dab in the middle of the living room floor. I recognized the ombré hair poking out of the top.

Sophie propped herself up on an elbow. She looked at me, her eyes widening. "Where have you been?" she asked.

"Santa Fe," I replied. "Oklahoma, Kansas, Missouri, too. I was doing some . . . soul searching."

"Okaaaaaay," she said. "You have been acting very peculiar lately."

"I know. I am figuring things out. Finally. What are you doing here?"

"You gave me a key. Duh." Sophie watched me nod. "You told me to come if I ever felt like I was in danger. And Roger has been calling me a lot. I was worried he'd come to my place like he did the last time."

I felt a flutter of happiness. Sophie wasn't back together with Roger. And I, in some small way, had summoned her here, on my floor, where she was free to pick herself up and launch herself toward her dreams whenever she was ready.

"Why are you smiling like that?" Sophie asked.

"Sorry," I said, forcing my face into a more sober expression. "Your hair is sticking up like a chicken," I lied.

"Like you're one to talk. That dress is something. And you look like Courtney Love after a rager."

"Impressive retro reference," I said.

Sophie smoothed her amazing hair and went on, "I didn't want to sleep in your bed because you left me that weird message about being on your way home. I tried calling but I couldn't reach you."

My shoulders hitched up closer to my ears as I tried to think of what to tell her. "Sorry, the phone reception was terrible."

She stared at me. "It's 2022, not the Stone Age."

"It's been a long, strange trip," I said.

"Evidently." She did that thing where she half-rolled her eyes and half-smiled.

"Can I ask you something?" I said, and tried to figure out a way to say what I was wondering about without giving too much away. "When was the last time you saw Alice?"

Sophie laughed. "You mean after she shut down the foundation to become a venture capitalist-slash-life coach? Never. Why do you ask?"

"Oh, I was just wondering," I said, relief flooding through me. We'd moved on from Alice, Sophie and I.

"Why are you asking?" Sophie pressed.

"I thought I saw her on my way over here," I lied.

"Well that would be weird. Considering that according to Instagram she is in Bali," Sophie said. "Okay, as much as I want to take a picture of you in this state, I'll let you shower first."

"Thanks, Soph." I could only imagine how disgusting I looked. I hadn't dared to glance at my reflection since a rest stop in St. Louis, when I'd seen a horrific mophead staring back at me in the mirror. I set my bag down on top of a chair and headed toward the kitchen.

I found a glass in the cabinet above the sink. I was midway through filling it when I noticed the bowl that Geeta had given me for my wedding present sitting on the counter. The last time I'd seen it had been in Alex's and my apartment.

The bowl was so delicate and beautiful, like the oatmeal lace cookies that my grandmother and I used to bake together when I was a little girl. Disjunctions, but the good kind. There was a postcard inside. I turned off the tap and picked it up. It was postmarked from Clinton Hills, New York. The message was to the point, written in Geeta's scrawl:

Find me.

41
····

CLINTON HILLS CORRECTIONAL FACILITY FOR WOMEN
CLINTON HILLS, NEW YORK
JUNE 20, 2022
AGE: 36

VISITING DAY WAS ON THURSDAY. I BORROWED SOPHIE'S CAR, A CUTE
little Prius. The dilapidated Honda I had previously shared
with Hal was still in the same parking spot, but no longer mine
to captain.

The route was almost identical to the one I had traveled
when I'd been heading to my reunion, feeling awash in shame
and self-pity. Now I was surprisingly calm. For the first time in
my entire life, I could accept my mistakes. They'd delivered me
to this moment, after all.

Geeta's mistakes felt similarly loaded with meaning and
possibility. I was hopeful that she would see this as some kind of
cleansing, a much-needed reset.

As I was merging onto Route 17, my mother called, just as she
had when I was driving to the reunion. This time I wasn't tempted
to press the "decline" button.

"Mom!" I said.

"What's that noise?" she shot back.

"I'm driving."

"Why are you talking and driving?"

"It's okay, mom. I'm all buckled in. You're on speaker."

"Where are you going? A job interview?"

"I'm going to prison."

"That's nice." I could detect a trace of humor in her voice.

"I'm going to visit Geeta."

"That poor girl flew too close to the sun," she said, clicking her tongue, not realizing how right she was or how it also applied to her own daughter. "What happened to her? She always seemed to make all the right moves."

"I guess I'll find out more when I see her."

My mom sighed loudly. "You're a good friend, but you should really focus on yourself, Jenny. You still have a lot to work out. How's that resumé coming along?"

Resisting the urge to react, I made myself remember how things had felt with my mom in the other realm. We'd been closer, comfortable in each other's presence. Back there, I wasn't a bundle of nerves around my mom. Wasn't there a chance we could achieve something like that here, too?

"I'm finally getting things together, mom," I said. "And I was thinking I might come visit you while I still have the free time. We can take a walk on the beach, hunt for seashells like we used to, and chat."

"The beach, you and me? Is something wrong?" My mom was dragging her words in a way that implied that I sounded crazy.

"I'm craving a mother-daughter weekend. And they don't have Long Island beaches in Pittsburgh."

"I guess they don't." My mom chuckled. "Let me know when you're thinking, and I'll get your bed ready."

When I hung up, I wiped my eyes and swerved to avoid an overly enthusiastic lane changer. My heart was thumping inside my chest as I narrowly averted a collision. My mom wasn't wrong about everything. I shouldn't be talking on the phone while driving.

The closest I'd ever come to paying a visit to an inmate was listening to true crime podcasts on my morning commutes. They'd prepared me for the basics: The metal detectors, the pre-meeting pat down, and the myriad rules, the clanging of cells opening and closing. No screaming, no hugging, no contraband. I knew better than to try to smuggle in a loaf of bread, but I did sneak a tiny bag of rosemary crackers—Geeta's favorite—in the pocket of my sweatshirt dress.

I registered with the guard at the front desk, who led me into the visitors area. The space looked cleaner than what I had imagined, but also felt surreal. How was this even possible? Geeta, the most conscientious person I ever met, had defrauded her investors to the tune of tens of millions of dollars. And she got caught. She was paying the price. But she hadn't boarded that plane with Levi. She was still alive. The rest didn't matter.

As I waited in the visiting area, I kept my eyes on the floor and tried not to eavesdrop on the meetings taking place around me. A mother-son duo was talking about a family dog. A pregnant teenager was pleading with her boyfriend.

Then an officer announced Geeta's name. She shuffled into the room, her handcuffs clanking. Her bangs were now down to her eyebrows and she looked even smaller than usual. Soon, though, I couldn't see much at all, given the tears flooding my eyes. She was crying too, and it took a little while for us to collect ourselves. "I've been thinking a lot," she said. "It's all falling into place."

"Same," I said.

Something about the way Geeta was looking at me told me all that I needed to know. She knew about everything that had happened, and everything that hadn't happened, in all its layered madness.

"You saved my life. In so many ways," she said.

She didn't get on Levi's plane that day because she had heard what I was trying to tell her. And she'd listened. She was finally free of the Memo. I was stunned.

"I want to thank you too," I said at last. "You believed in me. You trusted that I was . . . enough."

All those negative energy shockwaves—the jealousy, the regret, the sadness—that fueled my journeys through the unstable wormhole to fix my broken life had endangered our friendship. It wasn't just a matter of Player As or Player Bs. Our connection couldn't exist in the world scripted by the Memo. My rise had somehow caused her fall. "Thank you for sticking your neck out for me." She inhaled deeply and glanced around the room.

"Look where it got you," I said.

She cast her eyes down at her hands. "I kind of owed you."

"But you could have left me alone. I wasn't going to die in a plane crash—I was just going to drink dirt-flavored smoothies, swear off gluten, have babies with a handsome billionaire, and trample on some nuns in Tuscany."

"You would have hated it. Even more than I did."

"You hated it?" She deflected my question with a shrug. "But how were you so sure I would too?"

"I know you, Jenny."

"It goes both ways," I said, slipping a rosemary cracker under the table. Geeta took a stealthy bite.

"Now that's what I call a banger," she said.

"I added a bit of cinnamon to balance out the flavors," I told her.

"See? You were always innovating. It's in your DNA. You never needed a—" she looked around and mouthed the word, "Memo."

"But why didn't you ever say anything—about what you were going through?"

"I tried." Her eyes widened. "Did you not read the postcards I have been sending you since the beginning of time? I was trying to let you know how trapped I felt, how empty it all was."

I thought back to those messages she had written me when I was in Italy, about how she wasn't like me, she couldn't just quit her job and find something else. How she had to endure, push through. "I'm a slow learner," she said. "Now I know what you have always known: freedom is priceless."

"And because of me, you have no freedom," I said, my eyes welling up again.

"This," she said looking around the correctional facility's visitors' room, "is temporary. It's fine. Being here is like staying at a really intense, super austere meditation retreat. I have lots of time to reflect."

"Come on," I said.

"The food is inedible. Some—okay, most—of the other women are quite intimidating. Being apart from my girls is just . . ." Her chin was starting to tremble. "But . . . I'm alive."

I reached out to hold her hand.

"This is all temporary," she said. "I've had a lot of time to think things over. And I've made some big decisions."

"Such as?" I asked.

Her eyes twinkled. "I'm going to move to Pittsburgh when I get out of here."

No way. "*My* Pittsburgh?"

"Why not? That's where my best friend is, isn't it? Matt will too. Matt and I might not be together anymore, but he's an amazing dad, and we respect each other despite everything."

"You two were always so different."

She squeezed my hand. "I had to marry him," she said. "It was written."

"Right. I figured. Tell me this though. Did you ever love him?"

Geeta raised her shoulders in a shrug. "At first, yes. We were young. Which is what made everything so confusing for me. And I was a believer. Following the program fed into everything I always wanted. But then I had doubts and . . . then I had more doubts . . ." She sighed.

"I understand," I said. "It must have been horrible, putting on a front."

"I had my coping mechanisms. And thanks to being with him, I have my girls. And I learned a lot about chemtrails!"

I tried not to laugh.

"It's not going to be contentious," she said. "We're all grown-ups here, and the girls come first. Matt and I are dotingly detaching."

"Dotingly detaching," I repeated. "Is this part of the reboot? Geeta Brara rebranded as divorce-fluencer?"

She looked at me like I was crazy. "There is no reboot. There's no boot. No shoe! It's over. We're onto the next, all of us. Even Leigh, if you believe it."

"What? She gave up on her Memo too?" Geeta shot me a warning look. "Sorry," I said quietly. "But what happened to Leigh?"

Geeta shook her head and began speaking in a whisper. "She's still on board. I don't think that's ever going to change. But she's in another program: rehab!"

"Really?" I was shocked. "What happened?"

"She cut a little too loose at Alessandra's summer solstice gala." I remembered the party footage I'd seen inside the Consortium's transition chamber. Leigh had been acting extra, well extra, that night, dancing like a dervish on top of a cast-iron ram.

"When did she ever not do that?"

"Yeah, but Leigh was selling Molly to a trustee's daughter, and the girl freaked out and had to go to the ER. She was okay in the end but the parents are big-time collectors and started a smear campaign. Leigh's gallerist dropped her. Nobody else would take her on. She hit a real low."

"That's . . . terrible," I said.

"It's for the best," Geeta said. "Those celebrity vulva sculptures and influencer collabs were getting tired. I think she'll come to value this time out. A moment to regroup. I believe in her."

"You're good at that," I said. "Believing in people."

"Leigh is not that complicated when it comes to her motivations, but she's got talent. And she really misses you, Jenny."

"Okay, now you're believing in nonsense."

"I'm serious. You'll see soon enough. I hope you'll give her a chance. Is it possible you let your insecurities cloud your feelings about her?"

"I don't think that's what it was."

Geeta cocked her head. "Not even a little?"

"Maybe a little," I allowed. I thought about how happy Leigh was when I attended her art opening in my alternate existence, and how good it felt to correct my selfish mistake and show up for my old friend.

Geeta gave a satisfied nod. "What about you, Jenny? Now what?"

"I've been thinking," I said tenuously. Geeta made the go-on gesture with her hand. "This may sound ridiculous, but I can't stop thinking about it. There's a storefront in Pittsburgh, by the bus station. It used to be a bodega, and it has the most beautiful details—these ceiling tiles and moldings. It's just sitting there, empty."

Geeta's smile was a ray of light. "Empty for now."

"I know Pittsburgh doesn't exactly need another bakery," I said.

"It definitely doesn't," she replied. "So you'll show them what you've got and put the losers out of business." She winced. "Sorry, the destroy-the-competition mindset is a hard thing to shake off. Bear with me."

I looked at Geeta in her orange jumpsuit. She had on just one friendship bracelet, a thin red strand with a gold bead that I had given her a long time ago.

"What about funding?" Geeta said.

"None to speak of . . . yet. But I learned a thing or two working at Alice's foundation. I'm going to put my fundraising chops to work. I know who to ask."

"You already have my buy-in. My emotional buy-in," Geeta clarified. "I am dead-ass broke."

I bit down a smile. "Emotional buy-in is the best kind of buy-in. I don't need, like, major money. I just need to sign a lease and get some decent flour and yeast. I guess an oven would be good too. But it shouldn't be too outrageous."

"No, you're wrong. It absolutely should."

"Ever the hype beast."

"You know it."

We looked at each other, searching for the words. Everything was simultaneously wonderful and terrible. And here we were, riding it out together.

When it was time for the guard to escort my friend out of the visiting area, I vowed to come back the following week. But Geeta said no. She would be out soon enough, and she wanted me to focus on my project in the interim.

"One of us needs to make a living," she said. "And I want warm baguettes with salted butter the second I get out of this place."

I wasn't ready to turn around and head straight back to Pittsburgh. Sequoia Falls was only another thirty minutes away, just a slight detour. There was one last item to cross off my to-do list.

I stopped for lunch at Just a Peck, a local tapas joint, and ordered a mezze platter with warm pita bread. My friends and I used to come here to celebrate birthdays. It was where I'd ordered my first legal glass of wine as a twenty-one-year-old. So I couldn't help but get a glass of local Riesling, which I raised in the air, and make a quiet toast to Geeta. "To freedom," I whispered. I took a gulp, then dragged a triangle of pita through a pool of olive hummus. I needed some sustenance for my next plan.

The restaurant was only a few blocks from campus, so I left Sophie's Prius in the small parking lot and I wandered through the arts quad, winding my way through the paths I had traversed at our reunion. Then I found myself standing in front of the Simcott Center for the Study of the Soul. Staring up at the modern slab jutting out from its neoclassical foundation, I couldn't help wondering if the team was inside, performing experiments on some new subject who was a little less of a stubborn failure than I was.

I thought about all the young women who had gotten their Memos and had run with them. The army of supposedly lucky ones, the women who'd surrendered their lives and a sizable portion of their net worth to the Consortium and its ethos of optimization. To what end? Keisha, my roommate who just wanted to be a local veterinarian, but who was now chief scientist of a pharmaceutical behemoth. Leigh, in rehab after running too fast with an even faster crowd. Geeta, who'd revolted too late and was in prison.

We were all complicit in a broken system, even those of us who'd had the courage to walk away from it. We let it get to us, which meant we were all, to some degree, participants in a society that valued perfection at all costs. Everything always had to be an improvement on something else. You weren't making the grade unless you went in for an upgrade. Or you could hate the system, which so often meant hating yourself for failing to navigate it. And to think the Consortium called themselves feminists.

Suddenly, somebody on a motorcycle swept around the front of the building. "Please keep moving," the man said.

I hesitated, taking in one last glance at the mother ship, then walked away. That's when I heard a familiar voice that stopped me in my tracks. Desiree had come out of the center's side door. Her face looked sallow, her hair was unkempt, and her pantsuit was wrinkled. Evidently the Consortium had taken her back into its fold in some capacity, but she was a mess. She appeared to be about to say something to me, then thought better of it. "Don't pay her any mind," she said to the guard. "She's an utter nobody."

"It's true," I said, my tone probably too joyous for her liking. I was a nobody. And perhaps that was my greatest achievement of all.

42

• • • •

SEPTEMBER 2022
PITTSBURGH
AGE: 36

HYPE YEAST OPENED FOR BUSINESS ON LABOR DAY. AND THE CITI-zens of Pittsburgh were eager to check out their city's newest culinary offering. From the moment we opened, there was often a line out the door, which was pleasantly surprising. Hal and Brie were regulars—they still shunned gluten but enjoyed our matcha lattes—as did an assortment of other dog walkers, business executives, high-school kids, and carb-cravers of western Pennsylvania. My business was off to a great start.

We were a skeleton crew in the beginning. Geeta, who was living with me while writing her memoir, tentatively titled *Crime, Punishment, and Relaxation*, helped run the cash register and told anyone who would listen that she had named the bakery and designed our logo. With its simple geometric font, Hype Yeast looked like it had always existed in the world. Branding was always Geeta's strong suit. The media was fascinated with her presence at this low-key establishment in the middle of this small city.

Despite her fame, she had shunned national outlets but gave an interview to the *Pittsburgh Post-Gazette* stating that she was just the first example in my overarching mission of hiring formerly incarcerated women. As our sales increased, I doubled down and hired more women, offering them good pay and benefits. I was finally supporting women in a tangible way instead of organizing Father's Day parade parties and convincing myself that these efforts would somehow narrow the gender gap.

Sophie was busy working two phones documenting our activities, since one of her main responsibilities was running all of the @hypeyeastbaked social media accounts. By the time we had been open a couple of weeks, we already had more than 1,500 followers, including a couple of assistant editors at food magazines. The Crave, my favorite foodie website, published a profile of me with the following headline: "Jenny Green Once Burned Down a Bakery. Now She Owns One."

Ugly breads were our specialty. Sophie had done the research and identified the rising aesthetic of *jolie laide*—the French phrase describing an unconventionally attractive woman—baked goods. Our product was messy, imperfectly perfect. We weren't a factory. We were artisanal, like the bakery I had nearly destroyed, except we were on fire in a different way. By our third Saturday in business, we'd sold out of everything but the buckwheat croissants by noon.

"I could have told you that would happen," Geeta said after closing. She was reviewing a stack of credit card receipts.

"I know, I know," I said. "I always forget how much the world hates buckwheat."

I was wiping down the top of a marble table I'd salvaged from a yard sale, my arm moving in rhythm with the Counting Crows piping through our speaker system. Now that we were closed for business, my friends had allowed me to switch from the tasteful playlist that Sophie had made to all the bad rock ballads I missed singing with the Looney Tunes. (I hadn't been to practice since

I had returned from Santa Fe due to my busy work schedule, but fully intended to resume attending once things calmed down.)

Geeta balled up a damp dishrag and threw it at me. "That's not what I meant, Jenny. I meant that I always knew you could do it. You just needed to believe in your own power."

"Oh yeah—that," I said with a laugh.

"I never said it was easy. But it was possible. And you did it."

I cocked my head. "We did. And I'm still a work in progress."

"Who isn't?" Geeta asked.

She was right. Even Leigh, the most impenetrable member of our triad, had vulnerabilities to overcome. After her stay at a rehab center, she was working hard on her recovery as well as her comeback. She was making amends, part of which involved checking in on me on a regular basis. She was also putting in the hours in her studio, and had found an emerging art gallery to represent her. And she was painting landscapes again.

The one holdover was her Memo, the one thing she'd never let go of. And I didn't begrudge her that. We were each doing our own thing, going our own ways, but friends. Imagine that! All those years, I'd told myself that Leigh had changed, as if that was a bad thing. Of course she'd changed. We'd all seen some wear and tear. Underneath the surface, she was still the charismatic painter and crew-team member I'd befriended our sophomore year. Leigh and I were back in touch—in a real way, one where I wasn't just making excuses and keeping her at arm's length because I was too jealous.

When Leigh came to Pittsburgh for a meeting she had with a big collector—Alice's cousin, as it happened—she stopped by the bakery and offered her characteristically bold opinion: "Finally, Jenny, you are getting your act together. Promise me you're going to do something about the lighting in this place, though." A few days later she sent me an email with lighting recommendations at various price points. Thanks to Leigh, a bright red fixture now hung above the cash register.

As for Alice, she was busy crafting her own new identity following the dissolution of the Aurora Foundation. Despite her complaints about our incompetence, she was lost without my fundraising expertise or Sophie's social-media savvy. Once she returned from her extended trip to Bali, Alice decided to invest in one of the foundation's early grant recipients, an entrepreneur who wanted to save the planet by eliminating disposable baby wipes from the marketplace. According to the website for Tender Biddles, which made portable bidets for toddlers, Alice was a vice president.

Sophie and I were torn about whether we should personally invite Alice to our own new venture. Ultimately, we decided not to. She could find it on her own. Our days managing the many moods of Alice felt so long ago. I sighed in relief and grabbed another dish rag.

When I'd cleaned down all the tables, I took a seat on the reclaimed church bench that Sophie and I had sanded and refinished, and allowed myself to enjoy a milky iced coffee. I reached into the bookshelf containing a lending library for our customers and pulled out the first thing my fingers touched. I smiled when I saw what it was: *Stacey Plunkett Gets a Life*, the book that Gabe had lent to me that fateful night when I had just found out that I didn't get the Memo.

Before I could decide whether to re-shelve the book or crack it open, I heard the jingle of the bell affixed to the door.

"We're clo—" I started, pointing to the sign that stated that fact in no ambiguous terms. But when I saw who had come to check out the bakery I felt the blood rush to my face. It was as if I'd summoned Gabe by touching his book. There he was, accompanied by Ramona. She was dressed in purple leggings with stars and an I Heart Tacos T-shirt. I cringed, half expecting them to be struck by lightning or get sucked into the oven. But they remained intact.

"Really?" Gabe sounded more amused than defeated. "We're just blowing it left and right today, aren't we kiddo?" He squeezed his daughter's shoulder. "We just showed up for a birthday party a week too early," he blurted to me. I remembered how much I loved his random declarations.

"At least you didn't miss it," I said.

"And now we're barging in on you," Gabe said.

"It's okay. What can we get for you?" Geeta asked. Then she gave me a funny look and motioned to her cheek. I quickly wiped away a crumb on my face.

"Your timing is perfect, really," I said, still in disbelief that this was happening. "There's no line anymore."

"Do I know you from somewhere?" Gabe asked.

"Maybe?" I said. No matter how much I'd thought about him, I still hadn't seen him since my return from Santa Fe. "I have a familiar face." I could feel my heart rate quickening. I had to look away.

I turned to Ramona and smiled. "Hi," I said. "We don't have much left, but would you like a buckwheat croissant? They might not look perfect, but there are gobs of honey inside."

"Sounds delicious," her father said.

"Thank you." Ramona seemed shy, and sweet too. I'd heard so much about her, and seen her across park paths and Los Angeles traffic, but this was our first actual meeting.

"I'm Jenny," I said, handing her the treat. "And let me guess your name."

She raised her eyebrows.

"Are you . . . Raven?" The girl took a bite and shook her head.

I waved my fingers as if I was feeling the vibes of the universe. "I think it starts with *R*."

"Very good," Gabe said.

"Rapun— Never mind, that's not it . . . Rebecca, no that's not it either. Is it . . . Ramona?"

Gabe looked at me with astonishment. Geeta and Sophie were staring at me too.

"Well done. And I'm Gabe," he said.

"I'm Jenny," I told him.

"Right. You mentioned. And I read about you. We've been wanting to come here for a while to see what all the fuss was about."

"Do you two live around here?" I asked.

Gabe shook his head. "It's a bit of a hike. Ramona's mom is traveling with her husband this weekend, so I thought I'd do something exotic, take the kid to a new neighborhood. I love all forms of bread."

I could barely concentrate beyond one word. Did he say *husband*?

"They're in Iceland," Ramona said, her lips covered in flaky crumbs. "They have unicorns there."

"Lucky them. I don't have unicorns here, but I have something else you might like," I said, proffering the paperback that I'd promised to hand over to Ramona once-upon-a-pub outing.

"*Stacey Plunkett Gets a Life*," Gabe said, tilting his head to study the cover. "'A powerful tale of personal awakening—with a side of crinkle-cut fries.'" I could tell that something was happening inside of him, a blast of déjà vu tugging at him. "Thanks so much. We have a little collection of old paperbacks at home."

"It's a lesser-known classic," I said. "A friend once gave it to me and now I'm paying it forward."

"Well, thank you," Gabe said, taking the book and smiling. "We'll let you know how it was. We'll be back."

When the door jingled shut, Sophie looked up from her phone. "What the hell was that all about?"

"Yeah," Geeta said. "What's the deal? I could practically hear your ovaries singing."

I considered this for a second. I'd had enough intervention with my ovaries, but my heart was bursting—and not only for Gabe. Seeing Ramona again had pricked me with a sense of possibility. I wanted to get to know this quirky kid, be there for her. I was getting ahead of myself, but I couldn't deny that I'd felt a strange connection.

Maybe it had something to do with the renewed warmth I'd been feeling for my own mother. She was back to her old loving self, sending me novelty pajama sets she found at Target and calling me, not with an agenda, but because she just wanted to chitchat with her daughter. I needed to let go of the past and meet my mom where she was. I was trying, and it was making a difference. My mom had recently told me she'd been feeling blue. She never used to open up to me like that.

"Shhh," Sophie hissed, plastering on a smile. The door was opening again, and Gabe took a step toward me. I looked into his blue eyes and felt my heart bump.

"Listen, Jenny?" he said. "I just took a bite of Ramona's croissant and . . . I wanted to offer my compliments to the chef."

"Compliments are warmly accepted," I said.

"And . . . I should probably figure out a way to email you or something but . . ." He stood before me, ready to take his shot. "Would you possibly want to get a drink sometime?"

I could feel the smile stretching across my face. "A drink?"

Gabe took half a step back. I glanced through the window at

the girl waiting outside. Ramona and I exchanged a secret smile before I looked back up at her father. "Or not!" he said awkwardly.

"No, no," I replied, "a drink sounds great."

"Really?" He appeared to be confused as to what to say next. Maybe he wasn't expecting a yes. "There's this place I know that's sort of cheesy but it's also kind of fun—"

"Desmond's Tavern?" I jumped in.

Gabe's face lit up. "You know it?"

"Yeah, I've been there," I said. "I've been meaning to go back."

Acknowledgments

WE ARE PROFOUNDLY GRATEFUL TO FRIENDS AND FAMILY MEMBERS who read early drafts and provided thoughtful feedback and encouragement. Huge thanks to Pooja Bhatia, Dana Chieco, Grace Farris, Donna Freitas, Ben Greenman, Mia Levitin, Sharon Mechling, Laura Moser, Allie Valasek, Stephanie von Behr, and Lynn Weingarten.

Big ups to Rebecca Soffer, who connected us with Gráinne Fox and her talented colleagues Kelly Karczewski, Melissa Chinchillo, and Maddy Hernick. Thank you all for making difficult things seem easy.

Sarah Stein, thank you for bringing us into your stable and looking after us with such smarts, passion, and care. You are a dream editor. Heather Drucker, Lisa Erickson, David Howe, and all the other folks at Harper who have made the publication process as frictionless as possible, you have our enduring admiration.

We are in awe of Hillary Zaitz-Michael, who read an extremely early outline and stuck with us till the end—alongside the unflappable Nicole Weinroth. We had been huge fans of Aline Brosh-McKenna and Mark Roybal long before they came along and dove into the Memoverse. It is an honor to be working with all of you.

Our gratitude travels overseas to Christina Demosthenous and Sharmaine Lovegrove at Dialogue Books, our brilliant UK publisher.

ACKNOWLEDGMENTS

And of course we could not have pulled this off without the love and patience of our families, who believed in us as we locked ourselves away day after day to work on this project. Ben, Henry, Louisa, Josh, and AJ, none of this would have been possible without your support. And Coco, thank you for the unconditional cuddles.

About the Authors

Rachel Dodes is a freelance culture writer. A regular contributor to *Vanity Fair*, her work has also appeared in *Town & Country*, *ELLE*, *Esquire*, the *New York Times*, *Wall Street Journal*, and *Buzzfeed*, among other publications. She was previously a staff writer at the *Wall Street Journal* for a decade where she covered the fashion and film industries. She lives in New York with her husband, son, and dog.

Lauren Mechling is a senior editor at *The Guardian* (US), and has written for the *New York Times*, *Wall Street Journal*, *Slate*, *The New Yorker* online, and *Vogue*, where she wrote a regular book column. She's worked as a crime reporter and metro columnist for the *New York Sun* and a features editor at the *Wall Street Journal*. She has written a number of young adult books and the novel *How Could She*. A graduate of Harvard College, she lives in Brooklyn, New York, with her husband and two children.